The LETTER from the ISLAND

BOOKS BY ROSE ALEXANDER

The Lost Diary
A Letter from Italy
A Santorini Secret

The LETTER from the ISLAND

ROSE ALEXANDER

bookouture

Published by Bookouture in 2025

An imprint of Storyfire Ltd.
Carmelite House
50 Victoria Embankment
London EC4Y 0DZ

www.bookouture.com

The authorised representative in the EEA is Hachette Ireland
8 Castlecourt Centre
Dublin 15 D15 XTP3
Ireland
(email: info@hbgi.ie)

Copyright © Rose Alexander, 2025

Rose Alexander has asserted her right to be identified as the author of this work.

All rights reserved. No part of this publication may be reproduced, stored in any retrieval system, or transmitted, in any form or by any means, electronic, mechanical, photocopying, recording or otherwise, without the prior written permission of the publishers.

ISBN: 978-1-80550-174-9
eBook ISBN: 978-1-80550-173-2

This book is a work of fiction. Names, characters, businesses, organizations, places and events other than those clearly in the public domain, are either the product of the author's imagination or are used fictitiously. Any resemblance to actual persons, living or dead, events or locales is entirely coincidental.

PROLOGUE

'Run!' The voice is frantic and desperate. 'Run for your life!'

The sound of gunshot and artillery fire explodes in her ears as she scrambles to her feet. Her heart pounds and strains as, clutching the terrified, wailing baby to her chest, she stumbles uphill over cobblestones that give way to tussocks of rough grass, stones, brambles. But however hard she tries to make her legs go faster, she doesn't seem to be making any progress.

She's aware of footsteps behind her, and her already laboured breathing becomes even more ragged as her fear intensifies, yet still she isn't getting anywhere. Terrified, the exhausted infant now whimpering pitifully in her ear, she glances back over her shoulder, aware that they are almost upon her.

A face looms up, an arm raises a pistol and—

The woman wakes with a start, sitting bolt upright, hand clamped to her chest as if to stop her heart escaping. As always, it takes her a minute to come to her senses, to realise that her nightmare is just that – a dream. There is no army at her heels, no gun pointed at her head. Her life, the child's life, are not in danger any more. She is no longer fighting for survival on an enemy-infested island but safe in bed in her basement flat in London.

She slumps back against the pillows. She's eighty-five years old and she's been having this recurring nightmare for over six decades. The terror has never faded. The memory of that day, and the months and years that preceded it, has never faded.

The guilt has never faded.

It's as strong now as it was in 1943. She has given up thinking it can ever be assuaged. Stiffly turning over onto her side, she stares at the wall. If only she could bring her loved ones back from the dead. If only she could put it all right.

If only.

CHAPTER 1

LONDON, 2005

The letter lay on the doormat, the address handwritten in an untidy, scrawling and uneven script, as if writing were a skill unfamiliar to the person who had penned it. Callie stared down at the envelope disbelievingly. She did not get unexpected letters. Why would she? Almost everyone she knew had died by now. Sometimes it seemed to her that she was the only one of her generation, the war generation, still alive.

Putting a hand against the wall for balance, she bent down creakily, her knees protesting at every movement. She reached out for the envelope, tentatively, as if it might leap off the mat and bite her if she made a sudden move. Once it was securely in her grasp, she hauled herself upright and walked, a little unsteadily, into the kitchen, where she hoped she might find her glasses. There they lay, exactly where she had thought they were – she wasn't forgetful like all the old biddies at church, oh no! – on the little Formica table, with its chipped edges and stained top. She hadn't decorated or bought new furniture in decades. Ella was always encouraging her to, but then, luckily for Ella, she hadn't grown up in a war so she didn't understand mend and make do like her grandmother did.

Seated at the table, specs on the end of her nose, Callie studied the envelope. The stamp was Greek, the postmark faint and smudged, but she could just about make it out. Her heart lurched and her palms became moist with nervous perspiration.

Chania.

The second city of Crete, her homeland. Who would have written to her from there? She couldn't think of anyone. There was no one there who would remember her, or at least no one who could possibly know where she was now, where she had been for the last sixty-odd years.

Callie put the letter carefully down on the table and scrutinised it anew. Should she take the risk of opening it? It wasn't as if there could be anything dangerous inside, was there? No bombs or anthrax spores... What a ridiculous thought. But hadn't there been an anthrax attack campaign, in America, a few years ago, after that terrible disaster when the planes flew into the tall buildings...? People had died, Callie was sure of it. She could ask Ella – she'd know how to look it up on that World Wide Web thingy she was always going on about – *it's a revolution, Grandma,* she'd say, *it's going to change the world.* Well, maybe it would, but that would be a world that Calliope Smith wouldn't be a part of as she'd be long gone by then, six feet under and—

Abruptly, Callie stopped herself. Such nonsense. Who on earth would care enough about her to send her a poisonous letter? She really must nip such absurd notions in the bud.

The envelope was a bit battered, she noticed. Royal or not, they didn't take care of the mail these days like they used to. She should just open it. She would, in a minute. But she'd make her morning coffee first. Stick to her routine. That was the best way to deal with the unexpected. Don't let it put you out, or put you off.

Callie was big on routine. Her days followed a regular pattern. Sundays, she went to church, Mondays it was off to the library to choose a new book. Tuesdays she took a walk in the park, Wednesdays she met her friend Sheila for coffee, if Sheila didn't have one of her numerous hospital appointments. Thursdays, she called 'freedom day', when she took her Freedom Pass and went on an adventure on a red London bus – preferably a double-decker, because there was a better view from up top, but one couldn't pick and choose. Her aim was to cover all the routes in London by the time she kicked the bucket. She loved that British expression for dying, so irreverent and unsentimental. Friday was laundry day and then it was Saturday.

On Saturday, she penned a letter that she didn't post. She'd written every week for the last sixty-two years but she'd never sent a single one. They were all in boxes in the wardrobes and under the bed, harbouring memories and gathering dust. This was what was so odd. Callie wrote letters, but she didn't receive them.

The envelope still lay on the Formica tabletop, staring accusingly up at her. Or maybe it was staring innocently. Invitingly. It was hard to tell.

And after Saturday, back to Sunday again, with the trip to church, followed every other week by the event that was the highlight of her fortnight. A visit from her granddaughter Ella, for whom a packet of Bourbon creams always stood ready.

Callie's gaze fell once again upon the letter. A noise seemed to fill the room, the sound of low-flying aircraft, of droning engines, the roar of flames and the stench of burning, gunfire exploding in staccato rallies, screams, cries, howls...

Silence.

The planes and the bombs and the shooting ceased and an emptiness occupied the space, vast and desolate. Callie stared down at the floor, overcome by emotion. She clenched her fists tightly until the voices of all those she had once known and loved had faded and receded.

Exhaling deeply, Callie slowly unclenched her fists and flattened her palms against her knees, breathing as slowly and regularly as she could. She stayed like this until her head stopped spinning and her heart rate had returned to normal.

Then she reached out and turned the envelope over, placing it face down on the table so as to hide the handwritten address. It wasn't possible. It simply wasn't possible. Ghosts cannot write letters.

But as she made her way to the laundrette, Callie's hands trembled and her legs shook beneath her, because there was no doubt about it. It might have been decades since she had last seen it, but she knew for certain that the writing on the envelope was that of her long-dead sister.

CHAPTER 2

CRETE, MAY 1941

Out of the shelter of the trees, a fresh breeze blew across the valley. The spring grass underfoot was long and lush, studded with brightly coloured poppies, anemones and daisies, and beyond the meadow the jagged limestone crags of the White Mountains rose majestically upwards. Calliope paused and stood for a moment, lifting her face to the rising sun and letting it warm her cheeks, while keeping a tight hold of her little brother George's hand.

It dawned on her that, for the first time in days, there was no screech of planes in the sky, no distant dull explosions from falling bombs, no sound of anti-aircraft fire. Instead, in place of the Luftwaffe's relentless bombardment, all she could hear was the tinkling of goat bells, the buzzing of insects and, beyond that, the calm quiet of the countryside. Across the island, people were nervous and on edge, but they tried to reassure themselves by remembering the battalions of Allied troops stationed on Crete, recently bolstered by the Greek army on retreat from the seemingly unstoppable advance of the Germans across mainland Europe. And being surrounded by sea also protected them, didn't it? Everything would be all right.

After just a few moments of enjoying the sun, a sharp tug alerted Calliope to George's impatience; he wanted to chase after the animals, pet their stubby horns, let them playfully butt him with their hard heads. He loved the goats as he loved all creatures: cats, dogs, sheep, cows, rabbits, anything soft and furry, and innocent like him.

Looking down at him, Calliope smiled indulgently. 'Where do you want to go? You show me.'

Eagerly, George launched himself forward, and Calliope had to quickly lurch into action, tightening her grip to make sure he didn't fall. When he had been born there hadn't seemed to be anything wrong with him, but, over time, problems had emerged. His left arm and leg did not work quite properly and, even though he was now four, he still hadn't spoken. In the village, people muttered about him, saying that Calliope's mother and father had been too old to have another baby, that not having fallen pregnant for so many years after Calliope and her twin sister Calista had been born was God's way of telling them that it wasn't meant to be.

It upset their mother but Calliope ignored all of it. Let them talk. She couldn't have loved George more and, when anyone implied that he was not perfect, not quite right, she had to temper her rage and hold back from retorting, 'and what makes you think that you are?'

Calista felt the same way but she never got angry about it; anger simply wasn't part of her character. Their parents joked that, despite being identical, their two girls were chalk and cheese. Hot-headed and impulsive, Calliope loved to be out and about, roaming the meadows and river gorges, climbing the slopes and crags, always on the move, whereas quiet, gentle Calista was a homebody, wanting nothing more than to be washing and cleaning, laundering and dusting, and concocting delicious meals for her family. Nevertheless, despite their differences, the sisters adored each other just as they adored their little brother, and the bond between the siblings was as strong, unbreakable and necessary as a ploughshare.

As Calliope helped little George to navigate the uneven terrain, grasping him under his arms and swinging him bodily over the hillocks and mounds, crying, 'whee' as she did so, it occurred to her that the silence was not benign, that there was something unnatural and odd about it.

Uncanny.

Previously, she had thought that there was nothing worse than to hear the ear-splitting sirens that heralded a Stuka dive, and to see the bomber plunging through the air towards its target. Now the absence of such dives struck her as ominous. The wind got up and Calliope shivered, goosebumps rising on her forearms. Did the halt to the aerial bombardment signify that the attack was over? Or that it was only just beginning?

A dreadful sense of foreboding swept over her and she let go of her brother for a moment so that she could tighten her shawl around her shoulders. George sank to the ground, plumping onto a spongy tussock of meadow grass with a chuckle that sounded like rainwater gurgling down a drain during a winter storm. Calliope couldn't help but laugh too, despite her unease. Bending down, she hoisted the small boy to his feet. She was assisting him to stand firm when she heard it.

Straightening up, she stared into the sky, shielding her eyes with her hand. The noise grew gradually louder, a low rumbling that soon became a heavy growl. In the distance she could make out aeroplanes. Lots of them. They were approaching rapidly, flying in formations of three, the chugging of the engines becoming louder and louder as they advanced. Suddenly, they were almost overhead. Calliope knew enough about aircraft by now to know that these were not the dreaded Stukas. But they were definitely German. She looked wildly around her. She and George were out in the open, completely exposed, nowhere to hide when the bombs started. Urgently, she pulled George close in an instinctual protective motion. Panic rose in her throat as George began to cry, his laughter turned to terror in an instant.

The planes were even closer now, close enough to touch, it seemed. But still no bombs. As Calliope stared helplessly upwards, she saw black specks filling the sky. Confusion fuddled her mind. What was happening? Narrowing her eyes and straining her ears, she forgot about everything, about George and the goats and her family and the village. Up above, the specks were transforming, morphing into things with legs and a canopy. It took a moment for her to realise it was parachutes unfurling. Suddenly the heavens were full of falling men. For a few brief seconds, Calliope stood transfixed, imagining what her island would look like from above; the green pastures, remote valleys and meandering rivers, the massifs and high peaks still dusted by a covering of snow, the broad sweep of golden sand beaches framed by a sapphire sea. It must be so beautiful, she thought...

George, twisting and turning in Calliope's grasp, was also gazing upwards. Fascinated, he stared and pointed, chattering in his wordless way. His babyish babble brought Calliope to her senses. Bracing herself to bear his weight, she picked her brother up. Thank goodness he was small for his age.

A heavy thud sounded from somewhere behind her. She whirled around, and all her breath left her body as she saw that, only five hundred or so metres away, a parachutist had landed. Paralysed with fear, she watched, motionless, as another one joined him, further from her but still far too near, and then another, and another.

One thought seared through her mind. She must get George back to the village, back to safety. The goats would have to fend for themselves. Forcing her body to action, she ran. At first she was fleet and fast, but before long she began to tire, her brother becoming heavier and heavier in her arms. Stumbling and tripping over the uneven ground, she struggled to keep up her pace, battling the protests of her labouring lungs.

The planes had been joined by silent gliders, more and more of them, flying lower and lower. Calliope was dimly aware of the rattle of anti-aircraft fire coming from further down the valley. Her heart leapt into her throat as, before her eyes, a plane was hit. A dark plume of smoke erupted from the fuselage, staining the sky like a smudge of ink upon a sheet of blotting paper. As she stared, appalled, the pilot baled out but the plane kept flying, flames licking at its wings. With another jolt of shock, Calliope realised that it was heading in their direction.

Panicking, unable to think straight, Calliope halted. George was wriggling, unsettled by the terrible din, the smell of burning fuel, the thick pall of smog that had descended around them. Only a few hundred metres ahead of them, the plane crashed and exploded. Fear stilled the blood in her veins as Calliope's stricken mind registered the danger but struggled to formulate a plan. *Think, think,* she told herself. She must get to the village by another route, the back way, through the grove of tamarisk and oak trees and over the stone bridge, past the bakery.

As Calliope faltered, she lost her grip on the squirming George, who dropped awkwardly to his feet. Grasping frantically for his hand, she turned towards her escape route. And came face to face with another enemy parachutist, still recovering from his fall, parachute billowing behind him like the jellyfish that came to the bay every summer. The airman was on the ground, disorientated, not yet managing to stand.

But his gun was ready. And pointed straight at them.

Shock and desperate fear felled Calliope. Pulling George to her, she dropped to her knees, her gaze momentarily locking onto the man's before he looked away.

Then pulled the trigger.

CHAPTER 3

CRETE, MAY 1941

Calliope's scream splintered the air, an awful sound that seemed to be wrenched from the depths of her being. Despite her efforts to shield him, George had been hit. He lay, flat on the ground, blood oozing from a wound in his chest.

She crouched over her brother as another shot rang out. This one was for her, Calliope thought. How long did it take for a metal bullet to rip the life out of a body of flesh and bone? She waited to die.

But instead, she saw the German airman slump forward, a stain spreading out beneath him, turning the green grass red. Before she could react, strong hands were gripping her forearms and she was being dragged away, her feet slipping out from under her.

'George,' she yelled. 'Let me go. George!'

Struggling violently, she flailed and thrashed, but she couldn't get away. A voice in her ear told her to be quiet and, as she was trying to process the request, in the next moment she saw a uniformed man flash past her and bend to pick up her brother.

What was going on? Having shot George, were they now going to steal him and kidnap her?

Heart pounding, Calliope's breath was coming in ragged bursts. Her thick dark hair had come loose and fell across her eyes, obscuring her vision, while her ears registered the terrifying noise of the planes, still coming in their droves overhead, their low drone seeming to be inside her head... And now the din was augmented by the frantic ringing of church bells as the villagers sounded the invasion alarm. All was confusion and the only thing Calliope could focus on was the need to save George, to rescue him from whoever had got hold of him. She resumed her struggling, to little avail. The grip that held her was iron-firm.

'We must get out of here, and quickly,' the voice said, in a tone of measured urgency. 'The little lad – he's taken a bullet. I'll let you go but you have to come with us.'

Swiping her hair away from her face with her newly released arms, Calliope managed to focus on the person who had just spoken. A soldier, in a British uniform. Thank God, thank God. Not a German.

'He's my brother,' she gasped. 'My only brother. We have to get to the village, to our parents... there's a short cut. Follow me.'

Quelling her panic, Calliope raced ahead, through the grove of tamarisk and oak trees and over the old stone bridge, past the bakery, towards her parents' house. Glancing over her shoulder, she saw the second soldier carrying George's limp and bleeding body in outstretched arms as if he weighed no more than air.

In the village, the pealing of the bells was deafening. All along the crowded main street people gathered together, huddled in groups, staring at the sky, expressions of shock and confusion on their faces. As Calliope pushed her way through the multitudes, the gazes of her friends and neighbours turned towards her and the British soldiers, and then down to little George.

Screams erupted, yells and shrieks and desperate entreaties as to what had happened. Calliope barely heard. At one point she caught the eye of her friend, Eliana, saw her expression change from fear to appalled shock at the sight of George's limp form. Calliope did not stop to explain. Instead, she looked away and carried on running, through the mayhem. Her blood throbbed in her ears and her head felt as if it might explode, but she couldn't stop. The only thing that mattered was to get George home.

They reached her parents' front door and Calliope flung it open, gesturing to the soldiers to enter. For want of anywhere else to put him, they laid George on the large wooden table that stood in the centre of the room. Calliope rushed to him, cradling his head in her hands, her tears dripping onto his little body.

'Mum! Dad!' she shouted. 'Call the doctor. Calista! Where are you all?'

It dawned on her that they must be outside somewhere, among the throng. Still shouting, she seized up a bundle of cloths and applied them to the wound in George's chest, desperately trying to staunch the bleeding.

She heard footsteps outside, pounding up the cobbled side alley that led to the house. Looking up, she already knew who it was. Calista.

Of course her sister had come immediately. Despite their contrasting personalities, they had the twin connection, a deep intuition that told them when the other was hurt or in pain or sad. But this time it wasn't Calliope who needed help, it was George, their gorgeous, funny brother who they competed to love the most fiercely. When their mother had fallen pregnant with him, after all the years of wanting another baby, the twins were already nearly seventeen. They had regarded it as a miracle, and still did. If the infant was different, who cared? Well, it seemed lots of people, quick to pass judgement, did, but not Calliope or Calista, nor their parents.

All of this flashed through Calliope's mind as her sister pelted through the door and over to the table.

'Oh my God, my God, what happened, why George, what...?' Her eyes filled with shock and horror, Calista's words petered out.

'Fetch the doctor,' Calliope yelled, 'now.'

At that moment their parents stumbled over the threshold and immediately fell upon their son, kissing and hugging him, heedless of the dark-red blood that still oozed from his wound. Soon after, the doctor arrived and began to work on the small body, his face set grim and hard with concentration.

Now that George's care was in expert hands, all the terror and stress rose up in Calliope so that she shook from head to toe, suddenly feeling so exhausted she could hardly stand. Calista motioned to her to sit down, pushing her knitting from a chair onto the floor in order for her to do so, and brought her a glass of water. Only then did the whole family seem to remember the two British soldiers, standing awkwardly in the background with caps in hand. As the combined gaze of four pairs of eyes landed on them simultaneously, one of the soldiers, who Calliope now noticed was wearing an officer's uniform, stepped forward.

'Major Laurie Wynn-Thomas,' he announced, reaching out his hand to shake Calliope's father's. 'But call me Laurie.'

Calliope noticed the other soldier discreetly wipe his palm, stained by George's blood, on his uniform jacket, before also offering it in greeting.

For a moment, Calliope almost laughed at the ludicrousness of the situation, them all politely exchanging handshakes while George lay right next to them, clinging to life by a thread. But these men, these British soldiers, had appeared when she had needed help the most. It was only now that it occurred to her that they had shot the parachutist who had fired at George, and left the battleground to help her bring her brother home. They had undoubtedly saved her life. She needed to thank them, but at the same time she couldn't stop thinking, why me? Or rather, why not me? Why not me who was hit and George spared? He was too young to be part of this war, too young to...

The little boy uttered a few pathetic whimpers and immediately the family's attention turned from the soldiers and back to their beloved son and brother. Calliope's mother wept and keened, and even her father, usually so stoic and undemonstrative, had to wipe his eyes with his pocket handkerchief.

The two British soldiers left and, unable to cope with the tension in the room and overwhelmed by guilt because it was her fault that George had got shot, she who had failed to look after him properly, Calliope stepped outside. Parachutists filled the sky, their number seeming infinite. In the distance, the sonic boom of explosions sounded dully, providing punctuation to the frantic pealing of the church bells. Round the corner on the main street, the villagers were beginning to galvanise themselves to action.

Old and young appeared and reappeared, going to their houses empty-handed and returning armed with anything they could find. Men brandished ancient hunting rifles, cleavers, axes and pitchforks, women wielded rolling pins, kitchen knives or scissors. In the short amount of time since the men had started falling, the truth had become clear. This was an invasion on a huge scale, far greater than anyone could ever have imagined or foreseen.

In an instant, Calliope's guilt was swept aside and replaced by a sudden, intense fury. Clenching her fists, she imagined using them to inflict blow upon blow on the enemy. But hands were not enough. Determinedly, she returned to her house to find something that could be a weapon.

Stepping into the cool, dark interior, she was filled with a sudden, terrible understanding. The doctor, her parents and her sister were gathered around the table where George lay.

Creeping silently towards them, Calliope got there just in time to see the medic, whose fingers were pressed against the child's wrist, let go his touch.

'I'm sorry,' he said, slowly and simply. 'I did what I could.' A look of profound weariness mingled with sorrow settled on his craggy face. He was an old man now and had seen much fighting during the war against the Turkish. In his expression Calliope could read the dread of what was to come.

Calliope's mother's hands had been covering her face but now she let them fall, instead using them to tear at her hair as her sobs of grief became howls of unbearable pain. Her father sank to the ground and dropped his head between his knees as his tears dampened the earthen floor. Calista just stood, transfixed to the spot as if petrified, turned to stone by the terrible calamity.

Fiercely, Calliope swung back her hair, then leant forward and gently lifted George's fragile body, hugging him to her. As she did so, she silently made a vow to him that, come what may, she would somehow find a way to avenge his death. She would not rest while there was breath in her body to do so.

CHAPTER 4

LONDON, 2005

On her return from the laundrette, Callie made tea, carefully taking the pot from the cupboard, a spoon from the drawer and the milk from the fridge, stirring for a lot longer than was necessary. Then she re-boiled the kettle to steam the envelope open, rather than slit it with a paper knife. That way, she could reseal it if necessary. Why it would be necessary, she couldn't imagine. If she didn't want to engage with what was inside, perhaps?

The envelope became limp and floppy as she held it to the spout. It took less than a minute for the heat and moisture to do its work. Cautiously, Callie slid her finger along the flap, teasing it open. Then she pulled out the letter, unfolded it and began to read.

When she'd finished reading, she went through to the living room and sank down into her comfy armchair, the flimsy airmail paper still in her hand. She felt as if someone had punched her in the diaphragm. How could it be true? It simply couldn't be. There was no way. If it were true, then the whole of the last sixty-two years had been – had been what? A mistake? A lie? And why a letter now, after all this time?

Lost in thought, suddenly an idea crystallised about what

might have led to this extraordinary moment. A month or so ago she'd noticed a newcomer, a young man, in the congregation at the Greek Orthodox church she'd been attending for half a century. After the last beats of the closing hymn had faded away, Callie had, as usual, headed to the parish room for a cup of coffee. As she'd sipped the welcome hot drink, she'd sensed the newcomer hovering nearby, staring intently at her. She'd had a sudden feeling of recognition, of knowing this person from somewhere.

And then the stranger had approached her to say hello. Callie didn't want to chat. She wasn't unfriendly but she found small talk difficult – always had. And she'd been increasingly silent in recent years, having lived on her own since her husband Harry had died. Never particularly loquacious, she'd almost entirely lost the ability to have casual conversations. The only person she really spoke to in depth was her beloved Ella. But the arrival of the letter posed a terrible threat to that relationship, the only truly meaningful one Callie still had.

The stranger had told her that his name was George and that he was from a village near Chania, in Crete.

Callie's head had spun and a spell of dizziness overcame her. She almost fell, would have done so if George had not rushed to her side and caught her, then helped her to a chair. When she had recovered her senses, she realised that she was being utterly foolish. Of course this George was not her little brother. Her George would have been in his seventies by now, not a young whippersnapper of no more than twenty-five. Even after all these years, she still sometimes dreamt that it wasn't true, that George hadn't died. And when she remembered that of course he had, all the terrible guilt about his death swept back in because it had been her fault. She never spoke of the matter. To anyone. But now this stranger had made her confront it when she was least expecting it.

This new, young George asked her all about herself, where

she was from, how long she'd lived in England, exactly whereabouts she lived in London and all sorts of other stuff. Callie had to answer; it would have been rude not to. And Callie, though often reticent, was never rude.

After a while, George had said he'd like a picture of the church and the congregation to send to the folks back home. Callie had been astounded to see him pull a phone out of his pocket and take a photo with it. She had only ever seen one of these new-fangled mobile communication devices before, Ella's work BlackBerry, which as far as she knew, wasn't also a camera. All this new technology bemused, confused and wearied her.

Reluctantly, Callie had posed for the photo, along with a couple of other lingerers. As soon as she could, she'd got away, and had puzzled about the morning's events all the way home. Who exactly was this mysterious George and why was she so sure that they'd met before, when that could not possibly be the case?

The arrival of the letter so soon after George's appearance at church could not be a coincidence. The two must be connected in some way. But how? And why?

Slowly, Callie looked back down at the piece of paper. She ran her old, tired eyes over the writing.

Dear Calliope

This will likely come as a huge shock to you, but I believe that you are my twin sister. I have spent all the years since we last saw each other believing you to be dead. But recently, I received information that seems to suggest you are alive and living in London. If it's really you – and how I hope that it is – I implore you to get in touch with me as soon as possible. We have important matters to discuss. I'm sure you'll agree that we need to talk about what happened. Why it happened. And what you did.

Hoping to hear from you soon,

Calista

It was the last thing Callie had expected, in her eighty-fifth year on the planet: to discover that the identical twin sister she had believed to be dead for the past six decades was actually not dead at all, but alive and kicking in their home village on Crete.

And with that revelation came a host of consequences that Callie had no idea how to deal with.

CHAPTER 5

CRETE, JUNE 1941

For days, the battle raged. The Allied troops were joined by ordinary folk, men, women and even children, determined to defend their homeland. They fought in fields and meadows, in mountain hamlets and major cities, in village streets and town squares.

The Papadakis family, Calliope and Calista and their parents Valeria and Yiorgis, sunk in grief after George's violent death, barely noticed. The day after his killing, the funeral was held. The whole village attended, laying aside their makeshift weapons for an hour to pay their last respects before going out again to fight.

A number set off for the settlement of Kandanos to join an ambush of German forces trying to cross the island from Chania to Paleochora, but, though the brave band of resistance fighters inflicted some casualties, after two days they were beaten back into the mountains. And in the end, it was all in vain. As May turned to June, Crete fell to the German forces. A profound sense of despair engulfed the island.

But families still had livings to make, and for the Papadakis clan that meant looking after their livestock. Now that the fighting had subsided, Calliope and Calista headed to the pasture so that the flock could graze. As Calista opened the gate, a cacophony of excited bleating broke out. The billy goat butted his head against Calliope's thigh and she reached down to pet him, scratching his forelock in the way he loved. As she did so, a sudden rush of tears gathered in her eyes, unbidden yet unstoppable. She remembered how George had loved to fondle the goats, shrieking and laughing as they pushed and shoved in their eagerness to get to the most desirable leaves and bushes first.

They set off along the narrow path, Calliope walking with her head down, burdened by the pain of mourning her little brother and by the guilt that gnawed away at her. The prospect of returning to the place where George had been shot tormented her, though explaining this at first felt impossible. But of course Calista was able, in the end, to get her to talk.

'I don't want to go back to where it happened,' Calliope murmured.

'We'll go to the meadows by the river instead,' suggested Calista, giving her sister's hand a sympathetic squeeze. 'It's going to be hot today, so we can find a shady place to sit under the plane trees and keep an eye on the animals from there.'

Calliope nodded. Calista shot her a shrewd glance. She knew what Calliope was thinking.

'It wasn't your fault,' she murmured, 'no one blames you.'

But Calliope could not be convinced. She shook her head. 'Who else's, then? I was the one who was supposed to be looking after him.' Tears pricked behind her eyes. Angrily, she blinked them back. What good would crying do? Nothing would bring George back.

For a few moments, the two young women proceeded in silence as they negotiated a rocky path that ran between high hedges, so narrow that they had to go in single file, the goats jumping and skipping, the sheep eagerly trotting, the sisters half-walking, half-running to keep up.

'But I blame myself,' Calliope burst out as soon as she was level with her sister once more, unable to hold her feelings in any longer. 'Whatever anyone else thinks, it *was* my fault. It took me too long to realise what was happening and I didn't get him to safety soon enough. As soon as I heard the first plane, saw the first black speck in the sky, I should have got George out of there...'

Distractedly, Calista ran her hand down her plaited hair, thick as her own wrist. 'If I had been with him, I know I wouldn't have done any different, or any better,' she tried to reassure her twin.

Calliope shook her head. 'Anyone would have dealt with it better than me. Anyone.'

'That's not so,' replied Calista, insistently. 'It simply isn't true.'

Calliope shook her head but didn't reply. There was nothing else to say and, anyway, she temporarily needed all her breath to ascend a steep incline. The path rose upwards before flattening out as it gave onto a wide, open expanse of grassland fringed by plane trees on three sides and on the fourth by a river that at the moment was dry but which became a raging torrent in winter or early spring, when the heavy rains came or the snowmelt began.

As they emerged onto the plain Calista, who was ahead, let out a shriek of horror. A vision of an armed man pointing a gun, pulling the trigger, shooting George, flashed before Calliope's eyes. Not again, please God not again. She bounded past her sister, pushing her roughly out of the way. She would take any bullet that was coming. Let them shoot her, not Calista, not her kind, gentle, caring twin.

But there was no one there.

Calliope saw that it wasn't an enemy soldier that had so alarmed Calista but instead, landed in the dried-up riverbed, lay a glider, its metal wings glinting in the strong sunlight.

Crouched amidst the tall rushes and sedge, Calliope thought it resembled a resting grasshopper. She hated grasshoppers, the way they came into the house, following the light, and leapt around, sometimes landing in her hair, making her skin crawl. She knew it was silly, that grasshoppers were entirely harmless, but she simply couldn't stand them.

Another yelp from Calista brought Calliope back to the present with a jump. Silently, unable to speak, Calista pointed. Calliope's gaze followed her finger.

Beneath the wing of the glider lay a body.

Clinging to one another, the sisters froze, paralysed by fear. For long minutes, they stared. There was no sign of movement.

'I think he's dead,' whispered Calliope.

Calista nodded, still dumbstruck.

They had seen dead people before, of course they had, grandparents and great-grandparents, friends and neighbours, dressed in their finery and laid in their coffins so that all could pay their last respects. And George, only days before...

But those deaths were different.

This was an enemy soldier and, once she had got over the shock, Calliope realised that she was glad he was dead, glad he wasn't one of those rampaging across the island, leaving carnage in their wake. Already stories were circulating of the brutality of the German forces, who were inflicting upon innocent locals at best vicious beatings and, at worst, summary executions. The word on the street was that the Nazis believed violent repression to be the best way to ensure the population was cowed into obedience to their tyrannical rule.

Little do they know us Cretans, Calliope thought, as she continued to regard the soldier's lifeless body. We'll show them! *I'll* show them. She noticed he still had his weapon slung round his neck. It was resting beside him, gleaming in the sun. After the fightback during the invasion, a resistance movement had formed; it had already met in Chania just the day before and adopted the creed of liberty or death. Anyone could join.

Calliope could join...

'I'm going to take his gun,' she muttered under her breath to Calista, as if to make sure the soldier didn't hear.

Calista snatched at her wrist. 'No!' she protested. 'Don't be stupid, don't go anywhere near him. He might—'

'Might what?' retorted Calliope. 'Might come back from the dead? I don't think so.'

'Why do you even need a gun?' asked Calista, desperately. 'What are you going to do with it?' An edge of fear, of knowing but not wanting to know, infused her tone.

Impatiently, Calliope threw off her sister's hand. 'Why do you think? So I can fight.' She was always the daring one, reckless some would say, headstrong and impetuous. Calista, so much more considered and cautious in all her actions, was usually a steadying influence. But Calliope wasn't listening to her now.

'You can't, you mustn't, if you got hurt it would kill Mama and Papa, you—'

'I'm doing it and no one can stop me.' Calliope bounded forward and headed for the glider.

'Stop! Halt!'

The cry rang out, echoing between the steep hillsides that rose up all around them. Instinctively, Calliope looked over her shoulder and, as she did so, tripped over a tangle of brambles. She fell heavily, winding herself. Gasping for breath, she scrambled to her feet. The need for the gun was even more urgent now, to protect her sister and herself. Not that she had the first idea how to use it, but still. She could pretend, she could—

'Stay where you are.' The voice, hard as iron, was much closer now and, though terrifying, oddly familiar. It was speaking Greek, with an accent, but still easy to understand.

Turning her head to see who had spoken, Calliope clenched

her fists, ready to run again if need be. She found herself face to face with the officer who had rescued her on the first day of the invasion, and who, along with his fellow soldier, had brought George back home. Major Laurie Wynn-Thomas, that had been his name. *But call me Laurie.*

What was he doing here? The British were supposed to be leaving, evacuated by ship or submarine or caique or any means possible from the south coast, all those who could make it there, that is. Presumably he hadn't been able to do so yet.

'What were you trying to do?' he asked, his tone less harsh now, amiable even.

Calliope shrugged and looked bashfully at the ground for a moment, before raising her gaze and meeting his. 'I wanted the gun,' she mumbled. 'I thought, if I had a weapon, they'd let me join the resistance.'

There was a short silence and then he began to laugh, but not unkindly. Calista appeared beside them. Her face was blanched by fear and her expression showed her bewilderment at this outbreak of mirth.

'So join it,' said Laurie to Calliope. 'I admire anyone who does. And it's a good idea to take the enemy's weapons to do it. But not that one. Some of these gliders are booby-trapped. Go a step nearer and the whole thing might go up in smoke, you included.'

At this warning, the two women shrank backwards as one, clinging onto each other.

'What about the goats?' asked Calista anxiously. 'Will they set off a bomb? I don't want them to get hurt. And besides, they're our family's—'

Calliope elbowed her sharply in the ribs before Calista could say the word 'livelihood'. There was no need to advertise the Papadakises' slender means, their hand-to-mouth existence, to this handsome soldier of the British Empire. Calliope had her pride.

Laurie chuckled some more. 'No, the weight of a goat is unlikely to trip a bomb. I'll come back tonight and throw a grenade at it. That'll sort it out, even if it does remain an eyesore in this idyllic valley.'

Calista's face paled still further. 'Is that... safe? Shouldn't you be leaving, along with all the others? What will happen if the Germans—'

She stopped short, unable to continue.

Laurie took a pack of cigarettes from his jacket pocket, tapped several loose and offered them to the twins. Both shook their heads. Contemplatively, he pulled one out and lit it.

'You're right, I probably should be off.' He drew on the cigarette long and hard, then released the smoke in a grey plume that momentarily obscured Calliope's vision. When the cloud cleared, Laurie's face had hardened, his eyes narrowing as he gazed into the distance, beyond the looming White Mountains and towards the distant south coast. 'I'll be on my way soon.'

Calliope's stomach lurched. This man had saved her life, he had tried to help her brother. Now he had saved her once more, and Calista, too. He had to leave, she understood that. But their island would need men like this if they were to overthrow the enemy. She had a sudden, urgent feeling that *she* needed men like this too, or a man like Major Wynn-Thomas anyway, always there to protect her and her sister.

Laurie threw the cigarette butt down and trod it into the ground. 'You people measure distance in the number of cigarettes that can be smoked in the time it takes to walk somewhere,' he commented, smiling wryly as he spoke. 'But I think reaching the south would take more packets than I have left on me.' He shrugged. 'So maybe leaving won't be possible.'

The trio stood for a moment without speaking, contemplating Laurie's words. A loud gurgle from his stomach cut through the silence, and all three burst into laughter, made louder and more hysterical by the sudden breaking of the tension.

Calista rummaged in the bag slung across her body, and pulled out bread, cheese and two ripe, red tomatoes.

'Here,' she said, thrusting the food at him. 'Have this. We have plenty more at home. It's goat's cheese, made from our milk.' She waved her arm in a wide gesture that encompassed the flock, spread across the pasture, gently filling the air with the tinkling of their bells.

For a moment surprise filled Laurie's face, before it broke out in a wide, gorgeous smile of gratitude.

'Thank you,' he said. 'Are you sure you can spare it?'

Calista dropped her gaze as if burned by the brightness of his smile. 'Of course,' she replied, demurely. 'Calliope and I can eat later.'

'We'll have to go back now anyway,' interjected Calliope. 'We shouldn't be here until you've... until that thing' – she pointed at the glider and wrinkled her nose in disgust – 'is... dealt with.'

Laurie nodded. 'I'll make sure it's done,' he promised. And with that, he turned on his heel, strolled away and disappeared beneath the plane trees.

Calliope and Calista did not move for a moment. Then they began to call the goats and sheep in, Calliope grabbing the doe who was the flock queen and who all the rest would follow. Lost in their own thoughts, neither spoke as they led the animals to another meadow, far from the abandoned glider.

And from Laurie.

Remembering how he had smiled as Calista handed him the food, Calliope had a sudden, irrational feeling of regret. Why hadn't she thought of that? She would not have admitted it to her sister, could barely admit it to herself, but she wished that it had been her who had touched Laurie with her generosity, who had been gifted that wonderful smile, bestowed on her and her alone.

She snatched up a switch of beech from the ground and nudged a couple of lingering sheep with it, encouraging them to get a move on. At the same time, she tried to rationalise her feelings. It was not as if either she or Calista would see the handsome soldier again. He would be evacuating from the island as soon as he could, not dropping round for mountain tea, a slice of orange cake and polite conversation. However much she wished things were different, Laurie, along with that gorgeous smile, was not going to be a part of either twin's life.

But if the British were leaving, then who was going to save the island from the Germans? At that moment, the idea she had so carelessly flung out to Major Laurie earlier rekindled in Calliope's mind and began to burn with an eager flame.

She could join the resistance. She *would* join the resistance.

CHAPTER 6

LONDON, 2005

'Grandma!' Ella's voice echoed through the letter box. She always alerted Callie to her presence this way, rather than by using the doorbell.

Callie, grimacing as her back protested at the sudden movement, hobbled to the door to let her granddaughter in.

'How are you?' asked Ella brightly, throwing her arms round her grandmother. She was always cheerful, which Callie found remarkable, given what she'd had to endure as a child. Ella's mother Louise, Callie's daughter, had been a single mum. She and Ella had moved in with Callie and Harry when Louise first fell ill with breast cancer, assuming it would be a temporary measure until Louise had recovered enough to be independent again.

That moment never came. Instead, Louise got sicker and sicker until, when Ella was just seven years old, she died. Callie had been heartbroken but she'd had to rally for Ella's sake. It had been hard to cater for a little girl's needs at the same time as nursing her own grief, but somehow they'd got through it. Ella had grown up happy, contented and well adjusted. It was a miracle, really.

Today they'd be making their monthly pilgrimage to the cemetery at Golders Green, where both Louise and Harry had rose bushes planted in their memories.

'Would you like a cup of tea before we go?' asked Callie, thinking that if Ella had a Bourbon cream then so could she. She hadn't had food like that when she was growing up and she didn't care what people said about it being unhealthy. *A little bit of what you fancy does you good*, she'd always believed.

Ella shook her head. 'No, let's make a move. We can go to the café afterwards, or stop off somewhere on the way home.'

Relinquishing the idea of a chocolate biscuit, Callie took her coat from the hook in the hall and started putting it on. Halfway through she paused, fixing her gaze on her granddaughter. There was something different about her today. Her initial greeting had been enthusiastic, but now she seemed subdued, not as sunny as usual.

'Is something the matter?' questioned Callie, probingly. 'Have you been having a tough time at work?'

Ella did something unfathomable, called marketing, which remained a complete mystery to Callie. Her poor granddaughter had tried to explain what it actually involved on numerous occasions, but it still didn't make any sense to Callie. In her day, jobs had been much simpler, she always thought. She herself had worked in a grocer's shop, stocking the shelves and, once her English was good enough, serving the customers. She'd had to learn the language fast but she'd been lucky to have a sympathetic and supportive employer, and essentially she'd just got on with it for the next thirty-odd years.

But times had been different, then. Callie tried to keep up but, honestly, it was getting harder and harder. Computers had been the first thing, and now there were all these other devices, pagers and mobile phones and what-not...

'Look, Grandma, I do have something to tell you,' said Ella, her voice cutting through Callie's thoughts. 'But let's go to the cemetery first.'

Burning with equal measures of curiosity and concern, Callie reluctantly agreed. Ella had always been one of those people who took things slowly, so different from her grandmother who tended to go at things like a bull at a gate.

In the car, Callie tried to change the subject, but there was something on her mind, too. The letter – or, more specifically, its contents. She had, eventually, replied. She was still sure it was something to do with young George at church, but hadn't mentioned anything to him. It was far too complicated and difficult a subject to broach with a stranger. Or with anyone, for that matter. Even Ella. Though of all people, Ella should know.

Suppressing an involuntary shudder, Callie looked out of the car window, at the front gardens with their rows of wheelie bins and moss-stained walls. An image of Crete in springtime flashed into her mind, the meadows strewn with the many colours of the wildflowers and, high above, the snowline gradually receding up the mountains. At the cemetery there was no trace of spring. Instead, a cruel north wind scythed across the rose garden, making both Callie and Ella shiver.

'Surely it should be getting warmer now it's April, shouldn't it?' complained Ella, buttoning up her coat. 'I'm so done with the cold.'

Her granddaughter really wasn't herself today, reflected Callie again. Although she also felt the cold and, however much she had tried, over the years, to banish memories of her homeland from her mind, she often thought of the sunshine that would be bathing her beautiful island even as the British rain lashed down or the grey sky lowered above. But of course it was more than just the seasons and the chill that ate away at Callie's heart. She had left her beloved sister there, all those years ago, knowing she would never see her again. And now all that had changed. Calista was alive, not dead. Callie had not even begun to process this fact.

She and Ella laid some flowers, checked the health of the rose bushes and, after a short stroll around the grounds, departed. Ella drove them to Hampstead, where there was a little café on the high street that they both loved for its people-watching potential.

But today, Callie wasn't interested in anyone else but Ella and what was bothering her. And she still had to work out how to tell Ella what she was considering. Fortunately, Ella took the initiative.

'OK,' she began, once the waitress had delivered their pot of tea to the table. 'There's no point beating about the bush.' She paused and took a deep breath. Callie felt increasingly unsettled. What on earth was wrong? Had Ella been fired? Losing her job had always been one of Callie's biggest fears. They'd absolutely relied on both her and her husband's income, and couldn't afford for one of them not to be working. Once Ella had come to live with them and become Callie's responsibility, life had been one long round of informal after-school and holiday childcare arrangements. It had been difficult but somehow they'd managed, and thank goodness they had, because Callie needed every single penny of her pension, given that everything seemed to have quadrupled in price.

'The thing is,' Ella continued, 'that I've handed in my notice.'

It took a few moments for the words to sink in, and, when they did, Callie wasn't sure she'd heard correctly. Had Ella resigned? But who in their right mind would voluntarily give up a job that paid decently and, most importantly, gave security? It was even worse than she had feared.

Callie opened her mouth to respond, but didn't manage to get a word out before Ella leapt in.

'I've just had enough. I don't like the job, the company, my colleagues – any of it. It all seems so trite and pointless. I've never lived anywhere but London, I've never even been abroad. So I've decided to go travelling. For a year or two.' As she finished speaking, she gripped her teacup tightly in both hands as if this was the only thing keeping her grounded.

'Well.' Callie was quite simply lost for words. What could she say? It sounded like a done deal. Perhaps she'd been wrong to believe that Ella had grown up happy and secure. She clearly hadn't. Wasn't. At first, all Callie could think about was worries for Ella's future, but then she thought about herself. If Ella went away for a couple of years, there'd be no more Sunday visits to look forward to, no one to share Bourbon creams with. Callie might well be dead by the time she returned.

It was a devastating realisation.

'I've put my little car up for sale,' continued Ella. 'And I'm working out my notice while I plan my itinerary. You can get round-the-world plane tickets, you know. So I'm thinking Thailand, Vietnam, the Philippines, and then Australia and New Zealand.'

Callie's heart sank further. The other side of the world. And so many of the young people who went to these places did not come back. Why would they? Australia was the land of opportunity, that was what everyone said. Sheila's nephew had gone for a working holiday and that had been that. Next thing Sheila knew, he'd set up home in Adelaide. So very far away.

'Can I store some of my stuff at your place?' Ella was asking. 'Would you mind? I'm getting rid of most things but there are a few bits and pieces I want to keep.'

Dumbly, Callie nodded. 'Of course,' she muttered.

There was a pause, and then Ella resumed, falteringly. 'I-I'm sorry, Gran. I'm sure it's a shock for you to hear.' She sounded anxious now, as if she knew how much Callie would be hurting and didn't like it at all. There was a clang as someone dropped a teaspoon, and the waitress rushed over to pick it up.

Callie was glad of the distraction. She gathered her breath to speak.

'I've got some news, too,' she said. She couldn't think of any way to respond to Ella's news other than to announce her own. 'I-er, well, I'm going to Crete.' The words tumbled out. 'I've got to. Th-there's something that I need to do there.'

As soon as the words were said, Callie wanted to take them back. When had she actually decided this definitively anyway? As in, fixed upon it rather than just considering it in an abstract way. It was as if she'd been taken over by another Callie, one who wasn't terrified by the letter's contents but who wanted to engage with them.

'Before it's too late,' she added. Too late for what? Hadn't it been too late for sixty-two years already?

Ella stared at her grandmother, dumbfounded. 'But you never go to Crete,' she managed to articulate. 'I've got to say that I always forget that you are even from there. You never mention it.'

That was a bald statement of fact. Callie didn't ever mention it. There were good reasons why and not ones she wanted to share with her adored Ella. But she'd had to tell Ella what she was planning. There was no one else.

'No, I suppose I don't,' she agreed.

'Can you even speak the language any more?' Ella continued. The question was a good one; Callie wasn't sure of the answer. The only time she spoke Greek was at church, with her friend Elena, and that was only small talk, comments on the weather and each other's health. Would she be able to remember the words she'd require to say what needed to be said? Did those words even exist, in any language? She wasn't sure at all.

Ella wasn't done with her questions. 'Why now, Grandma?' she asked, insistently. 'What's happened? What's changed?'

But Callie just shook her head. 'I can't explain yet,' she replied. 'You wouldn't understand.'

No one who hadn't lived through it could possibly comprehend the events of over sixty years ago. Callie thought of her sister's last word to her, the last thing she had heard her say, the terrible accusation she had made. She had spent so long trying to forget, but the memory still burned in her ears, crystallising her guilt. She'd been a fool to think she could just ignore it, push it out of her mind for ever. A letter from the sister she had always believed to be dead was as sure a way to find that out as there could possibly be.

The past always catches up with you at some point.

CHAPTER 7

CRETE, JUNE 1941

The stench of death combined with acrid smoke filled the air. From their vantage point high on a hilltop, Calliope and Eliana could taste the ash and cinders. In retaliation for an ambush of their troops, the new commandant of Crete had ordered the village of Kandanos razed to the ground. After executing one hundred and eighty people, the Germans had torched and burned every house. Gazing down on the ruins, Calliope's eyes stung, whether from tears or from the smog she wasn't sure.

On the way here she and Eliana had passed other villages, where the inhabitants were being herded through the streets at gunpoint, bent old ladies leaning on crooked walking sticks, mothers clutching whimpering infants to their chests, grandfathers keeping their heads held high in a show of dignity and pride while being humiliated. Calliope had heard stories of men shot with their hands tied behind their backs, of babies killed in their mothers' arms. Seemingly at random, anyone could be struck down.

Rage and fury filled Calliope's heart anew and she squeezed Eliana's hand. They'd risen before dawn to walk the long hours it took to get here, simply because they had wanted to see the destruction for themselves, and to understand what the enemy was capable of. Now they knew, and the knowing was not comforting.

'We should go,' said Eliana, quietly. Each word sounded like an effort, as if witnessing the horror had sapped her of energy.

With a heavy heart, Calliope nodded. After readjusting the scarf that protected her head from the sun, she followed Eliana along the narrow goat path that led back towards home. As the Nazis consolidated their hold over the island they were busy setting up checkpoints and machine-gun posts, and anywhere you went you might encounter a patrol. By keeping their eyes and ears sharp, the two women had managed to avoid coming face to face with any enemy soldiers on the journey here, and had hoped that, even if they did, the fact of being female might mean they garnered less attention than a man. But there were no guarantees.

Filled with trepidation, and once more keeping all their senses on high alert, Calliope and Eliana navigated the rough and rugged terrain, following the footpaths and donkey tracks that rambled across countryside bursting with all the life of summer. Lizards darted from beneath stones and disappeared into fissures, birds competed to sing the loudest and the shrubs and hedgerows fizzed with insects. It would all have been so beautiful if it weren't for the presence of hostile forces who, at any moment, might pop up from anywhere with their cruelty, violence and oppression.

Calliope contemplated this as she negotiated her way around a huge boulder. The resistance was gaining support every day, and the local people had the advantage of being on home territory that they were well used to navigating. But that was literally the only area in which they had the upper hand. In all other respects they were hopelessly outgunned and outnumbered.

Lost in thought, Calliope and Eliana let down their guard.

They were almost upon the patrol before they spotted it. Pulling up short in the nick of time, Calliope grabbed Eliana's arm and dragged her down into a crouch behind a clump of laurel bushes.

Screwing up her eyes in the strong sunlight, Calliope observed the soldiers. There were about five of them, led by one in an officer's uniform. Before them stood a local man, whose clothes were so ragged and filthy and whose face was so mud-streaked and dirty that Calliope could only assume he was a homeless itinerant. From the way he was responding to the Nazis' questions, he appeared to be unable to speak as well, instead answering with a series of grunts and groans and few discernible words.

Poor man, thought Calliope. Why didn't they leave him alone? He was clearly no threat to them at all, and was becoming more and more agitated as his failure to understand deepened. As she watched and listened, the officer's tone of voice became increasingly aggressive. She didn't understand a word of German, which the officer was speaking intermingled with a few Greek phrases, but she could tell that he was threatening the homeless wretch. She cast a glance towards Eliana; her friend had an uncle who had lived in Germany for years and had taught her the language. She would have a better idea of what was going on. Eliana couldn't explain though, as obviously they couldn't talk while they were trying to remain concealed. But from the horrified look on Eliana's face, Calliope was sure that the interchange was as hostile and intimidating as it sounded.

Suddenly, the officer cocked his rifle. Calliope froze. Was he going to shoot? But instead, the German stepped forward and jabbed at the homeless man, prodding him so sharply that he fell backwards and lay sprawled on the ground, legs flailing, like an overturned beetle.

Anger flared through Calliope once more, all the wrath

she'd felt at George's death rising up in her. How dare they do this to a defenceless man? It wasn't right and Calliope would not stand by and watch. Memories of George being teased and taunted for his disabilities flooded back and enraged her further. She leapt out from the cover of the bushes, heedless of Eliana's attempts to restrain her, and ran straight towards the patrol, her dark hair flying around her shoulders as it came loose from her scarf. Taken by surprise by her sudden appearance, the soldiers hesitated for a moment.

When she reached the officer, whose eyes, she noticed, were startlingly blue, Calliope forcibly pushed his rifle butt away. The metal, exposed to the full heat of the sun, burned her fingers and the flash of pain brought her to her senses. What on earth was she doing? But it was too late to pull back; she was in it now, for better or worse.

'Stop it,' she yelled, 'how dare you? You might be the winners at the moment but that doesn't give you the right to abuse people in this way. He doesn't understand, you can see that.' From somewhere deep in her soul, an old playground jibe rose to the surface. 'Why don't you go and pick on someone your own size?'

A few interminable seconds ticked by, during which time realisation of the huge misjudgement she had made descended on Calliope's shoulders. She would pay for this, without doubt. But come what may, she wasn't going to give in. She waited for the officer to raise his gun again, point it at her. She stared at him, silently challenging him, 'Go on, do it, if you think you're brave enough'. Another childish dare, but at least she didn't actually say it out loud this time.

For an infinitesimal moment, their eyes met, locked in mutual hatred.

And then the officer simply turned away, motioned to his band to follow him, and they marched off.

Calliope stared after them, stupefied. What had all that

been about? She didn't understand. She turned towards the homeless man. She would take a leaf out of Calista's book and offer him the food she had with her, the same simple fare as always, bread, goat's cheese and tomatoes, but he was obviously destitute and presumably hungry so he'd surely be glad of...

The man was gone.

She scoured the landscape and could just make out his ragged figure disappearing into the distance. He was able to move much faster than Calliope would have expected from the state of him. As she stared after him, she thought there was something familiar in his gait but could not place it as belonging to anyone she knew.

Eliana appeared by her side, her face pale with fear. 'Good Lord, Calliope, what on earth did you think you were doing?'

Calliope lifted her arms in a gesture of incomprehension. 'I don't know,' she admitted. 'I couldn't let them treat him in that way. They're bullies and I don't like people like that.'

Eliana snorted in disbelief. 'No one likes them, you silly billy,' she rejoined, half trying to make light of it and half still clearly appalled by Calliope's recklessness. 'But that doesn't mean it's a good idea to confront them head on! They could have shot you. And then what...'

Her voice trailed away as she tried, and failed, to put the awful consequences into words.

'I know,' sighed Calliope, taking a deep breath to calm her still-racing heart. 'It was foolish.' Sensing that now Eliana's fear was abating it might quickly turn into anger at the risk Calliope had taken, she worked hard to appease her friend. 'But they didn't shoot me, so I suppose I got away with it.'

'You did this time,' remonstrated Eliana. 'But I don't fancy your luck another time. You need to be careful. Even what we did today, going to Kandanos – I'm already realising that really wasn't sensible. From now on, I think it's better to keep our heads beneath the parapet and avoid drawing attention to ourselves. Don't you?'

There was a challenge in her voice that Calliope chose to ignore. After several hours of walking, they reached their own village main street, where their ways parted. Calliope stepped forward to embrace her friend in farewell. They had always been so close, her, Calista and Eliana, like siblings, triplets even. Calliope wanted the gesture to dispel the tension that had arisen between them, to rub out any disagreement and confirm that everything was just as it had always been. But Eliana's back was stiff and her hug lacked its usual warmth.

A sudden sorrow suffused Calliope as she watched her friend depart. Eliana had always been up for any adventure, before. Now she seemed to want to take a back seat against the invasion, and Calliope couldn't agree with that. Was this going to prove an obstacle to their continuing friendship? Calliope profoundly hoped not, as a life without Eliana as a lynchpin was barely comprehensible, but on the other hand she couldn't compromise on her own principles, of support for the resistance and any action that might overcome and oust the Germans.

With a sigh, Calliope set off up the alleyway that led to her house. She put her doubts about Eliana to one side, and instead replayed in her head the encounter with the German patrol and the homeless man. Still unsure what this bizarre scene signified or how to explain it to her sister, which obviously she would try to do, as they told each other everything, Calliope traipsed wearily homewards, head filled with the mystery. At the same time, her previous desire to join the resistance gained greater weight with every step she took. She was going to do it, whatever her parents and Calista thought or said.

Just let anyone try to stop her.

CHAPTER 8

CRETE, JUNE 1941

'I've got a job,' Eliana announced, as she laid out the last of her washing on a huge flat stone. She and Calliope were on the riverbank, where the rhythmic thumping and thwacking of wet fabric on rock echoed through the air and every boulder was strewn with laundry drying in the sun: bed sheets and eiderdowns, baby blankets and shawls, dresses, breeches, skirts and shirts.

Calliope frowned as she scrubbed a little harder. 'Really? Where? Doing what?' Most village women didn't work outside the home, and Calliope struggled to imagine what employment Eliana would be taking on. At the bakery, perhaps? Or the small grocery store – but the family who owned that usually managed to staff it themselves without extra help...

'In Chania,' Eliana replied, and then added, 'well, nearby anyway. I'll have to be on the early bus every morning.' She sounded doubtful, and a little contrite, though whether about the early start or the job itself Calliope wasn't sure. Eliana wasn't heading for the bakery or the shop, that much was obvious, but she hadn't really answered Calliope's question.

'So what's the job?' Calliope asked, unsure why her friend hadn't offered more details.

Eliana shrugged, and avoided meeting Calliope's eyes. Calliope regarded her a little impatiently. Why was she being so evasive?

'I'm going to be working at the army base, same as Dad,' Eliana said eventually, her voice almost a whisper. 'Look, I don't really want to,' she added, hastily, 'but you know the situation, Mama's health, so many mouths to feed.' Eliana's mother had been ill for a while and was almost bed-ridden these days, leaving Eliana to look after her many siblings. 'Eleftherios is old enough to watch over the little ones now,' she continued, 'so I need to do what I can to contribute.'

For a moment, blindsided by this revelation, Calliope didn't respond. She knew Eliana's father, who was a chef, had a job at the base cooking for the Germans. Well, it was a case of needs must, a way to support his large family and buy his wife's medicines. But it was a shock to find out that Eliana planned to join him there.

'He heard they were looking for translators,' Eliana continued. 'And as you know, I can speak German, so it makes sense to use it if it lets me get such good employment.'

Ever since their trip to Kandanos, Calliope had been puzzled and frustrated by Eliana's ambivalence towards the resistance, and now she knew the root cause of it. Eliana was going to work for the enemy.

'It's just a job,' Eliana concluded. 'And we need the money.'

This last was uttered with a note of defiance, as if challenging Calliope to gainsay it.

Of course Calliope didn't. Couldn't. Eliana's family had struggled financially for years, even more so than most in the area, so Calliope understood why the decision had been made. She wasn't happy about it but it wasn't her business. Except that, apart from Calista, Eliana was her best friend, and

Calliope didn't see how that could continue when said best friend was working for the Nazis.

'Right,' she said, unconvincingly. 'Well, if it's what you want.'

Eliana raised her eyes to Calliope's. 'It's not a question of want,' she replied, sharply. 'It's necessity. Guess what they're paying me?' Before Calliope had a chance to answer, Eliana named a weekly sum that almost made Calliope lose her balance and fall over. It was indeed a princely amount, far more than any Cretan business would be able to offer.

'I wish you luck,' Calliope concluded, as magnanimously and graciously as she could.

'Thank you.' Eliana's reply was somewhat prim, and there arose a tension in the air, as if something had broken between the two of them that wasn't going to be fixed. She gathered up her laundry, folded it into her basket and, with a brief, cursory wave, left the riverbank.

Calliope resumed her washing, pounding and pummelling each item as if she wanted to murder it. This war was changing everything. It had already taken her brother, and now her friend, even without the finality of death, was lost to her too. What more would be gone before it ended?

When she'd finished the scrubbing and rinsing, she sat on a boulder, knees drawn up to her chest, contemplating the river, wide and green, as it made its calm progress towards the sea. At least nature could be relied upon not to spring such nasty surprises as Eliana had just done. Calliope had been late getting started on the laundry, a job she detested, and was the last one still there. In the quiet and solitude, she almost drifted off to sleep, and only noticed the sound of approaching footsteps when they were nearly upon her.

It must be a farmer or labourer returning late from the

fields, she thought, spade thrown over his shoulder and dreaming of a hearty evening meal after a long day's work. She lifted her face to see who it was, ready to greet them with a cheery *kalispéra*, but instead her mouth dropped open in shock.

Rather than the familiar face of a villager, it was the ragged homeless man she'd seen being harassed by the Nazis. She expected him to recoil at the sight of her, as he clearly wasn't used to human company and the memory of the earlier encounter would still be fresh in his mind. But the man continued towards her with no hint of hesitation. Again, there was that familiarity in his gait, but Calliope still couldn't work out where she knew it from.

As he drew alongside her boulder perch, the man stopped. Calliope braced herself for him to say something meaningless and incomprehensible, as earlier it had seemed that he couldn't talk properly.

'We've met before, haven't we?' the man said. His Greek was accented but perfectly correct, and he seemed in full possession of his marbles. Calliope's mouth fell open a little wider.

'When your brother— I'm sorry, I don't want you to have to recall it. But we went with you and him to your house.'

Calliope gasped in surprise as recognition dawned.

'Major Laurie Wynn-Thomas,' the man continued, holding out his hand.

It took a moment for Calliope to gather herself together sufficiently to respond. 'But call me Laurie,' she murmured, shyly. She started to reach out her own hand but then, glancing at his, inadvertently hesitated. He really was very dirty, his hands as bad if not worse than his face.

Laurie's eyes followed hers and he grimaced, withdrawing his hand and putting it behind his back. 'Sorry, bad idea. But yes, indeed, call me Laurie.' Their eyes met and he flashed her one of his heart-stopping smiles. 'I'd like that.'

Calliope almost swooned. This encounter had gone from the ridiculous to the sublime in a matter of moments. Was she dreaming? She almost had to pinch herself to be sure. But as she prevaricated, not sure how to react, Laurie spoke again.

'I don't believe we've been properly introduced. Your name is?'

Calliope gulped. 'Calliope,' she squeaked, her nervous self-consciousness showing itself in the high pitch of her voice. 'And you also met my twin sister Calista and our parents.'

'Yes, of course I did,' Laurie agreed, as if there might have been some dispute about this. Calliope had a sudden urge to laugh. What was wrong with her? She pushed her shoulders back and jumped down from the boulder. Laurie was supposed to be on a ship to the Middle East like all the other soldiers who had managed to survive the invasion, so what had happened?

'What are you doing still here?' she asked, forcing her tone back to normal. 'Isn't it dangerous for you? Shouldn't you have gone by now?' She remembered him saying, when they'd found the glider, that he might not be able to leave, but she hadn't thought he was serious.

Laurie shrugged and smiled again. Calliope wished he'd stop doing that. It was so unsettling.

'Most have left, but some of us are staying. We're forming cells in the mountains. London is sending us additional personnel and radio operators so that we can work with your compatriots in the resistance to do all we can to rid your beautiful island of these monstrous invaders.' He paused. 'It's just the beginning, but we won't give up.'

He said this with such assurance, and his voice had a tone of such steely determination, that Calliope allowed herself to believe him. To believe *in* him, and the British in general, and the fact that this war could be won even while that also seemed impossible.

'In the meantime,' Laurie continued, 'I need your help.'

At these words, Calliope's heart leapt. Was he going to ask her to join the resistance? Even though she was a woman? Would this be her chance to put in place the plan she had formed?

'What do you need?' she replied, her voice coming out as a strange yelp in her excitement and anticipation.

'My disguise isn't too good,' Laurie continued. 'I took these rags from a dead man, but being this dirty is hell. I need to look like one of you. My moustache is coming along nicely but it's the clothes that'll do the trick. And I'm very hungry.'

As quickly as it had risen, Calliope's heart sank again. Not an invitation to join an underground cell, just a request for food and clothing. But, feeling Laurie's expectant gaze upon her, she rallied again. *Anything* she could do was worth it. Any act of defiance, however small, was a way of fighting back against the hated Germans.

'Of course,' she replied. 'Come back with me now and my father will give you everything you want. And you'll eat with us tonight.'

'Thank you,' said Laurie.

'But,' she ventured, hesitantly. 'I-I mean...'

Laurie turned to her. 'What?' he asked, encouragingly.

'Well, I-I...' Callie was struck by an uncharacteristic onslaught of self-doubt. It was ridiculous to think she could actually be part of the resistance. Wasn't it? But then again, why not?

'Can I join you?' The words tumbled out before she could stop herself. 'I'm young, and strong, I know the island really well. I'd do anything you wanted.'

There was a pause. Calliope held her breath as she felt a flush suffuse her cheeks.

'You're still keen then?' he replied, amusedly. Calliope hoped he was taking her seriously. She watched as he carefully selected and lit a cigarette.

'I can't answer that right now,' Laurie continued, speaking slowly as if carefully weighing up each word. 'There's a lot to organise, a great deal of logistics...' He took a long pull on the cigarette and blew out the smoke into the darkening air. 'But I'll bear it in mind.'

With that, it was clear that the conversation was over. Shouldering Calliope's bag of clean laundry, Laurie turned in the direction of the village, gesturing to her to lead the way.

Reeling from the unexpected turn of events, and hopeful that it boded well for her future ambitions, Calliope took Laurie into the village. She wasn't worried about any of the villagers seeing him, as everyone was against the Nazis. Or were they?

With a sudden shock of horror, she remembered Eliana. Translating for the Germans. What if she saw Laurie, took the information to work with her? Riven with fear, Calliope quickened her pace. They must get to the house as soon as possible, without passing Eliana's home. If someone in her own village betrayed him, she'd never forgive herself, just as she'd never forgive herself for George's death.

Calliope was shaking with nerves by the time she reached her front door. Hastily, she bundled Laurie inside, all decorum and politeness put on hold until he was out of sight. Her mother and father came running at her urgent calls, and Valeria quickly organised the hot water needed for Laurie to wash while Yiorgis sorted out some clothes to give to the British soldier.

Before too long, Laurie was ready. He entered the kitchen dressed in wide breeches, tall boots, a black waistcoat and a mulberry sash, with a black lacy *sariki* upon his head.

'You look fabulous,' cried Calliope, clapping her hands. 'No one would be able to tell you apart from a true Cretan now.' And it was true. Even after his wash, his skin was still dark from the tan he had gained in the days he had spent on the run in this land where the summer sun shone so fiercely.

At this moment Calista returned, looking remarkably fresh

considering she'd been outside all day, engaged in the laborious tasks of weeding and hoeing. 'Who's this?' she asked, bewildered. And then, behind her hand to Calliope, 'Why is this stranger wearing Dad's good boots?'

Calista was always so observant. Calliope hadn't even noticed that Yiorgis had given Laurie his prized footwear, but she wasn't surprised at his generosity. It was typical of their father.

Laurie turned his dazzling smile on Calista and in that moment she realised who he was.

'Major Wynn-Thomas,' she exclaimed, blushing hard. 'I'm so sorry I didn't realise it was you. You look... different.' She gestured towards Laurie's new attire.

'Do you like it?' he asked. His eyes sparkled and Calista flushed more deeply.

'Of course,' she replied, demurely.

'Then I'm happy,' Laurie declared. 'If I'm good enough for Calliope and Calista Papadakis, I'm good enough for anyone.'

The family and their guest sat down to eat, a hearty meal of lamb stew with potatoes, vegetables and bread. After they'd finished, Yiorgis broke out a bottle of his infamous *tsikoudia* and, in ones and twos, men from the village arrived, summoned by some invisible bush telegraph. The twins never touched the drink, the alcohol being far too strong for them, but Laurie downed shots with the best of them. One of their neighbours had brought his lyre and began to sing lyrical *mantinades*, which Laurie somehow managed to join in with, though how he knew the words Calliope couldn't imagine.

Eventually, as it got late but the party showed no sign of ending, Valeria shooed the twins off to bed. In their room, whispering while the music drifted up through the floorboards, Calliope couldn't help but make a confession to Calista.

'Major Laurie,' she began, not sure how to put into words

what she was feeling. 'He's so... so nice. And handsome. Do you think he's handsome? His lovely thick hair and that smile...'

Calista giggled and slapped her hand across her mouth. 'Calliope! You like him, don't you? You better make sure Papa doesn't find out. You know how protective he is. He can't seem to grasp that we're grown up now.'

Calliope chuckled and then stopped, a frown creasing her brow. 'We're twenty-one! If it wasn't for the upheaval of the war Mama and Papa would have had us married off by now, I'm sure. But I, for one, am glad I'm not, or I wouldn't be able to feast my eyes on Major Wynn-Thomas.'

'Stop it, Calliope!' Laughing harder now, Calista threw the aged rag doll she still kept on her bed at her sister. 'You're terrible. Though if Laurie was going to look at either of us in that way, it would definitely be you. I wish I were bold and confident like you are.' She hesitated, biting her lip in the way she did whenever she was thinking hard. 'But anyway, it's irrelevant. Laurie's here to fight a war, not fall in love.'

Her sister's words rang in Calliope's ears as she drifted off to sleep. Love, and war. The two could go together, couldn't they?

CHAPTER 9

CRETE, 2005

Callie's pupils contracted sharply as she stepped through the door of the plane. She'd forgotten how much brighter the Greek sun was, how much lighter the light. She hesitated for a moment, trying to take in the fact that she was here, landed on Cretan soil after so many decades. Only the tutting of a passenger behind her, irritated at the hold-up, propelled her into action. Ella took hold of her arm and helped her down the steps. With each one, Callie's trepidation increased, along with her misgivings.

What if this was all a huge mistake? What if it would have been better to have ignored the letter? To let sleeping dogs lie? In the days since the decision had been made that Ella would postpone her worldwide trip and accompany her to Crete, it had been hard for Callie to find answers to all of Ella's incessant questions.

'Why the sudden need to go back *now*?' she'd asked, several times.

Callie had tried to put her off by being vague. 'You just need to trust me,' she'd said. 'I'll tell you when we get there.' She could have gone on: guilt that needed to be assuaged, if that was even possible, ghosts that had been haunting her for over six decades to lay to rest, explanations for the unexplainable to attempt...

And the baby. At some point, the fate of the baby must be addressed.

A sick feeling in Callie's stomach rose up to her throat. This was a terrible idea. Why was she here? She had a sudden urge to run back up the steps, back inside the aircraft, and refuse to leave. But Ella still had a hold of her arm and was gently pulling Calliope in the direction of the terminal building.

There was no turning back.

Inside was thronged with tourists and locals alike. Callie had had no idea so many people wanted to visit Chania. Where had they all come from? What were they doing here? It was a far cry from the war-torn island, hungry and battered, she'd left all those years ago. As they stood waiting for their luggage, Ella questioned Callie again.

'We're here now, Gran,' she said, stepping aside for a man with a suitcase almost as big as him. 'So surely you can tell me what this is all about?'

Callie breathed out through her nose, a tad impatiently. 'I need to see someone,' she said, obliquely, her eyes fixed on the conveyor belt. 'Someone... important.' And then, 'Look, that's mine, isn't it?' she exclaimed, pointing at a small black case with a purple ribbon round the strap. Ella had told her to do that, to make it easier to identify. Ella leapt over and retrieved Callie's case, and then her own, and was distracted from further questioning by having to navigate their way through customs and in search of the car hire place.

Callie had not been at all sure about this. 'Are you sure you'll be all right driving on the wrong side of the road?' she'd asked Ella on more than one occasion, with the result that, in the end, Ella had retorted, 'I was until you kept putting doubt in my mind!' Her frustration was clear in her tone and Callie had got the message that she needed to back off a little. Nevertheless, she couldn't entirely quell her anxiety about it.

At least on this first day they were staying in the city, so there was only a short journey to the hotel to navigate. Once they'd arrived there safely and checked in, Ella was keen to go straight out exploring, if that suited her grandmother.

'Are you up to it?' she asked, anxiously. 'Not too tired after the flight?'

Callie resolutely shook her head. 'I'm fine, my dear,' she responded.

Ella threw her arms round her in an unsolicited hug. 'You are amazing,' she enthused. 'No one would think you were eighty-five.'

'No, they'd think I was ninety,' quipped Callie, wryly.

'Oh,' scoffed Ella, laughing. 'Don't be daft. Most sixty-five-year-olds would be lucky to be as fit as you are. You're indestructible!'

At that, Callie chuckled too, but as she followed Ella to the foyer her smile faded. She had seen war, seen the damage that bullets and bombs could do, seen people die before her very eyes. No one was immune, no one could defy deadly weapons used against them. Of those closest to her, first her brother George and then her sister Calista had succumbed. But now Calista had somehow risen from the dead to send her that letter, and here Callie was on Crete, summoned by some inexorable force to return and face all the mistakes she had made, everything she had fled from so long ago.

Her pace faltered as doubt and fear assailed her.

'Would you like a rest?' asked Ella, anxiously. 'A little lie-down?'

Callie shook her head. Stiff upper lip. She'd learnt that from the British and really it was the best way. The only way. 'Let's go,' she said.

'OK, so we'll have a walk around and then we can look for

something to eat.' Ella was buzzing with all the ideas she had about what to do and see; she'd been researching Chania and the area around it for weeks now, her interest in her Cretan heritage suddenly awakened.

'I wish you'd taught me Greek,' she said to Callie as they left the hotel and set off for the harbour. 'Why didn't you? Did you teach Mum? Could she speak it?'

Already feeling too hot, Callie didn't immediately reply. There were so many reasons. Too many. How could she tell Ella that, once she'd reached the sanctuary of England, she'd needed to forget all about what had driven her away? Events that the letter had brought hurtling back into the present, demanding attention that Callie did not wish to give.

'I thought it would confuse you, and your mother,' she replied eventually. 'You and she were living in England, growing up English. I believed it would be easier to focus on that, rather than for either of you to try to have two identities.' There was so much more to it than that, but Callie could not imagine how she would ever be able to explain.

Fortunately, Ella's attention was diverted towards Chania's gorgeous Venetian waterfront, busy and lively with cafés and restaurants, souvenir shops and bars. It was familiar to Callie but, at the same time, utterly foreign. When she had left, there had been bomb damage everywhere. Now the buildings were mostly restored, spruced up for the tourists, pretty as a picture. Callie appreciated the efforts made but underneath she had a strange feeling that, whatever veneer was put upon a place, it could not eradicate the horror of the past. Chania had been under occupation, the population fearful, traumatised and oppressed. She, for one, could never forget that fact.

They reached a building that had not been renovated but still lay in ruins, close to the old mosque, grass and weeds valiantly growing out of cracks and crevices. Ella stopped to gaze upon it.

THE LETTER FROM THE ISLAND

'You don't talk about the war, Grandma,' she ventured. 'Neither did Grandpa.' Her expression was puzzled. 'Why not? It must have been – well, it must have changed your lives.'

Oh yes, thought Callie. *In ways you could not possibly imagine...*

'So why don't you?' repeated Ella.

Callie attempted to straighten her creaking back. 'It was all so long ago, my dear,' she replied softly. 'People who lived through that era – they tried to forget about it. To move on. There was no point in going on about the past when we had a present to inhabit, a living to make. That's just the way it was.'

Ella regarded her grandmother intently. To avoid her scrutiny, Callie turned away and focused on the ruins. She could picture the Stuka dive-bombers and the Junkers Ju 88s, the screech and howl of the engines, the terrifying sound of exploding ordnance... She shivered involuntarily, despite the heat of the sun. The young people simply didn't understand that there was nothing to be gained from recalling that time. Even though, on this journey, Callie knew she was going to have to.

They moved on, back from the harbour and into the dense maze of lanes and alleyways that made up the old Jewish quarter, Evraiki. Nestled in a narrow, vine-covered street was the recently restored Etz Hayyim synagogue, which had been the focal point for the town's two-thousand-year-old Jewish community.

'Oh Gran, look!' cried Ella. 'I read about this. It was so awful. The Nazis rounded up all the Jewish people to ship them to Auschwitz but the boat was torpedoed by the Allies and everyone died. Such a terrible tragedy.'

Callie grimaced. What was there to say?

At the museum, Ella marvelled at the displays of war memorabilia: weapons and uniforms, charts and maps, bombshells and grenades. Callie retained a tight-lipped frown throughout. She passed through the photography gallery without looking to right or left, leaving Ella to study the black-and-white images alone. What if Callie saw a picture of someone she knew? Someone she knew the fate of? How would being reminded of all the island had lost be helpful in any way?

Her stomach roiled at the thought of what she must confront on this trip, and then a sudden, intense, stabbing fear gripped her. What if Ella saw a picture of the baby? Recognised a family resemblance in the image? Shaking, Callie somehow managed to stumble to a chair and lower herself into it before her legs gave way beneath her.

Clenching her fists, she desperately tried to calm herself. There was no way that could happen. There were no pictures of the infant on Crete, of that Callie was sure.

Nevertheless, when Ella came wandering out of the gallery and stood looking around her to locate her grandmother, Callie scrutinised her expression, and breathed a sigh of relief when she saw no discernible signs of upset, other than the concern that would be on anyone's face after viewing pictures of such a sad past.

The pair found a tiny café overhung with purple bougainvillea in a pretty cobbled courtyard and sat down at a shaded table.

'It must have been so scary,' said Ella once the food had been ordered, still fascinated by the history she had been learning about. 'The bombing. Those parachutists! What were they called? *Fallschirmjäger*. Wow.' She shuddered. 'Awful.'

Callie had not meant to get drawn into a conversation about the famous Battle of Crete; indeed, she'd been actively resisting it. But sitting here, in this place she had not seen for so long, the memories came crowding back, too many and too intense to suppress.

'It *was* awful,' she responded, slowly. 'We called them the Sky People. It makes them sound innocent, doesn't it, or like make-believe. But they were real. All too real. Thousands and thousands of them, raining down on us from the blue heavens.'

Ella helped the waitress to distribute the plates on the small table. She'd ordered meze and it looked delicious.

'What did you do, Gran? I can't imagine what I would do if such a thing happened in England. Run away and hide under my duvet, I think.' She smiled in an attempt to lighten the mood, but Callie didn't follow suit. Her eyes were fixed on some distant point, far back in history.

'We fought, tooth and nail,' she replied, eventually. 'Everyone did. Men, women, children. For four long years. We never gave up. The Germans couldn't understand it. It's said their general liked to watch the firing squads at work because he'd never seen people face their death with such stoicism and bravery as the Cretans. He admired us even as he slaughtered us.'

Ella stared at her grandmother, eyes wide with amazement. 'Gosh,' she said, quietly. 'So – were you involved, then? If everyone was?'

Callie smiled, a small, simple, wistful smile. 'Oh yes,' she responded. 'Of course I was.'

Now Ella's expression was full of admiration. 'Go, Grandma!' she exclaimed. She regarded Callie expectantly, waiting for more. When Callie said nothing further, Ella screwed up her eyes in contemplation. Callie could see her mind whirring, and braced herself for more questions.

'Let's eat,' Callie said, abruptly. 'I'm hungry.'

But the food only provided a temporary respite.

'When people fight, or resist an occupying force,' Ella began once she'd finished her meal, speaking slowly, choosing her words carefully, 'people die. Cretan families are usually large. But you don't have any relatives. So what happened to them?'

Callie picked up a napkin and methodically folded it, over and over, until it was as small as she could make it. In the spirit of adventure engendered by her forthcoming worldwide odyssey, Ella had gone along with Callie's plan to come to Crete without too much probing. Callie had known it couldn't last. Her granddaughter's interest had been aroused and there was no putting it back in its box.

'My little brother died during the invasion,' she said, eventually. 'He was shot by one of the Sky People.' As she spoke, Callie's gut twisted at the memory of George's death. But it was not just his passing that lay on her conscience.

'My parents and my twin sister – well, they met their fate later. Along with so many others,' continued Callie. Her guilt joined forces with the recollections of the mistakes she'd made. No matter how much she tried to push such memories down, they were always there, waiting to pop up and taunt her like a jack-in-a-box of retribution.

'Right,' said Ella, clearly shocked. 'I see.' She seemed lost for words, overcome by her grandmother's revelations. 'So there really isn't anyone left here?'

Callie nodded. She couldn't find the words to tell Ella the whole, terrible truth about the purpose of her visit, though she knew she'd have to, soon. In just a few days she'd see Calista. And then it would all come out. Every last shameful bit of it.

The waitress appeared and began clearing plates, a welcome interruption. But Callie knew better than to think that Ella would give up at that. Her granddaughter was nothing if not persistent. Ella asked the waitress for another Coca-Cola for her and an orange juice for Callie, and waited until she'd gone before saying more. She reached across the table and took Callie's hand.

'You need to tell me why we're here,' she said, gently. 'After all this time, and for no apparent reason. Something must have happened. I'd like to know what it is.'

Callie pursed her lips. The drinks arrived and she took several long, slow sips of hers. There was a piece of orange perched on the rim of the glass and Callie studied it, its vibrant colour, its juicy flesh.

'My sister who died,' Callie replied eventually. She'd known Ella would wheedle it out of her sooner or later, but articulating it was still incredibly hard. 'I received a letter from her.'

Ella's mouth fell open. 'What do you mean? She's dead. So how could she write to you?'

Callie shrugged. 'I don't know. That's why I had to come. To find out.'

Ella took a long slug of her Coke, then stifled a burp from the bubbles. Fizzy drinks had always made her burp. Normally the two of them would have laughed, but not on this occasion.

'So when are you going to see her?' asked Ella. 'If that's why we've come. Tomorrow? Shall we go tomorrow?'

Callie took the orange slice from the rim of her glass and sucked the flesh. It was as good as it looked: sweet and delicious. 'We will go. Just not yet. Not tomorrow.'

Ella sighed loudly. 'At some point I'm going to lose my patience with all this cryptic stuff, Gran,' she said. She looked sharply at Callie. 'Is this really all? Nothing more?'

She knows me too well, thought Callie, before saying, 'Of course.'

It was a lie. Another lie. Lie upon lie. And then there was the worst lie of all. The one that Callie had kept to herself for all this time. The lie that would cause Calista to regret contacting her and make Ella hate her.

Pensively, Ella twirled the ice in her glass. 'I don't believe that's all there is to this,' she said. Callie wasn't surprised that her granddaughter was unconvinced.

'And I really don't understand why neither of you made any effort to contact each other before now,' continued Ella. 'All that time, all those years, but only now?'

Callie met her look of incredulity with silence. Eventually, Ella shook her head as if acknowledging she wasn't going to get anything further from her grandmother today. She ordered coffee for them both and, as Callie sipped at the hot, black liquid, she thought about what other long-buried secrets this trip would unearth.

How would or could Callie ever explain what she had done back in 1943, and why?

CHAPTER 10

CRETE, OCTOBER 1941

A flash of sunlight caught Laurie's pistol as he checked that it was loaded before stashing it beneath his Cretan waistcoat. Watching him, Calliope's heart lurched. He was there with a signal-sergeant called Ben and, at their lair in the mountains, other members of the Allied forces were gathered, forming one of many resistance cells operating across the island. Laurie, with various men, came to the village on a regular basis to collect supplies, so she and Calista had got to know him over the weeks. And part of that knowledge was the awareness that he and all of the British soldiers were in constant danger. If something happened to Laurie, would Calliope and the rest of her family even find out? The thought of Laurie suffering harm and not knowing was unbearable.

'Calliope,' Laurie said, interrupting her thoughts. 'Would you walk with us a short way?'

At this request, Calliope bristled with pride. She shot a look towards Calista. Her sister had been bustling around, gathering together provisions: tomatoes and onions, beans and eggs, a little smoked meat. The soldiers needed supplies and Calista loved to feed people; she was in her element in the kitchen. But though food was, of course, essential, Calliope's ambitions still resided outside of the domestic arena. Anything she could do to prove her worth to Laurie, she would grab with both hands, even if it was just to show them out of the village. What she really wanted though was to help Laurie with his work, which involved documenting and mapping the entire occupation network in the Chania area, every machine-gun post, supply station, ammunition dump and checkpoint, gathering intelligence and planning actions against the Germans.

'Could you please go ahead and check that the coast is clear?' Laurie continued.

'Of course,' Calliope replied with alacrity, leaping from her seat and ignoring the concerned glance that her sister shot her. Their parents had forbidden either twin from joining the resistance, saying that they could not bear to lose another child. But Calliope had not given up on her dream.

'When will you be back for more?' Calista asked Laurie as she finished packing his bag with food. 'There will be grapes soon, and apples and pomegranates.'

Laurie smiled. 'I can't say when we'll return,' he answered. Calliope had known that would be the case; the men never gave their movements away in advance. It was too dangerous, both for them and for anyone who knew what they were up to. Ignorance was safer than having information the Germans might want, and would be prepared to torture someone to get hold of.

'Well, I will be ready with whatever you need when you do come back,' Calista assured him, blushing slightly as she spoke. Both she and Calliope yearned for these visits by the men, clinging on to every precious moment with Laurie. Each time they met, the sisters became more and more beguiled by his shrewd wits and intelligence, his command of Greek, which was growing all the time, and, of course, his good looks. He was even more deeply tanned now, and his brown hair had lightened in the sun, which gave him a boyish look. When he flashed that enchanting smile, his brown eyes twinkled to devastating effect.

'Thank you,' replied Laurie. 'You know how much we appreciate all that you are doing for us.'

Calista's blush deepened as Laurie turned towards Calliope. 'We'll follow your lead,' he said, indicating towards the door.

Calliope slipped onto the street, ignoring the silent admonition she could feel coming from Calista. In the villages, the Germans were usually easy to avoid, travelling as they did in groups of half a dozen or more, often with vehicles, but there was always the chance of being apprehended, or of being seen by a spy, or a traitor. These were few in number but they existed. Calliope thought of Eliana. She had to concede to herself that she didn't have any actual evidence that Eliana was doing anything for the Nazis other than her job, which was simply to interpret for them, but nothing could dispel Calliope's deep suspicions. Eliana's willingness to work for the enemy was something Calliope could not forgive her for.

She stepped round the corner onto the main street of the village, and came to an abrupt halt. There, just a few steps ahead of her, was the object of her distrust. Eliana herself, smartly dressed for work, her feet tapping officiously over the stones. Damn! Calliope had forgotten that it was about time for the early bus to leave for Chania. They'd have to wait until it had gone. She tried to slip unobtrusively back into the shadows, hoping that Laurie and Ben would see her and follow suit.

'Calliope!' The cry of her name echoed between the stone buildings.

Damn again. Eliana had seen her.

'Where have you been all summer? I've barely laid eyes on you.' Eliana came right over to her. Calliope moved out of the entrance to the alleyway, hoping that this action would divert

Eliana's attention away from where Laurie and Ben were presumably – hopefully – concealing themselves.

'I've been busy,' replied Calliope brusquely, and then, realising that Eliana might question what she had to do that was so pressing, added more genially, 'You know how it is, with the chores and the vegetable garden... always lots to do.'

It sounded unconvincing even to Calliope's ears, but Eliana nodded. Over her shoulder was slung a smart leather bag and in one hand she held a tall umbrella with which she stabbed at the gaps between the paving slabs. 'I've missed you,' she said simply, reaching out to take Calliope's hand.

I bet you have, thought Calliope, thrusting her own hands into her pockets and ignoring the gesture. *Missed hearing anything I might know that could be of interest to your bosses.*

'Sorry,' she responded. 'Just the way it is sometimes. Anyway, you'd better be going, hadn't you? The bus is due any minute.'

Eliana looked around her, down the hill to the stop outside the *kafeneion*, and then back towards Calliope. Or was it Calliope her eyes were trained upon? Calliope had the sensation that Eliana was scrutinising something behind her, over her shoulder. But of course she couldn't look round to check.

'You're right, I must get a move on.' Eliana turned away and then glanced briefly backwards. 'It was nice to see you anyway.' She looked and sounded like she really meant it, but Calliope wasn't fooled.

'And you,' she replied, coldly. Thank goodness for that, she thought as she watched Eliana stride off, walking faster now in case she missed the bus to work.

Laurie and Ben appeared from where they had been lingering, and the three of them got out of the village as quickly as possible. As they climbed higher into the foothills of the mountains, the temperature dropped a couple of degrees and the breeze became noticeably chillier. Calliope shivered. Winter was coming. After they'd walked for twenty minutes or so, Laurie suggested that they stop for a bit. Seated on a rock behind a thicket of oak trees, he turned to Calliope.

'You're committed to the fight against the enemy, aren't you?' he asked her.

Surprised, Calliope hesitated. She wasn't sure what the answer should be. Was Laurie in any doubt about her determination to end the occupation? He must be or why would he be asking?

'Er, yes,' she said, eventually. 'I would do anything.' She crossed her fingers and whispered a silent prayer that her parents would forgive her. 'I-I want a chance,' she continued. 'To show you what I can do.' She knew she was different from lots of the other young girls. Perhaps Yiorgis had not been a typical father but, having been blessed with two daughters and, for over a decade and a half, no son, he had brought the twins up to do whatever a boy could do – hiking, running, climbing. It meant that Calliope was fleet and fit, tough and resilient.

She didn't know what Laurie needed her for, why he wanted her to accompany him and Ben that autumn morning. But, even if she didn't want to spend every second she could with him, she'd still have said yes.

'I don't doubt your capabilities,' answered Laurie, with a flash of his dazzling smile. A frisson of electricity ran through Calliope. She was more composed with Laurie these days, but that smile still got to her every time, sending delicious tremors shooting through her body and setting butterflies fluttering in her stomach. 'It's clear to me that you and your sister are remarkable young women, brave and honest.'

Calliope glowed with pride.

'So I have something important I need to ask you,' Laurie continued.

Narrowing her eyes, Calliope stared at him. 'What is it?' she asked.

'There's a ship coming in two days' time, to a beach on the south coast,' Laurie replied. 'It'll bring letters, spare parts for the radio and a few other things we've asked for. I need someone to go and meet it, bring back the stuff.'

'Right,' said Calliope, a little more uncertainly now. Was Laurie asking her if she could suggest someone? There was little Stelios, their neighbour's son, who was always making himself useful carrying messages to and fro from one village to another. But he was only ten years old, and that was too young for such an important – and dangerous – mission.

Before she could say that she wasn't sure what she could do, Laurie spoke again. 'It should be someone local who knows the land and who won't arouse suspicion.'

An expectant silence filled the air. Suddenly, it dawned on Calliope. That someone was her. Laurie wanted *her* to go on this vital mission.

'Yes,' she blurted out, without giving it a second thought. 'Yes, I'll do it. Of course I will.' To be believed in by someone like Laurie was special indeed. And the fact that he trusted her with his own life – because that was what was on the line whenever he gave details away to anyone outside his small cell of soldiers – made her feelings for him even stronger.

Later, after Laurie had given her all the information she needed, and the men were on their way to the mountains, Calliope went to the churchyard on the outskirts of the village. On George's little grave she laid a bunch of autumn-flowering cyclamen she'd picked, deep in thought about the undertaking she'd been entrusted with. She'd wanted so badly to do something real to avenge his death.

Now, sooner than she'd ever expected, she had her chance.

CHAPTER 11

CRETE, NOVEMBER 1941

Calista drew her shawl around her shoulders and brushed a tear from her eye. It was three in the morning and she'd insisted on getting up to see Calliope off on her mission.

'Please take care,' she begged as she stood helplessly watching her sister prepare to leave. She knew how stubborn and determined Calliope was and that it was futile to argue with her twin now her mind was made up. But that didn't make it any easier to let Calliope go.

'I will,' whispered Calliope, trying to sound reassuring even while her hands trembled as she fumbled with the bolt on the front door. No one had ever locked their doors before the invasion, but now the fear of the enemy coming in the night to take people away was ever-present. 'Remember, don't say a word to Mama and Papa until nightfall – let them think I've gone into Chania to buy fish for dinner.'

Calista bit her lip. 'All right,' she said at last, her agreement clearly reluctant.

Calliope shot her a sharp look. 'You want to avenge George's death as much as I do, don't you?' she probed.

Hastily, Calista nodded. 'Of course. As much if not more.'

A noise from upstairs caused both women to freeze, waiting anxiously to see whether it was one of their parents waking. When no further sound came and silence once more reigned, Calliope moved towards her sister and threw her arms round her. Calista was the only sibling she had left and to leave her was a terrible wrench.

As they hugged, Calliope heard Calista's uneven breathing and knew she was holding back more tears. It hurt her to be hurting Calista but there was nothing to be done about it. She had to go. Releasing her hold, Calliope picked up the wool cloak that would keep her warm on her trek.

'Just a few days,' she reassured Calista. 'Not long.' The idea that it might be for ever, that she might never see Calista again, leapt unbidden into her mind and she forcefully pushed the notion away, unable to contemplate such an outcome. 'Don't worry about me,' she implored. And with that, she raised the latch on the door and let herself out into the cold, dark night.

The journey was one she had made as a teenager with her father several times, but everything looked different now she was alone and always aware that she could encounter enemy troops at any time.

She tried to keep to a regular pace, slashing at the tangled brambles, grown long and twisted over the summer, with her knife, using her hands to steady herself on the sharpest ascents. Pushing herself up the steep hills, navigating rocks and boulders, narrow ledges and deep gullies, she made good progress. Tomorrow she would reach and cross the snowline. For today, it was rain she had to contend with, which began to fall soon after she set off, heavy and relentless.

She walked all day, higher and higher into the mountains, with only two short breaks to eat some of the supplies Calista had prepared for her. That first night, she stayed in a long-abandoned *mitato*, a shepherd's hut, picking some wild rosemary first to lay her head upon to help her sleep, and wrapping herself tightly in the woollen cloak to keep warm. So far from civilisation, she found she was not frightened of the Germans; for them to find her here would be most unlikely. Instead, as the wind howled outside the drystone walls, she held on tight to George's favourite toy, a little knitted rabbit Calista had made for him when he was born and which he had always kept in his bed. She'd brought it as an amulet, and to remind herself, when the going got tough, why she was doing this. It smelt of her brother, earthy and musky, and she kissed its little head just as she used to do to him every night, before drifting off to sleep.

The next day she reached a vast pine and cypress forest. It was dark and gloomy under the branches, the thin light of late autumn hardly penetrating, but at least the trees provided protection from the rain. The higher she got, the further the temperature fell and, an hour or so after the forest ended, she reached the snow.

Like many people in rural Crete, Calliope only possessed one pair of shoes, stout leather boots that she'd wear all year, apart from in summer when she wore simple sandals or went barefoot. Also like most rural Cretans, her boots had been repaired and mended many times; she'd lost count of how often the cobbler had resoled them. But since the arrival of the Germans, shoe soles, along with so much else, were in short supply. As she tramped from rough rocks to slippery snow, Calliope became conscious of the thinness of her shoes. She could feel the outline of each stone and, despite the thick socks that Calista had knitted for her, the cold penetrated deep into her bones.

That night, there was no shepherd's hut to shelter in. Instead, she found a shallow cave under a towering crag. She made a bed of cypress branches and used her knife to chip off the end of a stalactite for water. It was freezing cold and

Calliope woke every hour or so, groaning and longing for her bed with its many blankets, unable to get warm enough to stay asleep for long. All alone in the vast, empty expanses of the mountains, in the darkness Calliope felt a sudden stab of loneliness, which, when the acuteness of the pain had faded, remained in her heart as a profound feeling of homesickness.

Her wakeful mind was assailed by thoughts of her family, of George and Calista, Mama and Papa, the sheep and the goats, all the characters who were the centre of her world. What if she didn't make it back to them? Or even more awful, what if she got back to the village and they were gone in some raid or attack by the Germans? She would not be there to protect them...

With so much tormenting her, it was a relief when the feeble light of dawn began to creep across the sky. Exhausted though she was, Calliope was glad to get up and continue her journey. That day, she began to descend, and before long she was crossing a wide plain, and then flitting through a silvery olive grove. At about midday she stopped short, her breath catching in her throat. There, before her, was the sea, sparkling in the winter sunshine.

At that moment, Calliope realised that she had doubted herself. Doubted that she could do it, that she could navigate those huge, towering mountains alone, that she had the strength and stamina. But she had done it. She had actually done it.

It took the rest of the day, into the evening, to actually reach the coast. She'd been worried about the logistics of meeting the ship. But in the end it was easy. It came as close as it could to the shore, and then a small boat rowed in to the rendezvous point.

With no fuss or bother, the rower clambered ashore and handed Calliope the parcel of letters and radio parts .

'*Efharistó*,' she said.

'No, thank you,' said the sailor. 'And – you might like these as well. If you can carry them.' He handed her a canvas bag that was heavier than it looked. Unbuckling the straps, Calliope peered inside to see a selection of tins with English labels. She pulled one out and scrutinised it in the moonlight, screwing up her eyes to try to make sense of it. The sailor couldn't help; he didn't speak a word of Greek. He handed her one more item, a pack of playing cards. Calliope smiled at the sight of them – she'd played cards at a cousin's house but never owned any herself. She imagined games of *diloti* or *xeri* with Laurie and his men, laughing as they forgot, for a short while, the stresses and strains of the war.

The sailor coughed.

The sound brought Calliope back to the present and she had a sudden urge to get out of there. The moon was bright and nearly full, and the beach was exposed, with no cover nearby. She wanted to put some distance between her and the coast, get back into the relative safety of the mountains' craggy peaks.

'I'd better go,' she said.

The sailor nodded and in seconds was back in the rowboat, oars rhythmically pulling through the water.

Calliope shoved the cards into her pocket, checked that the package of letters and parts was strapped securely inside her backpack, slung the canvas bag over her shoulder and trained her eyes on the path home.

Resolving to do the return journey at top speed, she picked up her pace. High on the success of her mission, she had already decided that she would continue to work with Laurie, that she would take on any further assignments he should wish to give her. She hated to go against her parents' wishes, but this was too important to walk away from because of fears of safety. The truth was that the occupation had put every citizen of Crete into constant danger; joining the resistance didn't make a huge amount of difference. That was how she justified her decision to herself, anyway.

Eventually, after walking for nearly twenty hours without

pause, she knew she needed to sleep. She'd put more than a safe distance between herself and the beach by now, and it was time to find somewhere to lie down. A few hours' rest would be enough; then she could get going again.

Reaching a small copse of chestnut and plane trees, Calliope sank down onto a fallen trunk, breathing heavily in and out. Too tired to even eat, she made herself a nest among the dropped leaves, snuggled under the woollen cloak and slept for five hours, until the rays of the sun filtering through the thick branches roused her.

Drowsily, she hauled herself upright. She was famished. She'd taken the bare minimum of food with her so as not to weigh herself down, but now she realised she hadn't brought enough. Remembering the canvas bag, she pulled it closer, fumbling inside for one of the tins. With sleep-heavy eyes, she regarded it. The label was white with mainly black writing: Nestlé's full cream condensed milk. On top of it, in red, was stamped Suppliers to H.M. Forces. Calliope had no idea what any of it meant. There were three pictures beneath; two looked like coins but the middle one was of a bird perched on the side of a nest. So did that mean that there were eggs inside? But who ate birds' eggs from a tin? And if it were eggs, once she'd opened it she'd have to cook them, which she didn't want to do as the smoke from a fire might attract attention...

In the end, curiosity got the better of her. Using the point of her strong knife, she bashed a hole in the top of the tin. Inside was a white liquid. Calliope raised it to her mouth and took a tentative sip. It was milk, but not like any milk she'd tasted before. This was pure nectar; thick, creamy, sweet and delicious, better even than the fresh sheep's milk she'd been brought up on. Hurriedly, as if someone were about to snatch it away from her, she upturned the tin once more and drank deeply, draining every last drop.

When she had finished, she sighed with satisfaction, and

then was immediately consumed by guilt. She should have saved the sailor's gifts for her family, not greedily guzzled a whole tin by herself. Checking inside the bag, she saw that two more tins of milk remained. She would definitely not touch these; they were for Calista and her mother and father.

Scratching a hole in the ground, she buried the empty container and stamped soil on top of it so that she left no trace behind her. Then, fortified by this delectable breakfast, she set off. Whether it was the homesickness, the milk or the fact that she was homeward-bound, Calliope's strong, fit legs ate up the miles.

By the time the moon came up again, she was approaching the village. She expected it to be dark and absolutely quiet, everyone long since abed and asleep. But at the bus stop on the only road wide enough for a vehicle stood a row of German army jeeps.

Calliope stopped abruptly. What on earth was going on? Her mind raced, imagining the possibilities. Another terrible raid like the one that had occurred at Kandanos, and that happened in countless other settlements since the occupation had begun? Everyone knew now the potential consequences of conspiring with the resistance: the burning of houses, massacres of entire valleys, forced expulsions and summary executions. The Germans thought that extreme violence was the way to win over the Cretan population, to cow them into capitulation. Instead, all it had done was fuel their hatred and opposition.

Had the Nazis found out about her family, and the many other families in the village who aided and abetted anyone working against the regime? Had Eliana seen her leave with Laurie and Ben and put two and two together? Calliope's heart stilled at the thought.

Pressed against the side of the solid stone buildings for protection, she ventured into the village. She heard the enemy troops before she saw them, loud cries in harsh tones, barked instructions, angry footsteps. And then, beneath the stentorian voices, female screams and the wailing of infants. Dreading what she was going to see, she poked her head round the corner onto the main street. Torches and searchlights blazed, throwing a violent, disruptive yellow glow over everything. Huddled outside doorways Calliope could make out groups of men, women and children, shivering in the cold, wearing threadbare nightclothes and expressions of horror and bewilderment.

As she watched, countless German soldiers emerged from the houses or paraded down the main street, each carrying sacks of potatoes or grain, strings of onions, baskets of carefully stored apples; anything edible, it seemed, that they could lay their hands on.

Disbelievingly, Calliope slunk along the side alley that led to her house. The sight that greeted her there was just as terrible. A wheelbarrow, parked outside and being rapidly filled with jars of Calista's lovingly preserved tomatoes, along with apricots, peaches and cherries, bottles of the family's homemade wine, olive oil and *tsikoudia* and, worst of all, their chickens, squawking loudly in protest as, legs tied together, they were thrown onto the heap.

Calliope stared, dumbfounded. Their hens. Their food. The provisions that were absolutely essential to get them through the long, cold months until spring. All being pillaged, right before her eyes. Rage pulsed through her body. How could the Germans do this? What gave them the right?

But of course she knew. Being the dominant force gave them the right. In that instant, Calliope's red-hot fury solidified into cold determination that was stronger than it had ever been before. She had just undertaken a vital mission for the resistance and, in that moment, she knew she would complete many more, as many as she could while there was breath in her body. She would do it for her family, her friends and neighbours, the island – and for Laurie, who had won her heart and her devotion.

From inside, frantic shouting and arguing erupted, breaking her trance. It was her mother, loudly protesting the theft. A thwack of flesh on flesh and then her father, screaming in pain. Calliope threw the canvas bag under a juniper bush and darted to the door, not caring if the Germans asked where she had come from and what she was doing out and about so late. Inside the house, she saw her papa lying on the floor, dazed from the blow he had taken.

Her mother and Calista were already bent over his prostrate body, crying. The Germans, ignoring them all, including Calliope, carried on with their plunder. When they left, the family sat in silence regarding their ravished home, the empty shelves and the trail of chicken feathers strewn across the earthen floor.

Later, they discovered that the same terrible punishment had been meted out across the province: retribution for the resistance blowing up a food storage warehouse. Their own provisions being spoilt, the Nazis had decided to take it out on the entire population.

How would the family, the village, any of them, survive the winter now? But if the Germans wanted this action to break the islanders, they were wrong. Staring at the wreckage of her home, Calliope's resolve to fight back only intensified.

CHAPTER 12

CRETE, 2005

'Today,' announced Ella, over a breakfast of Greek yoghurt, fruit and pastries, 'I thought we could go to Souda Bay, to the Commonwealth War Graves cemetery.' She looked at Callie expectantly. 'What do you think?'

For a moment, Callie didn't think anything. Couldn't. There would be headstones there to the fallen, and whose names would be upon them? She wasn't sure who had been buried where, and was even less sure that she wanted to find out. Even from the distance of more than sixty years, the thought made her tremble with fear.

Ella was regarding her patiently. 'I mean, if we can't see your sister, for whatever reason...' She tailed off here to look pointedly at her grandmother, 'we can at least explore some other parts of the island's history.'

Callie's lips quivered. It was clear what Ella was getting at. 'We *can* see my sister,' she insisted. 'Just not yet. I'm— we got here a little earlier than planned and she's not expecting me until later in the month.' It was a small white lie to cover the dread she felt at the prospect of the meeting and, having uttered it, she didn't have the energy to also explain why going to Souda

Bay filled her with terror. On the other hand, nor did she have the energy to resist Ella's proposal.

They drove out in the hire car, the air conditioning on full.

'Gran,' said Ella gently, her gaze fixed on the road ahead. 'If you stopped being so secretive and told me the whole story, and I mean *everything*, it might be easier for you. Take some of the burden off.'

You think that because you don't know, Callie wanted to reply. *You don't know what I did, the consequences it had, the way I brought disaster upon my family and my village, and then compounded it by...*

Callie gazed out of the window at the modern outskirts of Chania, the concrete buildings, strips of shops and showrooms, the traffic. It had changed beyond recognition from what she remembered, when cars were rare and far outnumbered by mule carts, and children herded their goats along the dusty city streets.

'If there is a burden, it is mine, not yours,' said Callie. 'However frustrating it is for you, please don't rush me. You know I'm no good if I'm rushed.'

'Oh Gran, were you always this stubborn?' sighed Ella, rolling her eyes. Then she uttered a short laugh and added, 'That question was rhetorical, by the way. You don't need to answer!'

Callie tried a half-hearted smile. There was no one in the world who knew her better than Ella. Which made everything worse. Because what would Ella think when she found out the truth? What would she do?

Glancing at her granddaughter, she marvelled at the way Ella seemed to be able to read the map and keep her eyes on the road at the same time. There'd been a time when Callie had had no need of maps to find her way around her part of this island.

She'd known the landscape like the back of her hand. As Laurie had once commented on, in those days distances were measured by the length of time it took to smoke a cigarette, which had been funny, because she had never smoked in her life. Smoking was something men did, back then. But somehow she'd always known how long a journey would take.

It was only on that last, fateful journey that she'd not known the way, or the time it would take to get there. And had had not only herself to look after, but also a dying infant. Callie closed her eyes, willing the visceral memory of that last hike to fade away and for the torment to diminish.

Ella drove on, in silence now, understanding that Callie was not going to reveal any more for the time being. As they neared the cemetery, the buildings thinned out and the road was lined with silver birch trees, trunks glowing in the sunshine. Ella pulled into the car park. 'I'll park as close to the entrance as possible,' she said.

Callie sniffed and stared out of the window. 'I *can* walk,' she responded. 'I'm not an invalid.'

'No, Gran, of course you're not, I was just—' Ella broke off when she saw Callie's stiff back and distant expression. 'Well anyway, here we are!' she continued, with exaggerated cheeriness, before jumping out of the car and rushing round to open her grandmother's door. Ella was usually a confident person, but Callie had seen her doubt herself over the last few days. She didn't know how to react to Callie's reticence, to her refusal to lay everything bare. Callie felt bad about putting Ella in this position, but at the same time powerless to do anything about it.

Creakily, but trying to appear as agile as possible, Callie clambered out of the passenger seat. Ella took her arm and they walked to the cemetery entrance. An expanse of immaculately manicured, emerald-green grass, studded by row after row of perfectly spaced headstones interspersed with bright-red roses, met their eyes.

'Ohh!' Callie could not suppress an exclamation of shock, distress and disbelief. She gazed out at the full sweep of the cemetery, hands clenched into fists. 'I didn't realise... of course I knew... but so many of them.' In her state of heightened emotion, she seemed to have lost the ability to complete a sentence.

Forgetting about Ella, she propelled herself across the grass towards the closest row of headstones. She read the inscription: *A soldier of the 1939–1945 war.* Beneath the chiselled cross were the words *Known unto God.*

It was enough. Callie turned abruptly on her heel and marched straight back to the car, leaving Ella staring after her in bewilderment.

It was some time before Ella returned. Her demeanour was sombre, as if she carried the weight of the loss and suffering the cemetery represented on her shoulders. She climbed into the car silently and turned on the engine. It was a relief when the air conditioning kicked in. Callie waited for her granddaughter to put the gear into reverse, turn the vehicle round and head for the exit. But Ella showed no sign of doing so.

'I didn't realise how many New Zealanders and Australians were involved in the Battle of Crete,' she mused, her hands clasping the steering wheel.

Callie stared out of the window. 'Truthfully, we called them all British,' she replied. 'They all spoke English and we couldn't tell the difference. I think the wireless operator Ben was from New Zealand though. I must have heard that from someone. Maybe from him.'

As soon as she'd said the words, she regretted them. Ella immediately seized on this titbit, as Callie had known that she would.

'So who was Ben?' she asked. 'How did you know soldiers?

Was that because you took part in the resistance?' She'd seen her opportunity to squeeze some more information out of her grandmother and she wasn't going to let it go.

'He was part of a cell operating in our area,' replied Callie, guardedly, wondering how little she could get away with saying. 'He worked with Lau— I mean, he was just part of the group. They came to the village occasionally to get food and clothes. We were all happy to help.' Why had she answered the call in that letter from Calista? All that could come of raking up the past was pain, mental pain to match the physical agonies of her old, tired body. She shifted awkwardly in her seat to release the pressure on her back.

'In fact, I became a runner for the resistance. I delivered messages, and fetched supplies from the boats. Sometimes people were my cargo – soldiers I had to take to a different cell, for example.'

'Wow, that's incredible, Gran. You're a war hero!'

Callie rolled her eyes. 'Hardly.' She breathed a silent sigh of relief. Her strategy had worked. Give Ella a titbit of information to stop her probing where Callie could not bear her to go.

'I want to hear all about it,' said Ella, distractedly, 'but we better get a move on now or the air con will drain the battery.' Despite her worries, she made no move to set the car in motion. 'I was thinking, in the cemetery, among the tombstones, that it's amazing Grandpa Harry survived,' she mused.

At her words, an image of Harry snapped into Callie's mind's eye, his height and his blond hair, his kind eyes that crinkled when he smiled, his dimpled chin. She had always told Ella that he had been her one and only love, the love of her life. Was it a lie? It was hard to say.

'But I suppose if he hadn't,' continued Ella, 'you wouldn't have been able to marry him and have my mother.'

A sharp stab of pain, like indigestion, almost made Callie cry out. She managed to stifle it.

'I suppose there must be fellow soldiers of his buried there, perhaps even friends.' It was clear that the experience had affected Ella greatly. Callie wasn't surprised. It had hit her in the solar plexus too, even though she had lived through it. Perhaps it was the distance of time, all the decades, that made it worse, not better.

'Do you know any of their names?' questioned Ella. 'Grandpa must have told you, mustn't he? Some of them, anyway.'

Callie shook her head. 'I don't recall,' she replied. This, at least, was not a lie. She genuinely did not know the names of anyone Harry had fought alongside in Crete, but the reason for her ignorance was not one that Ella would ever guess.

Ella regarded her quizzically. 'OK,' she answered, eventually. She scrabbled around in her bag and pulled out the guidebook that she had studied closely before their trip and still had her nose buried in half the time. Callie wished she'd put it away. What did any of the people who wrote these books know about war?

'There's a German military cemetery too,' Ella announced. 'It's in Maleme – is that how you pronounce it? About twenty kilometres. I'd like to go there, too. Shall we?'

Callie's heart momentarily stopped beating. She didn't want to go. Not one little bit.

'The Germans were our enemies,' she stated, hoping this might put Ella off.

'Yes, that's true,' replied Ella. She sighed. 'I get that you're not keen. We can go back to the hotel for a rest if you like, and then maybe the beach?'

'It's up to you, my dear.'

Ella pursed her lips. 'Just a quick visit then,' she said. 'I don't know why, but I feel I should go. Now that we're here.' She shrugged, as if making clear that her desire to see the cemetery was just one of those things that couldn't be helped.

Without waiting for Callie's reaction, she consulted the map for a few minutes, tracing the route with her finger as if committing it to memory. Then she released the handbrake and they were off. The road hugged the coast until the turn-off after the village of Maleme, from where it wound upwards through groves of trees, oranges and silver-leafed olives that glistened under the sun.

'Where are your parents buried, Grandma?'

The question blindsided Callie. For a moment, she was speechless. Once she had control of her vocal cords, she attempted to answer. 'I-I, er, in the village,' she muttered. Were they? How would she know? It wasn't as if she'd stayed around to—

The car hit a pothole in the road, the undercarriage slamming onto the crumbling tarmac, and Ella swore. 'I hope I haven't blown a tyre,' she groaned. 'Or the exhaust. That'll be all we need, stranded in the heat as we wait for a mechanic.'

'We could change a wheel ourselves, couldn't we?' protested Callie. 'I thought you young women liked to be independent.'

Ella smiled. 'I should know about car maintenance, I agree,' she said. 'But I'm afraid that I don't. Oh well. Anyway, it seems to be OK – it's running fine and there are no warning lights. I think we got away with it.'

'Jolly good,' Callie said, but her relief was for the fact that the near-accident had distracted Ella from her questioning about her family's graves. How could she explain that she didn't know where they were buried, could only assume that they would have been laid to rest alongside George and her grandparents? Where she had always thought Calista was, too, but had now found out that she wasn't...

When they reached the cemetery, the view across the bay of Chania was spectacular, the sea calm and deepest blue.

'I want to jump right into that ocean,' enthused Ella. 'I'm

definitely swimming later.' She released her seatbelt and looked expectantly at Callie, who was not moving.

'Gran? Are you ready?'

Callie remained immobile. 'I'll stay here,' she said. 'But take as long as you like.'

Ella reached out and put her hand on her grandmother's shoulder. 'It's far too hot to sit in a tin box,' she protested. 'You'll melt. I don't think your long-lost sister will be too happy when I have to tell her she won't be meeting you after all because you've expired into a puddle of sweat.'

Callie refused to take the bait. She knew that Ella meant well, and it was only to be expected that she wanted to meet her great-aunt, but she had to understand that this trip, odyssey, whatever it was, would go at Callie's pace.

'Ladies don't sweat,' she answered, stoutly. 'We glow.'

Shaking her head, Ella laughed briefly. 'Oh Gran, you are incorrigible. But fine, stay if you insist.'

'I'll get out if it gets too warm.'

'OK.' Ella handed her grandmother the key. 'See you in a bit.'

When Ella returned, she found Callie still in the car, weeping.

'Gran! What's the matter?'

Callie regarded her through bleary, teary eyes. 'Nothing,' she muttered, unconvincingly.

Ella didn't look happy with this explanation. 'You're going to have to tell me what's going on,' she said, clearly trying to be patient but unable to prevent a hint of exasperation from coming through. 'If it was just a sister who's alive when you thought she wasn't, we'd have visited her straight away, it would have been simple, not like this. I've gone along with it so far, let you be all enigmatic and mysterious. But I know there's stuff you're not telling me.'

Her final words contained a challenge that Callie knew she couldn't dodge for ever. Exactly as her granddaughter said, at some point she was going to have to come clean. She just wasn't sure she'd ever have the words to do so. How could she ever explain, in language that Ella or anyone else would understand, that, as well as the deaths and the destruction, she had stolen something from someone, the most precious and irreplaceable thing that anyone could have? Yes, she had done it for the best of reasons – but did that excuse her?

It was impossible to imagine that Calista – or Ella herself – would see her theft that way.

CHAPTER 13

CRETE, FEBRUARY 1942

Calista emptied the bucket onto the kitchen table with a loud clatter. Calliope, Valeria and Yiorgis looked on in silence. The muddy pile heaved and swelled as the snails poked their slimy heads out of their shells and slowly began their escape attempts.

Calliope's stomach gurgled and churned, partly from hunger and partly from revulsion. She hated snails, always had, always would. But over this starving winter, she had had to learn to eat a lot of things she would never have touched before. They all had.

'I think it's time,' she said, her eyes moving from her sister to her mother and then her father.

Valeria frowned. 'We should wait,' she replied. 'Until we are really desperate.'

'I'm desperate now,' Calliope stated bluntly, her eyes flicking towards the revolting snails. 'And I must go to the hideout today. Laurie might need me.'

Over the winter, she had achieved her aim, and could now claim to be an active part of the resistance. But though it was what she had yearned for, and though she was committed to continuing for as long as it took, constant hunger dulled all other feelings. It gnawed at her stomach, hollowing it out, making her feel always on edge.

For a moment, nobody spoke. And then Yiorgis broke the silence. 'All right,' he agreed. 'But you have it, my child. You need to keep your strength up for the important work you are doing.' That was the only positive about the starvation conditions. Her parents, so enraged by having their supplies stripped bare, no longer opposed Calliope's involvement with the insurgents. Hunger had changed a lot.

'Yes.' Calista spoke with firmness and surety. 'That's right, Papa.'

Calliope shook her head. 'We all have it, or no one has it.'

Her tone indicated that this was the end of the argument. She went to the cupboard in the darkest corner of the kitchen where the bottled fruit and vegetables were usually kept. In any year, by this stage of the winter, their supplies would be depleted. But this year the shelves were entirely empty, apart from one solitary tin. The last of the condensed milk that the sailor had given Calliope on her first trek to the coast. Since then, she had made numerous journeys across the mountains, through freezing rain and snow and ice, across towering peaks and through deep ravines, delivering letters, collecting new arrivals to the island sent to bolster those already covertly battling the enemy, taking messages between different cells of fighters.

The job of runner was perhaps the most demanding and gruelling of all resistance work, not to mention the loneliest and most perilous. Most of the runners were young men: those with the strength and stamina to take these trips, to live rough, navigating by the stars and the sun, relying for their survival on their knowledge of their land and their wits. As far as she knew, Calliope was the only woman.

Ever since that first mission, she had worked hard and tirelessly to show that she was as competent as any male. She made every trip with George in her heart, and in his memory. And so far, things had worked out. She was still here, wasn't she? She could only hope that her good fortune or blessed luck or whatever it was would continue.

Calliope picked up the tin and brought it to the table. Calista laid out four tea glasses. Yiorgis opened the can and Valeria solemnly poured out the white liquid, meticulously checking that the amount in each glass was exactly even. When she had finished, there was a moment before anyone moved. And then each picked up their share of the milk and drank. Calliope, always impulsive and rash, threw hers down her throat in one gulp. Calista, on the other hand, so much steadier and more measured than her twin, consumed hers in small sips, savouring each sumptuous drop.

Valeria placed her empty glass on the table, a curious mix of elation and devastation on her face. 'That was delicious,' she wailed. 'But we should have saved it. What if one of you girls gets sick and we need it then?'

Calista put her arms round her mother. 'That won't happen, Mama,' she said. 'We're not going to get ill, are we, Calliope? And if we were to, we'd find a way. God would provide.'

Calliope didn't share Calista's conviction. She wondered why God was letting this war happen, letting so many people suffer so intensely. But there was no point in that sort of questioning. Apart from anything else, she didn't have the energy.

Fortified, if only temporarily, by the milk, Calliope bade her family farewell. Her mother no longer cried every time she left the house, but Calista often did. Determinedly, Calliope never looked back once she'd crossed the threshold, in case she lost heart at the sight of her sister's wan face watching her depart. In her pocket, she could feel the comforting, hard solidity of the pack of cards she always carried with her. She and Laurie usually had a game of something if they had time; recently, they had been playing *koum-kan* and keeping a running tally of the score. Calliope was ahead at the moment, but only by a fraction. She wondered if they'd have a chance for another round that day.

The sky was overcast, huge clouds hanging low over the mountains, shrouding the highest peaks in a grey pall. By the time she was approaching the hideout, snow had begun to fall. The soles of her boots were almost completely worn through now. She'd packed the insides with newspaper, but this quickly became soaked through and her feet were blocks of ice. She hurried on and, as soon as she was within hearing distance, paused to make the bird call that was their signal. Only when she heard the answering call did she proceed to the entrance.

Inside the makeshift shelter, the men were huddled in their Cretan wool cloaks, donated by various families to see them through the winter, tin cups in their hands. At the turn of the year, Laurie and Ben had been joined by two others, John and Gerald; they had been roaming the hills since the invasion and had ended up here.

The soldiers couldn't light fires for fear of the smoke giving away their position, but they had a small paraffin stove on which they could heat water for tea, which Calliope had discovered British people drank a lot of. They liked to add milk to it, an utterly peculiar habit to her mind, and when she'd first tasted the drink she'd hated it – bitter and sweet at the same time, with a bad aftertaste. She'd tried to introduce the men to Cretan mountain tea, made from a local herb, but they hadn't been keen, preferring their weird variety.

'Calliope!' Laurie exclaimed as she entered, his generous, beautiful smile immediate and unreserved. 'Hot drink?' He gesticulated with his mug towards her. He seemed in good spirits, smiling and happy. But then again, she'd never seen him gloomy or depressed. He seemed to live in a state of eternal optimism, however bad the situation and despite the omnipresent danger.

·

Calliope shook her head. She crouched down on the floor beside him. As she did so, her stomach gurgled, long since done with the condensed milk and desperate for further sustenance.

'I've got some good news,' he announced. 'We've been promised a parachute drop to bring supplies, ammunition, clothing and more. It should take place in the next day or so.' He paused, peering out through a gap in the branches that formed the sides and roof of their temporary home. 'As long as conditions allow.'

Calliope's heart sank. There was no guarantee that that was going to happen. The planes needed clear skies to make a drop, but there had been thick cloud cover for days.

'The other news,' Laurie went on, 'is that we'll be moving from here soon. We've located a *mitato*, like the one your family has, which will give us a bit more shelter until the weather improves.'

'Right.' Calliope was puzzled, but tried not to let it show. How did Laurie know about the Papadakises' *mitato*, or what it looked like? Though on the other hand, all *mitata* were pretty much identical: drystone walls topped by a low, vaulted roof and with a semi-subterranean area for the storage of cheese. Laurie began to speak again and Calliope put the mystery to the back of her mind; she needed to concentrate.

'If you can stay for the drop, it would be helpful,' Laurie continued. 'We'll need as many hands as possible to collect the packages as quickly as we can, in case of detection. There should be food for you to take back to the village. I'm hoping for tinned salmon and corned beef, eggs, mutton, cabbage...'

As Laurie listed the goodies expected, Calliope began to salivate. She would stay here a week if it meant getting her hands on some of this booty. 'So we wait,' she said, simply. 'Cards?' She pulled the pack from her pocket. Laurie smiled. 'Why not?'

'Do you think we're making a difference?' asked Calliope as Laurie shuffled. 'Are we having an impact?'

Laurie paused, contemplating the cards he held in his hands. 'Oh yes,' he replied, eventually. 'Everything we do makes a difference, even if it isn't immediately obvious.' He dealt, then picked up his stack and examined them. 'Don't be disheartened if, at times, it seems futile. This is a war of attrition and, in the end, we will win.'

Calliope was filled with admiration for his confidence, his resolute determination. She wished she herself could feel so certain.

'I understand that it's harder for you,' Laurie continued, fanning out his cards and deftly swapping their positions.

Calliope held her breath. Was he going to cite her femaleness? She railed against such a suggestion. But her doubts were unnecessary.

'It is your family who is suffering, not mine. Your people, your parents, your sister—' He broke off, and a wistful look drifted across his handsome face. Calliope wondered what was behind it, but it seemed too intimate a question to ask.

'Your family must be hurting, too,' she remonstrated. 'Wondering where you are, what's happening to you – it must be awful for them.'

Laurie grimaced. 'You're right, I suppose it is.' He sighed. 'But at least my folks are more or less safe in England. They live in the countryside, far from the bombing of the cities. Food isn't abundant, but there is enough for everyone. They're in a very different situation from people here.'

Calliope was sure that it wasn't that simple for Laurie's parents, but she understood that he needed to look at the positives rather than the negatives. Trying to banish her fears for her own family, she turned her attention to the card game.

. . .

In the end, it was two days before the wind swept the clouds away and, via the radio operated by Ben, they received news of the plane's impending arrival. It would come to the nearby plateau, a suitably secluded place. The night arrived dark and cold and Calliope shivered as she and the soldiers, lying flat on the snow, anxiously strained their ears for the first sound of the engines coming from afar.

The hours and minutes until it happened seemed everlasting. And then, suddenly, it was under way, the swooping aircraft circling overhead, the parcels dropping in droves. Some of the parachutes caught in trees and hung there from the branches like stranded clouds. Calliope, Laurie and the others waited on tenterhooks until the drop had finished and it was safe to rush to collect what had fallen.

But what they found plunged their spirits into despair. The plane had misjudged the drop, or entered the wrong coordinates – whatever the cause, the result was that the majority of the parcels had fallen not on the plateau but into the gorge a few hundred metres to the left. Despondently, they gathered what they could salvage and began dragging it back to the hideout.

They were on their third or fourth journey when it happened.

Into the silence of the night, a shot rang out. And then another, and another.

Calliope froze in her tracks, cowering in the shelter of a pine tree. She heard the muffled sound of footsteps in the snow and suddenly Laurie, Ben and the two other soldiers were beside her. Without a word, Laurie pointed upwards. There, on a ridge high above them, silhouetted by the moonlight, was a band of resistance fighters, weapons poised. As Calliope watched, terrified, more shots sounded. Following their downwards trajectory, she saw a German patrol of many scores of men, some already hit and fallen, the others fixed in position like rabbits in car headlamps.

'We requested cover from the Cretans,' whispered Laurie. 'We didn't expect to have to use it.'

There was no time to ask how the Germans had found out about the drop. They had the capacity to listen in to radio messages. They had traitors and they had spies, living and working among the Cretans. Not many, but enough.

Eliana?

But how could she have known? Nevertheless, she was always Calliope's first suspect whenever anything went wrong.

Loud shouts in German erupted from just behind them. The patrol must have split in two. Chaos ensued. The troops who were being fired upon took flight, the ones behind them began to fan out over the widest area possible.

'Follow me!' hissed Laurie.

Calliope did as she was told. Laurie was beside her, Ben a little ahead as she desperately tried to keep up with them. In their path lay a huge boulder. The two men were big and tall enough to scramble over it, but Calliope wasn't sure she could do so.

'I'll go round the side,' she gasped. 'Don't wait for me.'

She veered off to skirt the boulder. But there, on the trail in front of her, stood a German soldier. Their eyes locked for one appalling moment and then Calliope's feet slipped out from under her. Instantly, she was falling.

Falling and falling, a fall without end.

CHAPTER 14

CRETE, 2005

Callie knew that Ella's patience was wearing thin. But the longer they spent on Crete, the harder facing up to the past was becoming. Those times of finding herself eye to eye with an enemy combatant pointing a gun at her now seemed far less frightening than what she was facing in the present. Calista had specifically said in her letter that she wanted to talk to Callie about what she had done. But whatever her sister imagined the truth to be, Callie was sure it couldn't be as bad as the reality.

'I'd like to visit this museum, Gran,' Ella had announced the previous evening. 'The Askifou War Museum. It says here that it's a family collection of artefacts and memorabilia gathered from all across the island. Shall we go tomorrow?'

Callie suppressed a shudder at the word Askifou. How could Ella begin to understand the images that place name conjured up? The row of resistance fighters belly down in the snow, watching the sky for an approaching aircraft. The sudden sound of gunfire, the cordite stench as bullets parted the air. She closed her eyes momentarily, as if she could wipe away the memories. Ella's tactics had changed in the light of her grandmother's continued refusal to tell her any more about her plans.

She had not asked about visiting Calista in twenty-four hours, but was merely ploughing on with ideas about what to do, as if that, eventually, would wear Callie down.

The drive up to the plateau and the museum was breathtaking. Through the car window, Callie watched the landscape passing by at a speed she could only have imagined as a young woman traversing the area on foot. They drove through rippling wheat fields, vineyards and green meadows, which gradually gave way to groves of orange and almond trees. As they climbed, the rise and swell of the mountain peaks loomed over them, wispy white streaks of cloud caught beneath the summits.

'It's soooo beautiful,' breathed Ella. 'I had no idea how gorgeous.' She glanced briefly at her grandmother, before focusing back on the road to negotiate one of the many sharp bends. 'Why didn't you ever come back to live here, Gran? I think I would have done.'

It was hard to know how to respond. Crete was, undoubtedly, gorgeous. But even though the Germans had left in 1945, vanquished, their tails between their legs, there were so many other reasons why Callie had never returned. Could never return.

'The British soldiers hid up here,' she said, changing the subject. 'In shepherds' huts, or caves and home-made shelters. Sometimes they stayed with villagers in their houses, but they never lingered for long as it was too risky. The Germans declared at the outset that all enemies, whether armed or unarmed, whether fighting or fleeing, were to be slaughtered. Even so, everyone – almost everyone – helped the British. The children idolised them. For all of us, what little we had, we shared. It's the Cretan way. The British operatives could not have survived without the help of ordinary civilians.'

Ella considered this for a moment. 'Do you think people would do that now?' she asked. 'Be that brave, and that generous?'

Callie gave a short, dismissive snort. 'I don't know. Remember, for us, it was only forty years since we'd fought for independence from the Ottoman Empire. Resistance was in our blood. Whether it still is, who can tell?'

At the museum, Ella quickly fell into conversation with the proprietor, grandson of the resistance fighter who had established the collection. Callie shrank into the shadows, pretending to be utterly absorbed in the exhibits, not wanting to be drawn into the conversation. She had to keep reminding herself that this grandson could not possibly know who she was, but, even so, she didn't want to talk.

Everywhere Callie looked lay objects related to the war: weapons, helmets, motorbikes, grenade shells, and even the propeller from one of the dreaded Stuka dive-bombers. Every possible type of gun adorned the wall – rifles, pistols, handguns, submachine guns – the sheer weight of firepower was incredible. At the sight of a swastika, that emblem of evil, Callie felt the same trembling fear that it had engendered in her all those years ago, and she shivered despite the heat of the day.

She stopped to read a framed notice addressed to soldiers of the British army, navy and air force, notifying them that their presence was known about and instructing them to hand themselves in. *Every OPPOSITION will be completely useless. Every ATTEMPT TO FLEE will be in VAIN. The COMMING WINTER will force you to leave the mountains.*

At the sight of the spelling mistake, a smile curled across her lips. Laurie would have had something disparaging and sarcastic to say about that. 'You'd think they'd get a decent translator on the job when they're issuing death threats, wouldn't you?' She could hear his voice now, his clipped English accent, feel the confidence his indomitable spirit and optimism had always inspired in her. Major Wynn-Thomas. *Just-call-me-*

Laurie... How she had loved, admired and adored him. She recalled the stricken expression on his face that last time she had laid eyes on him, as he realised that all he cherished was destroyed...

'What's on your mind?' Ella was beside her, eyes narrowed enquiringly. 'It looks serious.'

Callie shook her head. 'I was just thinking that they have amassed a vast collection,' she replied. 'It must have taken years.'

'That's what the owner said,' agreed Ella. 'Apparently they've done it all themselves – they don't get any support from the government. His grandfather scoured the island and the sea looking for anything interesting to add. It's incomprehensible to me how much got left behind or cast aside. And that's just here, on Crete, one relatively small island.' She spread her arms in a gesture of incredulity.

They reached a covered verandah from where anti-aircraft guns looked out over an idyllic view of terraced fields and wooded slopes. It was so peaceful, so quiet. Up above, too high to hear, an aeroplane left vapour trails in the azure sky. Callie thought of the last time she had been here. Her stomach roiled and bile rose in her throat.

No! Don't remember. Damn that letter, bringing all of this to the surface. Pack it away where it's been for all these years.

In the final room, the mounds of exhibits continued. Ella, intrigued by everything she saw, examined the contents of a glass cabinet.

'Hey Gran, look,' she called.

Startled, Callie turned round. Ella was intently studying one of the exhibits. 'Playing cards,' she said. 'I can just imagine the soldiers whiling away the hours with a card game or two.'

She pointed out the red-and-white-patterned card box, and then watched in horror as her beloved grandmother collapsed to the ground.

CHAPTER 15

CRETE, FEBRUARY 1942

Calliope tentatively opened her eyes. For a moment, she had no idea where she was or what had happened. And then it all came flooding back. She was freezing cold, probably injured, but she was alive – for now. Had the others got away? Calliope had no clue, and the idea that they might all be dead made it hard to galvanise herself to action. Eventually, she thought of George and roused herself. She had promised her parents and her sister that she'd be back, and she had to keep that promise. There was no other option.

Gradually, she tried to extricate herself from the ledge on which she was lodged, held fast by a thorn bush growing at an improbable angle out over the gorge. Vicious thorns tore at her clothing and ripped her skin. Gritting her teeth against the pain, Calliope gave one final tug at her skirt and freed herself.

Looking down, a wave of nausea swept over her. The riverbed lay far, far below, the depth dizzying. She paused for a moment, forehead resting against the scrubby grass and weeds that clung to the sides of the gorge. Then, mustering all her courage, she raised her head and looked up instead, at the sky, which today was china blue and cloudless. She imagined she could see George's smiling face, gazing down on her, chuckling in his enchanting way, encouraging her to be strong.

Hesitantly, she pulled herself up, one careful move of her feet and hands after another. Clumps of snow clung to the steep sides, and in sheltered pockets black ice lay in wait to trick her. She put her foot on one and it slipped out from under her, leaving her hanging from her outstretched arms. With a superhuman effort, she managed to find a more secure foothold and right herself. Her progress was glacially slow and all the time she had to be careful not to glance down. She had no idea whether there were German soldiers waiting for her at the top of the gorge, watching her progress and planning her demise. She couldn't think about this. She had to keep going.

It seemed to take for ever to reach the top. How far had she fallen? It felt like miles. Her whole body ached, particularly her ribs on the right side where she had been lodged against the bush. The pain was intense, and worsening all the time. She began to wonder if she had broken them. But there was nothing she could do about it.

Breathing through the pain, Calliope forced herself onwards. Finally she was there, pulling herself over the edge of the gorge, where she flopped down onto the icy ground, gasping for breath. As she clambered to her feet, her eyes caught sight of the bottom again and dizziness consumed her. How she had managed to overcome her fear of heights and get out of there, she had no idea. She tried to walk and an excruciating flash of pain radiated through her entire body, causing her to dry-heave.

Rubbing her hands across her face, she was suddenly aware of how thirsty she was. She had no water, and knew that eating snow could make matters even worse. Mustering all her resolve, she took a few small steps forward. Agony accompanied every movement. But there were no Germans around. At least as far as she could see.

It took hours for Calliope to get home.

When she fell through the door, the house was empty. She crawled to the sink and found the water pitcher where it always was. Grabbing hold of it, Calliope lifted it up, and was about to drink straight from it. But it was empty. With a groan, she slammed it down, and gripped the sideboard until the shooting pains subsided once more. For the first time, tears sprang to her eyes. She no longer had the resolve to hold them back, but instead let them fall. Yes, she was alive. But she was injured and already knew it would be some time before she'd be able to return to her job as a runner. And even worse than that, she had not managed to bring any food back to her family.

When Calista and their mother returned from the vegetable garden, where they'd been optimistically digging to prepare the ground for sowing seeds, they found Calliope lying on her bed, moaning in agony. On inspection, Calista found the skin over her ribcage was swollen and bruised, dark blue-black lesions as livid as her sister's pain.

Only when Valeria had gone out on the daily, desperate hunt for food, hoping to find a loaf of bread at the baker's or a rib of meat at the butcher's, did Calista ask Calliope what had happened. When Calliope explained about the German patrol, despite the thin February light she saw how her sister's face visibly blanched.

'What about the men?' she breathed, her voice barely audible. 'What about... Laurie?'

Tears pricked behind Calliope's eyes. Angrily, she blinked them back. She could not cry again. She would not.

'I don't know,' she answered miserably. 'I want to go to the hideout and find them, but I wouldn't make it there in this state. And anyway, Laurie said they were moving on. After what happened the other night, that will be even more urgent.'

Calista slumped back onto the bed, leaning her back against the wall. The movement sent searing agony shooting through

Calliope's entire body but she didn't say anything, just shut her eyes, clenched her fists and waited for the pain to subside.

'Perhaps he'll come here,' Calista said hopefully, her face still impossibly wan. 'To check up on you, if nothing else.' She ran her hands over her belly and Calliope could feel her sister's hunger like her own. She had hoped to be able to alleviate that, but had failed.

The twins fell silent, each lost in their own thoughts. Neither stirred until they heard the door latch click downstairs and their father come in, back from the animal pen where he was spending a lot of time now that it was close to lambing season.

Calista went to break the news. Calliope could just make out her gentle voice drifting up to her through the floorboards. She thought of Laurie, his handsome face and dazzling smile, his acknowledgement of her family's suffering that was so thoughtful and kind. She wanted to see him so badly, to know that he was alive. The longing hurt her heart almost as much as her physical wounds.

She had drifted off into a fitful half-sleep when a commotion disturbed her. A few moments later footsteps were thudding up the stairs, not slow, heavy ones that an adult might make but lighter, childish ones. For a moment, her mind fuddled by pain, she wondered if it were George. Then she realised that it wasn't his uneven gait as he dragged his bad leg behind him. And also that George was dead.

Seconds later, the door was flung open and little Stelios, their neighbour's son, entered, eyes alive with excitement.

'I've got something for you,' he shouted, unable to temper his obvious exhilaration. 'From the British man, the major. He gave it to me to bring to you.'

Calista had followed Stelios upstairs, and stood behind him now. At the mention of the British major her face visibly brightened, and Calliope too felt a huge wave of relief. That meant Laurie had survived the attack. Thank the Lord for that.

'Show me,' said Calliope.

Stelios ran over to her, brandishing a box.

'What is it?' Calliope thought she recognised one of the packages they had retrieved from the parachute drop, but she couldn't imagine what could have sparked such delight in a small boy. It flashed through her mind that she hoped it wasn't anything dangerous, explosives or guns. But then she came to her senses and realised that Laurie would never have given the little boy anything that would harm him.

Thrusting the box towards her, Stelios lifted the lid to reveal what was inside. It took a few moments for Calliope to recognise the strange objects that the box contained, but, when she did, despite everything she burst out laughing. And then immediately stopped as the agony was too intense.

She reached inside, plucked one of the items out and held it up.

'What?' questioned Calista, confused. And then she, too, understood.

'Shoe soles,' said Calliope, laughing. 'Which admittedly we can't eat, but which we certainly need.' It wasn't just her boots that were falling apart, but those of her whole family and indeed the whole village.

Stelios' little face glowed with pride.

'Take them to the cobbler,' Calliope instructed him. 'And my boots, too. He can mend them while I'm laid up in bed.'

'I will,' shouted Stelios, and careered off down the stairs and out of the house. But in just a few seconds, he was back.

'There are visitors,' he told the twins, still clutching the box of soles to his chest. 'British soldiers. Not the major, new ones. They're coming here now. Eliana is bringing them!'

Calista and Calliope looked at each other. Calliope's heart

sank. What could it mean that Eliana was on her way, and who on earth did she have with her?

Calliope tried her best to sit up, but immediately fell back onto the bed, the pain too great to overcome.

'You stay here,' Calista said. 'I'll deal with it.'

Reluctantly, Calliope agreed. As her sister went downstairs, with a huge effort she managed to position herself so that she could see down into the kitchen through a gap in the wooden floorboards. Straining her ears, she waited to see what this mystery visit was all about.

CHAPTER 16

CRETE, FEBRUARY 1942

'I didn't know who to ask for help.' Eliana sounded genuinely confused and desperate. 'I thought that—' Her eyes flicked between the three soldiers, who wore British uniforms, and Calista, as if suddenly aware that she needed to be careful with her words.

'You've always been so smart, Calista,' she went on. 'What do *you* think we should do?'

Calliope bristled at the word 'we'. Eliana was involving Calista, whether she wanted to be involved or not. On the other hand, Eliana did sound sincere and genuine. But Calliope couldn't forget the suspicions she'd been harbouring about her former friend for so long. She'd discussed them with her sister, but Calista had been resistant to believing that Eliana could be a spy. Through the ancient floorboards, Calliope silently transmitted her concerns to Calista via the twin telepathy that they shared. Her sister was apt to be too trusting, believing everyone was as honest and honourable as herself. She needed to be on her guard around Eliana.

The men were standing there, caps in hands. One of them interjected, in faltering Greek. 'I'm Corporal Stan Platt,' he said. 'And this is Sergeant Bob Butcher and Sergeant Phil Turner.'

There was an awkward moment of silence. Calliope still wasn't sure why Eliana had come to the Papadakis family home. It seemed unusual for three British soldiers to appear in a village together, by daylight, and undisguised. To Calliope, something felt off. But on the other hand, how could they turn away those who genuinely needed help?

Calista, with her innate sense of hospitality, began to bustle around, first bringing in water from the well to fill the pitcher. Stelios' family had given them a small bag of almonds, and predictably Calista poured some into a saucer and offered them around. However little they had, she would always share.

At this moment, Calliope noticed something that made her heart skip a beat. On the table still stood the empty condensed-milk can. Did it give away that they had contacts among the British troops? Who else would they have got it from? If the men were who they said they were, it would do no harm. But if not—

'We have heard that there are other British soldiers and officers living in the mountains around here,' piped up Stan. 'We need to know where to find them.'

Calliope listened with bated breath. Her ribs were screaming at her to get into a more comfortable position, but she couldn't take her eyes away from the gap in the floorboards.

Eliana opened her mouth to speak. 'I—'

A huge crash stopped her in her tracks. Calista stood, staring at the floor where the stone water pitcher lay in pieces.

Stan, Phil and Bob immediately sank to their knees and began picking up bits of stoneware, water swishing around their feet.

'It slipped out of my hands,' she explained, tearfully. 'I don't know what I'm going to say to Mama. She had that jug from her grandmother.'

It was unusual for Calista to be so clumsy, but Calliope hoped it would divert the men's attention from possibly noticing the condensed-milk can. As she squinted downwards, she willed her sister to spot it and move it, or throw a cloth over it – anything. But Calista's hands were trembling and Calliope doubted she was thinking straight. An icy-cold river of fear ran through her body, for the moment drowning out the pain from her ribs. Calista was worried about something, she was sure.

Calista turned to Eliana, who was shifting nervously from one foot to the other.

'We can't help,' she said, bluntly. 'I don't know why you would have thought that we could. We have nothing against the Germans or their occupation. We would never do anything to assist the British.'

A confused expression crossed Eliana's face, and she seemed lost for words. At that moment, there was a knock on the door and Stelios burst in.

'I took—' he began. And then, picking up on the atmosphere in the room, his voice petered out and he stood there, staring at them all. The soldiers were still plucking pieces of the pitcher from the floor.

'Eliana,' said Calista. 'You can show these men the way out of the village, can't you? Now, please.'

Her tone was not one which allowed for argument.

Standing up, the men put the fragments of the pitcher onto the table, replaced their caps, then gave small bows and followed Eliana out of the door. As soon as they had gone and were out of earshot, Calista was upstairs and beside Calliope's bed.

Calliope raised her eyebrows questioningly at her sister. 'What on earth?' she asked.

Calista grimaced. 'Their guns. They weren't British rifles, they were German ones, I'm sure of it. The British ones are longer and thinner and— oh, I don't know, I just thought they looked different.' She paused, biting her lip. 'But perhaps I was wrong, and I've sent those men to danger?'

Calliope shook her head. 'If that's what you thought, I'm sure you're right. Laurie has told me about German soldiers impersonating the British in an attempt to flush out those who are aiding and abetting the resistance. I think that might be what just happened here.'

Calista sank down onto her knees, her whole body trembling. She looked pale and nauseous. 'Did Eliana set us up?' she asked, her tone indicating that she could scarcely believe it. Didn't want to believe it.

Calliope clenched her fists. 'It looks that way.'

A scuffling from the kitchen made both women start. Through her spyhole, Calliope saw Stelios lingering there. She'd forgotten all about him in the drama. At first, she was relieved that it wasn't one of the soldiers returned. And then, with a jolt of fear, she wondered whether he'd heard the twins' conversation.

But before either of them had a chance to say anything to him, Stelios was gone.

A short while later, a commotion from outside drifted up to the bedroom window. Helped by Calista, Calliope managed to crawl over to look outside, her curiosity and fear temporarily overriding the pain of her ribs. The twins were greeted by the sight of a group of older villagers, black-clad women bearing rolling pins and white-haired men carrying sticks and shepherds' crooks, chasing the three British soldiers down the street, threatening a beating if they were caught. Behind them ran Stelios, yelling at the top of his voice with the best of them.

Calista and Calliope looked at each other. Stelios must have heard and then spread their concerns around the village, and this was the result. A lump formed in Calliope's throat. What if they were wrong?

Despite the oldest of those who were pursuing the soldiers being over eighty, they managed to catch them up. It was amazing how sprightly octogenarians could be when sufficiently motivated, thought Calliope. Without further ado, the men were tied to the plane tree and Stelios sent to the nearest German base to inform them of what had happened.

It wasn't long before an army jeep appeared. The three infiltrators were pushed, shoved, punched and handcuffed before being loaded inside and driven away.

Quite soon after that Stelios, who must have run like the wind, returned to address the throng, still assembled under the plane tree.

'They were German soldiers all along,' he cried, his voice loud enough for the twins to hear. 'When they got to the base, they just got out and went inside, and next time I saw them they had their Nazi uniforms on!'

An outpouring of elation erupted from the jubilant crowd on hearing this news. Calista and Calliope clung on to each other's hands and whooped and cheered from their window along with everyone else. The enemy had tried to trick them, but they hadn't succeeded. The taste of victory, even a small one such as this, was sweet indeed, and it was all down to Calista's quick thinking and powers of observation.

Perhaps she had underestimated her sister, thought Calliope. When Laurie heard, he would undoubtedly be impressed. A momentary twinge of jealousy stabbed at her heart. She wanted to be the one Laurie admired. Then she immediately dismissed such disloyal thoughts. Calista had been amazing and she should get all due credit for that, but Calliope did not need to worry about her twin eclipsing her. Calliope was the one who had made the countless trips, fraught with danger, through the mountains to help the resistance.

At that moment, Stelios arrived at the house, barged through the door and hared upstairs to the bedroom.

'Ooof!' Calliope exclaimed, unable to hold back the groan as she turned to greet him. And then what Stelios had to say wiped out all other thought, feeling or emotion.

'Calliope,' he cried, urgently. 'I hung around outside their headquarters down there, pretending to be looking for a lost goat. That was a good idea, wasn't it?' He beamed at her, bursting with pride at his own resourcefulness.

'It was,' agreed Calliope.

But then Stelios seemed to remember the rest of what he had to say and his expression darkened, his eyes clouding over with apprehension. 'I heard them talking from inside. I don't know who was speaking or what they were saying because I only know a few words of German. But they were describing you, Calliope; they said you'd been seen at a parachute drop. They sounded serious. I think you might be in danger.'

CHAPTER 17

CRETE, FEBRUARY 1942

For a moment, Calliope forgot about her aching body as alarm pulsed through her veins. So that brief encounter with the Nazi soldier at the scene of the parachute drop had been enough for him to give a description of her that, with the help of someone who knew her, had identified her. Eliana. It could only be her who had given Calliope away.

She caught Calista staring at her, mouth open in horror. 'What are you going to do, Calliope?' The decisiveness of earlier had deserted her and her voice quivered as she spoke.

Calliope clenched her fists and frowned, deep in thought. 'I need a disguise,' she muttered. She looked around her as if the answer might be lying somewhere in the room, and her eyes rested on Stelios, who still stood there, anxiously watching the twins.

'Can I borrow some of your brother's old clothes?' Calliope asked him. She knew this was a big request. People in their village didn't have much; at most, two or three outfits each. Anything belonging to Stelios's older brother Thanos would have been carefully packed away until Stelios himself grew into it. But right now, Calliope couldn't think of anyone else whose clothes would fit her. 'I need to disguise myself as a boy,' she continued.

Stelios, always happy to have a job to do, immediately scampered down the stairs and out of the house, rushing to fetch Calliope what she needed.

Groaning, Calliope hauled herself to her feet. 'Calista,' she said, 'come with me.' Somehow she managed to get down to the kitchen, where she paused, leaning against the table and exhaling deeply in and out, breathing through the pain. She took a pair of scissors from a drawer and handed them to her sister. 'Cut my hair off,' she instructed. 'All of it, until it's as short as a boy's.'

Calista gasped. 'No!' she cried. 'Not your beautiful hair. You've never once had it cut – it would be bad luck to do it now.'

Calliope drew in a deep breath. 'It'll be bad luck not to do it,' she insisted. 'I have to change my appearance. If I'm captured and put in prison – or worse – what good will I be to the resistance then?'

Reluctantly, her mouth twisted into a miserable grimace at what was required of her, Calista opened and shut the scissors a couple of times, as if testing their ability to achieve the task her sister had assigned her. Then, with a heavy sigh, she picked up Calliope's thick plait. She regarded it for a few moments before she was able to bring herself to apply the scissors to it.

The task was harder than Calliope had expected. The scissor blades, blunted from age and years of use, sawed and hacked at the hair, slicing through just a few strands on each cut. The sound was almost the worst bit, a rasping, scraping noise that went on and on. Throughout it all, she stood patiently, elbows resting on the table, not complaining when Calista's yanking or pulling hurt her scalp, focusing on managing the pain in her ribs.

Finally, Calista finished. 'There, that's it,' she declared, sadly. In her hand the plait lay thick and limp like a dead snake.

'Throw it away,' Calliope ordered. She didn't even want to look at it. It would take years for her hair to grow to such a length again, if it were ever safe enough for her to let it. Because who knew how long it would take to oust the Nazis?

Faithful Stelios returned, bearing a small bundle of clothing. Calliope needed Calista's help to take her own clothes off and replace them with the boy's breeches, sash, shirt and waistcoat. By the time this was done she felt sick with the pain and the exertion.

Their mother and father were still out in the fields. Calliope realised that she'd have to leave without saying goodbye. Mustering all her strength and willpower, she straightened herself up and stood tall. She took from a cupboard the canvas bag the sailor had given her all those months ago and placed inside it a few bits and pieces from the meagre resources the family had in the kitchen: a heel of stale bread, a sprouting potato.

Tearfully, Calista watched on. 'Where are you going?' she asked, tentatively.

'To Laurie,' replied Calliope, bluntly. 'I'll hole up with him and the gang for a while. If I stay here, I'll endanger all of you.'

She caught a strange look passing over Calista's face. Was it alarm or surprise? Calliope wasn't too sure. Whatever it was, she couldn't let it deflect her from what she had to do.

'How will you get there, all the way up into the mountains, with your injuries?' asked Calista, her voice full of apprehension.

Calliope shook her head. 'I don't know, but I'll have to,' she answered, a little bluntly because she was wondering this exact same thing herself and didn't want to admit it. While she fiddled with the canvas bag, adjusting the strap and tightening the buckles, Calista spoke to Stelios, her words too low for

Calliope to hear. The little boy left and the two sisters were alone together in the still quiet of the afternoon.

'I'll need my cape,' said Calliope, running through in her head whether there was anything else she should bring with her. 'And I'll take some mountain tea.' She shivered involuntarily, sending another spasm of pain shooting through her whole body, as she imagined the frozen world that awaited her so high up. Their house was not grand or luxurious but it was cosy and filled with the people she loved the most. A sudden pang of homesickness made her momentarily doubt herself. And then she remembered Stelios' words – 'they were describing you' – and her resolve redoubled. She had to get away, while she still could.

'Aren't you going to wait for Mama and Papa to get back?' Calista's eyes were moist, her beautiful face riven by an expression of pure woe.

Calliope shook her head. 'No time,' she replied, tersely.

The sound of a donkey's hooves clopping along the worn cobblestones drifted in from outside. Dread filled Calliope's heart. And then she remembered that the Nazis didn't travel by donkey like Cretans did. They had motor vehicles for the roads and, for where there were no roads, motorcycles. She let out an involuntary sigh of relief. They hadn't come for her.

Yet.

Breathing through the pain as she shouldered the bag, she turned to the door. There, on the threshold, stood Stelios, holding a rope by which he was leading his family's donkey. He regarded Calliope expectantly.

'Shall I give you a leg-up?' he asked, his kind brown eyes full of concern.

Calliope frowned, her brow creasing as she tried to take in what he was suggesting. Stelios shifted from one foot to the other as he waited, watching her at first expectantly and then in puzzlement, as if wondering what the delay was.

'You mean I'm to ride there?' Calliope was still confused.

Stelios nodded. 'Yes,' he replied, in a tone of voice that said, 'What else could I have meant?'

Calliope almost laughed, but didn't as it would be too painful. Though not as agonising as trying to climb aboard a donkey. Somehow she managed to do this, with the help of Stelios and Calista. With no further ado, Stelios led the donkey up the alleyway outside the house, across the narrow plank bridge over the gully and onto the goat path that led to the high mountains. It wasn't what Calliope would call a comfortable ride; in fact, there were times when the poor beast of burden was scrambling around rocks and up the icy scree when she was sure she was going to fall off, or the donkey itself was going to trip up. But eventually they neared Laurie's camp.

When the *mitato* to which Laurie and his gang had now moved hove into view, Calliope gestured to Stelios to stop and help her off. She descended to the ground with an excruciating thud, hugged the little boy to her, then released him quickly because that, also, was beyond torturous.

'You mustn't tell anyone where you've brought me,' she said to the child, holding him by the shoulders and making him meet her gaze. 'You don't know anything. You understand, yes?'

Solemnly, Stelios blinked twice, before nodding forcefully. 'Of course,' he replied, confidently. 'Anyway,' he added, 'I know how to deal with Germans.'

It would have been funny if it weren't so sad, the precocious confidence of a little boy forced to grow up too soon due to the invasion of his homeland and the brutality of its captors. He had no idea what those Germans were really capable of. Or maybe he did, and that was even worse, that he should have to. So much for childhood innocence. For a moment Stelios morphed into George and a familiar rage against the occupiers seethed inside Calliope that she struggled to suppress.

'Goodbye, Stelios,' she said, eventually. 'Hurry home, all right?'

Holding her body awkwardly in an attempt to make moving as painless as possible, Calliope limped towards the *mitato*. There was no one there, that much was obvious. If there had been, they would have come out to see who had just arrived. Stumbling inside, she lowered herself onto one of the beds made from fragrant stems of mountain shrubs and lay, trying to focus on something other than the pain until, exhausted, she fell asleep.

She dreamt uneasy dreams, in which her thick plait of hair came alive and attempted to strangle her, which she couldn't understand. *But you're my hair,* she kept telling it in her sleep, *so why are you trying to harm me?* The hair didn't listen.

Waking with a start, she saw that it was pitch dark now and she was still on her own. It was bitterly cold and the wind blew fiercely through the open doorway. Hungry and thirsty, her body pulsing with pain, Calliope lay on her bed of leaves and branches and felt tears well in her eyes. She wanted to go home, to curl up in her bed next to her twin, to hear Calista's regular, rhythmic breathing and to know she was safe.

The sudden, terrible realisation that she had been suppressing ever since Stelios had brought her his message resurfaced, refusing to be ignored any longer. If she ever had been safe since the German invasion began, she certainly wasn't now.

She would probably never be safe again. It was an awful thought to bear, far from home, all alone and freezing half to death. The tears began to fall and Calliope was unable to stop them.

CHAPTER 18

CRETE, MARCH 1942

By the time two weeks had passed, Calliope's ribs, though still tender, were a lot better.

'I think they were just badly bruised, not fractured or broken,' Laurie said, feeling them with gentle fingers. Little jolts of electricity thrilled through her every time his flesh grazed hers, no longer from pain but instead from his delectable touch. Now she was almost fully recovered, and not constantly starving hungry courtesy of supplies the British had got from somewhere, she found herself more in Laurie's thrall than ever. His deft, firm hands on her body was almost too much to bear.

'But,' he continued, fixing her with a stern look, 'you still need to take it easy for a few more days. You've got to respect the injury.'

'I will,' replied Calliope demurely, secretly crossing her fingers behind her back. She had no intention of staying out of the action a moment longer than was absolutely necessary. She smiled at Laurie and was rewarded by one of his lovely smiles in return. For a moment the cold and the damp were replaced by a glow of warmth, in which Calliope basked for the next few hours.

In the depths of winter, up in the mountains, the days passed slowly. Ben was usually busy with the wireless, and the rest of them would huddle around the paraffin stove, seeking warmth from the feeble flame. Their food was limited and repetitive; tinned meat and fish, sometimes peas and beans, but it satisfied the appetite, which hadn't been the case for most Cretans since the summer before.

Calliope knew that, if Calista were here, she would be able to whip up even such basic ingredients into something tasty, but she herself entirely lacked such culinary skills. Instead, she and the men ate their boring meals and passed the time playing cards. So many card games involved chance or luck, and the same was true of war, it sometimes seemed. Who lived and who died was as much a matter of fortune as of skill and cunning.

During those long hours, Calliope felt herself growing ever closer to Laurie as they talked long into the night. Calliope did not dare voice her love for him – it was too soon, their world too fragile just then to broach such a subject. But she was as sure as she could be that her growing feelings were reciprocated.

She pined for him when he was occasionally absent for days at a time. On his return, he would give nothing away about what he had been doing. Calliope burned to know but at the same time understood that it was pointless to question him. Instead, she probed him about his past life, before the war, in that country called England about which she knew so little.

'What job did you do?' she asked one day as she dealt the cards for another game of *biriba*. 'Before...' She paused, and then gesticulated around the cramped hideout, meaning 'all this'. The others were all out on reconnaissance missions, apart from Ben, who was in the nearby cave where the battery-charging equipment was kept.

Laurie smiled. 'I was training to be a doctor,' he replied. 'Only in my second year, so I don't know much—'

'Oh!' cried Calliope. 'So that's how you knew my ribs weren't broken.'

The smile intensified, until it became so dazzling that Calliope was quite overcome and had to drop her eyes until she'd recovered her composure.

'Well, I'm not sure I needed medical training for that diagnosis,' Laurie responded, modestly. 'I could have carried on my studies but I wanted to enlist. I was sent to Albania, but it wasn't too long before the fact that I can speak Greek came to my superiors' attention. And that led to me being dropped in here just before the invasion.' He paused to take a long draw on his cigarette. The smoke blew across his face in a grey cloud and, when it had dissipated, Calliope saw a wistful look in his eyes. 'We wanted to stop the Germans taking over but, as we all know, we failed.'

Calliope's heart turned over. It was still hard for many Cretans to understand the commitment of these foreign fighters to their cause, their passionate desire to rid the island of the oppressor and set its people free.

'You'll win in the end, though,' she said, determinedly. '*We* will.'

Laurie laughed. 'Yes, I hope we will.' He spread out his cards in his hand and began arranging them, pulling out one at a time then slotting it back into another place. 'I really hope so.' He laid a card on the ground between them. Calliope couldn't help noticing that he seemed less certain about the war's outcome than he had previously.

'And what about you, Calliope Papadakis? What were your ambitions for the future, before this war came along to disrupt everything?'

Calliope blushed with embarrassment, and hastily covered her face with her fan of cards. How could she admit to Laurie that all she'd really wanted was to get a job rather than go straight into being a wife and mother? It had felt like an ambition at the time, but now it seemed laughable. Then she remembered George and her wish to look after him and make sure he grew up surrounded by love, sheltered from those who wished to belittle and spurn him. If Laurie believed he had failed because of the German takeover of the island, how much greater a failure was Calliope's? Her brother was dead.

'I wanted to take care of George,' she replied, simply. 'So I failed, too.'

Laurie eyed her contemplatively. Then he put down his cards and reached across to her, pulling her head against his shoulder. 'It wasn't your fault,' he said, soothingly. 'You did everything you could.'

He held Calliope's face between his strong, dextrous hands. For the tiniest second, she thought he was going to kiss her. And then he released his grip and sat back on his haunches. 'Our hatred of the enemy is what drives us,' he said. 'If anything brings us victory, it will be that.'

Later that day, Calliope saw him preparing to go out.

'What are you doing?' she asked him.

'Going to have a scout around,' he replied. 'There's a new guard post been erected down on the plateau, by the junction where two paths meet. It's a couple of hours' walk. You want to come?'

Calliope didn't need to be asked twice. After so much inactivity, she was desperate to get out into the open air. 'Of course,' she answered, leaping up. She suppressed a groan at the residual pain in her ribs. She did not want Laurie to know that they still gave her any bother in case he instructed her to stay behind.

Laurie was as sure-footed on the rocky, narrow path as a native Cretan these days, and was familiar with much of the surrounding terrain. Calliope, having hardly moved for the last fortnight, had to almost run to keep up with him and had no breath left for talking.

Eventually, they came within sight of the guard post. Laurie paused behind a cypress tree, pulling Calliope in beside him to shelter under its evergreen branches. 'We're just simple shepherds, all right?' He pulled out a pair of binoculars and trained them through a gap in the foliage. 'There are three of them on guard today,' he said, to himself as much as to Calliope. Then, after slipping the binos back into his pocket, he gestured to her to follow him.

Stepping out into the sunlight, Calliope shivered at the contrast in temperature. Or perhaps it was fear. Laurie didn't seem to have considered whether Calliope should be here, so close to the enemy. Was her disguise good enough? What if the Germans on duty recognised her? And what, exactly, did Laurie intend to do anyway?

She soon found out.

With breathtaking insouciance, Laurie strolled right up to the guard post, Calliope following behind, feeling as if she were going to the gallows. What madness was this? The soldiers spotted the pair of them and immediately stood taller, shoulders back, guns at the ready. Calliope broke into a cold sweat. This was ridiculous. What was Laurie playing at?

By now they were right beside the guard post, the sentry box to the right of them, the roadblock straight ahead.

'*Kaliméra*,' Laurie called out and then, without waiting for a reply, asked, 'Do you have any cigarettes?'

Calliope was astounded and horrified in equal measure. What on earth? Desperately, she tried to compose her expression into one of simple incomprehension. Her cropped hair made her look a lot younger than she really was, and she hoped the Germans wouldn't think her worthy of notice.

'*Nai*,' replied one of the German soldiers. 'You want one? All right, here you are.' He pulled a cigarette out of a packet and tossed it dismissively over to Laurie, where it fell on the ground. Calliope noticed that Laurie didn't take his eyes off them – or their guns – as he stooped to pick it up.

'Now clear off,' said one of the other soldiers, whose eyes were a piercing shade of blue. Transfixed, Calliope was shocked by a sudden bolt of recognition. This was the soldier who had harassed Laurie when he was dressed in a dead man's rags.

Oh my Lord, she thought to herself. Forget about any of these Nazis recognising her. It was Laurie they might recall. She screwed up her eyes and scrutinised him, trying to remember how he had looked on that first occasion she had seen him. Did he look different enough? She wasn't sure...

Just as she was trying to convince herself that he did, a radio crackled with an incoming message and the soldiers' attention was diverted.

Laurie waved a casual goodbye as he turned round. Calliope tried not to gallop after him, instead steadying her pace in a way she hoped made it look like she had nothing to hide, even while she could barely take in oxygen for the fear that was consuming her. As soon as they reached a sheltering grove of olive trees, she halted for a moment, bending over as she tried to catch her breath.

'What was that all about?' she gasped. 'I thought... those soldiers... they could have shot us.'

Laurie grinned and butterflies immediately began dancing in Calliope's stomach. Damn her feelings for this impossible man. He'd nearly got them both killed!

'I wanted to check out their weapons,' he responded calmly, his eyes narrowed in thought. 'See what kind of capability they're putting on these guard posts. As it turns out, the firepower is fairly minimal. They will not be difficult to take out.'

Calliope rolled her eyes, about the only bit of her that didn't hurt with movement. Trust Laurie. There was always a plan, always a strategy. She couldn't prevent herself from grinning back, even though she was still furious with him. He could at least have warned her. But then again, if he had, it might have affected her behaviour or demeanour, which could have blown their cover. She had to admit that, as always, Laurie had played the whole thing perfectly.

'You were fabulous,' he continued, fixing his eyes on hers. 'You didn't give anything away. We'll make a fine SOE operative out of you yet.'

Calliope felt a flush rise in her cheeks at the unexpected compliment. 'Thank you,' she said, her voice coming out as a high-pitched squeak as she tried to control her pride in herself. When she'd recovered, she remembered what she had noticed.

'Did you see who one of the officers was?' she asked Laurie. 'The one with the blue eyes.'

'Oh yes,' he replied. 'My old friend who thought it was fun to use a rifle butt to intimidate a broken old man. Well, we'll see how he likes it when the shoe is on the other foot.'

Puzzling over what he meant by this expression, which he must have translated from English into Greek, Calliope had another thought.

'I'll make my own way back to the *mitato*,' she said. 'It's probably better if we go separately anyway.'

Laurie took a drag on the cigarette. 'They're not bad, these Sulima fags,' he mused, regarding the white stick in his hands. 'But things tend to taste better when you've taken a risk to get hold of them.'

Calliope considered this remark. She and Laurie were taking risks all the time. And if – when – their mutual attraction came to any kind of fruition, she could only imagine how sweet-flavoured that would be.

Stubbing out the cigarette, Laurie gazed into the distance. 'Fine,' he said, responding to her earlier statement of intent. 'I've got a few more things I need to do.'

And with that, he was gone, marching off towards the horizon.

Slightly surprised that Laurie hadn't questioned her further about her plans, Calliope turned in the direction of the village. She knew it was incredibly hazardous to go there. But up in the hideout she had no way of getting news from her family, and she was desperate to know that they were well. She would pay a fleeting visit, just to put her mind at rest.

As Calliope wended her way through familiar fields and meadows, she felt again the swell of emotion that Major Wynn-Thomas, *just call me Laurie,* caused in her. She tried to push the feelings away. This was war. Laurie was British. What would he possibly see in a lowly Greek girl – especially one now dressed and looking like a boy? But on the other hand, his warmth and friendliness, his obvious admiration for her pluck and resilience, meant that she couldn't help but dare to dream... Surely it was only a matter of time before he made a move and declared his feelings for her?

In a daze of happiness, Calliope barely felt the residual pain in her ribs and the miles passed quickly. She arrived at the village just as dusk was falling. In the sheepfold, she heard the distinctive bleating of a newborn lamb. She hoped that he or she would be one of many. If it was a boy, it was destined to have a short life. She salivated at the thought of a plate of lamb stew, or lamb cutlets with spring greens.

Taking the back route beside the gully, she could hear from inside the houses the sounds of families gathering to eat whatever meagre meal they could put together. And then a louder noise drifted up to her. There seemed to be some sort of kerfuffle going on further down the lane, but she couldn't see clearly which house it was. She slowed down, flattened her body against the stone walls and crept a little further.

A cry rang out and her blood stilled in her veins. She'd recognise that sound anywhere. Her sister. Desperate to get closer, Calliope slunk past a few more houses. And then was confronted by an appalling sight.

Calista being dragged through the front door by two mean-faced Nazi soldiers.

Abandoning all caution, Calliope stood in the middle of the narrow alley and watched. Her parents were silently weeping as Calista was manhandled along the road. She appeared to have gone weak and boneless from fear and, even as slight as she was, the men were having to almost carry her in order to move her in the direction they wanted.

Calista glanced up and, along the length of the alley, her eyes met those of her twin in one desperate glance.

Calliope had a sudden, terrible realisation. Why hadn't they thought of this? Why hadn't *she*, Calliope, thought of this? She and Calista were identical to all but those who knew them well. The Germans didn't know they were twins – Corporal Stan, and Sergeants Phil and Bob, had only laid eyes on Calista. They had obviously compared descriptions with the soldier who had seen Calliope at the parachute drop, put two and two together and made one. As in, only one girl, who they believed to be Calliope.

Stunned, Calliope froze to the spot in horror as she watched her twin sister being bundled along the lane and into the waiting army jeep.

CHAPTER 19

CRETE, 2005

Ella wiped her eyes with a tissue and sniffed. Every time she looked at her grandmother, the tears restarted. Callie hated to see her so upset.

'It was just a funny turn due to the heat and being on my feet in that museum for too long,' she insisted, reaching out and patting Ella's hand. 'I'm not used to the climate here any more.' She shifted awkwardly in the hospital bed. She had no idea why they had brought her here; a total overreaction. She'd have been fine if they'd just let her be. But Ella, panicked, had called an ambulance and, once those health people get their hands on you, well, you've got no chance. Heart rate, blood pressure, oxygen saturation, whatever that meant... all of it was apparently wrong and so here she was, when what she very much wanted was to be somewhere else. Anywhere but here.

She squeezed her granddaughter's hand. 'Can we go back to the hotel now?' she asked, trying to pull on Ella's heartstrings by pleading rather than being cross.

Ella regarded her for a few moments, a complex mix of emotions flitting across her face: relief, concern, confusion. And when she spoke her scepticism was obvious. 'Gran, I think it was more than the weather. So do the doctors. That's why they're keeping you in. They might want to do some more tests on your heart and—'

'My heart is absolutely fine,' scoffed Callie dismissively. 'Nothing wrong with it at all. There's no need for me to be here. And how much is all this costing?'

'I don't think we have to pay,' Ella replied with a sigh. 'And if we do, the insurance will cover it. We paid an arm and a leg for the policy, given your age, so at least we're getting our money's worth, I suppose.' She tried to make it a joke, but Callie could hear the strain she was under. That was why she wanted to leave. There was no need for Ella to be so worried. Callie knew what had happened, what had caused her legs to buckle beneath her. She knew only too well. And it wasn't something medicine could fix.

'Please just ask them, Ella. Ask them if I can leave now, and tell them I'll come straight back to the hospital if I feel the faintest twinge, pain, ache, whatever.'

'Grandma! You're not listening. They don't think you're well enough to go.' Ella's anxiety came out in something that sounded very close to anger. She grimaced and then took Callie's hands in hers. 'Please do what the doctors want you to do.' Her voice quavered and she paused to fight back more tears. 'You're all I've got, Gran. There's no one else. If you go, I'll be completely alone. I need you, more than I could ever put into words. I can't lose you. Not yet. Not now.'

Guilt suffused Callie. Her granddaughter was the world to her, the shining light in her often dull, pedestrian life. Ella's father had never been on the scene and, after Louise's untimely death, Callie had always been paranoid about her own health and that of Harry, terrified that disease or illness might take them also, leaving Ella to be brought up by the care system. Callie shuddered at the thought of that. The authorities did what they could to help children in their charge but it wasn't the same as being with family, was it? How could it be?

And of course it wasn't a one-way street. Ella had more than repaid the devotion Callie had poured upon her. She was the most loving, caring, thoughtful grandchild anyone could want. She had postponed her travels so that she could accompany her grandmother to Crete, and, though Callie had insisted otherwise, she was secretly relieved that Ella had made herself available. Though she hated to admit it, even to herself, the thought of undertaking the plane journey and then the logistics of getting around the island on her own had been daunting to say the least. And that was without considering what she was here to do, the past she must lay to rest. The forgiveness she must seek.

Callie's cold hands squeezed Ella's warm ones. 'I'm not going anywhere, I promise you,' she assured her. 'Truly, I'm fine. Absolutely fine.'

'OK,' replied Ella, sniffing loudly. 'Good.' She dropped Callie's hands and began fumbling around in her backpack for another tissue.

Sinking back onto the pillows, Callie gazed at the tiled ceiling. Thank goodness it was cool in here, but then the hotel was too. She couldn't imagine how they had got on in the olden days, without artificial heating and cooling and lighting... they'd had to put up with the heat, put up with the cold, put up with the dark. Everything was different now. Despite her reassurances to Ella, Callie suddenly felt incredibly old, ancient even, so much so that the thought of ever getting out of bed again loomed like an impossible task. Perhaps she should just stay here without protest, do what they all wanted her to do, rest up like everyone seemed to think an octogenarian should.

Then she wouldn't have to face the consequences of the letter. The time to confront her sister, and her past, was drawing ever nearer. Callie was suddenly struck with nostalgia that hit like a body blow. All the wasted years, all the time spent mourning and missing someone who had been alive the whole time. She wondered if Calista had been happy and if it were the slightest bit possible that they could make up the years they had lost. She supposed this was unlikely, once everything had come out. Calista wouldn't want to know her then.

Ella dabbed at her eyes with the tissue, then loudly blew her nose. She looked at Callie expectantly.

'Okay,' Callie said. 'Even though there's nothing wrong with me, if it makes you happier I'll stay. But one night only.'

Ella beamed at her. 'Thank you,' she enthused and then, under her breath, 'Thank God for that.'

Callie couldn't help but smile, but the smile soon faded. That God Ella had just mentioned had taken so many people away from Callie, including Louise, who should have been here now, going through whatever this was with Callie and her daughter. For over sixty years she had thought God had taken her sister Calista. Really, when she thought about it, she had no idea why she went to church every week to converse with this person-stealer of a God. Perhaps she'd simply needed something to believe in, through all the hard times. And now? Now that Calista had seemingly risen from the dead, unearthing long-buried secrets, Callie was left facing demons she had never thought were going to see the light of day.

Once Ella had gone, and the nurse had completed another set of observations, it was early evening. A meal was brought round, which Callie could only pick at. She thought of the packet of Bourbon creams in her suitcase at the hotel. She fancied something sweet and familiar, something that reminded her of Sunday afternoons with Ella rather than the memories that had been assailing her here.

Eventually, exhausted from the day, Callie fell asleep. That night, the nightmare came again, as it always did. But this time, when she tried to run, someone was holding on to her legs, not letting her get away. At first, she didn't realise who it was. She had just recognised the person when she awoke, shaking and sweating.

'You're dreaming, Mrs Smith,' the nurse said to her softly. 'I'm going to give you something to make you more comfortable.'

Mutely, Callie took the pill. Afterwards, she fell into a slumber that was deep and, thankfully, dreamless.

In the morning, Ella returned. She sat with Callie for a while and then, when the doctor appeared on his rounds, disappeared off to speak to him. The pill must not have worn off yet because Callie felt distant and disconnected, as if she were watching the hubbub of the ward around her from inside a fish tank. The sensation was weird but not unpleasant. It was nice to feel divested of all responsibility or decision-making for a while. Perhaps she should ask for some of these tablets to take away with her.

But there was no time. Ella bustled over, car key at the ready.

'OK, you're free,' she announced with a broad grin. 'They're letting you out for good behaviour.' She chuckled and Callie smiled with her. You could joke about being in prison when you had never experienced it. A sudden vision of Calista, in the clutches of uniformed soldiers, being taken away to who knew where, flashed through her mind and she shivered involuntarily.

Oh God. Calista. Callie observed Ella's bright and sunny expression as she gathered up Callie's handbag and took the package of medication the nurse handed to her. Her granddaughter didn't know about any of what had happened. There was too much to tell her. She'd never be able to make her understand...

'Right, upsadaisy.' Ella held out her hand for Callie to help her out of the bed. 'I'll come to the bathroom with you and wait outside while you get dressed,' she said. 'I've brought you clean clothes.'

Resignedly, Callie let herself be led to the facilities, where she put the clothes on, washed her face and cleaned her teeth.

In the car on the way back to the hotel, Ella summarised the doctor's instructions. 'Rest and relaxation,' she declared. 'Those are your orders. Quite simple really. No more strenuous outings – well, that was my fault, insisting on going to that museum. So I thought this afternoon we could go to the beach by the hotel – I checked it out already. There are loungers with lovely soft cushions and parasols, and a stall selling cold drinks. We can chill out there for a couple of days. I'm well up for that.'

Callie nodded. 'Very good, my dear,' she agreed. Ella shot her a glance, clearly surprised at her easy acquiescence.

After lunch, they headed for the beach. Callie was feeling a little spaced out. Surely that sleeping pill couldn't still be affecting her? Once they'd taken up residence on a couple of loungers, placed the sunshade exactly right and settled down, Callie realised she'd forgotten her book.

'I'll pop back and get it,' suggested Ella immediately. 'It's no problem.'

'You might as well bring my whole bag,' Callie said. 'My reading glasses are in there as well.'

While Ella was gone, Callie gazed out at the blue water. Children splashed and played in the shallows, their excited shrieks splitting the heat-heavy air. Further out in the bay, sun-worshippers floated face down on lilos that swayed from side to side on the gentle swell. She still found it hard to understand how much Crete had changed, how many holidaymakers flocked here for those commodities that, as children, she, Calista, Eliana and all their friends, family and acquaintances had taken for granted: the sea, the beaches, the sunshine, the food and wine, the honey and olives. Though not so much the latter during the hungry years of the occupation, that was true.

Ella was taking a long time fetching Callie's bag. Where was she? But it was so peaceful and relaxing that Callie, waiting, nodded off to sleep.

She woke with a start to find Ella returned, lying on her lounger, dark glasses over her eyes. At first Callie thought she was asleep too. But as soon as Callie sat up, so did Ella. She lifted the glasses from her face and immediately Callie knew that something was up. Her granddaughter was so easy to read.

But Ella didn't say anything. Instead, she simply handed Callie her bag and announced that she was going for a swim. She stayed in the water for a long time. Callie watched her slender arms slicing through the surface as she front crawled, back and forth, back and forth, as if she were training for the Olympics. When she stopped lapping, she remained far out at sea, fair head bobbing up and down.

Callie opened her bag to retrieve her book. She saw it immediately. The letter. Everything became obvious in a heartbeat. Ella had seen it. Ella had read it. Ella knew.

A little, choking sob erupted from Callie's throat. She'd known the moment of revelation had to come. But now it was here, nothing seemed any clearer or easier than it had before.

CHAPTER 20

CRETE, MARCH 1942

The snow lay thick on the ground. There'd been a storm the night before; Calliope had been caught in the white-out as, numbed from the shock and the cold, she had stumbled back to the *mitato* with the terrible news about Calista's capture. The person she had wanted to see there, thought she would see there, was Laurie. But she had arrived to discover that Laurie was absent, that he'd already left for a conference of resistance leaders in Heraklion. It was terrible news.

Now she, Ben, John and Gerald were gathered around the paraffin stove, Calliope holding her hands to the flame in an effort to get warm. Down in the valleys and by the coast, spring was gathering pace and the sun, when it shone, had some warmth in it. But up here, it would be May at least before the snowmelt.

'We've got to get her out,' said Calliope, her voice wavering. Pausing to fight back tears, she gulped, and then resumed. 'Quickly, as soon as we can, before...' Unable to put her worst fears into words, she stopped again. Despite her best efforts, big salty tears were rolling down her cheeks. She hated to cry in front of all these tough men, but it was impossible not to when she imagined what Calista was going through, what might happen to her in Nazi hands.

Ben's expression was dark and serious. 'Calliope, I...' he began haltingly. 'We... look, I don't think we can do anything until Laurie returns.' He coughed and shifted awkwardly on the hard ground. 'He'll be back in three days,' he concluded, somewhat apologetically.

Three days! He might as well have said three years. Three centuries. There was no way that Calista's rescue could be put on hold for so long.

'We can't wait that long,' Calliope responded. She wiped her eyes with her sleeve and stared at the flame intently, mouth set in a hard grimace. '*I* can't wait that long.'

Ben adjusted his position again. 'I'm sorry, but I can't come with you right now,' he said. 'It's essential that I'm here operating the radio in Laurie's absence. He charged me with that task and I can't let him down. The intelligence is coming through thick and fast and I must keep on top of it. If the Germans get the slightest whiff of this conference, they'll bomb it or torch it or shoot every attendee. I'm responsible for a lot of lives. John and Gerald – well, they're busy too.'

Calliope dropped her head into her hands. Yesterday, she had been with Laurie all day, and he'd not breathed a word about this dratted conference. Why had he not told her? They were so close now, all this time spent together up here in the mountains, the attraction between them that she was surer than ever was both real and mutual. Wouldn't he have wanted to share the information with her, discuss the aims of the meeting, gain her opinion? Or maybe he hadn't told her because it was dangerous for her to know and he was concerned for her welfare and safety. Yes, that must be it, undoubtedly so.

She lifted her head and looked at Ben. She couldn't expect him to abandon his duties; it was unfair of her to even ask him to. But every moment spent here, not knowing what was happening to her sister down there, was agony.

As Ben made tea before getting ready to fire up the radio, Calliope ran through the options. She could go to the Nazis and own up. Tell them that it was her they wanted, not Calista. But what if that just led to her own capture as well? Then she wouldn't be able to assist in any operation to get her sister out. And knowing that both their girls were in enemy hands might destroy their parents completely.

Fists clenched, Calliope hatched a plan. Her disguise was as good as it could be. When she looked at herself in the shard of mirror the men kept to shave with, it was a shock every time. Who was this young boy looking back at her? If she could even fool herself, she could be more or less assured that the Nazis would be fooled also.

Getting up to stretch her legs, easing out the pins and needles, Calliope made her decision. The British soldiers had got their hands on some flour from somewhere and made flatbreads with it – they had no yeast, so this was all that they could concoct. There was some tinned cheese from a parachute drop that she could wrap in paper to make it look local. Playing the innocent, concerned brother, Calliope would take these meagre provisions to the prison and beg to be allowed to see her sister. After that – well, she'd think on her feet, the way this war had taught her to do.

The intense cold made her still-recovering ribs ache badly and it took nearly three hours for her to reach the German garrison and the camp they had hastily erected for prisoners-of-war and anyone else they deemed to be a miscreant in any way. Before fear could overtake her and put her off her mission, Calliope marched right up to the main gate.

'I'd like to see Calista Papadakis,' she said, politely but firmly.

The guard stared at her as if she were a particularly

disgusting and repellent insect that had crawled out from under a stone. In the distance, a dog barked, a bloodcurdling sound that echoed through the chilly air. Beneath her facade of brash bravado, Calliope quailed inside. The guard called inside to someone and another German soldier stuck his head out of the sentry box, sneered and then retreated again. Calliope stood, entirely unsure what was happening.

'She's my... relative,' she continued, refusing to be intimidated. 'I-I brought her some things. Just food,' she stuttered, unwrapping the cloth and thrusting the bread and cheese forward to show him.

The guard said something in German that she didn't understand. Then he went back to pacing up and down in front of the sentry box, completely ignoring her. This went on for several minutes.

Just as Calliope was summoning her courage to speak to him again, she became aware of someone hurrying along the path from the main garrison block towards the gate. For a moment, Calliope did not recognise who it was. And then the person got near enough for her to see that it was Eliana.

Of course it was. She worked here. She was in the pay of the Nazis. With a sudden, chilling realisation that momentarily took her breath away, Calliope understood that it was Eliana who had given her away. Eliana, her childhood friend, with whom she and Calista had played dolls and practised different ways of plaiting their hair and discussed boys, three girls growing up together, bonded by girlhood's rites of passage. But now Eliana had betrayed her. She must be the one who had told the Nazis where Calliope could be found.

Bile rose in Calliope's throat and nausea turned her stomach over. Damn, damn, damn. Why had she come here? What a stupid, stupid thing to do. Calliope hadn't even considered Eliana when she'd made her plan, had not even thought about the possibility of running into her. Laurie would be disgusted by her idiocy. Everything he did was thoroughly thought through, impeccably planned to the smallest detail. He would never act impulsively and recklessly as Calliope had done.

'*Kaliméra*,' said Eliana, primly. She ran her hands over her smart wool skirt, smoothing out non-existent creases. 'I've been asked to come and translate.' She cocked her head a little to one side and regarded Calliope curiously. Calliope knew she recognised her. Of course she did. The sick feeling grew until, if she'd had anything other than a dry crust of bread that day, she would have thrown up.

Eliana and the guard had a short exchange of words in German. Then Eliana turned back to Calliope.

'So what is it that you want?' she asked.

Calliope gulped. 'I'd like to see Calista Papadakis,' she replied, struggling to keep her voice steady and to not let her panic show itself in her eyes. 'Her parents are worried about her.'

Eliana's dark, almost black, eyes narrowed. 'She's a prisoner of the German forces,' she responded.

A flame of anger rose in Calliope, stronger than her fear. 'She's done nothing wrong,' she retaliated, and then immediately regretted it. *Don't antagonise*, she silently screamed at herself. 'I mean, I don't know what she's done,' she corrected herself. 'But please can I see her. Just for a few minutes. To give her some food.' She displayed the pitiful handful of bread and cheese again.

Up to this point, she'd been avoiding looking directly at Eliana. But now she did meet her one-time friend's eyes. There was the hint of something in them, an emotion Calliope couldn't name. And then in a flash it was gone, and Eliana was talking to the guard, hard, harsh-sounding words that Calliope longed to know the meaning of.

'Literally two minutes.'

For a moment, Calliope didn't understand, struggling to separate the Greek from the German. But yes, she had understood correctly. Eliana gestured for Calliope to follow her. Accompanied by a soldier who had appeared at just the right moment, Eliana led Calliope through the camp to a long, low hut with a corrugated-iron roof and barred windows.

'He'll be waiting outside,' Eliana said, pointing at the soldier. 'And there are dogs all around. So don't try anything.'

Another bolt of fury threatened to derail everything. Who was Eliana to threaten her? If Calliope did what she wanted to do, which was seize Eliana by the throat and throttle her, she'd be shot in an instant. She managed to restrain herself.

'*Efharistó*,' she muttered. Forget Eliana, she told herself as she stepped inside the cold, dark cell that the soldier had unlocked.

As her eyes adjusted to the dark, she made out her sister's limp form, lying on a hard wooden plank bunk covered by a thin, threadbare blanket.

'Calista,' Calliope whispered, crouching down beside her.

Slowly, her sister opened her eyes. She stared at Calliope for several seconds before seeming to realise who it was.

'Calliope,' she murmured, disbelievingly. 'What are you doing here? How did you get in?'

Calliope shook her head. 'Don't worry about that,' she replied, reaching out her hand and stroking Calista's matted, dirty hair. She would hate that, Calliope thought. Calista was always so particular about her hair, washing it even in the coldest of winters when it would take twenty-four hours to dry, combing and brushing it repeatedly so that it shone and gleamed. 'I'm here now. How are you?'

'I'm all right.' She patently wasn't, but Calliope didn't challenge her. There was no sense in pointing out the obvious.

Calista bit her lip. 'At first they didn't tell me anything,' she continued. 'But then Eliana informed me that I'm accused of assisting the resistance. I don't know what the punishment will be.' She gasped, the very thought winding her. 'They say that, if they don't get executed, prisoners are sent to Germany, to camps over there.' She began to weep, silently and pitifully. Calliope's belly turned over in fear and compassion. Her sister, shipped hundreds of miles away to a foreign, northern land. She'd never make it. She hated to be away from home, even for one night. Being here would be torture enough. Going elsewhere would kill her.

'We won't let it happen,' Calliope put her lips right next to her sister's ear as if kissing her and spoke as quietly as she could. 'We're going to get you out of here,' she promised. 'Me and Laurie, and Ben and the others. You need to stay strong so that you're ready to run when we come.' In her head she was thinking, it can't wait until Laurie returns from Heraklion. Calista might not last that long. Or she might be on a boat to northern Europe by then.

Conscious of the guard waiting by the door, Calliope straightened up. 'I brought you this food,' she announced, and passed Calista the little bundle of bread and cheese. Her sister's eyes lit up momentarily.

'Thank you,' she said effusively. 'They don't give us much to eat.' Calliope hoped the guard didn't understand Greek and so wouldn't be angered by this accusation, even though it was obviously true. 'And I'm hungry all the time now.'

Calliope sat down again, placing herself in front of her sister, blocking the guard's view of her.

'We all are,' she sympathised. As if in full understanding, her stomach gurgled and groaned. If circumstances had been different, they'd both have laughed at that. But this dank prison was no place for mirth.

'This is more than that,' Calista said. Something in her tone filled Calliope with even more alarm.

'What do you mean?' she asked.

Calista bit her lip so hard that a bright-red drop of blood appeared there. Calliope reached out and wiped it away with her thumb. 'What is it, Calista?'

Her eyes full of fear, Calista grasped Calliope's hands. 'I'm pregnant,' she said in a hushed, reverent tone. 'About two months.'

Calliope's mouth fell open in shocked disbelief. Her sister was expecting a child? But how? When had this happened… She couldn't understand. How could this be possible?

'We were going to tell you,' Calista whispered, her agony evident in her desperate expression. 'Me and the father – we're in love and planning to get married. It would have been some happy news amidst everything – and then this happened.' Tears were gushing down her cheeks now and falling onto the dirty, dusty floor. Calliope still hadn't recovered enough to speak.

'What if something happens to the baby?' Calista sobbed. 'You've got to help me get out of here,' she implored Calliope. 'The baby's life depends on it.'

Utterly blindsided, Calliope nodded mutely. When she had come to the prison today, this was the last thing she had expected to hear. Then suddenly she got her voice back. There was a question that she had to ask.

'Who's the father?' Even as she said the words, a terrible feeling assailed her. No. It couldn't be. Could it? Surely not. But then who else?

'It's Laurie.' Calista's eyes lit up momentarily as she said his name. 'The baby's father, the man I love and who loves me, is Laurie.'

CHAPTER 21

CRETE, 2005

Of course Ella hadn't read the letter. It was written in Greek. She couldn't understand a word of it. That evening, seated at a table in the hotel garden, shaded by a grapevine pergola and drinking iced tea, Ella cleared her throat in a way Callie knew meant business.

'Gran,' she began, 'um, look, I appreciate that there's something going on here that I don't know the half of. But I really think, after what happened yesterday, that you need to tell me now. I've waited long enough. And if it's making you ill, giving you funny turns, well...' Her words petered out but the meaning was clear.

Callie clenched her fists in her lap. As she did so, Ella bit her lip, something Callie had never seen her do before. For a second, she looked exactly like Calista, making the habitual gesture that Calista had always made when she was nervous or unsure or simply thinking hard about something. Waves of nausea swept over Callie just as they had when she'd seen George at church, and had that ridiculous notion that he was her brother, back from the next world. The living and the dead seemed to be all mixed up and Callie didn't know how to separate them.

'I looked at that letter in your bag,' Ella admitted. 'I'm sorry, I appreciate that reading someone else's mail is a terrible thing to do. But' – she smiled wryly – 'as you know, I couldn't make head nor tail of it. It was all Greek to me, literally.' She coughed and took a sip of her iced tea. 'But it seems pretty obvious that it's from Calista. So can you explain how your sister, who you thought had been dead for decades, suddenly found your address and was able to write to you?'

Callie's lips trembled as she formulated her reply. 'It was someone at church, I think. A young man, called George. He reminded me of my brother. I even had a senior moment and thought it *was* him. Right after I met this George, the letter arrived. The two things must be connected.'

Ella frowned. 'OK,' she said, cautiously. 'Can you show the letter to me now?'

It was as if all the air had been sucked out of the garden. Slowly, Callie pulled the envelope out of her bag and handed it over. Time seemed to speed up and slow down, warping before her eyes.

Ella prised open the flap, which was quite easy to do since the steaming Callie had subjected it to. She took out the letter, together with the other item the envelope contained, which she laid on the table.

A red-and-white-patterned playing card, identical to the deck at the museum.

'It was seeing the pack of cards that made you faint, wasn't it?' The question was rhetorical and Callie didn't answer. 'So why, Grandma? Why did Calista include a card from a similar pack? It clearly had a huge impact on you, so why?'

A blackbird trilled, its clear tones filling the air.

'It just brought back memories,' Callie replied. It was too soon to tell Ella exactly what the cards had come to mean, the role they had played in Callie's journey across the island as she and the baby struggled to escape.

'Gran, forgive me for doubting you. It just doesn't make sense. "Identical twins, separated for over six decades, are cagey about being reunited." Anyone hearing that would be puzzled, if not downright suspicious. So forgive me for remaining unconvinced that you're telling me the whole story.'

Callie looked away, her eyes searching for the blackbird. She remembered that terrible moment when Calista had announced her pregnancy and told her who the father was, how blindsided she had been, almost unable to comprehend her sister's words. How could she explain any of this to Ella? The unforgivable thoughts she had had, the time it had taken her to do what she ought to have done straight away – congratulate her sister, be happy for her, pray for her.

'Gran?' Ella's tone had changed from exasperation to concern. 'Look, sorry to keep pushing you. I suppose that I'm so interested in Calista because she's family and – well, as I've said before, I've only got you... To find I have a great-aunt as well, and potentially a whole lot of other relations – this George, for example – well, it's a big thing to me. It matters.'

The blackbird flew past, coming to rest on the grape pergola, its beady, inquisitive eyes darting here and there. It seemed to be listening, and Callie wondered what it would make of her story if it knew everything. Would it judge her as she feared being judged? As Ella would judge her? Callie did not know how she could ever explain about her family, which was Ella's family too, the relationships between them.

'I'm so desperate to meet my Cretan family,' Ella continued. 'To get to know them and spend time with them. It's frustrating that it's taking so long to do that.'

The accusation hung there, suspended in the heat-heavy air. The blackbird's melodic song rang out once more, and then it flew away. Callie remembered reading an ancient legend that held blackbirds responsible for guiding the souls of the dead into the next life. She hoped that her brother George hadn't had to wait this long to reach heaven.

Clenching her fists under the table, Callie stared at the card. At least seeing it hadn't made her faint again, as she had the day before, like some frail old biddy. Like someone with things inside her head that were too hard to face.

'I was given an identical pack by a British sailor one day, after I'd gone to the coast to pick things up,' she explained. 'I loved those cards. They kept me company on all the long, lonely nights away from my family, up in the mountains. We used to— I mean I used to play with them all the time. It was just a sh— a surprise to see a similar pack at the museum. That's all.'

Ella narrowed her eyes and regarded her grandmother with an air of suspicion. 'So, Grandma. You've told me you met a young man at church who you thought was your brother George, even though George would be an old man by now if he had lived. Then you faint at the sight of a playing card. And in your bag I find the mysterious letter that you've brought all the way here but won't tell me anything about, other than that it's from the sister you always believed to be dead. Do you understand why I'm a bit concerned? Not just that there's something you're not telling me. But also that you might be losing your marbles.' She stared defiantly at Callie as she uttered the final words.

She knows just how to play me, thought Callie. *She knows that the worst thing she can think about me is that I'm going doolally.*

'All right,' she replied, resignedly. 'I give in. There is more to say. But I'm too tired at the moment.'

Touché. Ella couldn't argue with that, after all her fussing over Callie and instructing her to follow doctor's orders.

'Give me a day or so more to rest,' she concluded. Previously, she'd protested that she didn't need to take it easy, that she was fine. Now she was happy to use her little dizzy spell as an excuse to buy herself time. But even she knew that that time was running out. She didn't have long now before she'd have to face up to everything the letter would reveal.

Not long at all.

CHAPTER 22

CRETE, MARCH 1942

Calliope left the prison reeling, a million mixed emotions tumbling over each other in her mind. She barely noticed who escorted her out, or how she got to the exit gate in the first place, in her struggle to take in what Calista had told her.

Somehow, she managed to put some distance between her and the prison, which bristled with guards and watchtowers, before collapsing to the ground, where she sat, hands dug into the cold, hard soil, welcoming the pain of the stones against her flesh as a relief from the agony in her heart and head.

For some time she couldn't work out what she was feeling. There was fear for her sister and the unborn child, astonishment as to how the relationship between Calista and Laurie had been going on right under her nose and she hadn't noticed, and finally, when she forced herself to be nice, happiness at the thought of a new life amidst all the death and destruction.

But overriding all of it was a deep and profound sorrow, combined with a terrible feeling of embarrassment. Had Laurie noticed how she gravitated towards him, how she hung on his every word, how she regarded him with devotion? How could she have seen attraction in his every smile, felt desire in his every touch? How could she have thought that her dedication to the resistance would win his heart? It was humiliating how she had misread all the signs so completely. She had been wrong, so very wrong.

All along, it had not been her who Laurie loved, but Calista.

Calliope was so numbed with shock that she couldn't cry. She just sat, running over the past year again and again, trying to work out what she had missed and when. She became angry, and thumped furious fists against the stony soil until her knuckles were bruised and bleeding.

After a while, the anger subsided and a terrible sense of shame overcame her. How could she be selfishly thinking of herself when Calista, pregnant and vulnerable, was in prison, taking the punishment that should be hers?

As she trudged back to the hideout, feeling more miserable, lonely and scared for the future than she ever had before, even in the midst of the airborne invasion, she tried desperately to think of what to do. Laurie was not due back for another two days, but Calista's rescue could not wait until his return – especially if there was a danger of her being transported to Germany. Calliope sifted through everything that she had heard about prison breaks; she knew that numerous such events had occurred and several escaped prisoners had had contact with Laurie's group, and had been given assistance to reach the coast and escape off the island.

But then she remembered the barbed wire fences, the guards and the dogs. All those who had probably tried to get out and failed, and who had never been heard of again. There were two lives at stake here: Calista and the baby's. That was the terrible reality.

Calliope cursed herself inwardly. If she'd thought things through the way Laurie would have done, she'd have planned the rescue straight away, smuggled a message into the prison so that Calista knew what to do. She'd wasted her visit by giving her sister nothing more useful than a bit of food. *Idiot!*

At the *mitato*, there was no sign of anyone. Calliope made a mug of mountain tea to warm herself. Its herby aroma was usually comforting and consoling. But it was going to take more than the taste of home to make her feel better today. She got up and rummaged in a box stashed in the place designed to store cheese. She pulled out a pad of paper and a pencil. Chewing the end of the pencil, she screwed up her eyes and frowned.

Hesitantly, she began to sketch out what she remembered of the layout of the prison and the position of Calista's cell. While she was there, she had tried as best as she could to take it all in, the way Laurie would. The thought of how she'd always admired him, emulated him, brought her up short. Emitting a choking, strangled sob, she laid the pencil down, put her head on her knees and, finally, she wept, for everything she had hoped for but which was no more, for everything that was lost. Desolate, she cried and cried, not caring that Ben or one of the others might come in at any time and witness her wretchedness, and her weakness.

Nobody came. Calliope wept alone for hours. She thought through the past months again. She had been surprised when Laurie had seemed familiar with the Papadakises' *mitato*, but now she realised that he and Calista must have used it as a private meeting place where they could— Calliope couldn't bear to take this thought further. And occasionally she had spotted a certain look on Calista's face when Laurie was around, or when his name was mentioned, that should have given her a clue as to what was going on, if she hadn't been so oblivious to anything but herself and her own feelings.

Calliope forced herself not to contemplate the pair's clandestine trysts. It hurt too much. To think that she had internally disparaged her sister for her homeliness, her lack of ambition, her contentment with staying in the domestic sphere, how she had secretly, shamefully, believed that Laurie would see Calista as somehow inferior to Calliope because of their different character traits. How wrong she had been. How horribly, arrogantly judgemental, and how blind.

Lost in thought, she jumped out of her skin when a voice said, 'Calliope.' She had not heard anyone approaching. It was dark and at first she could not make out the identity of the figure in the low doorway, apart from the fact that it was far too small to be Ben or either of the other soldiers.

'Calliope,' the voice said again, and now she recognised it.

'Stelios,' she responded, hastily wiping the tears from her eyes. 'What are you doing here?'

'You need to come at once,' the boy replied. 'I found Calista, but she's not well. She fell down. I couldn't get her up. Please, Calliope, come quickly.'

Dazed by the news, unable to work out what it could possibly mean – Calista was in prison, how on earth had she got out? – Calliope leapt to her feet. She debated with herself for a few moments about whether she should go to look for Ben in the cave where he kept his equipment, but almost immediately she decided that there was no time for this. However it had come about, Calista had collapsed; she must get to her sister's side as soon as possible.

It took over half an hour to get to the place where Stelios had seen Calista. At first, in the gloom of the night, they couldn't locate her. And then Stelios found her, nestled into the base of a tree, curled up among its roots like a wood nymph or a poor, lost girl from a fairy tale or myth. She was shivering with cold, teeth chattering, and at the same time emitting small, painful moans. Calliope whipped her wool cloak from her shoulders and tenderly wrapped her sister in it. She was burning with questions to ask her, but this was not the time or the place.

'Go back to the village,' she instructed Stelios. 'Don't tell anyone about this, apart from my parents. Go to them and explain that they must pack a few belongings and come to our family *mitato* tomorrow at first light. Don't say anything more than that.'

Nodding, the little boy turned in the direction of the village, and galloped off. Calliope's heart turned over as she watched his small frame disappear from view into the darkness. He was so brave and reliable, and his desperate desire to be part of the effort against the Germans had brought out a wily fearlessness in him that made him as useful as an adult – if not more so, because as a child he attracted less attention and potential suspicion.

Calliope hoisted her sister into her arms and, determinedly gritting her teeth, set off back to the mountain hideaway with her precious cargo. Many times she had to stop to rest, her muscles screaming in pain. But determination made her strong and eventually she made it back to the lair. After laying her sister down, Calliope fired up the paraffin stove and brewed mountain tea. She lifted Calista's head and raised the cup to her lips, urging her to drink. The warmth of the hot liquid soon revived Calista enough for her to sit up and look around, but she still didn't speak. Calliope made a meal for her: beans and bread. At first Calista poked and prodded at the food, but once she'd had a few mouthfuls she began shovelling it into her mouth, eating as if it was the first time she'd done so in a month.

Eating for two, Calliope thought, and the same, uneasy feelings of sadness, joy and devastation assailed her once more. She shoved them away.

'What happened,' she asked, softly. 'How did you get out of the prison?'

Calista's eyes were wide with bewilderment. 'It-it was so strange,' she explained, falteringly. 'I-Eliana came. She said I was to work in the laundry, washing uniforms. They don't do this on the stones by the river like we do, but in a room with big sinks and huge urns of hot water. She took me there and locked me in. It was very odd because I was on my own. I kept thinking someone else would come, to watch me or perhaps to work alongside me, but nobody did.'

Calliope, listening intently, frowned. It did seem most peculiar. Was this a punishment Eliana had decided to subject Calista to? Eliana was supposed to be a translator, nothing more. But Calliope had long suspected her of greater involvement with the occupying forces, and this seemed to be further proof.

'After a couple of hours,' Calista continued, 'I began to feel faint because it was so hot in there. There was a door, not the one I'd entered by but another one. For some reason, I decided to try to open it, to see if I could let some air in. I turned the handle, expecting it to be locked. But it wasn't.'

Calliope's frown deepened. This still didn't explain how Calista had got away. 'So then what did you do?' she asked.

'I looked around and there was no one about. I could hear sounds of prisoners in the other huts, but there didn't seem to be any guards in that area. Perhaps they had all gone off shift, I don't know.' Calista faltered and Calliope saw that she had a strange expression on her face, as if she were still mystified by her experience, still couldn't believe what had transpired. 'I'd tried to pay attention to where we were going when Eliana took me to the laundry room, and I knew I was right at the back of the camp, on the far side to the main entrance. I could see a gate in the wire fencing and I don't know what came over me but I decided to go over there. And when I got near enough, I noticed that it wasn't quite closed. I gave it a push and it opened enough for me to get out.'

Calista halted, looking aghast, her eyes wide with fear and confusion. 'Suddenly I was outside the camp and no one had even seen me. I was so scared I thought about running back inside, back to the laundry, and pretending I'd never left. But then I thought of Laurie, and the baby, and I knew what I had to do. Get away from there as fast as I could. Come and find him, and you, so that you could keep me safe.'

By this time, tears were running down Calista's smooth, pale cheeks. Calliope handed her a rag to wipe them away and tightened her grip on her sister's hand.

'You did the right thing,' she crooned, 'we will keep you safe, don't you worry.'

So Eliana had messed up. That would serve her right for going against her community. Calliope hoped she was punished for her carelessness, allowing a valuable prisoner to escape, and then admonished herself for being spiteful.

As for her plan for what Calista should do next, she decided not to share that now. Calista needed to rest, and sleep, and eat, for the baby's sake. In the morning, Calliope would tell her. Tomorrow would be time enough.

CHAPTER 23

CRETE, MARCH 1942

Ben, John and Gerald came back not long after Calista had fallen asleep. Calliope explained to them about Calista's miraculous escape and her ideas about what should happen next. As she was talking, she tried to read Ben's expression. He was the natural leader when Laurie wasn't around.

'So, Calliope,' he said, when she'd finished. 'You don't need Laurie these days! You're thinking tactically yourself.'

In other circumstances, Calliope would have burst with pride at this compliment. But the suggestion that she didn't need Laurie made her curl up and die inside. She did need him, in every way. She'd thought that they were destined to be together, that they were soulmates. And then, with that shattering revelation from her sister, all her dreams had come crashing down around her ears. The fact that her love rival was her own twin made everything even more complicated, and bewildering. She could never hate or resent Calista, her own flesh and blood. But being gracious and generous when Calista had what Calliope had longed for was extraordinarily hard. She hadn't seen Laurie since then and, the more time that passed, the more frightened she was of doing so. What would she say to him? She'd have to congratulate him on the relationship, and the baby, and of course she was happy for him for both of those things – if she kept herself out of the equation.

But as soon as her own emotions rose to the fore, it all felt impossible.

Calliope hardly slept that night. She kept waking, checking that Calista was breathing normally, that her body felt warm under the woollen cloak. Long before first light, she gently shook her sister awake.

'We need to get up now,' she whispered. 'Get ready quickly.'

She had mountain tea waiting, and some scrambled eggs she'd made with powder that had come in one of the parachute drops. They ate and drank, Calista still seeming half-asleep.

'How are you feeling?' asked Calliope, anxiously. She could just make out Calista's grimace in the half-light.

'I'm so tired all the time,' she said. 'I just want to lie down and sleep. It's worse every day.'

Calliope patted her hand sympathetically. 'It'll get better,' she reassured her sister, even though she had no idea whether this was true or not. She thought of the village women who were always having babies, or their own mother when she was pregnant with George. She had seemed to carry on as normal throughout the whole nine months. But then, as she searched her memory, Calliope did recall Valeria sleeping longer each siesta time.

Leaving the stone hut, the two sisters slunk along goat paths and mule tracks under the ghostly light of the moon. Calliope kept a careful eye on her sister, taking her hand and helping her over any rocky, steep or precipitous parts, anxious that Calista should not fall for fear of harming the baby.

After a couple of hours of strenuous hiking, they reached a small hidden valley ringed by majestic peaks. Here lay the family *mitato*, the place where, for centuries past, their ancestors had brought their flocks to spend the summer months, a tradition that continued to the present day. On seeing the familiar surroundings, Calista halted in her tracks, bending over with hands on hips as she caught her breath. 'I need a rest,' she gasped.

'I'm sorry,' Calliope whispered, although they were so far from everywhere it was impossible to imagine anyone being able to hear. 'You can take a few minutes. But you're not stopping here, or at least not for long. Just a short break and you'll be moving on.'

At this, Calista stood bolt upright, fear and alarm written across her pale face. 'What do you mean?' she asked, an edge to her voice that indicated she was about to cry.

'Mama and Papa will be here any minute,' explained Calliope. 'You're all three going to our cousin's village over the other side of the pass. You'll lie low there for...' Calliope paused, her own voice breaking as she forced back tears. Taking a deep breath to calm herself, she continued, 'for as long as necessary.' Seeing Calista looking increasingly agitated, she reached out a hand and rested it on her sister's forearm. 'It's not safe for you at home just now. We need to get you far away from anyone who knows or might recognise you – anyone who might think you are me.'

Calista did not respond, apparently blindsided by the news.

Calliope moved closer, enveloping Calista in a huge hug. 'It won't be for ever,' she reassured her. 'Only for a while. We have to think about what's best for you both.' She stood back a little, glancing down at Calista's belly, where it was far too early to see any visible signs of the new life growing, but which harboured such a precious cargo.

'But what about Laurie?' breathed Calista, stricken at the prospect of being parted from him.

'He'll visit you, of course he will,' promised Calliope. 'And so will I. But you have to understand, Calista, that this is the only way. There are no other options.'

Calista began to cry. 'I just want to be with him and the baby,' she sobbed, 'to live together like a proper family, the way we would have done if not for this awful war. It's the only thing I've ever really wished for – to be married and have a family, lots of children running around and me cooking them good food and making sure they grow up strong and healthy.'

The voicing of her sister's simple desires brought tears to Calliope's eyes. They were so modest, so ordinary, wishes that should be so eminently achievable but because of circumstance were not.

'I know,' she replied, stroking Calista's hand. 'I know that's what you want. And you shall have it one day, I promise you, just not quite yet. And in the meantime, you need to look after yourself and the little one. That's your priority.'

Calista's sobs intensified. Calliope handed her a piece of rag to wipe her eyes. 'Try not to exhaust yourself with crying,' she said, gently. 'You need your energy for the journey.' And gradually, Calista's weeping subsided and she sat quietly, tear-stained face looking unutterably woebegone, until Valeria and Yiorgis arrived.

By now, the moon had faded and the hint of the dawn glowed pink in the east. There was no time to lose.

'You need to go,' Calliope said firmly, clenching her fists to stop the tears flowing. All this crying, it was no good. No help to anyone.

Not able to be so restrained, her parents and sister bade her a tearful farewell and then turned resolutely towards their destination. Calliope stared after them until they disappeared into the distance.

She'd held herself together throughout the journey and the parting, but, once her family had gone, Calliope slumped to the ground and curled up in a little ball, feeling desperately lonely once more. Even when Laurie returned there would be scant comfort or consolation, now that she knew his heart had been claimed by another.

Eventually, she hauled herself to her feet. She didn't want to go back to the lair and sit there, cold and alone. *What would Laurie do?* she asked herself. Despite everything, she still wanted to impress him, and nothing would put her off her desire to work against the occupation. The answer came to her: *put his misfortune and despondency to good use, take his mind off it all with decisive action.*

Throwing back her shoulders, Calliope made up her mind. Laurie wanted as full a picture as possible of all German activity in the area, but the problem was that the Germans were always changing positions, dismantling old machine-gun posts and setting up new ones. She would go on a recce, find out if anything had changed since Laurie had been away. This would be making herself useful and would hopefully show him that she hadn't wasted her time in his absence.

Now that she had descended so far from the high mountains she felt, for the first time this year, real warmth in the rising sun. It was luxurious and life-giving after the harsh, cold, hungry winter. Revelling in the prospect of the approaching spring, Calliope let her guard down. Emerging from a copse of chestnut and oak trees, she came face to face with a German patrol. How she had not heard them, she had no idea, but in any case there was no way to escape them now. Ice-cold fear trickled down her spine as she halted and stood, frozen to the spot, regarding the enemy troops who were regarding her with a similar amount of suspicion.

It felt like there was an inevitability to this encounter; the final blow after the crushing disappointment of having to give up on ideas of a future with Laurie.

The German soldiers approached, mean eyes and poised guns fixed upon her. Though her legs trembled beneath her,

Calliope held her ground. To run would mean certain death. Far from any grazing flocks, she had no idea what she would say if they asked what she was doing there. And her chilling fear only increased as the lead officer came closer. Close enough for her to recognise him.

It was the man who had bullied Laurie, and who Laurie had taken a cigarette from on their last outing together before he went to Heraklion, the man with the piercing blue eyes. Would the officer recognise her from either occasion? As long as her disguise protected her from being spotted as the woman from the parachute drop... Who was also the woman who had subsequently escaped from custody.

As this thought chimed in her mind like a death knell, Calliope's stomach heaved. She quailed as the officer stopped right in front of her. There was no hope. If they knew who she was, they would shoot her. They might shoot her anyway, just because they could.

Standing firm, Calliope refused to show her intense fear. In her mind's eye, she saw Calista, the Calista of the future with a tiny tot clasped to her chest, or pattering around her feet, clutching hold of her skirts as he or she tried to stand. If for nothing else, she wanted to live to see her niece or nephew, who she already knew she would love as she had loved George, fiercely and eternally. The officer's eyes were expressionless, giving away not one flicker of emotion. Calliope waited to see what he would do.

It turned out that he did nothing, other than to bark at her, 'Get out of our way, boy.'

Stunned, Calliope shrank back under the trees. With a flick of his head, the officer indicated to his men to keep going. Their jackboots thudding on the stony path, the soldiers marched past. Calliope stared after them, trying not to look as fearful as she really was in case one of them turned round. After the intensity of the fear, the let-down left her exhausted. She was also mystified. Why had she not been questioned, her route examined, her purpose scrutinised?

If something seems too good to be true, it probably is, she thought. Deciding that she'd had enough for one day, she moved off back up the mountains. She'd had a lucky escape, but this encounter had left her dreading what it all meant.

CHAPTER 24

CRETE, APRIL 1942

The scent of almond blossom filled the air with its delicate aroma of nuts and honey. Calliope breathed in a huge gulp of it as she and her parents stood outside the church, waiting for the newly married pair to exit. As Laurie and Calista appeared in the doorway, Calliope readied herself with a handful of petals to throw upon the couple. It was a miserable apology for a wedding compared to usual Cretan standards, when every relative as well as the entire inhabitants of a village would get together to celebrate the nuptials and dance a *mantinade* or twenty. But Calliope was determined to make it as special as possible for her sister, even if there were only three guests: herself, Valeria and Yiorgis.

Calista laughed as blossom blew into her face, settling on her head and shoulders like delicate snowflakes. She was utterly beautiful, wearing their mother's wedding dress, her silky black hair plaited and wound round and round her crown so that she resembled an ancient Greek goddess. The sun was out, the winter already receding from memory with the hope of the new season and, now, this marriage of the British soldier and his Cretan bride.

The priest emerged, smiling. It was fortunate that all the men of the cloth were on the side of the resistance, although many had suffered badly for it. One monastery had been burned down by the Nazis after they discovered that Allied troops travelling to the south coast for evacuation had been fed and sheltered there.

'Thank you for such a lovely ceremony,' said Laurie, ever the perfect gentleman.

'Yes, thank you so much,' added Calista, her eyes shining with happiness. Laurie put his arm round her waist and kissed the crown of her head. He murmured something to his new wife that Calliope couldn't hear, and Calista smiled and blushed in response. Watching them together, her heart yearned to have a connection with someone like this pair had. The connection she had thought existed between her and Laurie. If she had got it so wrong about him, how would she ever know in the future if the love she felt was reciprocated?

Hastily, she pushed such thoughts away. She was still working on herself, on the disappointment that ate away at her in the silent watches of the night, but had found that the best way to deal with it was to convince herself, on an hourly basis, how delighted she was for her sister and Laurie and how eagerly she awaited the birth of their baby. She hoped that, if she forced herself to think these thoughts often enough, they would become true.

Back in the home they had borrowed from relatives who had long ago abandoned their rural life and gone to live in the city, Valeria bustled around preparing the wedding banquet. She had managed to get hold of enough flour to make honey cake and sweet bread rolls, and somehow she conjured up cheese and olives to go with them. There was wine and raki, and Yiorgis had brought his lyre with him, upon which he played some traditional tunes as they drank a toast to the future.

Before Calliope left, she embraced her sister so tightly that Calista begged to be released.

'Look after yourself and the baby,' she implored. 'I'll come whenever I can.'

Calista nodded. 'I know you will,' she replied, simply. 'But please don't endanger yourself on my account.' Even after all she had been through, Calista was still thinking of others before herself. 'I'll be fine here with Mama and Papa.'

Calliope hoped that this was the case. Was this tiny mountain village the sanctuary she had envisaged it to be? Only time would tell. She was haunted by the thought that the enemy might come in the night and take her entire family away, and that she would not know it had happened until she arrived to find the house empty and abandoned, door swinging open on rusty hinges—

Stop it! she instructed herself. She had to stop letting her imagination run away with her.

Giving her parents and Calista one last hug, she departed. Laurie, Ben and the others had left the *mitato* and moved to a cave; they could never stay anywhere for long for fear of being found, but Calliope was not going there with them.

The old shepherd who had taken the family's flock to the summer pastures every year for donkey's years was now too old to continue working so Calliope would go in his place. It would mean forgoing her role in the resistance for the time being, which she did not welcome. But on the other hand, she was weary and heartsore, and a part of her longed for the simple life of solitude that awaited her in the tranquil valley far from civilisation.

The only person she would see from one week to the next was Stelios, who would help her out, relieving her every now and again so that she could visit her family. Her other company would be the old shepherd's dog, who was being lent to her to help her protect the flock. Though Crete had no natural predators, no bears, wolves or foxes, sheep rustling was a major problem and, in these times of hunger and hardship, no one could afford to lose any of their animals.

In the *mitato*, Calliope soon had things arranged comfortably. She'd been living rough for so long that she was used to it now, and the extra woollen cloaks she'd brought with her seemed like the height of luxury. Many of the sheep and goats had had their babies already, but there were still some expectant mums and Calliope knew she'd be up and about at all hours, supervising labour and delivery. Sheep tended to have their lambs at night, just to be awkward, Calliope always thought, but goats seemed to like to give birth by day, and to choose a nice day at that, though just how they were able to do this Calliope had no idea.

One morning about a week after the wedding, when the sun rose bright in a cloudless sky, Calliope knew she was going to be busy. She got ready her can of iodine for painting the umbilical cords and, as the kids were born, stood by to ensure that they found their mother's teats. Meanwhile the dog, who had been doing this job since he was a puppy and needed hardly any supervision, patrolled the furthest extent of the meadow, always on the lookout for any hapless animals straying too far from the others.

Finally, as the sun began to sink and the strengthening breeze chilled the air, Calliope called to the dog and, obedient as ever, he rounded up the flock and drove them back to the safety of the fold. Calliope fastened the gate and headed to the *mitato*; she was parched with thirst and desperate for some water. But as she crossed the stony area between the fold and the hut, she saw two tiny lambs huddled beside a rock, bleating pitifully. There was no mother nearby and Calliope knew immediately what this meant. These poor little mites had been rejected.

Her heart sank. In previous years the shepherd would have

had powdered milk and bottles with which to feed such lambs, but none had been available this terrible year of war. She could take the lambs back to the *mitato* and try to keep them warm, but without sustenance they would soon die.

This was a mini-catastrophe; the family needed every lamb possible to survive. They were all they had, their livelihood. Calliope was responsible. And the fact that these two were twins, like her and her sister, made her especially desperate to save them. She cast her eyes around her in all directions, as if somewhere might lie a solution to this problem. Of course, there was nothing.

She called the dog to her and trudged miserably towards the little hut nestled in the crook between two hillocks, her thirst almost forgotten in her distress. As they drew near, the dog paused, the hackles on his neck rising. He growled, long and low, and then let out a volley of frenzied barking. Alarmed, Calliope took hold of his collar. 'What's the matter, old boy?' she murmured to him. 'What's wrong?'

As she spoke, a hundred unanswered questions flooded her mind. What had set the dog baying with such ferocity? Who would come here, to this remote and inaccessible place? *Why* would anyone come here?

When she reached the low, narrow entrance in the drystone wall of the *mitato*, she bent to enter. The dog was no longer barking but instead wagging his tail enthusiastically, which was just as odd. He rushed on ahead, his eyes quicker than hers to get used to the semi-darkness. When she did finally manage to make out what was inside the hut, she nearly collapsed at the sight.

There, sitting on the floor with a lamb in his hands, which he was in the process of skinning, was a Nazi officer. And not just any Nazi officer – the very same one who Calliope had encountered three times now, bullying Laurie and leading patrols. Her heart stilled and the blood froze in her veins. She had thought it was strange that she had not been challenged when she had seen him so recently, and had wondered if it foretold trouble to come. Now she knew she was right. But what a terrible rightness.

All of this flashed through her mind as she stood there, mute and immobile.

The officer raised his blue eyes to hers, at the same time stretching his arm out to the dog, who had lain down beside him as if he were an old friend, and patting his head with a bloodied hand. Now Calliope was even more confused. Dogs were supposed to have the best instincts, right? But this one seemed to like the officer. Maybe it was a myth; maybe, for all their intelligence when herding sheep, dogs were incredibly stupid in other matters.

Calliope's eyes darted back and forth, from the officer to the half-skinned lamb. Just what exactly did this man think he was doing on her property and with her property?

Emboldening anger pulsed through her. 'What are you doing?' she demanded, coldly.

The officer smiled, and in that slow, small smile all the cruelty Calliope had seen before melted away and was replaced by a sadness that seemed to hold a million memories of better times. 'There are two abandoned lambs out there,' he explained, as if it were perfectly normal for a Nazi officer and a Cretan woman, disguised as a boy and wanted all over the island, to be chatting in a stone *mitato* in a hidden valley in the White Mountains. It categorically was *not* normal, but somehow Calliope went along with it. 'They won't make it on their own. But then I spotted a dead lamb, its mother hopelessly licking it and pushing at it to try to wake it up. So I picked it up and brought it here to skin it. If we put the skin on the twins and rub the smell into them, the mother will accept them as her own and feed them. Hopefully she will, anyway.'

Before he'd finished speaking he'd looked back down and

resumed his task. 'We don't have long,' he added, intent on his labour. 'It's been an hour or so already and they won't survive another without milk.'

Flabbergasted, Calliope did not reply. She didn't have the words. Her heart thudded in her chest. This was all so weird. Everything the officer was saying was true. But how did he know all this? And why did he care enough about some poor Cretan family's flock to go to such lengths to help?

'Right,' said the officer, laying his extremely sharp-looking knife to one side. The poor fleeced lamb was a wretched bundle in his bloodied hands. 'Your dog will appreciate this, I'm sure,' he continued. 'But we need to get to work – no time to lose.'

Still speechless, Calliope followed him outside.

The two little lambs were still in the lee of the stone but, already visibly weaker than they had been, they were no longer bleating. Calliope's unexpected guest was right about the urgency of their task. Skilfully, he draped the skin loosely over the backs of the two small, frail babies, then picked them up in his huge hands and gestured with his head towards the fold.

'The mother we want is the one with the black muzzle,' he said. 'I made a careful note of what she looked like so that I could remember her. With any luck this adoption will go well.' He sounded cheerful now they were on the road to success and, turning to Calliope, grinned broadly at her, looking completely different to how he had seemed in the gloom of the hut. He was walking quickly and Calliope had to almost run to keep up. He didn't bother opening the gate to the fold but just swung one leg and then the other over the low stone wall. Not wanting him to see her clambering inelegantly after him, Calliope detoured to the gate and entered that way.

By the time she reached him, he had already begun introducing the mother to her new offspring. As Calliope watched on, she saw the lambs searching for the teats and, when they found them, suckling for all they were worth. Spellbound, she could not tear her gaze away as, before her eyes, the lambs revived, seeming to visibly grow bigger and stronger with every suck.

Eventually, they had both had their fill and broke off. The mother licked them, nudging them gently to their feet. When she trotted away, the two babies gambolled after her, not a care in the world, and took their place with the rest of the flock, all huddled together now in preparation for the night to come.

The urgent job attended to, the officer turned to Calliope and reached out a hand to make a formal introduction, then hastily withdrew it at the sight of all the blood.

'Sorry,' he said. 'I'd better give myself a good wash.'

Wordlessly, Calliope pointed with a shaking hand towards the spring that gushed with pure mountain water. She watched in a daze as he strode towards it and spent a while scrubbing and dousing until the blood was gone. Then he returned to where she still stood, numb and motionless. Now the lambs had been dealt with, her fear had returned in spades.

'Do you have any tea?' he asked. 'It's getting cold, don't you think?'

Calliope nodded silently and led him back to the hut, where she lit a fire in the blackened fireplace and put a pot of water upon it.

'Just mountain tea,' she said, her voice now she had found it again sounding strange to her own ears. This was surreal. Was she about to sit down and share a hot drink with a German, a man who was one of her arch-enemies, and for whom she had, up to now, only felt the most intense hatred?

'That's fine,' replied the officer. 'I like Cretan mountain tea.'

Extraordinary.

'I grew up on a farm,' he volunteered, as if Calliope had asked him the question. 'In southern Germany, in the Alps. They're mountains too,' he added.

This brought Calliope to her senses. She shot him a withering glance. Though she was a poor Cretan girl who'd left school at fifteen, she wasn't completely ignorant. She knew about Europe. Bits of it, anyway.

'We had sheep, and cows,' the German continued. 'Mostly cows, if I'm honest. But a few sheep, so I knew what to do when I saw those poor mites. And I also know how important it is that every newborn survives. That's no different in Germany to how it is here.' He held his hands in front of the fire and then rubbed them together. They were still red, but from the stinging cold of the spring water rather than blood.

Calliope opened the tin containing the tea leaves, but her hands trembled so violently that she dropped the lid. The sudden clatter sent her heart rate shooting upwards again.

'The tea will be ready soon,' she said. She sounded monosyllabic after all his chattering, but she couldn't think of what to say. She was still waiting for him to suddenly turn, to become that cruel Nazi she had assumed him to be. But there was no sign of it yet.

'*Efharistó*,' he replied. He spoke good Greek. He must have spent some time learning it since he'd been here. A sudden rush of horror ran through Calliope. Perhaps Eliana had taught him. She'd heard that her old friend was giving lessons these days. It was a good way to trick and entrap someone; lull them into a false sense of security by being able to communicate and, once their guard was down, take advantage.

'How's your sister?' the officer asked.

Now it was the spoon that fell out of Calliope's hands. Oh God. She knew it. He'd been playing Mr Nice to catch her out, make her give herself away. She'd be arrested any minute, if not killed.

The officer picked up the spoon and handed it to her. His bloody knife still lay on the ground next to him. What would it feel like to be stabbed? thought Calliope, her stomach turning over in fear.

'Look,' he went on, sounding more serious now, but still sincere. 'I know who you are. I know you've got an identical twin and I know you're the one who was at the parachute drop, but not the one who was arrested.'

Methodically, Calliope spooned tea leaves into the pot. She almost laughed. How did this person she had thought was a complete stranger know so much about her? It was disconcerting to say the least, if not downright terrifying. And what was the point of making the tea if she was about to die? But then again, what was the point of not making it? Did anything matter, when you were facing your own imminent death? She poured the water.

'By the way, in case it's not obvious by now, I also know that you're a girl, not a boy.'

Calliope filled a cup with mountain tea and handed it to him. She wasn't sure if this was really happening. Perhaps she was in the middle of a particularly vivid dream?

The officer took a sip. 'God, that's good,' he sighed. He put the cup down and rubbed his eyes with his knuckles, then took off his hat and ran his hands through his hair.

'Please don't be afraid of me,' he went on. 'You have nothing to fear. I want you to know that I hate this war, the mindless violence, the subjugation, the pointlessness of it all. As I parachuted in, I almost hoped that I'd be shot down, that I wouldn't make it, so that I'd be out of it for good. But when that didn't happen, I knew I'd have to choose another path. The executions, the destruction of villages, the killings for no reason – they sicken me.' He gestured to her to sit down and then picked up his cup and gulped down some more tea. 'I'm on your side,' he concluded.

Cautiously, Calliope sat. It was cold now and she pulled her woollen cloak around her.

'Why would I believe any of that?' she responded, mechanically. It was a question she had to ask, but what would the answer mean? Everything was so extraordinary, she felt disconnected from her own life.

'My name's Heinrich Schmidt, by the way,' the officer said, not immediately answering the question. 'And you're Calliope Papadakis aren't you?' Without waiting for her affirmation, he continued. 'I can't make you believe me. But if it wasn't true, you'd be dead by now, or at least I'd be marching you down to the prison in Chania, where you'd probably be tortured to give away the names of all the British that you're working with.'

Calliope was glad of the thick woollen cloak, not only for protection from the cold but also so that he could not see her shaking.

'All I can do is beg you to believe me, and let me help you,' Heinrich went on. His voice was soft and his words heartfelt. Perhaps he was speaking the truth. Calliope relaxed a little. It was certainly the case that he could have done away with her immediately if he'd wanted to, given how defenceless she was. And the dog liked him. Perhaps it would be all right.

'And if I say I believe you,' Calliope ventured. 'What then?'

'Then I'll do everything I can to help your cause,' replied Heinrich, more animated now. 'And all you have to do is keep it a secret. Keep me a secret. Don't tell anybody. Not the British, not your sister. Do you understand?'

Calliope considered this. She didn't think she was good at keeping secrets, probably because she'd never had any. But then again, she would have said the same about Calista, and look what a secret Calista had kept from her. And anyway, she was in it now, whether she liked it or not. Heinrich knew who she was. On the other hand, she knew his betrayal of his country.

Slowly, Calliope nodded. 'All right,' she agreed, trance-like, still wondering if this were really happening.

Taking her hand to shake on it, Heinrich spoke. 'It's a secret that can never be revealed,' he insisted, with utter gravity. 'Or we will both die.'

CHAPTER 25

CRETE, 2005

'How do you feel today?' asked Ella, as she passed Callie a plate of pastries she'd collected from the buffet breakfast.

'Good,' answered Callie and then quickly added, 'a little better than yesterday anyway.' She was wary of letting Ella think that she was completely recovered because, from that moment on, it would be harder than ever to resist the pressure to make the visit to the village, and her sister, that loomed over her.

'Do you think you'd be up for a little trip?' Ella went on. 'The receptionist told me about an olive oil and cheese tour that's happening today, by minibus – there are two places left. She's knocked thirty per cent off the price for a last-minute booking, so it's very inexpensive.' She knew how much Callie liked a bargain.

Callie considered Ella's proposition. It couldn't hurt to go, could it? It would buy Callie some more time. But still, it seemed utterly improbable that olive oil and cheese was a touristic activity in this day and age. When Callie had lived on the island, they'd consumed these substances because they were all they had, were what the land provided. To think they were now desirable and exotic, coveted artisan products that foreigners were happy to pay what Callie regarded as silly money for, was preposterous, really.

'So shall I go and confirm with reception?' persisted Ella. She was halfway out of her chair before Callie nodded her assent.

An hour later, Ella was helping Callie up the steps into the minibus. They visited an olive oil mill that proudly boasted a three-thousand-year-old olive tree whose branches had been used to create wreaths for the winners at the previous year's Olympic Games. As Ella exclaimed about the size and great age of the tree, and read the information panel about how olive trees have always been regarded as sacred and symbols of peace, Callie just stared at the enormous, gnarled trunk, the heartwood of which had long been lost. This tree had already been one thousand years old when Columbus first set out across the Atlantic and since then it had seen everything, survived everything – including the war.

While Ella went into the museum to have a look around and buy some oil, Callie stepped forward to touch one of the olive's silvery-green leaves. She wished this tree, so ancient and so wise, could help her understand how to deal with the situation she now faced.

They clambered back aboard the minibus and headed towards the mountains. The driver pulled off the road and drove along a dusty, rocky track, past thorn trees and cistus bushes, beneath oak and plane trees. The vehicle rocked from side to side on the uneven road surface and Callie remembered a journey by donkey when she'd been black and blue from a fall, how the animal's lurching gait had been almost as bad as trying to walk herself. Everything had changed so much, it was hard to remember that that past had ever existed. It felt like another world.

'We have to stop here,' announced the tour guide. 'And then

we have a short walk, about five or ten minutes.' She regarded Callie anxiously. 'The ground is quite rough underfoot, so—'

'I'm fine,' interjected Callie, tersely. 'I was brought up in these mountains.'

The guide smiled apologetically. 'I'm sorry, I didn't mean to offend.'

'No offence taken,' said Ella hastily, bustling Callie off the bus.

They followed the rest of the group along the path, eventually rounding a corner to see, nestled at the foot of a rocky hillside studded with wind-stunted trees and squat bushes, a stone-built hut with a domed roof and a low, narrow doorway. Callie stopped short, breathing shallowly as if she'd been winded. A host of memories came flooding back, of her and a dog, and a German officer, in a *mitato* just like this...

Ella went inside to listen to the guide explain how the cheese was made, while Callie sat on the low wall outside surveying her surroundings. This hut was remote, but not as remote as her family's. Or perhaps it just felt less remote because they'd driven to it in such a short amount of time. At any rate, at least it was cooler here. She breathed in the clear, sharp, dazzling air and looked up at the jagged mountains towering in the distance, their purplish outline interspersed with the shining white of the limestone peaks.

Ella rejoined her and handed Callie a bottle of water from her backpack. 'What are you thinking, Gran?' she asked.

'Just remembering how things were, back in the olden days,' she replied, her eyes half-closed in contemplation.

'If you and Calista are identical twins,' mused Ella, 'then you must have the same skin colouring?' She rubbed some sunscreen into her face and neck as she spoke. 'Mum was a bit fairer than you, wasn't she? I suppose that's because Grandpa was so fair. And I'm a little fairer again. Which is a pain when it means I'm constantly getting sunburnt.'

Callie wondered where on earth Ella was going with this. If she started to get on to family trees, it would lead her even further into deception. Far from clearing up the lies, coming to Crete seemed to be creating a whole bunch of new ones.

'Well, it's not an exact science, is it,' she pronounced. 'And anyway, Hei— what I mean is, why are you thinking this just now?'

Ella shrugged and stowed the sun cream in her bag. 'Wondering whether I'll look like any of Calista's family, or have the same colouring as them – her children or grandchildren. I mean, if they're my cousins or second cousins or whatever, I might do.'

The glug of water Callie had taken went down the wrong way and suddenly she was coughing and spluttering. Anxiously, Ella jumped up and started patting her on the back.

'Are you OK, Gran? Here's a tissue... are you all right?'

Unable to reply for a moment, Callie nodded at the same time as she continued to cough. Damn Ella's inquisitiveness. When they'd embarked on this journey, Callie simply hadn't given enough consideration to how deeply Ella would probe. But of course she was bound to do that. And she had a right to know. But the thought of losing Ella as a result of the truth being told was too terrible to contemplate.

The guide signalled that it was time to return to the minibus. As she trudged back along the stony track, Callie gazed at the mountains. They hadn't changed. They were just as they had always been, a source of danger but also safety, a place to flee to and to hide among. Implacable. Unmoving. Uncompromising. The mountains knew everything.

'It's so beautiful here,' sighed Ella.

It was true. Everything *was* so beautiful.

It made it all worse, somehow.

CHAPTER 26

CRETE, APRIL 1942

Over the next days, Calliope played and replayed the encounter with Heinrich in her mind. It had been so bizarre. It was all wrong, to be fraternising with the enemy. But he'd made it plain that he didn't consider himself her enemy, or the enemy of any Cretan. And she had to admit she'd liked him, as had the dog.

She glanced down at the faithful animal and rubbed his soft head. He had never had a name before but now Calliope gave him one – Orion, after the constellation – because he was a star in her life and because Calliope often went outside at night to gaze up at the sky. She would imagine all the galaxies out there where maybe there were no wars that killed and destroyed, that ripped families apart and ruined futures. The dog would snuggle in beside her, also looking upwards, and Calliope liked to think he was stargazing, too.

Every few days, Calliope set off to visit Laurie and the other soldiers. It was on one of these trips that he delivered some devastating news.

'I've been called back to Cairo,' he told her, as they sat on a ridge that gave on to a panoramic view of miles and miles of crags and peaks, valleys and plateaux, river gorges and limestone boulders.

Calliope looked at him, aghast. 'Why? What for? You're needed here, not there!'

Laurie grimaced. 'I know. But the situation is changing all the time and our role in tying up German forces in Crete and thus preventing them being deployed elsewhere is crucial. We need all the intelligence we can get, plus as many new ideas about how to continue our campaign as possible. To achieve all this, I need to spend some time in Egypt.'

This was a terrible blow for Calliope, but her overriding concern was what it would mean for her sister. She could imagine how difficult it was for Calista, with Laurie only able to visit intermittently. For the duration of the time he spent in Cairo, they wouldn't see each other at all. An awful thought struck her.

'Will you be back in time for the baby's birth?'

Laurie took a long draw on his cigarette. 'I hope so,' he replied. Calliope waited for him to say more but he didn't. She took this to mean that his return by late September, when the baby was due, was not certain. Calista would be devastated.

Calliope stared out across the undulating landscape where, far in the distance and almost lost in the haze, lay the blue of the Libyan Sea, the sea that Laurie would have to cross to reach Egypt. What if he didn't make it? What if he was caught trying to reach the coast, or his ship was hit by a bomb or torpedo, or— She forced herself to stop catastrophising. Laurie was a survivor, one of those lucky human beings who, catlike, had nine lives. He would be all right. For Calista's sake, and the baby's, she had to believe this was true.

The problem was how dependent they all were on Laurie, how naturally he led, how much devotion he inspired in others. Being without him for any length of time was going to be a challenge. She wasn't sure if it was better or worse for her that she wasn't currently an active resistance member. It meant that perhaps she wouldn't feel Laurie's absence so deeply, but, on the other hand, she would also miss out on fully supporting Ben and the others while their leader was gone.

She comforted herself with the knowledge that she regularly passed on information gleaned by Stelios. The child, sharp-eyed and clever, had turned into one of the most assiduous members of the cell, often acting on his own initiative to stake out German garrisons and control points, memorising troop positions and numbers, observing checkpoints to see how conscientious – or not – were the soldiers manning them.

And of course there was Heinrich. After that first time, he came to the *mitato* as often as he possibly could, and Calliope collated every piece of information he provided and added it into the mix of what Stelios had brought, therefore disguising that she actually had not one, but two, sources reporting in to her.

'While I'm gone, Ben will be in charge here,' Laurie said, taking one last drag at his cigarette and then grinding it out on the stone beside him. 'So keep bringing him everything Stelios uncovers. That boy is a godsend, that's for sure.'

Calliope nodded. It seemed that Laurie had no idea about Heinrich, which was good – and essential, given the promise she had made to keep their friendship and collaboration a secret. She glanced towards the sun, checking its position in the sky. It must be late afternoon; time to make a move. Heinrich had said he would visit at dusk today and, in April, that meant in only two and a half hours' time. She should be there when he arrived, and not only that but Orion was guarding the flock, and she didn't like to leave him for too long.

She stood up, and Laurie did too, and faced her, squinting into the strong sunlight. Up so high the heat of the rays was intense, although as soon as you went into the shade, you'd start to shiver.

'Goodbye, Calliope,' Laurie said. 'You've been amazing. You *are* amazing. You've done so much to help us, and for the cause. I'm constantly impressed by your bravery. And – well, we're family now, aren't we? So we'll always have those bonds to connect us, however far apart we are.'

Calliope blushed, avoiding his gaze. She still adored him but all deeper, romantic feelings had now of necessity evaporated. He belonged to her sister, and that was that. 'I've only done what anyone would do,' she murmured, self-deprecatingly.

Laurie shook his head. 'Cretans, maybe,' he agreed. 'You lot are incredible. The Germans had no idea what they were taking on when they decided to invade. Not everyone would step up the way you have.'

The pair stood, both seeming overwhelmed by the moment. Then all of a sudden, Laurie stepped forward, flung his arms round Calliope and held her in a tight embrace for many minutes. When he finally released his grip, he met her gaze. 'Look after Calista for me, won't you?' he asked. With the last words his voice went weak and croaky, and Calliope realised that this strong, indomitable man was trying not to cry. 'And the baby,' he managed to blurt out, before his voice broke again.

'Of course I will,' she replied, her voice also breaking. Her poor, darling sister, living in semi-exile, soon to bring a new life into a world filled with evil. 'I'll guard them both with everything I have. You know that.'

Laurie, unable to speak, merely nodded. Of course he knew it. He slipped a small package into her hands, and gestured to her to get going.

Eyes smudgy with moisture, Calliope left. She did not look backwards. She didn't want what might be her last glimpse of Laurie to be him forlornly waving after her, knowing that, in the time he was away, his baby might be born.

At the *mitato*, Orion ran to greet her as soon as he picked up her scent on the breeze.

'Good dog,' praised Calliope, reaching down to pat his thick, wiry coat. 'Are you hungry, old boy? Is it dinner time?'

She had some meat and bones for him in the hut, but for herself there was not much. Just some beans and a heel of stale bread. Her stomach gurgled as she tried to calculate when Stelios would next appear. Tomorrow? Or the day after? Sadly the latter, she realised. After drinking several cups of spring water to dull her hunger, she fetched Orion's bowl and put some food in it. As she bent to place the bowl on the ground, she felt the bulk of something in her pocket. The package Laurie had given her, fighting for space with the pack of cards that she still carried everywhere with her. She used them often to pass the time with solitary games of patience, an activity that filled her with nostalgia for the old days of playing with Laurie.

Though her dreams of a future with Laurie were long since over, she still longed for companionship and all the things her sister now had: the sure knowledge of being loved, the prospect of forging into the future as a partnership, rather than alone.

Slowly, she opened the package. Inside was a note telling her to collect food from Ben whenever she needed to, and a couple of bars of chocolate. Calliope salivated at the sight of them. She wanted to rip them open and devour them, then and there. She imagined the rich taste in her mouth, creamy and delicious, how it would linger on her tongue so delightfully. As she luxuriated in these thoughts, Orion suddenly broke off from eating and rushed out of the *mitato*, barking in welcome. Heinrich. The dog always greeted him like some long-lost best friend, which made Calliope laugh and which she knew Heinrich liked immensely.

Calliope put the chocolate down where Orion couldn't get at it – that dog would eat anything – then ducked under the low threshold of the door and followed him outside. To the west, the sunset striped the heavens, a vivid line of orange fading to amber between the white limestone mountains and the clear blue of the sky. As he approached, the light cast upon Heinrich a golden glow, making him resemble a god or figure from myth and legend.

'*Kalispéra*,' she greeted him. Her heart gave a little leap of excitement at seeing him at the same time as her belly emitted a loud rumble. Embarrassed, she frowned at her stomach, but Heinrich merely returned her greeting, laughing.

'You're hungry,' he said, sympathetically.

Calliope nodded, thinking that, if she ate now, she'd have to offer food to Heinrich too, and she had so very little – *Shame on you!* her internal critic scolded her. How hunger turned people into beasts. Of course she would share whatever she had, and gladly.

As if he were reading her mind, Heinrich swung his backpack onto the ground. 'I brought you some supplies,' he announced. 'Some boiled ham, potatoes and cabbage. And a couple of loaves of bread.' He looked at her apologetically. 'Sorry it's nothing more exciting than that. But at least it's something.'

Calliope's eyes had already widened at the sight of this bounty. 'No, it's wonderful,' she enthused. 'My stores are a little low, so this is amazing.' She didn't want him to know exactly how low, as in, almost non-existent, didn't want to seem desperate. Even though she pretty much was.

'I'll get some plates.' She went into the *mitato*, Heinrich following. He had to practically get onto his knees to fit through the low doorway. It wasn't until the food was plated up and they were back outside, eating it while sitting in the shelter of a large boulder, that Calliope noticed Heinrich's ears. They stuck out from the sides of his cap and the tops of them were bright red, beginning to blister.

'What happened to your ears?' she asked, thinking how sore they looked.

Heinrich grinned ruefully. 'Sunburn,' he said. 'I was outside for hours the last two or three days and suddenly the sun has got so much stronger. My poor lugholes are not used to it!'

'Oh dear,' responded Calliope, grimacing sympathetically. She regarded Heinrich, who was so handsome but whose looks were so different from the local men and even Laurie. Heinrich's skin was pale and freckled, and even though his hair was cut close to his scalp, you could tell that it was strawberry blond. The Cretan sun, especially at this time of year, had the ability to burn even those with the darkest of skins, and someone so fair was bound to suffer. 'I've got some salve,' she said. 'We make it from the aloe vera plant and it's really good – very soothing. Let me get it – it will definitely help.'

She retrieved the little jar from the *mitato* and brought it back to Heinrich. He regarded it dubiously, a look that made Calliope laugh. 'I promise you it's good stuff,' she insisted. 'I'm not a witch doctor!'

At this, Heinrich laughed too. 'All right,' he said. 'What do I do with it?'

'You apply it to the affected area,' responded Calliope. 'Or – if you like – I could do it?'

'Please,' responded Heinrich. 'I'm sure you will have a gentler touch than me. My hands are too big and clumsy for such delicate work.'

Calliope glanced down at his hands. They were large, but didn't look clumsy at all. Instead they seemed deft and dextrous, with long, supple fingers that she could imagine playing the piano, the bouzouki or the lyre. For a moment she imagined holding those hands, or being held by them, caressed by them – and immediately swatted the thought away. She remembered the way Laurie had looked at her sister outside the church, his eyes so full of adoration. Calliope longed for someone to look at her like that.

She unscrewed the lid of the jar, scooped out some of the precious salve and, gently and carefully, applied it to the tips of

Heinrich's ears. His high, chiselled cheekbones were a little red as well, so she smoothed some there, too. As she worked, he sat motionless, eyes half-closed as if he were meditating, while Orion observed them both curiously. Despite her best efforts, Calliope's thoughts kept straying back to those hands, to how they would feel on her body—

'Oops!' Heinrich's laughing exclamation broke through her daydream as a dollop of the salve missed its target and fell onto his neck.

Glad that she was standing behind him and he couldn't see the flush rising on her cheeks, Calliope wiped it away, apologising.

'I think I'm done now anyway,' she said. It might have been a signal for Heinrich to get up, or for Calliope to move away. But for a moment both of them remained motionless.

And then Heinrich let out a heartfelt sigh. 'That feels better already,' he declared, turning to face her. 'Thank you so much.'

Calliope shrugged off his gratitude with a careless wave of her hand. 'You're welcome,' she replied. 'Here, take the jar. I can get—' She halted abruptly. She'd been about to say she could ask Stelios to bring some more, but she didn't want Heinrich to know about the child's visits. She trusted Heinrich, she really did, but, just as the two of them had to keep their meetings a secret, she felt that Stelios should be one too. 'I can make more if I need it,' she continued.

It was so good to see Heinrich and it felt so comfortable sitting here with him. She realised now that, with Laurie, she had always been a little on edge, anxious to impress him, whereas with Heinrich she felt no need to do that and could just be herself, normal, ordinary, everyday Calliope. She remembered the chocolate and suddenly thought how nice it would be to have some now, the perfect end to the perfect day. She went inside to fetch a bar.

Back beside Heinrich, she carefully snapped off a couple of

pieces and handed them to him, then took a couple for herself. Before putting them in her mouth, she rewrapped the bar. She would save the rest for her family, to give to her mother and father, and to Calista, who with the pregnancy craved sweet things.

'What was your favourite food or drink when you were a child?' Heinrich asked her. 'For me, it was the *Lebkuchen* we had at Christmas. Just the smell of the chocolate and cinnamon reminds me of those times, all the family gathered together around the tree and nothing to worry about apart from whether the present you received would be what you really wanted.'

Calliope smiled. It was sweet to hear Heinrich reminiscing about a happier past.

'What about you?'

Hugging her knees into her chest, Calliope screwed up her eyes in concentration. 'I can't think of one favourite,' she said, eventually. 'But if we're talking Christmas biscuits, then mine would have to be *kourabidies* – almond biscuits dusted with sugar. So good,' she added, putting her fingers to her lips and kissing them.

'We'll have these things again one day, for sure.' Heinrich's voice carried a certainty that comforted Calliope. When survival was always in doubt, it was often hard to believe in the future.

She and Heinrich finished eating the chocolate in silence, watching the last throes of the setting sun paint the sky pink before fading to darkness. Calliope felt a strange sensation descend upon her that for a few moments she could not name. And then it came to her. Contentment. For the first time in many months, if not years, she almost felt happy. Relaxed. She glanced at Heinrich, nibbling contemplatively on his chocolate ration. He sensed her eyes upon him, turned towards her and smiled.

It wasn't Laurie's dazzling smile, but one that was more

thoughtful and considered, and not so often bestowed, its rarity giving it great value. Calliope smiled back and, in that moment, something changed. She knew in her bones that everything he said was the truth, that she could trust him implicitly – and perhaps there was more than that. A shiver ran through her as goosebumps rose on her arms.

'Come on,' said Heinrich, immediately. 'It's getting chilly. You go inside to warm up. I'll wash the dishes.'

Surprised that he was willing to do a woman's job, Calliope followed his instruction. When he'd finished, he came to say goodbye. He shook her hand, his touch electric, his grasp lingering just a little longer than necessary. When he left, she stood at the door of the *mitato*, wrapped in her trusty woollen cloak. A little hankering of her heart niggled at her as it always did on his parting, wondering if he would return, not because she doubted his desire to do so, but because it was always possible that he wouldn't be able to.

While war raged across the island, nothing was certain, and so Calliope waved and waved until Heinrich's figure had faded into the distance, in case that was the last time she ever saw him.

CHAPTER 27

CRETE, MAY 1942

Over the next weeks, Calliope's fears remained unfounded as Heinrich appeared more and more frequently at the *mitato*. At first, he would make an excuse for his presence – needing to get away from the barracks, the fact that the mountains reminded him of the Alps of his homeland and so quelled his homesickness, his concerns about whether Calliope needed help with the flock or more food. But one day, things changed.

It was late May now, the snow mostly melted away, the meadows and plateaux alive with wildflowers and the sun steadily growing in intensity, heralding the summer to come. Though the nights were still cold, Calliope no longer wore the woollen cloak during the daytime. She was sitting on the low wall beside the *mitato*, drinking mountain tea, listening to the bleating of the lamps and the birdsong that filled the air and thinking how the tranquillity of the scene belied the reality of the war that raged upon the island, when Heinrich appeared beside her.

She jumped out of her skin, exclaiming in shock and surprise before recovering enough to breathlessly gasp, 'You frightened me!'

Heinrich grinned remorsefully. 'Sorry,' he said. 'I didn't mean to. I thought you'd hear me coming.' He glanced around him. 'Speaking of which, why didn't Orion announce my arrival? That's odd.'

'I don't think so,' replied Calliope, shaking her head and pointing to a squat thorn bush some distance away. 'Look at him! He's so used to you now that he doesn't bat an eyelid.' Heinrich's gaze followed the direction she indicated, and he laughed when he spotted Orion, fast asleep beneath the branches.

'Would you like some tea?' she asked, ready to jump off the wall and fetch him a cup.

Heinrich stretched out his arms and lifted his face to the sun. 'No, not right now. Maybe later.'

He sat down beside her. 'It's so beautiful here,' he said. 'So peaceful.'

Calliope nodded. 'That's just what I was thinking,' she agreed. 'Up here, it's easy to forget what's going on down there.' She waved her arm in the general direction of the coast.

They sat for a while in companionable silence.

'What are you doing here, by the way?' The question suddenly occurred to Calliope; Heinrich didn't usually come during the daytime. 'Won't you be missed?' she added anxiously. For multiple reasons, she didn't want him to draw attention to himself or his illicit whereabouts. Her own safety was at risk, but his was just as important. Calliope was always fearful of him being found out and the awful consequences for him that would entail.

Heinrich didn't reply immediately; his gaze remained fixed on some faraway spot for several minutes. When he did speak, it was with caution, as if he were choosing the words carefully. 'I came to see you,' he said, simply. 'I find that, these days, when I'm away from you I miss you. You're always on my mind. I think of you all the time.'

Winded, Calliope stared at him. It was so unexpected, so out of the blue. Or was it? When she was honest with herself, she acknowledged that she felt this way, too. Her life in these times was simple in the extreme, stripped back to its bare essentials, just her and Orion and the flock, spending the majority of the time alone, the sporadic appearance of Stelios or her occasional visits to her family and the cell the only things to break the monotony and the solitude.

Apart from Heinrich. She had been refusing to let herself accept how much she looked forward to his visits, how she lived for them, because, even though she knew in the depths of her being that he was good and true and honest, every now and again it still felt wrong, to be fraternising with a German, to be developing feelings for one of the enemy.

'I'm sorry,' Heinrich apologised when Calliope still didn't reply. 'I shouldn't— I've said too much. It was stupid of me. I'll get going, leave you to the view and—'

'No!' Calliope's exclamation exploded out of her. 'No,' she repeated, managing to modulate her tone to something more normal. 'Please don't go. I don't want you to. I-I love you being here. I love being with you.' She clenched her fists and worried that now she was the one who had said too much, given too much away. When she had been in love with a British army officer, things had seemed complicated. Now that her affections were directed towards a German soldier, how much more impossibly difficult had everything become? But what could she do?

Feelings were feelings, after all.

Heinrich was regarding her, his head tilted to one side. 'Do you really mean that?' he asked softly, his expression filled with hopeful longing.

A wave of emotion whipped Calliope's breath away. 'Yes,' she managed to whisper. 'I do. I really do.'

A second later, Heinrich's arms were round her and he was

pulling her tight and holding her so close she could feel his heartbeat through his thick uniform jacket and it was as if they were not two people but one, joined together by love and loss and fear and courage and all the many adversities each had to face in order to be where they were, in this lonely valley perched amidst the crags of the White Mountains.

They remained entwined in each other's arms for long minutes. When eventually they broke apart it was momentary, just enough time for Heinrich to brush a strand of hair away from Calliope's face before he bent to kiss her. Calliope had never kissed a man before; it was something she and Calista and Eliana had often chatted and speculated and giggled about, back in their innocent girlhood. These days, Eliana wasn't someone either of the twins would talk to about anything, and anyway as adults it seemed inappropriate to question each other about intimate relationships. The result was that Calliope was as ignorant as she had been five years ago. And yet somehow, when Heinrich's lips met hers, she seemed to know what to do.

They kissed and kissed, occasionally breaking off for a few moments before their mouths immediately reunited again. They slipped from the wall to the ground, Heinrich pulling Calliope away from the stones and onto a patch of soft, springy grass, where they continued to touch and kiss for minutes more, that stretched into hours. Somehow, half a day passed, during which time they forgot about everything: the sheep, the dog, the war, all of it.

Towards evening, they lay on their backs beside each other, gazing up at the puffy white clouds.

'What's your favourite colour?' asked Heinrich.

Calliope chuckled. 'Blue,' she answered. 'Yours?'

'Green. Favourite month of the year?'

'Ooh, that's a good one.' Calliope considered her answer for a few seconds. 'May.' She said the word and then almost choked on it. In her drowsy state of contentment, she'd momentarily forgotten what May was now associated with: the airborne invasion. 'I mean, it used to be May because it's so beautiful, with all the wildflowers, and there's lots of sunshine but it's not too hot, but since last year—'

'Everything's different.' Heinrich finished her sentence for her. 'I'm sorry,' he added.

Calliope reached out and grasped his hand. 'Don't be,' she reassured him. 'It's not your fault. Anyway, what's your favourite month then?'

'I would have to say January,' he answered. 'Because it's a new year and new possibilities.'

'Yuck, I totally disagree with you,' said Calliope, laughing. 'It's so cold and dark and nothing to look forward to once Christmas is over. I don't like January at all.'

'Perhaps by next January the war will be over,' mused Heinrich, wistfully. 'And then you'll have to agree with me.' He rolled over and propped himself on one elbow so that he could look down at her. Calliope noticed how his blue eyes were no longer steely, but softened by love, and fancied that her reflection in his pupils showed the same.

'If that happens, I will,' she murmured.

When it eventually came time for Heinrich to leave, they could hardly tear themselves away from each other. Once he'd departed, Calliope sank down beside Orion and held him close to try to fill the aching of her heart. It was a long time until January would roll around again. But she was pretty sure the war would still be going on, even all those months into the future. And even if the conflict had ended, didn't that just throw up a whole different problem?

The problem of how a Greek woman could confess to a relationship with a German. The problem of how Calliope and Heinrich could ever be together.

CHAPTER 28

CRETE, SEPTEMBER 1942

'Keep going, Calista. Breathe!' Valeria's voice was low and insistent. On the surface she seemed calm, but Calliope could tell that this was a veneer. Beneath her brisk and businesslike facade, her mother was starting to panic. Calista had been labouring for hours now, over twenty-four, and was clearly not only in agony but also exhausted.

Calliope dipped the cloth she held in trembling hands into a bowl of water and gently dabbed Calista's brow. It was late September but still hot, even up here so high in the mountains. Calista, lost in pain, did not appear to notice. Another scream rent the air and Calliope saw Valeria wince as her sister, experiencing another contraction, gripped her mother's hand as tightly as a vice.

Why wasn't the baby coming? What was taking so long? Was it supposed to be like this? From the expression on her mother's face, Calliope assumed it was not. Earlier that day, Yiorgis had set off on the long trek to the nearest town that had a resident doctor. Hopefully he would have a donkey to enable him to travel more rapidly through the rugged landscape and so get back to Calista in time.

In time for what, Calliope didn't really want to dwell on. In time to help Calista get the baby out, she reassured herself. Not for anything else. No one had mentioned fetching the priest yet, thank God, but Calliope could not keep from her mind the knowledge that every village had a family deprived of a mother who had died in childbirth, and every year infants were stillborn.

Calista screamed again, more faintly this time than the last, indicating her fading energy. Valeria looked desperately around the room as if somewhere, hidden in a corner, might be some source of help or succour. But of course there was nothing. No wise woman, experienced in all matters of childbirth, no nurse or midwife. Such people did not exist in a remote backwater such as this, where hardly anyone of childbearing age even lived any more. Until the doctor arrived, it was up to Valeria and Calliope to do what they could to assist Calista.

'Do you feel like pushing yet?' Valeria asked, urgently. Calista shook her head.

'She should be pushing by now,' Valeria whispered under her breath. 'I don't know why she doesn't feel the urge.'

Calliope did not respond. What could she say? She knew nothing at all about childbirth. And in the light of what she was seeing now, she was in no hurry whatsoever to experience this horror for herself.

It felt like hours later when Calliope finally heard the rattle of the front door's rusty handle, followed immediately by the sound of heavy footsteps ascending the staircase to the first floor. The doctor was already taking his stethoscope out of his case as he entered the room, and within seconds had it pressed against Calista's belly. He listened for a moment and then stood upright. His face bore a friendly smile but Calliope did not miss the slight shake of his head that had accompanied whatever he had heard. Speaking briskly, he asked for warm water and more cloths, and was pulling on his white coat as Calliope sped out of the room to fetch what he had requested.

Downstairs, her father stood in the entrance, breathing heavily and seeming bewildered, unable to take in what was happening.

'Is she all right?' His voice was low and tentative, as if he didn't really want to know the answer.

Calliope grimaced. 'I don't know,' she replied honestly, too tired and anxious to worry about sparing her father's feelings. 'But the doctor needs hot water, so I must get the stove going—' She broke off as she bustled around the primitive kitchen, stuffing olive wood logs into the fire and stoking it so that she could heat the water. Yiorgis looked on, helplessly, lost in apprehension.

After setting a pan upon the hob, Calliope gathered up what clean cloths and scraps she could lay her hands on. There was so little here; almost everything had been left at home. She rushed back with what she had found, but the sight that met her eyes as she reached the threshold of the bedroom stopped her in her tracks. The doctor was wielding a fearsome-looking object, made of metal, a bit like giant tongs. As she watched, he approached Calista with the tool, and it disappeared beneath the sheet covering her lower half and bent legs.

Oh my Lord. Calliope could hardly formulate her thoughts as she realised what was happening. The doctor was using that medieval-looking implement to get the baby out! Just as this realisation crystallised within her, Calista screamed, a howl of pure torture and terrible distress.

Calliope cast aside the pile of cloths and ran down the rickety stairs and back to the kitchen, where she filled a bowl with some of the water. It hadn't quite boiled yet but it was warm and, as it came straight from a mountain spring, she knew it was clean. Her breathing was shallow and panicked, her heart thumping painfully in her chest. How could Calista bear what was happening to her? How would she ever recover? Was any baby worth this trauma and torment?

And then, through the thin floorboards separating her from the room above, she heard it. It was faint at first, a whine rather than a cry, like the mewling sound made by a lost or hungry cat. But it quickly grew louder and developed a rhythm and became unmistakably what it was. The wail of a newborn baby.

Calliope could not get back up those stairs quick enough. The water in the bowl sloshed from side to side, slopping onto the treads, but she did not care. She raced into the birthing room and put the bowl down any old how, just in time to see her mother help the doctor wrap the baby in a cloth and hand it, still screaming at the top of its tiny lungs, to Calista.

As she took hold of her infant, Calista's appearance transformed before Calliope's eyes. The pain and anguish that had riven her brow melted away to be replaced by an expression of pure love. Valeria propped her up on some pillows as Calista gazed down on the infant. Calliope had the strangest feeling of being in the presence of the divine, of the baby as some kind of deity, worthy of worship. The sensation was so strong that she got down on her knees and knelt beside her sister and the child, unable to take her eyes away from the two of them.

She opened her mouth to speak, to say how beautiful the little one was, but then remembered that she didn't yet know if it was a boy or a girl.

'What is it?' she asked.

'A little girl,' burst out Valeria, crossing herself as she spoke. 'And healthy, praise the Lord, despite everything.' She turned to the doctor and began genuflecting, and repeating 'Thank you, thank you, thank you', over and over again.

The doctor smiled. 'All's well that ends well,' he said, simply.

Calliope noticed for the first time that there was blood all over his white coat and his hands. The hideous implement that was presumably what had finally ended Calista's labour lay on the bed, also covered in blood. Calliope shuddered. She had never thought of herself as squeamish before – it was hard to be so when one dealt with livestock on a daily basis – and she'd seen countless sheep and goats give birth, but before this day she had had no idea that, for humans, the experience of childbirth was of an entirely different order. She thought of the village women who had six, seven, eight children or more. They'd had to go through that horror multiple times! She couldn't bear to dwell on the awfulness of that reality.

Instead, she rested her eyes upon her sister and her niece. The baby was suckling already, her hair still matted and wet from the birth, her face red and blotchy. But nevertheless, Calliope thought that she'd never seen anything or anyone more lovely in her life before.

'Ariana,' whispered Calista, her voice croaky and hoarse after all the screaming. 'I'm going to call her Ariana. Laurie can choose an English name for her second name. But for her first, she will be Greek.'

'I love that name,' enthused Calliope, as their mother also nodded her approval. 'It suits her perfectly.'

As if in response, Ariana opened her huge dark eyes and fixed them on her aunty so that Calliope fell in love with the tiny scrap all over again.

'Would you like to hold her?' asked Calista, already proffering the baby.

Calliope opened her mouth to reply and then closed it again. It was a grandmother's privilege to have the first hold, wasn't it? But the doctor intervened.

'Calliope, please take the baby downstairs,' he instructed. 'And Valeria, fetch some more of that hot water and then come back to help me. We need to...' He paused, clearly choosing his words. 'We need to make Calista more comfortable.'

Nervously, Calliope took Ariana from her sister, whose face had now blanched white and bloodless, her eyes barely open. It was clear she was weakened and exhausted by the ordeal. The baby in Calliope's hands weighed almost nothing, like a little bird or the tiniest lamb. Terrified of holding the little mite too tightly or dropping her, she descended the stairs at a snail's pace, placing both feet on each tread before stepping onto the next one. Yiorgis was nowhere to be seen. Calliope assumed he'd escaped outside, unable to bear hearing his daughter suffer so terribly. Sitting down on the one good armchair, Calliope cradled Ariana in her arms as the infant slept, eyes tight shut now, breathing low and rhythmic. Brushing her finger across her cheek, Calliope marvelled at the softness of her skin. She put a finger against the baby's hand and Ariana's tiny fingers instinctively uncurled and wrapped around it.

Adoration for her niece swelled Calliope's heart as she clutched Ariana, the newest addition to the family, the most precious, the most wonderful. Out of this terrible war had come this most miraculous of things. Ariana, whose name meant 'most holy', was all of their dreams for the future, a future without war and destruction, without fear and hunger, a future where they could all live happily again like they had done before. Ariana had brought that most precious thing of all.

She had brought hope.

CHAPTER 29

CRETE, OCTOBER 1942

Away from the shelter and protection of the high mountains, Calliope was constantly on her guard. She'd brought the animals back down to the village as winter approached, and was waiting there for the arrival of her parents. They and Calista had judged enough time to have passed for it to be safe to return, a decision compounded by their fear that they, and the baby, would not survive winter in the remote hamlet. Once they got back, Calliope would leave, and rejoin the resistance cell. In the meantime, she could not relax for a moment. Nevertheless, when she saw a man approaching in the distance, she thought nothing of it. From his clothing he was clearly local so there was no need to worry.

She picked up a stick and used it to scratch the bearded billy goat behind his ears. He enjoyed it without moving for a few moments and then shook his head, quivering in delight and setting his bell tinkling. By the time Calliope looked back round, the man had drawn nearer. She knew immediately from the man's gait and posture who it was and her heart missed several beats. Heinrich! But what on earth was he doing here, so close to the village, dressed as a Cretan?

Seeing her startled reaction, Heinrich chuckled. 'Don't worry,' he hastily reassured her. 'There's no one around for miles.'

Calliope rolled her eyes. 'Thank goodness,' she responded, primly. 'You nearly gave me a heart attack.' She wanted to be really cross with him, but it was impossible. He was so tall and handsome standing there, smiling down at her. 'Where did you get the outfit?' she asked. 'Why are you wearing it?'

'I bought it in Chania,' Heinrich told her. 'Luckily these baggy trousers your men wear aren't full-length anyway, so it doesn't really matter that they're a little too short for me.'

Calliope regarded him quizzically. 'Wasn't that taking a bit of a risk?' She ran her hand through her cropped hair. 'Didn't the stallholder think it was odd that a German was buying Cretan clothes?'

Heinrich shrugged. 'Maybe so, but a sale is a sale in these times. I don't think he's doing much business with the locals, and I'm pretty sure he wouldn't say anything. Who would he tell, anyway? Most Cretans avoid any contact with us if they can help it.'

A silence descended after these words. Calliope shifted uneasily from foot to foot. *You should avoid contact with Germans, shouldn't you?* a little voice whispered in her ear. But this was different. She and Heinrich – it was different. He was a good German – more than that, a German who wanted to help the resistance drive his own countrymen off the island. He'd told Calliope that defeat would come to the Nazis eventually. How could it not, when they were the ones in the wrong?

Calliope wasn't so sure. She had once been so confident in the outcome of the war, sure that the Allies would win. But as the conflict dragged on, her conviction had faltered. Now she made herself believe in victory because it gave her the strength to do what she had done before, and would do again, for the resistance. In the meantime, it was a question of biding their time, storing up as much intelligence as possible, ready for when the moment came.

'Even with the disguise, it's dangerous for us to meet somewhere so open,' she said, keeping her voice low as if the fields and the olive trees and the grass had ears.

Heinrich took her hand. 'I know,' he murmured. 'But I had to see you. I can't stop thinking about you. Being with you is the only thing that makes sense at the moment.'

Calliope's heart turned over. She knew what he meant; she felt the same. Since that moment at the *mitato* when they had first kissed, their love for each other had only grown deeper. In the midst of all the upheaval and uncertainty, it was the still point of the turning world, the part that made all the rest seem peripheral.

As they stood in the meadow, the sun beating down on their heads, she felt Heinrich's hand tug at hers.

'Do you fancy a swim?' he asked her, his tone light and easy once more and full of fun, as if there were no war, no danger, no uncertain future.

For a second, Calliope hesitated. And then she grinned, and nodded her head.

'Come on then!' cried Heinrich. 'Race you!'

Simultaneously, they both turned and hared towards the river that cut through the lower half of the pasture. Of course Heinrich was faster than her, but Calliope wasn't too far behind. When they arrived at the reeds alongside the river, grown thick and tall over the summer, they were both hotter than ever. Orion, who had been snoozing in the shade of an oak tree, joined them, panting hard, also eager to cool down.

Parting the reeds with one arm, Heinrich gestured Calliope through. They stumbled along the riverbank until they reached a little sandy patch like a tiny beach. Orion, who'd forged ahead of them, was already in the water, swimming strongly against the current, tongue hanging out of one corner of his mouth. Calliope giggled at the sight of him.

'He looks so funny,' she said, laughingly. 'He's such a character, that dog.'

Heinrich nodded in agreement. 'I miss the dogs at home, on the farm,' he said, a tinge of nostalgia in his voice. 'One of them, Rufus, was old even before I was called up. I don't know if he'll still be around when I get back. If—'

'Stop!' Calliope's voice cut across his. 'I know what you were going to say. *If I get back*. But I don't want to talk about such a thing, nor think about it.' She clenched her fists as her eyes met Heinrich's. 'Let's not worry about the future on this lovely day.'

Orion emerged from the water and loped towards them. 'Watch out, he's going to shake!' cried Calliope. As Orion did, indeed, begin to shake she ducked behind Heinrich for cover, shrieking as a few of the cold droplets fell upon her. The sombre mood was immediately dispelled.

'Last one in is a coward,' Heinrich called out, already pulling off his jacket and shirt. Within seconds, they were both splashing into the water, Heinrich's pale limbs flashing in the bright light of the sun. Taking a giant stride forward, Calliope plunged herself beneath the surface and swam with brisk, long strokes, then bobbed back up again in the middle of the river.

There was no sign of Heinrich. Spinning round and round, Calliope scoured the water. Nothing. Where was he?

Suddenly she felt a strong tug on her legs. She was being pulled under the surface, down and down. Opening her eyes, she saw Heinrich, smiling broadly. He released his grip and within seconds her head was above water again, and so was his, and they were laughing and spluttering together.

'You beast,' she said. 'I should have known you were going to do that.'

'I'm sorry,' apologised Heinrich. 'The temptation was just

too much to resist.' He moved nearer to her, put his arms round her and pulled her towards him. The warmth of his skin contrasted with the water's chill and she felt his vitality and his desire. Slowly, they spun themselves back to the riverbank, where Heinrich laid her tenderly on the sandy beach.

This is insanity. So dangerous. So irresistible. The thoughts arose but Calliope banished them, closing her mind to anything but Heinrich, how much she loved him and how much she wanted him.

Afterwards, Heinrich went back into the water, but Calliope stayed on the shore, basking in the sunshine, drowsy and sated. A rustle of the reeds made her eyelids snap open. Silence. It was just the breeze rattling the fronds. And then another rustle. It must be an animal. Orion would bark, otherwise.

Just as she was thinking this Orion, who had also been dozing by the water, emitted a long, low, ominous growl, which then erupted into a torrent of barking. Terrified, Calliope sat bolt upright, grabbed her clothes and hastily pulled them on, hands trembling. Heinrich was right over on the other side of the river. He'd heard the barking but it would take him a minute or so to get back. Once dressed, Calliope beat her way through the reeds. Orion, in sheepdog mode, crept beside her. He knew not to run until he had the order.

Emerging into the open, Calliope cast her eyes to the right, back towards the village. There was no one there. She looked straight ahead and then to the left. At the edge of the field she just caught sight of a figure disappearing into the olive grove. A female, dark skirts swishing.

Oh God. Eliana? It must be. In fact, it definitely was. Calliope would recognise her brisk gait anywhere. Spying on her and Heinrich. What would her friend-turned-enemy do with this information?

Nausea rose in Calliope's stomach and she vomited up bile.

There was nothing either she or Heinrich would be able to do or say that would get them out of this one. Orion whined, thumping his tail on the ground. Instinctively, Calliope reached out her hand and patted his kind head. At this moment, Heinrich burst through the reeds and rushed towards her.

'What happened?' he demanded. 'Who was it? Did they see us?'

Calliope made her decision. She shrugged. 'It was nothing,' she answered. 'Probably a rat or a marten. Or sometimes Orion just barks at the wind.' She grinned at Heinrich as if there was nothing to worry about.

'I better go,' he replied, not seeming wholly reassured by Calliope's brushing-off of the incident. 'I don't want to put you in danger.' He bent forward and kissed her lightly on the lips, and then he turned and marched away into the distance.

Calliope waited until he was out of sight before trudging back to the flock, a profound sense of disquiet lodged in the depths of her being. Was this the beginning of the end? She had evaded capture for so long, but her luck had been bound to run out sooner or later. The possibility of it being sooner hit her like a steam train. She gazed around her at the tranquil meadow and the grazing animals. She had always thought that she'd rather be dead than see the Germans triumph. But perhaps that wasn't the case. The thought of never seeing her family again, of not watching Ariana grow up, of being parted from Heinrich, was devastating. In that moment, Calliope came to realise something for certain. She did not want to die. But it was highly likely that she would.

CHAPTER 30

CRETE, DECEMBER 1942

Arriving at the cave, at first Calliope thought her eyes were playing tricks on her. One of the men gathered around the paraffin stove looked exactly like Laurie. As she approached, the man stood up and, to her utmost incredulity, it *was* Laurie.

'Laurie!' she cried, rushing towards him. 'When did you get here? Does Calista know you are back? Are you staying? Please say you're staying.'

Chuckling at the barrage of questions, Laurie slapped her back in greeting.

'I just arrived an hour or so ago,' he told Calliope. 'There's some business to sort out here and then I'm going to visit Calista – and my daughter.' As he said the last three words, his eyes misted over with something that looked very like tears.

'She will be overjoyed,' replied Calliope. 'She's been pining for you for so long.'

For a fleeting moment, Laurie's expression was wistful. And then, as Ben returned from the wireless battery-charging station, he snapped back into military mode and summoned all those present to him. Men appeared from nowhere, British but also several Cretans, some of whom Calliope recognised, some who she didn't. They must have been gathering here while she was away, ready for Laurie's return. Crouched beside the fire, Calliope pulled her trusty woollen cloak around her and listened intently to what Laurie had to say.

'This year to come, 1943, is going to be crucial,' he explained. 'The Americans have got on board with what we are doing here and they are going to provide much bigger parachute drops than we've had up to now, giving us plentiful supplies, especially weapons, guns, ammunition and so on. It will change everything in terms of how well equipped we are. The British are sending more men from the Special Operations Executive and the Special Boat Squadron. The Cretans will be better armed and better organised than ever.' He paused to look around at the expectant faces, all eyes trained on his. 'If we can keep inflicting casualties, destroying capability and demoralising our enemy, we can achieve the kind of success that no guerrilla organisation in the world has ever dreamt possible before.'

Calliope suppressed an involuntary shudder at these words. It was fighting talk indeed.

Laurie lit a cigarette and took a long draw. 'For the meantime, we continue as we are. We have big plans for spring and summer; sabotage of enemy facilities on a huge scale, destruction of airfields and ammunition dumps, raids on army bases, the details of which I'll share with you at the right moment.' He looked around the group, meeting everyone's eyes. 'To liberty and freedom.'

'To liberty and freedom,' came the chorus of responses, the Cretan voices loudest of all.

In the end, Laurie could not get away early in the morning on Christmas Day; an important message was due in from Cairo and he had to wait with Ben to receive it. He'd be on his way as soon as he could. Calliope knew that he was desperate to see Calista and the baby but that, as a soldier, duty had to come first. So she set off alone, through the blanket of white, down through the mountains, where the air was crystal clear and cold enough to freeze the lungs, to the foothills and into the valley.

On her way, she encountered the indomitable Stelios, gathering firewood from the forest, trudging stoically through the drifts, many of which came up to his waist.

'Season's greetings,' she said to the youngster. 'Why are you not home celebrating with your family?'

Stelios shrugged. 'I needed some fresh air,' he replied. 'Collecting wood was a good excuse.'

Calliope regarded him quizzically, but did not say anything. Sometimes silence was the best way to get someone to confide in you.

'I'm bored of being a child!' Stelios exclaimed. 'I want to fight with the British men. I'm old enough now.'

Calliope stifled a chuckle. 'You're still only eleven,' she protested.

'Exactly! Eleven. That's a good age for a soldier.'

'Well, I think a little older,' Calliope replied, keeping as straight a face as possible. 'The thing is that you're most useful when you're fooling the Germans into thinking you're a kid with nothing more in his head than an interest in engines and a desire for German chocolate.'

Now Stelios grinned, stamping his feet in the snow in acknowledgement of his cunning. 'That's true,' he said. 'But even so, I want to be taken seriously,' he went on, his expression suddenly darkening.

'But you are, among the people that matter,' remonstrated Calliope. 'No one is taken more seriously than you.'

'They say that Crete surrendered,' Stelios continued. 'But we didn't, Calliope. The island fell, but we never surrendered. And we will win, in the end.'

Calliope thought anew about her own faltering conviction that this was the case. Watching Stelios marching doggedly away across the snow, she wished she could summon up the small boy's confidence, or use his to reinvigorate her own. Lodged somewhere deep in her heart was a terrible premonition that the worst was yet to come.

She arrived in the village just as the church service was finishing and waited, hiding behind a plane tree as the crowd spilled out of the ancient building and milled around, everyone chatting and exchanging Christmas greetings. Eliana was among them, joining in the gossip, smiling innocently for all the world as if she wasn't a Nazi spy. Calliope bristled with antipathy towards her. It was obvious that Eliana, as someone who knew her well, would see straight through her disguise as a boy, and yet nothing had happened to her as a result of either her visit to the prison or the incident on the riverbank. It should have comforted Calliope, but it did the opposite – made her even more fearful about Eliana's motives, what she might be planning.

Despite the cold, it took for ever for the villagers to begin dispersing to their homes, the conversation now turning to the Christmas meal. In normal years it would be a veritable feast, but these days there was precious little available, and no luxuries at all. Calliope didn't care though. She'd brought a couple of tins of fish and more of the delectable condensed milk, and she'd be able to add those to whatever her mother had managed to put together. More than that was unnecessary; all she wanted was to spend a few precious hours with her family.

She'd asked Laurie if she should tell Calista that he was on his way and he'd said that she should. He thought it would be the best Christmas gift he could give to her, and Calliope did, too. When the little courtyard in front of the church was finally empty, Calliope slipped through the winter-cold streets and along the alleyway to her family home. Quietly pushing the door open, she found her mother and Calista in the kitchen, bustling around peeling potatoes and carrots, while her father sat holding little Ariana in his strong labourer's arms, crooning lullabies. From the oven emanated the most delicious aroma of roasting pork, and already on the table was the *Christopsomo*, the special, sweet and spiced bread of Christmas.

Calliope almost choked up at the sight, so homely and cosy, so *normal*. How she longed for a return to the life of old. Or did she? Because what place would there be for Heinrich in such a world? Could he even feature in it? The thought of losing him was unbearable. But if that was the price of liberating the island, how could she not wish it to happen?

These dilemmas troubled her more and more often these days, just as her love for Heinrich grew stronger and stronger. Though Calista faced many of the same difficulties, it was also completely different for her. Laurie was on the right side, whereas Heinrich was not. And Laurie and Calista were married, and parents now, two things that bound them inextricably together for all time. Calliope had neither of those things.

Unconsciously, as she stood on the threshold waiting for someone to notice her, she ran her hand over her belly. Heinrich had things he used to stop her getting pregnant, and, after seeing the terrible ordeal Calista had had to endure, Calliope wasn't sure she could ever face having a child of her own. But on the other hand, perhaps she should try to conceive, because if she had a baby she would always have something of Heinrich, whatever happened.

As she was thinking this, Calista looked up from her bowl of potatoes and shrieked. 'Calliope! What are you doing just standing there? How long have you been there?' She dropped the knife she was holding, rushed over to her sister and embraced her. 'I've missed you so much,' she murmured as she held Calliope tight.

'Me too,' Calliope responded. 'And all of you.' She hugged

her mother and father and then crouched down next to the crib where Yiorgis had placed the sleeping Ariana. 'And you too, little one,' she whispered, stroking the baby's cheek.

'Why don't you hold her?' suggested Calista.

Calliope stood up. 'Can I?' she asked, timidly. 'Won't it wake her up?'

Calista laughed. 'It's Christmas Day! And better if she wakes now and sleeps later, so that I can have my dinner. I rarely get a chance to eat more than two mouthfuls at a time these days.'

Another reason not to have a baby, thought Calliope to herself, only half in jest. She sat down in a chair and Calista tenderly passed Ariana into her waiting arms. While Calista returned to her cooking chores, Calliope simply sat and stared at the baby, unable to take her eyes away from her sweet, innocent little face, only half-listening to what her mother and her sister were telling her about village life. Eventually, Ariana began to stir. She opened her huge dark eyes, fixed them on Calliope's and then, suddenly, a smile broke out on her rosebud mouth.

'She's smiling!' Calliope almost shouted. 'She's smiling at me!'

Calista beamed with pride. 'I know,' she said. 'She's been doing it for a few weeks now.' She bent over her baby and addressed her in a high, lilting tone. 'Haven't you, clever girl?' Then her expression clouded over and she bit her lip. 'I wish her father could see her. She's changing every day and he's missing all of it.'

Calliope remembered what she had been supposed to tell her sister. She'd been so overcome with emotion at being among her family that she'd clean forgotten.

'Calista, sit down,' she instructed. Calista's face became immediately stricken, though she followed the instruction.

'It's fine, it's fine,' Calliope added hastily. 'More than fine.

What I mean is – Laurie's back. He's on his way here now. We would have come together but there was some emergency. He said he'd try to get here by three.'

Calista exclaimed in shock and clutched her hands to her heart as she digested the news. 'Oh, thank you Lord,' she muttered. 'Thank you for bringing my husband to me on your birthday...'

The next hour or so flew by as the lunch was cooked and the table set, ready for Laurie's arrival. There was a palpable sense of excitement in the air. Yiorgis opened a bottle of wine and put the raki on the table. By three thirty, the anticipation was at fever pitch. By the time the clock had ticked to four, Calista was in pieces and Ariana, picking up on the tension, had begun to wail.

Suddenly the front door flew open and in burst Stelios.

'They've taken him!' he yelled, as if the Papadakis family were miles away rather than right in front of him. 'They've got him!'

Valeria screamed in horror, Calista's face blanched pure white, Ariana howled and Calliope felt as if someone had punched her in the diaphragm.

Stelios was trembling with fear and panic. Clenching her fists as she tried to gain control over herself, Calliope stepped towards him. 'Tell me exactly what happened, Stelios,' she said, forcing her voice to stay calm and even.

Stelios took a few deep breaths and then, when he'd restored a bit of his equilibrium, spoke again. 'They were out looking for men to take part in a forced labour squad,' he panted.

'On Christmas Day!' Valeria's shock rang through every syllable. 'Is nothing sacred? Do these heathens care about absolutely nothing?'

'Mama,' reproached Calliope, 'quiet for a moment. Let Stelios speak.'

Valeria pulled an apologetic face. 'Sorry,' she murmured, as Stelios resumed his account.

'There were lots of Germans out searching, looking for anyone they could find. Any men, that is. They grabbed Laurie and shoved him into the back of a truck.'

'Where did they take him?' Calista's voice wavered as tears poured down her cheeks. Calliope could hardly bear it for her. All this time waiting for Laurie's return and now this. He was gone again, and not to a safe place like Egypt.

Stelios held out his hands in a gesture of despair. 'I don't know. I asked some of the soldiers as the jeep drove off but they just laughed and said if I wasn't careful they'd take me, too. So I ran away.'

'You did the right thing,' Calliope reassured him, even as Calista's sobs intensified, understanding that the young boy felt dreadful that he didn't know more.

His news imparted, Stelios left. 'I'm wanted at home,' he explained. 'You know, Christmas...'

Of course they knew. Christmas was the time for families to be together. Even Stelios had had to give in to that in the end. It was also the time when Laurie should have been reunited with his wife, and finally have the opportunity to get to know his tiny daughter. But instead he was in German hands. And who knew what would happen to him there, or if he would ever be let free? Seeing her sister's reaction, Calliope had a sudden, terrible jolt of fear that, having survived the hunger years, imprisonment and childbirth, the loss of Laurie would kill her.

CHAPTER 31

CRETE, 2005

The scenery grew more dramatic as they approached the foothills of the White Mountains, the limestone crags and peaks glistening in the sun. The day had finally come to make the trip to the village to see Calista.

Callie directed Ella down a small side-turning that led to hairpin bends with plummeting drops. A newly built house here and there indicated the outskirts of a settlement. They reached a crossroads and Ella asked, 'Which way?'

Callie tried to speak but instead a choking sob erupted from her throat.

Shocked, Ella pulled over onto the grassy verge. 'What's the matter, Gran?' Her voice was full of tender concern.

'I don't know the way,' Callie replied through tears. 'I haven't been here for so long that I can't remember. I don't know if I'll recognise anything about it.'

Ella stared through the car windscreen, seeking inspiration. 'It looks like there are more houses down there,' she said. 'So let's try that way. We can always turn round.'

They set off down a single-track road fringed by trees and full of the sound of birdsong. Eventually they reached a place where the road widened. There was a bus stop and shelter next to a lane that rose steeply upwards and had a big sign indicating *No vehicle access.*

'That looks like the village up there.' Ella pointed up the narrow lane. 'We'll have to leave the car here.'

Without responding, Callie opened the car door and climbed out. She stood looking upwards. The village lay nestled beneath the mountains, just as it had always done. The church tower pierced the blue sky, just as it had always done. High up above, among the clouds, an eagle soared, just as they had always done.

Ella came to stand beside her.

'It looks... the same,' breathed Callie. She felt her legs trembling beneath her and hoped they weren't going to give way again.

'We're not that far from the city,' observed Ella, 'but it seems like another world here.'

'It was always like that,' said Callie. 'Cretan villages were very self-sufficient, independent places, as were their inhabitants. We didn't have any choice.'

'Shall we walk up there?' Ella regarded her grandmother expectantly. Callie tried to step forward but could hardly make her legs work. Seeing her struggle, Ella held out her arm. 'Come on, lean on me. What are we looking for?'

'I'm fine,' muttered Callie, through gritted teeth. Rejecting Ella's arm, she mustered all her strength and set forth. She was not ready for her bath chair yet. If she had her way, she never would be. No matter how her body aged, her pride did not diminish.

'We're looking for my old family house, where I used to live,' answered Callie, speaking sporadically through shortened breaths. 'George will be there. The young George, of course, the one I met in church. And so will Calista.'

Ella stopped short, eyes wide with confusion. 'They do

know you're coming today, don't they?' she demanded. 'They're not going to have heart attacks when you suddenly appear, unannounced?'

Callie pushed her shoulders back and attempted to straighten her ancient frame so that she stood tall and unafraid. Though her body had aged and weakened with time, she still had inside herself some of that indomitable spirit that had enabled her to take part in the resistance. She tried to summon it now, to give her the strength to do what she had to do. Face her sister, ask her why she'd made that final accusation, and answer for everything she had done and not done.

High up above them, the church bells tolled the hour.

'Let's go,' she said to Ella. 'They are expecting me.'

CHAPTER 32

CRETE, JANUARY 1943

The days after Laurie's kidnapping by the press-gang were awful. Calliope couldn't put the awfulness into words. She spent as much time as possible with her sister, trying to persuade her to wash, and eat, and drink, and brush her beautiful hair. She didn't think Calista would have done any of those things without Calliope's reminders. But throughout it all, Calista tended to Ariana as conscientiously and tenderly as always.

Calliope knew that staying in the village was risky, but that was her life these days. Everything was risky. Every action was potentially perilous, holding danger both for herself and all those around her. Death could come in an instant. The future was not worth thinking about because there was every likelihood that she didn't have one.

A few things kept her going. Her love for her family. Her love for Heinrich. And her adoration of Ariana. Now four months old, the infant was exactly how Calliope had always imagined a baby to be, no longer skinny and raw-looking like a plucked chicken, but gorgeously soft and plump, with chubby ringlets round her wrists and ankles and round, red, dimpled cheeks. Despite everything that her mother, the family and the island were going through, Ariana was thriving.

When the knock sounded on the door, the women's first reaction was horror. Things were not as they used to be, when villagers walked in and out of each other's houses without ceremony or inhibition, coming and going as the mood or necessity took them. Now any unexpected approach chilled the blood; there had been too many terrifying early 'visits' by German soldiers that had resulted in friends, neighbours and relatives being hauled out into the street and either carted away or summarily executed.

Calliope's eyes flitted towards her sister's, which were wide with shock and fear. They'd been playing a game of *biriba* to pass the time, and the cards lay on the table.

'Take Ariana and go out into the garden,' she hissed towards Calista. 'Hide there until I come to find you.'

Calista bit her lip as, hands trembling, she snatched her baby from the crib by the fire. She swiftly wrapped her in a wool blanket and slipped outside. Once the back door was closed, Calliope hastily pushed the cards into a single heap to hide the fact that two people had been playing with them and went to the front door. With her heart in her mouth, she summoned all her resolve and flung it open. No dithering around opening it a crack and checking who was there. She wanted whoever it was to know that she wasn't afraid. Even though she was.

But instead of the phalanx of uniformed officers staring grimly at her that she had expected, she came to face to face with the last person she had expected to see.

Laurie.

And far from looking beaten and downtrodden by his time

in captivity, he appeared jubilant, a huge smile on his handsome face.

'L...' Calliope was so stunned she couldn't even get his name out.

By stepping over the threshold, Laurie invited himself inside.

'How did you get here?' Finally Calliope managed to formulate her words. 'Where have you been? What's been happening?'

Laurie smiled even more broadly. 'I'll tell you everything in a minute. There's something more important to do first—' He broke off and looked around the room, clearly searching for something. A cloud descended on his face, eradicating the good cheer of moments before. 'Where are they?' he asked, his voice full of trepidation. 'Where are my wife and daughter?'

Calliope clapped her hand across her mouth. In the shock of the moment, she'd forgotten about poor Calista and Ariana, outside in the cold.

'They're here,' she squeaked, her voice high with emotion and excitement. 'I'll get them.' Rushing outside, she found Calista trembling and frozen, while Ariana, wrapped up in blankets, slept on in her arms, oblivious to the frigid weather.

'Come inside,' Calliope said to her sister.

'Who was it?' Calista questioned anxiously.

'You'll see,' replied Calliope.

In the kitchen, Laurie was waiting, his usual calm demeanour replaced by obvious agitation. As Calista appeared, the baby against her shoulder, Calliope observed how his eyes filled with love and wonder. For a moment, he was rooted to the spot, transfixed by the sight of the two people he had been parted from for so long. And then he was upon them, flinging his arms round both of them and enveloping them in a bear hug, almost crying with joy. When he let them go, he stood back a little to regard Ariana properly.

'She's so beautiful,' he breathed. 'So perfect. Like a little angel.'

Calista, unable to hold back her tears, merely nodded her agreement. She wiped her eyes with the edge of the baby's blanket, then held Ariana out to him. 'Would you like to hold your daughter?' she asked, shakily, as she wept tears of happiness.

Silently, Laurie took hold of the little bundle that Calista offered to him and gazed reverently down upon the infant.

'I can hardly believe it,' he whispered. 'I had no idea she'd be so lovely.' He sank down onto one of the old wooden chairs and rocked Ariana gently back and forth. The baby stirred, opening her huge dark eyes and fixing them on her father. It was the first time she had seen him but it seemed to Calliope that she knew who he was, and how much he loved her, and what a good, brave man he was.

Later, when Valeria and Yiorgis had returned and much tea and raki had been drunk, Laurie cradled Ariana in his arms as he told them his news.

'It was perfect,' he explained. 'I couldn't have planned it better myself. The Germans were rounding up fit, able-bodied men to work in a forced labour gang. Our job? To build a new runway at the airfield!'

He beamed round at the four expectant faces listening so intently to him. Calliope wasn't sure what was so marvellous about being made to labour for the enemy for free. But Calista, who Calliope had so underestimated in the past, understood immediately.

'So you got inside the airfield,' she replied, pensively. 'And I suppose that means you saw everything?'

Laurie almost jumped out of his chair in excitement. Calliope had never seen him so animated – he usually kept his true feelings under wraps, preserving the same cool, calm, authoritative manner at all times. 'Absolutely. I was able to check out the number of aircraft they have, the amount of fuel in the stores, the size of the patrols, the shift pattern of the guards... everything.' He chuckled triumphantly as he shook his head, presumably reflecting on the unexpected bounty that had fallen into his lap.

'So,' he continued, turning towards Calliope and addressing his next comments to her, 'we have a huge boost to our plan for the airport sabotage. There are still things that need to fall into place, and we're not ready yet, but I've got a much better idea now of what will be needed when the time comes.'

Calliope nodded. While she had been sitting here, surrounded by the people she loved best in the world (apart from Heinrich), the war had been feeling very far away. There had even been a few moments when she had forgotten about it entirely. But Laurie's pronouncements thrust her back into the middle of the action, into that world in which the constant fear of death underpinned everything. Calliope felt suddenly tired, weary of the strife, weary of the sheer physical, mental and emotional toll this conflict was having on her.

Ariana stirred, then woke and almost immediately began to cry, the low, urgent, insistent sound that Calliope now knew meant she was hungry. Laurie handed the baby to Calista, who took her and attempted to soothe her.

'I have to go,' he said, standing up and gazing regretfully at his wife and child. He turned to Calliope. 'What we have coming up is huge,' he warned her. 'Get as much rest as you can. We need everyone firing on all cylinders.'

Having spoken, he abruptly turned away. Calista moved with him towards the door. Calliope, still trying to absorb his words, bustled around, clearing up the teacups and wiping down the old table. Seeming to pick up on her cue, Valeria and Yiorgis also stood, turning their backs on the young couple so that they could have a semblance of privacy in which to say their goodbyes.

When Laurie had gone, Calista sat back down by the fire to

feed Ariana. The room felt very quiet once the infant's wails had ceased and she was sucking contentedly away. Calliope regarded the serene tableau with equal amounts of love and fear.

Ariana had been born into a dangerous world. Calliope would do everything she could to keep the child safe. But what if that wasn't enough? A deep sense of dread and foreboding settled on her soul as she, too, took her leave. Ariana was no safer than any of them were. And that was a terrible thought.

CHAPTER 33

CRETE, JUNE 1943

It had been a long trek on goat tracks through the deserted landscape to the rendezvous point near a village on the other side of a large plateau. There, Calliope had delivered radio batteries and messages rolled inside empty bullet casings to another resistance cell. But the cargo she was charged with bringing back with her was far more valuable. It was people or, more specifically, operatives from the Special Boat Squadron who had arrived from Turkey to help with what Laurie hoped would be the biggest blow yet to the Germans on Crete – the airfield sabotage. It was to be a coordinated attack across the island, focusing on several different locations, and Calliope was responsible for guiding half a dozen of the recent arrivals to Laurie's new lair in yet another cave system, from where they would make the final preparations.

For months now, Calliope and Stelios had been spying on the airfield, using binoculars issued by the British government that they kept hidden among their clothing, ready to keep to their usual cover story, if they should be challenged, that they were simple goatherds out with their flock. Calliope had not seen her family or Heinrich in all that time. It was necessary for the cause, she knew, but every now and again she was struck with intense loneliness that not even Stelios' ever-cheerful banter could dispel.

'It's godforsaken country around here, isn't it?' observed one of the SBS men. His name was Captain Andersen and Calliope found him an intimidating presence. He was tall and well-built, with an expression of grim determination that never left his darkly tanned face. 'Just rock and stone, then more rock and stone, as far as the eye can see.'

He lifted his hand to shade his eyes and gazed into the distance. Calliope tried to see the landscape that was so familiar to her through a stranger's viewpoint. It was hard when every towering peak and jagged crag was beautiful in its own austere, forbidding way, the bare limestone glaring white under the summer sun just as it did when snow-covered in winter.

'I'm sure you love it, because it's yours,' interjected one of the other British men. Calliope had done her best to memorise their names. He was Sol Baker, she recalled, and quite different to Andersen. All of these men were tough and battle-hardened, but Sol was quiet and thoughtful, with a gentle demeanour that belied his strength and resilience. They were each carrying huge packs that Calliope could see weighed a ton, and some of them wore shorts, which wasn't ideal when they reached the thickets of thorn bushes that peppered the mountainside. Their shins and ankles bore the scratches that were testimony to the ferocity of those thorns.

The sun was fierce and the men constantly thirsty. Calliope had her work cut out, not only in guiding them but in seeking out the mountain springs and streams that provided them with water. The journey was taking longer than she had anticipated and she hoped that they were going to get back to Laurie's lair in time. The whole plan was carefully calibrated and needed to run like clockwork to be a success – including getting the SBS men on and off the island successfully.

Despite her fears, they eventually reached the caves at about two in the afternoon, only an hour later than intended. Laurie greeted his British compatriots with his usual equanimity, but Calliope could tell that beneath his calm exterior he was taut as a wire. This was his big chance to shine, and to achieve something that had been tried before and had failed. Perhaps once he would have wanted this victory for himself, for his chance of medals and glory back home. But now Calliope knew his motivation was completely different. Just like her, he wanted the win for Crete and its people – most of all, for Calista and Ariana.

Thinking of the bond shared between Laurie and her sister intensified the feelings of loneliness and isolation that Calliope had been experiencing on this mission. She missed her family and Heinrich with an ache that was like a band tightening round her heart. She knew it was crazy to love Heinrich, a German and a soldier in the Nazi army, like this but she couldn't stop herself. She'd never experienced such a connection with someone before, not even with her identical twin. It was as if she and Heinrich were made for each other, made *of* each other. Everything he said and did was so right, so perfectly pitched at whatever she needed from him at that precise moment. She hungered for him. Was this what addiction was like, she wondered: knowing something was probably bad for you but wanting it so greatly? The problem of how they could ever be together in the post-war world, if either of them survived that long, was never far from her thoughts. But these days she was much better at focusing on the present, not the future. Living in constant danger did that to a person, she'd discovered.

She would not stay at the caves between now and the raid. Laurie thought it was better if she and Stelios were elsewhere, in case of a German attack. Though the vast majority of the

Cretan people were on the side of the resistance, there were always those who weren't.

Like Eliana, thought Calliope, as she trudged away from the lair. Her intention had been to sleep in the family *mitato* that night, but she was struck by a sudden sense of despair at the prospect. If only she had Orion to keep her company.

Calliope glanced up at the sky, judging the hour by the position of the sun. If she headed back to the village she could visit the family's vegetable garden, where for sure her parents would be working, and at least see them briefly. This would be her last opportunity before the raid, and what if she didn't make it? She needed to tell them how much she loved them, to hug them one last time and drink in the familiar, homely smell of them.

Her mind made up, she picked up her pace. In a few hours, as the sun was dipping in the sky, she was nearing home, crossing the pasture where she and George had been when the Sky People began raining down on them. She shuddered at the dreadful memory. There had been so much death since then, so much destruction. What was it all *for*, she wondered. There didn't seem to be any justification for what the world was enduring in these times.

Lost in thought, she reached the vegetable garden on autopilot, her feet taking over while her mind drifted. At the gate, she paused, having sighted her mother and father toiling away just as she had anticipated. Their backs were bent double as they weeded the beds and tied tomato vines to their supports. Valeria stood and, turning, caught sight of her daughter. With a cry of delight, she came rushing over and clasped her shoulders in soil-covered hands.

'Calliope, *kardia mou, moro mou*, my heart, my baby,' she said, kissing Calliope's forehead and cheeks over and over again. Her mother was always demonstrative in her love, but this was excessive, even for her. Far from reassuring Calliope, it only increased her sense of foreboding. What if this was the last time she held her mother's hand or felt the softness of her touch?

Angrily, she tried to shake such feelings away.

'Bye-bye, Mama,' she murmured, burying her head in her mother's shoulder, breathing in the familiar smell of her, rosemary and onions, sunshine and fresh air. 'I love you so much. Stay safe, stay strong.' Just words, all she had to offer. Nothing she could say seemed adequate at such a moment.

After a brief hug with her father, who was the complete opposite of Valeria in such matters, Calliope reluctantly dragged herself away. Crossing back over the stone bridge, she paused for a moment to look down at the water. The river was summer-slow and sluggish, the current barely perceptible. She had the urge to put her feet into the cooling water, and hurried across to the bank, where she removed her boots.

Sitting with her feet submerged was bliss but stopping still a mistake. Waves of weariness swept over her and, though she kept trying to get up and get going, she simply couldn't make her body obey her orders. Calliope's eyelids closed, and she was unable to stop them.

The touch on her shoulder jolted her abruptly awake. Her eyes snapped open to see a figure clad in the field-grey uniform of the German army looming over her. So this was it. This was how it was all going to end. Right here by the river, because she'd been stupid enough to fall asleep in the open.

And then she recognised the man. Heinrich.

Before she could say anything to him, he was speaking urgently to her. 'We need to go somewhere private. Somewhere not too far away.' He looked up, his gaze sweeping their surroundings. 'Quickly.'

Calliope scrambled clumsily to her feet, searching her mind for an answer. 'The sheepfold,' she said, 'this way.'

In just a few minutes, they were ducking under the low

threshold of the small shelter that lay in the corner of the now empty sheepfold; the flocks were at their summer pastures with a new young shepherd boy.

'What's going on?' asked Calliope, breathlessly. 'Why are you here?'

Heinrich sank to the earth floor and ran his hands through his cropped hair. He shook his head but didn't immediately reply. Eventually, he reached out and took Calliope's hand. 'I've left,' he mumbled, as if he could hardly bring himself to say the words out loud. 'I've deserted.'

Calliope's mouth fell open. This was huge. Barely comprehensible and utterly terrifying. Deserters were shot on sight. There was no mercy, no leniency or forgiveness.

'I can't do it any more.' Heinrich's voice was strained and mournful, and every word sounded effortful. 'The brutality, the killings... it's too much. If I take part, then I'm complicit, I'm as guilty as everyone else. If I don't take part, the attention that would bring would put me under suspicion and I'd probably be locked up, if not worse.' His expression was desperate, his eyes wild. 'I've been pretending for so long – faking behaving like a true Nazi, and I've hated every moment of it. I never wanted to bully anyone, to frighten or intimidate anybody.'

Calliope had known this to be the case without Heinrich explaining it; it was obvious. She recalled her first encounter with Heinrich when he'd been questioning the man she now knew was Laurie, prodding at him with his rifle butt. She recognised now how half-hearted Heinrich had been, even though his actions had enraged her at the time. And then there were the times she'd run across his patrol, and he'd clearly seen through her disguise as a boy, but taken no action against her. He'd been struggling to play the part of a mean soldier for too long, and he'd reached breaking point.

'So here I am,' Heinrich continued. 'I've left. I didn't even stop to put my Cretan clothes on, just brought them in my bag.'

Calliope knelt down beside him and pulled him into her arms, letting his head rest on her shoulder. As she stroked his hair, his breathing slowly became more regular. She hadn't worked out what it all meant yet and wasn't sure when she would. It was so unexpected. Her muddled thoughts were all over the place. But right then, the only thing that made sense was Heinrich's proximity, the delicious, musky, masculine smell of him, the firm hardness of his muscular body against hers.

Outside, the sun sank lower and the birds quietened as dusk began to fall. The only sound was the deafening whir of the cicadas. After they'd made love, they lay together, Heinrich's uniform, hated because of what it represented, piled up in a field-grey heap beside them. Lazily, Calliope traced lines across his strong back with a fingernail. She was half-asleep again, and knew she must stir herself. As she struggled to pull herself out of her soporific state, the shelter suddenly darkened. For a moment, Calliope felt pure terror sear through her. Were they outside, the Nazis, already searching for the missing soldier? But the darkness lasted only moments before it lifted and the muted light of dusk returned. She must have been mistaken. There was no one there.

Heinrich, disturbed by her movement, sat up. He reached out for his backpack and pulled out his Cretan disguise. It suddenly occurred to her that, all that time ago when he'd bought the clothes, he must have had the idea of desertion at the back of his mind. She wished she could stay with him, in his hour of need, to make sure he was all right. But she couldn't.

In a few days, she would be risking her life in the airfield sabotage. And Heinrich would be on the run for ever now. The Germans would never forget about him. They would track him down, seek him out, make him pay for what he'd done.

For a moment, Calliope felt hopeless. It was overwhelming. Forcibly, she pushed her despair away. She had a job to do, one that would be make or break for the resistance, and Heinrich would survive. He was resourceful and resilient. He'd be all right.

She had to believe it.

CHAPTER 34

CRETE, JULY 1943

'Go!' Laurie issued the instruction in an urgent whisper. At his command, he and the SBS men began their approach to the airfield. Calliope could hardly bear to watch. She and Stelios had equipped them with all the information they had gained over their months of surveillance and this, along with Laurie's detailed maps from his time on the forced labour project, meant that the raiders were as well-prepared as they could be. It was still a heart-stoppingly perilous mission.

The airfield's perimeter was protected by a high fence, which itself was guarded by a ring of sentries. Inside, each of the dozen Stuka dive-bombers had its own guard positioned under the wing. As well as these aeroplanes, the aim was to also put out of action the four Junkers Ju 88 bombers, and to destroy the fuel dump.

The blood thumping in her veins, Calliope clenched her fists and dared to look up to see the men's progress. They had split up now, with Laurie and Sol Baker heading to the northern side, and Andersen and Salter, one of the other SBS men, aiming for the south, with the rest of the band providing backup. Each man carried Lewes bombs and wire-cutters.

Barely able to breathe, Calliope flung herself down, flattening her body into the ground, as the beam of the searchlight sliced through the dark.

After that, the men melted into the obscurity and she could see nothing more of them. She knew the plan – the men would place a bomb on the left wing of each plane, on the basis that all airfields carried spare wings, but only a limited number of each. In the unlikely event that the explosive didn't destroy the entire aircraft, this strategy would take the maximum number out of service.

The seconds seemed like hours, the minutes like years. Time expanded into the black void of the night. Stelios and Calliope, hidden behind some scrubby bushes, felt the agony of each pregnant moment.

Suddenly, a single shot rent the air. Just a few seconds later, a volley of gunfire rang out, reverberating across the deserted countryside. Calliope imagined the spatter of bullets that the British men were facing; they were hugely outnumbered – how could they succeed and get away unscathed?

Just a short while afterwards flares illuminated the velvet sky, before a deafening roar signalled the first of the Lewes bombs exploding. A fireball erupted, visible even from Calliope's distant vantage point, followed shortly by the wail of fire engine sirens. And then another fireball, and another, until the entire airfield seemed to be engulfed in flames.

They had achieved their aim. But had any of the men made it out?

A terrible wait ensued. Calliope crept across the stony ground to Stelios, needing to be near someone rather than all alone. By the faint light of the stars, she saw his white teeth shining as he smiled at her.

'I have a good feeling,' he whispered. 'I think they're all right.'

Calliope did not share his optimism and so didn't

respond. Instead, she peered cautiously around the side of the bush. Out in the open, nothing moved. In the distance, the furore at the airfield continued, the shouting and yelling, together with the roar of the fire, clearly audible in the stillness of the night. The voices didn't seem to be getting any nearer, indicating that all the activity was focused on the airfield. Did that mean that everyone was too busy to go out searching for the men?

Minutes passed, interminably slowly.

And then, looming up out of the darkness, the figures of the British soldiers, stooped low to the ground, weapons in hands, faces flushed with exertion and excitement.

'Get away,' ordered Laurie. 'Go back to the village. It'll be better for you there than with us, in case we are caught. Tell Calista I love her.' And with that he turned away, and led the SBS men back towards the relative safety of their hideout.

When Calliope reached the house in the pre-dawn hours, all was quiet, no one yet stirring. She was too agitated to sit, her body still flooded with adrenaline, her nerves on edge. She swept the floor and tidied up some plates and cups that had been left on the table. Then she pulled the trusty pack of cards out of her pocket and began a game of solitaire. She played game after game as she waited for the slumbering household to wake.

Ariana was first, her lusty cries signalling her hunger. Calliope heard Calista singing softly as she picked her up, and then silence fell once more as the baby began to feed. Mother and daughter must have fallen back to sleep, because the first person downstairs was Valeria, quickly followed by Yiorgis. Both were astonished and delighted to see Calliope, but knew better than to ask exactly why she was there, playing cards in the kitchen in the feeble light of dawn.

Valeria was making tea when the door burst open. Stelios ran in, his eyes wild.

'The Germans are coming!' he cried. 'A whole patrol of them.'

Calliope's heart missed a beat and her stomach turned upside down. She was glad she hadn't had the tea yet, as she would only have brought it straight back up again. There were two possible reasons for the Nazis to be out en masse at this hour of the day. Either they were looking for Heinrich, or they were looking for those who had destroyed the airfield. Probably both.

If she were caught, would she be able to keep quiet under torture? Calliope had no idea. Was she that brave? She didn't know. She couldn't afford to stay around to find out.

'Let's go, Stelios,' she said. 'The mountains are the only safe place for us.'

After briefly embracing her mother and father, she hastily gathered up the cards and stuffed them back inside the box, which she shoved into her pocket, not noticing the one that fell to the floor. Just as she and Stelios were about to cross the threshold, Calista appeared at the top of the stairs. Calliope hesitated, hoping to give her sister a final hug before leaving. But instead of descending, Calista stayed stock-still. As Calliope gazed at her questioningly, she saw Calista mouth a single word.

Traitor.

It took a moment for the word to sink in and, once it had, there was no time to ask Calista to repeat herself, or to demand to know what she meant. The awful accusation ringing in her ears, Calliope grabbed Stelios by the arm and ran out of the house.

Outside, various villagers stood around in the main street, anxious expressions on drawn, war-weary faces. Calliope, intent on getting out of the village, ignored them all. She and Stelios tried several routes, but each time had to stop in their tracks when they spotted Nazi soldiers blocking their path. Soon it became obvious. The entire settlement was surrounded. Perhaps the Germans knew that people from this village were involved in the destruction of the airfield. Or perhaps not. It was just as likely that they merely intended to wreak their terrible style of revenge on any random settlement. It had happened before.

'Stelios, we must separate,' Calliope told the boy. 'You are a child – they're less likely to take their wrath out on you. Take the back route through the gully and up the goat track. Don't try and stay quiet as that will make you look suspicious. Pretend you're searching for a lost animal – go loudly, shouting its name. It's your best bet.'

Stelios nodded. The child was really remarkable, thought Calliope. Nothing seemed to faze him. He was young enough for the Germans to ignore him. She, on the other hand, was not.

Unable to think of anywhere else to go, she headed for the shelter in the sheepfold. She'd hole up and hope for the best. What else could she do?

CHAPTER 35

CRETE, JULY 1943

Traitor.

As Calliope huddled in a corner of the sheepfold, her mind kept returning to Calista and that word her sister had mouthed as she stood at the top of the stairs. She worried and worried away at the memory. She must have been mistaken. Or perhaps she had understood correctly, but Calista had been talking about someone else. But who? Not Stelios, no way. Eliana? Yes, that must have been it. Because surely Calista could not really think that Calliope, her own twin, was that word?

Calliope had many faults; she was too headstrong, too opinionated, too obstinate. But she was not a traitor.

Tormented by what on earth Calista had meant, Calliope stayed hidden while the Germans searched. It went on all day. At one point, a platoon of Nazi soldiers passed the perimeter of the sheepfold. Calliope, heart pounding, listened as they paused to discuss something in staccato tones. She had picked up a fair bit of the language now, but they were using words that weren't familiar to her. Then she heard something she did understand. *Sheiße*. Shit. When it had sunk in, Calliope almost laughed. The soldiers were arguing about whether or not to enter the sheepfold, several objecting because they didn't want to get animal muck on their beautifully polished boots.

If it hadn't been so terrifying, it would have been hilarious. Shooting an unarmed villager at point-blank range was quite easy for these men. But stepping in sheep and goat dung was anathema to them.

It seemed to take the soldiers ages to conclude the argument. Calliope sat huddled in the shelter, knees drawn up to her chest, trying to make herself as small as possible. It was ridiculous – she would be seen in an instant if they entered the field. She wondered if she was playing this all wrong. Perhaps she should brazen it out like she had instructed Stelios to do. Act as if she had nothing to hide and hope they believed it.

No. Something told her that this would not be a good idea. So she stayed hidden, and prayed.

Eventually, after what seemed an age, the German soldiers moved on. Calliope didn't relax. She couldn't. For the rest of the day, she remained rigid and still. Her legs went numb and her back ached, but she did not dare move. Hours passed. Every now and again, her head began to nod and her eyes to close, and then she would jerk awake, all her senses on high alert in case she had missed the sound of approaching footsteps.

Eventually, worn out from gnawing anxiety and endless rumination, Calliope fell asleep. Despite everything, she must have slept for hours, because when she woke dawn was breaking again. Throughout her childhood, daybreak had been a source of optimism and pleasure at the prospect of the new day ahead. Not any more. As Calliope came back into consciousness, the familiar sense of dread consumed her.

She lay still for a moment, curled up in a ball, not wanting to face whatever was waiting for her, already sure that it couldn't be anything good. And then something began to filter through to her fuddled mind. A strange smell. A smell that signified danger, fear and death.

Fire.

Calliope sat bolt upright and her blood ran cold in her veins. Fear shivered down her spine. There. A hint of the smell came again, acrid and pungent. Oh God. A terrible realisation began to percolate in Calliope's very being. Something was burning. Something big.

Hauling herself to her feet, staggering and stumbling on numb legs, she lurched to the open side of the shelter. Now she was upright the smell was more intense. Hesitantly, she stepped forward. The village was not visible from here as it was blocked by a cluster of pine and cypress trees. But the sky above was dark with smoke. Suddenly overcome by the urgency of the situation, Calliope began to run, heedless of who might be around to see her. The air tasted of ash, and small particles of black soot landed on her cheeks and arms as she raced along the narrow path and over the stone bridge. She rounded the corner, and stopped still in her tracks.

The village, her village, was burning.

As she watched in paralysed horror, she heard the distant sound of jeep engines and then the screech of brakes being suddenly applied. Moments later, a stream of Nazis appeared, brandishing weapons and a terrible air of determination.

Villagers were gathered in the main street, women clutching children to their breasts as they wept at the sight of their homes consumed by flames. Old men watched helplessly on, empty buckets held in impotent hands as they realised that they were powerless to extinguish this inferno, while younger men dragged family members and neighbours from upstairs rooms, valiantly entering and re-entering houses even as walls collapsed and ceilings caved in. The Germans had set fire to the village while the population was asleep in their beds. There would be many casualties.

And as if that were not enough, now they started shooting,

firing indiscriminately into the crowd. Silent tears of terror poured from Calliope's sore and smoke-filled eyes.

Men, women and children fell to the ground as the shooting continued, bodies piling up on the ancient cobbles. Suddenly, Calliope came out of the trance-like state she had fallen into. She must get to her house, rescue her parents and Calista, and most importantly of all the baby, little innocent Ariana, who bore no part of the responsibility for this war.

Calliope slipped through the bushes at the end of the main street and managed to reach the alleyway that led to her home. All was chaos and confusion, and she knew it was only a matter of time before the Germans moved away from the centre of the village to the side streets and passages.

It was hot, a searing heat that threatened to melt her skin, and the smoke-filled air was noxious and suffocating. She pulled off her waist sash and wrapped it round her nose and mouth. Taking snatched, shallow breaths, she continued a few paces further. Then she saw them.

Smoke billowed from the open doorway as Laurie emerged, carrying Calista, who had Ariana clutched in her arms. He caught sight of Calliope and it seemed to trigger something in him. Sobbing, he sank to his knees and laid his wife and daughter on the rough, uneven ground. Instantly, Calliope was beside him, kneeling down. She reached out for Calista's wrist, held her fingers against it. No pulse. Nothing.

Ariana, still enveloped by her mother's embrace, also lay still and unmoving.

They were both dead. The awfulness of it, the cruelty and savagery, threatened to destroy Calliope too. Her heart broke into a million pieces. As she collapsed onto her sister's body she wondered if dying would be the best option. She should have known that the nearest village to the airfield would suffer a reprisal. If only she hadn't fallen asleep in the sheepfold. If only she'd got here earlier, rescued her sister and the baby, her parents too of course. But little Ariana was the one who most deserved to live. To have her life cut so tragically short reminded Calliope of George's awful death.

Moments later, she felt the ground vibrate with the weight of many footsteps. Through slitted eyes, she saw German soldiers advancing. She heard firing. A cry. Feet pounding the cobbles. More gunfire.

Calliope wanted to howl and wail as she watched the obliteration of everything she loved and valued. Instead, she played dead, lying as still as she could over her sister. Above her, a cacophony of gunfire blended with the crackling of the blazing fires to drown out all other sound. Eventually, the shooting receded into the distance. The soldiers had moved on. But the flames still raged, creating a heat so intense that Calliope expected it to consume her at any moment.

When she heard Laurie's voice she assumed that she'd woken up in heaven, and that he was there with her, helping her through the pearly gates, welcoming her to that peaceful place. But then she felt a tugging at her arm. Her eyes flickered open.

Laurie's face was sooty and blackened, his eyes bloodshot. He must be real. No one in heaven would look this bad. She still couldn't move, couldn't rouse herself from her stupor.

A shot rang out. A second later, a body fell, landing on her legs. It was heavy and motionless, trapping her. She stared at it.

Laurie's empty, lifeless eyes stared back at her, his beautiful smile erased for ever.

CHAPTER 36

CRETE, 2005

They walked slowly through the village, partly because Callie was struggling with the steep streets and partly because she had to look so closely at everything, checking it out, running what she saw against what was in her memory, trying to make sense of the new village from what she remembered of the old. The whole place had been reconstructed after the war, stone for stone, building for building. In the centre was a new plane tree, not as large as the old one but plenty big enough by now to provide the shade that is so necessary for a Cretan summer. But though everything was the same, nothing was the same.

Eventually Callie stopped, and pointed. 'Our house was up there,' she said, indicating a narrow alleyway that wound up and up towards the high crags. 'There's a gully alongside the path and right at the top, if you are deft and sure-footed, you can escape over the bridge and into the mountains. That route saved me, once.' She finished speaking but did not move.

'Shall we go then?' asked Ella, gently. It was clear that this was not the time to rush her grandmother.

Silently, Callie nodded, and took a step forward. She could hardly believe she was doing this. Despite what she'd read in the letter, she still didn't fully trust the words it contained. How could Calista be alive, when she herself had seen her lying prostrate and motionless, had felt for her pulse and found nothing?

At the house, which looked just like it had before, but newer and cleaner and more robust somehow, Ella knocked on the door. They heard footsteps approaching on the other side, and then the door swung open. Callie couldn't breathe. This was utterly foolish. They were both too old for this, her and her twin, too old to put right all the mistakes of the past. Too much time had passed and—

'Hello!' A small boy grinned cheekily at the two strangers on the doorstep, his arrival cutting short Callie's panicky ruminations. His dark brown eyes had a mischievous gleam to them, and he reminded Callie of Stelios, the youngster who had proved so indomitable and invaluable to the resistance. The boy looked at them expectantly and, when neither Callie nor Ella immediately spoke, he turned and scampered back into the bowels of the house, shouting, 'Mama' at the top of his voice.

'We shouldn't have come,' whispered Callie, feeling weak and breathless. 'I don't know what to say. I can't do this...'

'Shh,' soothed Ella. 'It'll be fine. We'll work it out.' But nevertheless the expression on her face revealed her apprehension.

At that moment, a woman appeared in the doorway, gently greying hair piled up on top of her head, a pair of spectacles dangling from her neck. She looked elegant and sophisticated in a way that would have been extraordinary in a village like this in Callie's youth.

'Hello there,' said the woman in Greek. 'How ca—' She stopped short as her gaze rested on Callie. 'Oh my God,' she exclaimed, a sudden flush reddening her cheeks. 'Oh my...' Her hand flew up to her chest and rested there, as if to calm her palpitating heart.

Ella took a step backwards. She couldn't understand the

woman's words, but the impact of her and her grandmother's arrival was obvious. 'I'm sorry,' she said. 'We didn't mean to shock you.'

The woman regarded her blankly. 'No English,' she replied, 'sorry.' Then she turned towards Callie, grabbed her hands and began a torrent of emotional Greek as she ushered both her and Ella inside.

The interior of the house was cool, and beautifully decorated in natural tones, with ceramic tiles and stoneware vases. It was nothing like the home Callie remembered, with its rough walls, hand-hewn furniture and earthen floor.

The courtyard behind the house was also utterly transformed, no longer an extension of the vegetable garden where hens had pecked among the rows of beans, peas and tomatoes, but now a tranquil haven with a gnarled olive tree at its centre and sweet-smelling jasmine clambering up the walls. Bees hummed among the fragrant blooms, and a plump ginger cat slumbered on an old wicker chair. Seated in the shade was an old lady who looked just like Callie.

Calista.

Callie stood stock-still, unable to believe her eyes. Even though she had known that this moment was to come from the minute she'd stepped on the plane to Crete, if not the moment that she'd read the fateful letter, she still couldn't take it in. Calista, her beloved twin sister, her soulmate, the person most like her in the whole world, was sitting there in front of her.

As Callie struggled to find any words to express what she was feeling, another figure slipped into the garden. It was George.

'Calliope!' He rushed over to her and embraced her, kissing her on both cheeks. 'And you're Ella, Calliope's granddaughter?' He hugged Ella, too. 'You've met my mother, Sophia?' he added, still speaking English, gesturing towards the elegant woman. 'And here is Grandma Calista.'

Slowly, as if in a trance, Callie crossed the small garden until she stood next to her long-lost sister. George hastily pulled up a chair and helped her lower herself into it. The twins stared at each other, both dumbstruck and overcome with emotion. Tentatively, as if this person beside her might not be real at all but the ghost she had spent the last sixty-two years thinking she was, Callie reached out her hand and rested it on Calista's, and her sister picked it up, raised it to her lips and kissed it.

'I thought you were dead,' said Calista, her voice trembling with age.

'And I thought you were,' replied Callie.

There was a moment of utter and profound silence, as if the world had stopped turning. And then suddenly they were both crying, tears streaming down their cheeks, clasping each other's age-spotted hands.

'Tea,' interjected Sophia determinedly, as if overcome by the need for decisive action of some sort. 'We need tea.'

She disappeared into the cool interior of the house, and soon Callie could hear the sound of cupboard doors opening and shutting, cups and saucers clinking together, the whistle of a boiling kettle. She regarded her sister, her twin, and marvelled at the fact that this was what they looked like now, old and withered, a lifetime's experiences, both good and bad, etched upon their wrinkled faces. She could see the same image any time she looked in the mirror, but somehow it only seemed real now it was reflected back at her from another person. God, they were old, her and Calista. How had they both survived this long? The odds had been against them throughout the war years and yet here they were, sitting in the very same spot where their lives had begun eight and a half decades ago.

Just thinking about the reality of Calista's existence, seeing the proof in front of her, made Callie feel dizzy and light-headed. Ella was eyeing her quizzically, as if waiting for her grandmother to say or do something, but Callie could do neither.

Sophia returned with the teapot, followed by George, who'd gone to help, carrying a tray full of cups and saucers, a sugar bowl and platefuls of Cretan sweet snacks, *loukoumades* and *kalitsounia*. The young boy, who George introduced as his brother Christos, grabbed some treats and then disappeared, George explaining that he'd gone out to play with his friends. Once everyone had been served, Callie opened her mouth to speak but then abruptly shut it again. Ella eyed her with an air of wariness mixed with expectation. Callie tried again.

'I never thought this moment would come,' she murmured, almost as if she were talking to herself.

Sophia smiled as George translated, but Calista seemed to have drifted into a trance, her eyes half-closed, her tear-stained cheeks pale in the shade. Callie understood. Intense emotion was exhausting at their age. She was feeling pretty done-in herself.

She took Calista's hand in hers. In her mind, she trawled through what Calista had written in her letter. *We need to talk about what happened. Why it happened. And what you did.* She had not used the word 'traitor', but her meaning was clear and had haunted Callie since the day the letter had arrived. At some point it had to be discussed. But not right now.

Calista sat up a little straighter in her seat. It seemed to cost her a great effort. Callie was surprised that her sister seemed older than herself; she'd thought the climate and the Mediterranean diet, all that olive oil and fresh food, were supposed to bestow longevity and healthiness. 'We have so much to catch up on,' she murmured.

Ella, hovering awkwardly beside her grandmother, interjected encouragingly. 'There'll be lots of time for you two to reconnect and chew the fat. We got open-ended tickets, so we can stay as long as you both want.' Callie thought again about how generous it was of her to put her plans on hold.

'The thing is that we don't,' responded Calista, her voice frail and wavering. 'We hardly have any time at all.'

Callie frowned and looked at her questioningly. 'Are you going somewhere?' she asked.

'No.' Calista shook her head and chuckled dryly. 'Well, unless you count a journey to the next world.' She paused, bit her lip. That old gesture she'd always done when unsure, doubtful or frightened. A tight band of fear tightened around Callie's chest.

'I have cancer.' Calista's words cut through Callie's worst imaginings. 'It's incurable. The doctors tell me I haven't got long to live. Maybe a few months if I'm lucky. So no, we don't have plenty of time. We have almost no time at all.'

CHAPTER 37

CRETE, 2005

Her sister's shocking revelation shook Callie to the core. Calista had not mentioned her condition in the letter and Callie had assumed that, as her identical twin, Calista enjoyed the same good health as she did. Of course she herself had her aches and pains, some of which, especially the shortness of breath and chest pain, had been getting worse recently, but that was to be expected in one's ninth decade on this earth. They were mere niggles, inconveniences, annoyances, not serious. They would not kill her, she was sure. They were not cancer.

Sophia came over to her mother and patted her shoulder, reassuring her that the whole family was there for her, that they would make sure she didn't suffer. Such platitudes were comforting, Callie could see that, but how true were they? She suppressed a shudder at the thought of the agony her sister might have to endure, at the idea of the slow diminution of being until, eventually, Calista slipped away.

Sophia, sensing the tension that fizzed in the air since her mother's revelation, decided that it was time for lunch and proceeded to produce a simple but delicious meal of salad, crusty bread, cheese, olives and wine. It was so Greek, this hospitality that involved plying guests with a constant flow of meals and snacks, but Callie could hardly touch a thing. She blamed her lack of appetite on all the emotion, though she knew it was more than that. She'd faced her fears and got here, met Calista and some of her family, and now they were all confronting the fact that this wondrous reunion might be short-lived. That they might not get the chance to say all the things that needed to be said.

Once the food had been cleared away, Sophia suggested to Calista that she go inside for a nap, and George asked Callie and Ella if they'd like to take a walk around the village. But Calista resisted Sophia's entreaties.

'I'll have plenty of time to sleep once I'm dead and gone,' she said, bluntly. Callie saw how Sophia blanched at this bald statement, expressed so unemotionally.

So instead, only Ella accompanied George. Sophia went inside to busy herself with some chores, leaving Callie and Calista alone together. For a while, the sisters sat in silence, both lost in thought. A warbler sang from the boughs of the olive tree, its metallic trills repeated over and again.

'I'm sorry about the cancer,' Callie began, eventually. Her Greek was rusty and faltering, compounded by the fact that she didn't really know what to say. She had had difficult conversations about health and unexpected diagnoses with all sorts of people over the years, including her husband when his coronary heart disease had been discovered. But consoling a sister and a twin from whom she had been separated for most of her lifetime was a different matter. Uncharted territory, as dangerous and hard to navigate as the jagged crags of the White Mountains.

Calista smiled wanly. 'It's all right. I've come to terms with it. I've had a long life. Like anybody, I am not without regrets, but I am ready for the end to come.'

Callie's heart turned over in her chest. How could Calista

be so sanguine? She felt that she herself would be raging against the dying of the light. But rage had never been Calista's way.

'I wish everything had been different,' she responded. 'Most of all, I wish there had never been a war. It caused our separation and nothing can give us back the missing years.'

Calista reached for her water glass and took a few refreshing sips. 'I wasn't sure if you would come,' she said. 'It seemed preposterous, that chance meeting of you and George at church, too much of a coincidence, a story that you wouldn't believe if you read it in a book or saw it in a film.'

Callie nodded. 'Though they say the truth is stranger than fiction,' she replied.

A pause ensued. Callie knew that it was now or never. She had to raise the subjects that had haunted her across the decades.

'Calista,' she began, haltingly. 'I-I... well there's something I've never understood. On that last day, right here in this house, I saw you mouth the word "traitor". What did you mean when you said that? Who were you referring to? I have always tried to convince myself that you were referring to Eliana.'

'Eliana?' Calista sounded bemused. 'I know you had doubts about her, as did I. She was one of the few who survived the destruction of the village. She was at work at the time. But I know for a fact that Eliana had nothing to do with it.'

'Humph,' snorted Callie. 'How can you be so sure?' Calista was going to have to work harder than this to convince her of Eliana's innocence.

'I'm certain,' insisted Calista. 'After the war was over it transpired that Eliana had been double-crossing the Nazis all along, handing on the names of those the Germans were looking for to the resistance so that they could escape. Her contact was with another cell, not Laurie's, as she wanted to keep some distance from— Well, from you, because she knew of your involvement.

She thought it would be better that way. She absolutely was not a traitor.'

Callie stared at Calista, open-mouthed. 'She was on our side all along?' It was scarcely credible. For so long, Callie had been convinced of Eliana's culpability, of her treason towards her homeland. To find out that it wasn't true blindsided her. But on the other hand, there were all the times when she had been sure that Eliana knew of her involvement with the resistance, and wondered why her former friend had not handed her in.

As Callie was thinking this, Calista's words broke in. 'Remember what happened in the prison?' she said. 'That was Eliana. She set it up so that I could get out. She got into terrible trouble for that.'

Callie remembered hoping that Eliana would be made to pay for her mistake, as punishment for being a turncoat, and she now knew that she had – just for all the wrong reasons. But now that Eliana was in the clear, was not the person Calista had referred to as a traitor, there was only one other option. The option Callie had always feared. Calista had meant her, Callie. Despite her certainty, she still had to ask, to hear it from her sister's lips.

'So who were you talking about?' she asked, a familiar feeling of dread filling her heart.

Calista sighed. Her liver-spotted hands trembled in her lap. 'I was talking about you,' she murmured, so quietly that Callie had to strain to hear her.

It was only what Callie had suspected, and yet it still hit her like a body blow. 'But why?' she almost pleaded. 'What did I do that could possibly have made you think such a thing of me? I worked tirelessly for the resistance, I put my life in danger over and over again...' Her voice rose as she spoke the last words; the injustice of the accusation still cut deep.

Calista took a deep breath. 'I didn't want to believe it either,' she sighed. 'But I saw you with a man in the sheepfold. He had a German uniform, so he was obviously one of them. I was constantly crazy with worry about Laurie, you, Stelios, everyone in the resistance coming to harm, and when I saw you fraternising with a Nazi... well, what was I supposed to think? I assumed you were betraying the cause, and that put Laurie at terrible risk.'

The tears of earlier threatened to return as Callie contemplated her sister's words. How could her own twin have believed she could be so evil? But she remembered that time in the sheepfold, when she'd seen a shadow cross the entrance and been sure that someone – Eliana – was spying on them. The significance of the moment had faded quickly in the devastation that followed but she'd never forgotten it.

'The man you saw,' she began, 'his name was Heinrich. Like Eliana, he was double-crossing the Germans, helping the resistance. Helping me. He gave me so much information to pass on to Laurie, and he brought me food, he was my stalwart prop and companion. When you saw us together, he had just deserted. He *was* a traitor, but to his homeland, Germany, not to the Cretans or the British. He was on our side. He hated the Nazis and helped to defeat them.'

Calista stared straight ahead of her, lips trembling. 'I see,' she said, simply. 'I understand now.'

A dead weight settled in Callie's stomach. That was one topic dealt with. But what about all the rest? Ones that went even deeper than an accusation of betrayal. When she thought about it now, in the tranquil courtyard of her childhood home, Callie wasn't quite sure how so many secrets had been allowed to develop. How *she* had allowed so many secrets to develop.

At that moment, Ella and George returned, Ella full of compliments about the beauty and tranquillity of the village, the gorgeous flowers on every windowsill, the amazing view from the church tower at the top of the main street. Callie was glad of the interruption, which prevented her from having to say what needed to be said – for the time being at least. She suddenly felt absolutely exhausted and, observing her sister, saw that she looked done-in, too. Sophia, who'd come back outside with the two young people, must have thought the same thing, because her eyes narrowed with concern.

'Mama, you are tired,' she murmured, going over to her mother and tucking a blanket round her knees although it was not cold.

Calista nodded. 'A bit.'

Sophia's tone when she spoke next was uncompromising. 'I think it's time to call it a day. You mustn't wear yourself out.'

Picking up on the cue, Callie nodded. 'We should go, leave you in peace.'

Ella leapt up and helped her grandmother out of her chair.

'But come back tomorrow, won't you?' cried Calista. 'I want to have every moment possible with my twin and my great-niece. There's still so much we have to discuss.'

Callie's stomach turned over as she and Ella made their farewells. For so long she had tried to convince herself that Calista's accusation that she was a traitor was the most important thing to address. But of course it wasn't. Nowhere near. It was everything else that had gone on during and after that traumatic final battle on the streets of their village that needed to be confronted. The decision she had made about Calista and the baby, on the spur of the moment, in desperation, that would now be laid bare for a scrutiny that it would not survive.

However much she put it off, the truth would have to be faced sooner or later. After which, neither Calista nor Ella would probably ever speak to her again.

CHAPTER 38

CRETE, 2005

So that Callie and Ella would be closer to the village, George had found them a nearby B&B to move into. It was converted from an old olive mill and inside was all exposed stone, wooden beams and beautiful local artwork and ceramics. Outside lay a series of terraces studded with vibrant bougainvillea, olive and fig trees, and set about with parasol-shaded sunloungers and cosy reading nooks built into the low walls.

'Wow, Gran, I love it!' exclaimed Ella as they were shown to their room. 'Don't you?'

Callie nodded at the same time as inwardly marvelling at how places that were working, functioning buildings when she was a child were now set aside for luxury and relaxation, all traces of their industrial past reduced down to charming relics and artefacts. In her village of old, no one could have imagined the lives that people led nowadays, the modern conveniences, the possessions. When she and Calista were growing up in the 1930s, you felt lucky if you had two changes of clothes and a rag doll to your name. It was all so different now; stuffed wardrobes and overflowing toy boxes were the norm.

Opening her suitcase, Callie took out her nightclothes and laid them on her pillow. She had to concede that the little two-bedroom apartment that George had booked was perfect for her and Ella's needs, and just a ten-minute drive from the village. She wanted to spend as much time as possible with Calista, of course she did. Though whether Calista would ever want to see her again, once Callie had made her confessions, was doubtful.

The weather seemed to be getting hotter every day now they were in July. The next day, Callie and Ella spent the morning lazing in the garden. After a light lunch, Ella insisted on Callie having a nap before they headed to the family home.

'Calista will want to rest, too,' she reminded Callie, which of course Callie knew. She suspected this enforced sleep was as much Ella worrying about her as about Calista, but Ella knew how Callie hated to be treated like the old person she actually was.

The heat was still simmering when they finally set off. Air that smelt of honeysuckle and dust pressed down on them, throbbing with the incessant roar of the cicadas.

'I really want to learn Greek,' announced Ella, as she negotiated the narrow, potholed road.

'Ha!' exclaimed Callie. 'Good luck with that! You know that it's pretty tricky, don't you?' Then, catching Ella's frown, she added, 'But you're so smart, you'll have no trouble.'

Ella laughed. 'I'm not sure that's quite true,' she said. 'But George has said that while we're here he'll give me a few lessons to get me started. And I don't know, in the future perhaps I'll come to live here.'

'That would be... interesting.' Callie didn't know what else to say. She should be happy to see Ella embracing her Greek heritage. But it was more complicated than that. Despite the unexpected unearthing of a family still existing, thriving, here in Crete, Callie knew she could never settle here. Once this was all over and done with, she would go back to her basement flat in London and resume her old life with its familiar routine. She'd always assumed Ella would be close at hand, company for Callie as her twilight years faded to heavy dusk, then eventual night. It was hard to contemplate the idea that this would not be the case.

'So this afternoon,' said Ella as she turned the air con up. 'I hope we'll hear the story of how Calista survived. And then... well, what about you, Grandma? You haven't explained how you got away. I'm dying to know.'

Dying to know. It was a funny phrase, when you thought about it. Knowing things could definitely have led to dying, in the war years. These days, was it knowing or not knowing that was the more dangerous? It was a conundrum Callie could not get her head around. When she did finally confess all, Ella would probably never speak to her again. As for Calista, such revelations might kill her even quicker than the cancer.

Whatever happened, it would all be Callie's fault.

They arrived at the village and Ella had to resist taking Callie's arm to help her up the steep streets to the house. She knew her grandmother would shake her off if she tried.

'I know that I'm a tourist and therefore this is extremely hypocritical,' she said. 'But I really don't want this place to become a tourist magnet, like Chania.'

Callie snorted, then paused for a few seconds to catch her breath. 'That's hardly likely, when there's no access for cars to most of it. People don't like to walk in this day and age.'

'That's true,' conceded Ella. 'So, maybe there's hope that it will retain all its charm and uniqueness.'

An image of the village on fire, white-hot flames bursting through red-tiled roofs, huge wooden beams crashing downwards, crushing anyone below, the air thick with grey ash and black soot, flashed into Callie's mind. She had been surprised to find a village still standing here on her return. It was remarkable that anyone had wanted to rebuild on a site of such carnage. But, she reminded herself, Cretans don't give in so easily.

At the house, Calista was seated in the same spot as before in the shady courtyard garden. Sophia served tea and cakes as they sat around chatting, making small talk, George on hand as usual to translate. Callie marvelled at how they, herself included, could be behaving so casually, as if it wasn't absolutely momentous and scarcely credible that they were all together, that they were all alive.

There was so much ground to cover, all those missing years and years of memories to discuss. Although, on the other hand, did anything in the past really matter? Could they simply write it off, start from now, go from here? In many ways, that would be preferable. But in reality, impossible. The events of 1943 could not be ignored or brushed over. Callie knew that, if Calista didn't ask, Ella would. And she wanted to retain some semblance of control over a situation that constantly threatened to take on a life of its own, to catapult her towards recollections that she did not want to see the light of day.

'Calista, I know it will be hard to talk about,' Callie began. 'But how did you survive the destruction of the village, the aftermath? Where did you go, what did you do?'

Calista grimaced, perhaps from pain or perhaps from the idea of confronting the deep trauma of the past. Sophia, who was sitting on her chair facing her mother, cast her a concerned glance.

'It's all right,' Calista assured her. She paused, smoothing imaginary wrinkles out of her skirt, before slowly, with lots of stops and starts, beginning her story.

'I think I must have been knocked unconscious during the attack. Presumably because of that, the Germans missed me during their final murderous rampage through the burning streets. When I came to, I found myself entirely alone amidst the charred remains of the village. The only signs of life were the vultures circling overhead.'

Calista halted. Her eyes were moist and the trauma of her memories was written across her face. Sophia got up and whispered something in her ear, but Calista waved her words away and continued.

'I dragged myself to my feet, stumbling around in the ashes, frantically searching for my baby, Ariana. I was unable to find her but I couldn't accept that she was gone. Perhaps I've never truly accepted it.'

When Calista said those words, it was if all the air was sucked out of the courtyard, leaving the listeners gasping. The idea of a lost child hit everyone like a body blow. Calista, seemingly almost in a trance now, continued her narration.

'Eventually I came across a couple of other survivors and, a while after that, help began to arrive from other villages. We identified many of the dead – Laurie and our parents among them – but some of the bodies were so badly burnt that we couldn't tell who they were. We assumed that anyone missing had passed away.'

She looked at Callie then, reaching out her hand to her twin. 'We didn't find your body and, though I knew you must be dead, I still held out a tiny smidgeon of hope that maybe you'd been captured and imprisoned in Chania. I waited for you, even after the Germans finally left. But you never came.'

Sophia was watching Calista with narrowed eyes, checking whether her mother was all right to continue. With an almost imperceptible nod, Calista indicated that she was.

'For days following the fire, the other two living souls and I sheltered in the sheepfold. Every waking hour, I searched for Ariana. I could hardly function, I was so crazed and mad with grief over my lost daughter. I contemplated drowning myself in the river, or throwing myself into the gorge. But I didn't have the energy to do either. And I thought: if she is out there, somewhere, I have to stay alive for her.'

Tears pricked behind Callie's eyes. Ella was already crying. It was hard to establish what George was feeling. He was busy translating for Ella, and seemed perfectly composed. Perhaps he'd heard the story before.

'I'm not sure how much time passed,' Calista continued. 'At some point, a kindly distant relative from another village took me to the mountain hamlet where I'd spent my pregnancy, and stayed with me there until the war ended, and for several years after that. I thought that my grief would never leave me. But then, in 1949, I met my husband, my' – Calista's eyes flicked towards Callie as she said these words – 'my second husband, Manolis. We married and, over the next ten years, we had four children, the youngest of whom is Sophia.'

Sophia gave a smile that encompassed both gratitude and sorrow. Callie, weeping now, could only imagine how strange it must have been for her to have heard this story over the years.

'I managed to find some happiness in life,' Calista sighed, tears beginning to stream down her face. 'And I thank God every day for the blessing of my children and grandchildren.' She smiled a sweet sad smile towards George, her grandson. 'Then George went to London to study for his PhD – very clever, he is – and told his mother that he'd met someone at the Greek Orthodox church who was from Crete and looked exactly like me. The photograph that arrived in the post a week or so later confirmed what he had claimed. As soon as I saw it, I knew. I knew that my sister had not died in the massacre after all. She was alive and well and living in England. I could not begin to understand how this had happened, only that it was a miracle. A God-given miracle.'

Callie was weeping harder than ever, her eyes red, her skin blotchy.

Calista let out a huge, gulping sob. 'And now y-you're here,' she spluttered, 'and I can't believe that it's been so long, that it's taken all these years for us to find each other again.'

By now, everyone in the garden was crying, George included. Callie reached out and held her sister's hand. They had got through this part of the reminiscences. Only Callie knew the worst was yet to come. What still needed to be said.

CHAPTER 39

CRETE, 2005

Callie got up late the next morning. She had a headache and everything hurt: her back, her legs, her feet. She felt not eighty-five but a hundred and five. A sick, dizzy feeling overcame her when she thought about the tale she still needed to tell.

In the breakfast room, she found Ella nose-deep in her guidebook, even though Callie was sure she had read every word ten times over. She sat down heavily and ordered coffee.

Ella put the book down and smiled at her grandmother. 'How are you? Did you sleep well? How are you feeling after yesterday?'

Callie stirred her coffee cup vigorously. The whirling black liquid reflected her mood: sombre, confused, full of foreboding. 'Fine,' she answered blandly.

One of the B&B dogs came to their table and sat beside Callie, staring up at her. Ella giggled. 'He likes you, Gran,' she said.

Managing a smile, Callie reached out to pat the dog's head. Its fur was smooth and cool, its ears silky-soft. The way it gazed at her with melting chocolate eyes reminded her of Orion, her faithful companion over that long summer at the *mitato* when, temporarily removed from the heat of war, love developed between her and Heinrich, at the same time as Ariana was growing in her sister's belly, unaware of the cruel and hostile world into which she would be born. For a moment Callie thought she might weep, for all the losses: Orion, her youth and innocence, her sister, who until so recently she had thought was long departed, Laurie, her parents, Ariana and Louise, Heinrich.

'So we'll go to the village today as usual, yes?' Ella asked. She'd pulled her hair up into a high ponytail that bobbed and swayed as she spoke as if it had a life of its own. Callie thought it quite lovely, and also quite funny. 'Sophia said to go a bit earlier, in time for lunch.'

'I like your hair that way,' Callie said, ignoring Ella's suggestion and gesturing towards the jaunty ponytail.

'Oh.' Ella instinctively put her hand to her hair and grinned. 'I've been so hot,' she explained. 'It's not high fashion but getting it off my neck should be cooler at any rate.'

Callie thought of the hair she had had as a young woman – and Calista's had been the same – how long and thick and strong it had been, how, on special occasions, she would plait it and wrap it round her head like a crown. Now with age her hair was grey and scant, wispy fronds that barely covered her scalp, no longer lush and pretty, far from covetable. She looked down at her hands, liver-spotted, criss-crossed by raised veins that resembled the branches of an overgrown fig tree. God, getting old was frightful.

'Gran? Are you listening?' Ella's tone was anxious and plaintive, reminding Callie of when she had been a little girl, always anxious to be heard in a world that was often confusing and frightening for a child who had lost her mum.

'Sorry, dear,' she replied. 'I was miles away. What were you saying?'

'I thought that perhaps we could drive down to the beach

later on this afternoon. It would be lovely to have an evening swim. I'm missing the water.' She paused and then added hastily, 'I mean, it's wonderful being here and learning about everything that happened, and healing for you and Calista, I'm sure, it's not that I want to get away. It's just nice to swim...' Her words tailed lamely off, as if she were embarrassed.

Callie spread her aged fingers against her hands, contemplating their only adornment, her wedding ring. 'Of course,' she replied. 'I understand.'

As if in a trance, or one of those dreams you can't get out of where everything is going wrong, Callie followed Ella to the little hire car. She was going to have to do it. Today. And then afterwards she could swim with Ella, but go further out, further and further, until she disappeared into the blue.

Sophia had prepared fresh lemonade with fruit from the courtyard tree. It was ice-cold, sour and tangy, delicious. Once everyone had a glass and they were settled in the shade, Ella began asking questions, via George and his assiduous translation. She wanted to know about Calista's other children, all the other cousins she had never met but hoped to one day, soon maybe. Callie only half-listened, not because she wasn't interested, but because she was too preoccupied.

Calista could tell there was something up. When Sophia went back into the house to fetch more refreshments, and Ella and George were chattering happily away, she leant towards Callie and whispered, 'What's wrong? You're distracted. And you're clenching your fists like you always used to do when you were worried about something.'

Callie glanced down to see that those hands, whose antiquity and general decrepitude she had contemplated earlier in the day, were indeed clenched tight as if gripping an imaginary object that she must not let go. She shook her head. 'It's nothing,' she lied.

But Calista knew that it was.

'I'd like to hear your story,' she said, louder now, at a volume that interrupted George and Ella and made Sophia, returning with another jug of lemonade, raise her eyebrows. 'How you survived. How you got away. How you ended up in London.'

It had to be done. Callie knew it. She took one last, long look around the courtyard with its blossoming flowers and overflowing pots of herbs, and past the blue shutters into the welcoming kitchen, drinking it in because she would never see it again. Once her story had been told, Calista would not want her back and Ella might want nothing more to do with her. Callie would be left all alone.

Taking a deep breath, she began to tell the tale.

CHAPTER 40

CRETE, JULY 1943

In the midst of the smoke and ashes, face down in the dirt, Calliope sensed movement beside her. She opened her eyes to see Ariana scrambling out from where she had been half-buried beneath her mother's body. The little tot sat up and looked around her with an utter lack of understanding. She wasn't crying; she just seemed dazed.

Seeing her alive brought Calliope to her senses. She tried to move, not sure if all her limbs were whole and complete, whether they would still work. Laurie's body was a dead weight on her legs and she whimpered in horror at having to move him to free herself. Ariana bent forward towards Calista, crying Mama, Mama over and over again, patting her with her chubby hands, unable to comprehend why her mother was lying there and not responding. It was the most pitiful sight.

With a struggle, Calliope got to her feet. She stumbled over to Ariana, picked her up, grabbed her to her chest. She cast one last glance towards Calista before she ran, tripping over the debris, the charred remains of what had once been simple but much-loved homes, over bodies lying lifeless on the blackened ground. If she had allowed herself to register the horror of all that surrounded her, she would have collapsed and given up. So she didn't. She had no idea where the German troops were, whether a soldier was about to step out from behind a still-standing tree and shoot her. She couldn't think about that possibility. She just had to run.

She headed for the top of the alleyway, the only possible route of escape. As she neared the end, a figure appeared from nowhere, looming up ahead of her. Her heart stopped still in her chest. She was about to drop Ariana to the ground, hold up her hands and beg for mercy for the two of them, although she knew such mercy would never be given, when a familiar voice said her name.

It was Heinrich. Somehow, impossibly, he'd found her, found them. He grabbed Ariana from her, took Calliope's hand and led her through the gap at the end of the alley from where it was possible to pick one's way over the narrow ledge above the gully and into the foothills of the mountains. Calliope's eyes still smarted from the acrid fumes of the fire and her smoke-filled lungs laboured with every breath. At the ledge, panic threatened to overcome her. She couldn't see clearly where she was putting her feet, and she was shaking so much she was sure she would make a false move and plunge down, into the river far below. She had a vague awareness of Heinrich managing the crossing, and of Ariana screaming as if she'd suddenly realised that she was being taken away from everything she had ever known.

Poor child. Poor orphaned child.

Just as she was almost across, Calliope's foot slipped out from under her. She fell, half her body dangling over the chasm, her hands clinging to a hardy cistus bush as she tried desperately to pull herself to safety. By some Herculean effort she righted herself, and crawled to safer ground, gasping and spluttering, crying hysterically, breathing short, shallow breaths that barely gave her enough oxygen to function.

On the other side, Heinrich stood waiting, his face buried in Ariana's curly brown hair as if he needed to fill himself with the innocent, babyish smell of her in case they didn't make it. Once Calliope was by his side, they moved cautiously forward, using the pine trees for cover. Calliope edged ahead; she knew the place, knew the terrain. She also knew that this little copse soon gave way to open ground, which they would have to cross to get to the mountains.

Suddenly, Heinrich's hand was on her shoulder. She turned to look at him and he shook his head. He'd heard something. He passed Ariana back to her and inched forward, scanning the area to left and to right. His ears must have been wrong because he signalled to her the all-clear. As they emerged from the shade into the light, Calliope looked at the distance ahead of them. Five hundred metres of pasture before the next hiding place. Her stomach roiled.

They were halfway across when the German soldier appeared. He was one of a patrol, fanning out across the bottom of the meadow, rifle in hand, ready for use.

He shouted something as he spotted them, but his words were lost on the breeze. He was quite far away. But not so far that he couldn't hit them if he was a good shot.

'Run!' Heinrich pushed her forward. 'Run for your life!'

Calliope ran as she had never run before. It was hard to do so while keeping hold of Ariana, and she nearly fell numerous times as she lurched across the tussocky grass. She heard a barrage of gunshot but had no idea if Heinrich had been hit. She couldn't stop to check; she had to carry on.

She reached the edge of the pasture, where the ground rose steeply upwards and was studded by huge boulders. She crouched down behind one to catch her breath and surveyed the route she had just taken. Heinrich, bent almost double, was still moving. The firing had stopped. In a few moments, Heinrich was beside her. In his hand he held his service revolver.

Calliope was glad to see it. At least they had some way of protecting themselves. Although one gun against the firepower of the incensed Germans was laughably inadequate. But it was better than nothing.

Cautiously, keeping their eyes peeled for signs that they were being followed, Heinrich, and Calliope with Ariana clutched to her, crept up the hill, darting from rock to rock, staying as low to the ground as they could. Once they'd crossed the summit and were in the dip of a small valley before the next hill rose up, Heinrich dared to speak for the first time.

'Oh God, Calliope,' he croaked, his voice hoarse with emotion. 'I thought I'd never see you again. I thought you were—'

'I'm all right.' Calliope's words cut across his. She was shaking and shivering with nerves and exhaustion. She wanted to fall into Heinrich's arms and cry and wail and mourn the loss of her family and her village. But there was no time for that. They were still in utmost danger.

Heinrich surveyed the child held awkwardly in Calliope's arms.

'We need to find a better way to carry her,' he said, 'so that we can move faster.' He untied the sash that formed part of his traditional Cretan outfit. 'Here, let's try this.'

He made as if to wrap it round his body but Calliope stopped him. 'Let me carry her,' she said. 'At least until she gets to know you. She'll be more comfortable with me, more settled.'

'I wanted to take the extra weight,' Heinrich protested, 'so you don't have to.' But at the same time he complied, using the cloth to fashion a sling for Ariana to nestle against Calliope's chest. For a split second Calliope imagined them in another life, taking their baby out for a stroll on a beautiful summer's day, smiling at strangers who stopped to admire Ariana's curly hair and melting chocolate eyes.

And then she was back in the present again and facing a

different future. One where they must cross the mountains in the searing July heat. One where they had no protection from the scorching sun of the day or the piercing cold of the night. And one where they had no food, no water and no milk for the child. Calliope was desperately thirsty. But her own needs didn't matter any more.

Now, the only thing that mattered was Ariana.

CHAPTER 41

CRETE, JULY 1943

Once they were sure that the German patrol had moved away, Heinrich and Calliope began the climb up the steep, rocky slope that led to the high mountains.

'We've lost them,' Heinrich said. 'For now.'

'Do you think they're going to come back with reinforcements, more troops, to find us?' Calliope thought that Heinrich might understand the German mindset and their intentions better than she did.

Heinrich paused, turning his back to the sun to survey the distance they had covered. 'The Germans don't like to think that anyone has got the better of them. So yes, they will come after us. We must be constantly on our guard.'

'They are no good in the high mountains,' stated Calliope, definitively, as if wanting to convince herself of this. 'They can't function, they get disorientated. Once we reach the peaks, we will have the advantage.'

Heinrich did not say anything. He looked tired, as if he held the weight of the world on his shoulders. Calliope understood. Once they'd put enough distance between themselves and the village and airfield, she could hope to become just another

Cretan peasant going about her business. But as a deserter, Heinrich would be shot on sight.

Ariana, in the makeshift sling, whimpered. She had fallen asleep, obviously exhausted from the trauma, but was stirring now. Calliope knew she must be thirsty, and hungry too. But there was nothing she could do.

'We need to find water. And food.' She rubbed her eyes, which were still sore and stinging.

'We'll find a spring soon,' Heinrich reassured her. 'And there are summer pastures everywhere – you know that better than anyone. I'm sure we'll find a goatherd who'll give us some milk and cheese.'

Calliope wasn't so certain. They should keep going higher, as that was the best way to evade the Germans. But that also meant that they'd soon be well above the altitude where goats and sheep thrived.

'Perhaps,' she replied. 'But our main problem is that we need to work out which direction we need to go in.' The British were constantly changing their landing and embarkation points to try to stay one step ahead of the Germans, and the most recent beach they had used was much further afield and not one that Calliope knew. She was familiar with her own patch of the White Mountains and the south coast, but Crete was a large island and there was much of it that she had no knowledge of at all.

Heinrich narrowed his eyes and turned to look towards the south. 'We must keep going and hope for the best,' he said.

Before too long they found a small stream bubbling between lichen-covered stones. They had no drinking utensils, no cup or bottle. Calliope tried to capture the sparkling water in her hands and pour it into Ariana's mouth. Some of it went down the child's throat but a lot spilled all over her instead. This was not good; wet clothing would soon make her cold when the sun went down. Her nappy had not been changed for hours and was soaked through. Calliope had no idea what to do about it. She had nothing to replace it with.

Suddenly, confronted by the impossibility of their situation, how utterly ill-equipped and unprepared they were for this perilous journey, despair swept over her. She imagined Calista in heaven – would she be there already? How long did it take? – looking down upon her and crying to see Ariana in such dangerous and dreadful circumstances.

Heinrich's pale skin was already reddening with sunburn. His complexion wasn't suited to the climate, as his burnt ears had demonstrated all those months ago, and neither was Ariana's, whose colouring was more like English Laurie's than Cretan Calista's.

'Perhaps we should stay here for a few hours,' Calliope suggested. 'I can let Ariana's things dry out and we can rest in the shade while the sun is so strong. Then we'll get going again later in the afternoon.' The little girl was sitting by the stream, dabbling her hands in the water, fascinated by the way it bubbled around her fingers and sparkled like diamonds in the sunlight.

Nodding his agreement, Heinrich bent down to the stream to take another drink. Calliope followed suit and, as she did so, something fell from the pocket of her skirt. Looking down to see what it was, she saw the pack of cards with its distinctive red-and-white pattern.

'Ha, look!' She picked the cards up to show to Heinrich. 'Fancy a game of *biriba*?' she joked, half-heartedly.

He smiled weakly. 'Not right now,' he answered.

'I'll get rid of them,' said Calliope. 'They're just more weight to carry.' She raised her arm above her head, ready to hurl them into the distance. But before she could let them go, Heinrich snatched them out of her hand, then lost his grip so that they fell into the stream.

'What did you do that for?' Calliope protested.

'We mustn't leave any trace of ourselves or the path we have taken,' answered Heinrich. 'Nothing at all that would make it easier for them to find us.' He reached into the water to scoop out the cards. Several had fallen from the box and, wet from the stream, were separating out into layers of card and paper. 'They're ruined now, anyway. We'll bury them somewhere.'

Calliope took the cards from him. She was so fond of this pack; they'd been with her through thick and thin and had helped to pass the time on so many occasions. She stared fondly down at them, regretting her decision to abandon them. After all, they weren't *that* heavy. As she scrutinised them, she noticed something wondrous, and scarcely believable.

'Look, Heinrich,' she said excitedly. 'There's something printed on the inner layers. It looks like maps...' Gently, she prised a couple of the layers apart. 'They are maps – see!'

Forehead creased in puzzlement, Heinrich watched Calliope as she busily wetted and peeled the remainder of the pack, then laid them on a flat stone next to where she'd put Ariana's nappy and cardigan to dry. When the whole pack was complete, he crouched next to her and they moved the pieces around until they had a map of almost the entire island. One of the cards was missing, but they had the whole of the south coast, which was where they were headed to try to meet up with a boat that could evacuate them.

'That's the beach,' cried Calliope, stabbing her finger down. 'Oh my God, I don't believe it. With these maps, we can find our way there!' Her forehead furrowed as she calculated the distance. 'About three more days from here,' she judged. 'Not too far.'

She looked triumphantly at Heinrich. The feeling of elation was like nothing she'd ever experienced before. After so much horror, here was a stroke of good luck. A gust of wind sent the cards flying and immediately the pair of them launched into action, frantically chasing after the dancing cards before they were lost for ever. Seeing them dashing so madly and chaotically about, Ariana began to chuckle, and then to laugh. She laughed and laughed and it was the sweetest, most adorable sound Calliope had ever heard. She lifted the child up and danced a little *pantozali* with her, whirling her back and forth until both she and the little girl could scarcely breathe for laughing.

Eventually, panting for air, Calliope sank to the ground, hugging Ariana to her. Heinrich had gathered up the cards, and he stowed them now in his waistcoat pocket. He collected together all the pieces of paper that had preserved the secret but were no longer needed, and scratched out a hole in the ground with his fingernails, then covered it with a large, heavy rock.

It was stiflingly hot by now and the three of them crept into the shade behind a boulder and dozed for a couple of hours. As the sun began to sink, they woke. Calliope put Ariana's now dry nappy and cardigan on and wrapped her in the sling.

They would walk through the night for as long as they could manage. The discovery of the maps had brought some relief from the tension and given them fresh energy. But Calliope was aware that they were going to need a whole lot more of the same luck, plus some sound judgement, if they were going to survive this journey.

CHAPTER 42

CRETE, JULY 1943

The goat track climbed steeply upwards for a short way and then, as they squeezed through a narrow gap between two huge rocks, emerged into a wide, wild valley. Calliope asked Heinrich to carry Ariana for a while and used the last of the fading light to gather *horta*, edible wild greens, which she stashed in her pockets. The greens should be cooked and then served with olive oil and lemon juice, but they'd have to eat them raw. It would be better than nothing for Heinrich and Calliope – but for Ariana?

Calliope had thought that the little girl would be howling with hunger by now, her poor empty belly shrivelling up as she was given nothing to eat. But instead, after a short crying spurt, Ariana slept. It was as if her body knew that, if she wasn't going to get fed, she should preserve her energy.

As she was picking mountain sorrel, dandelion and mustard leaves, Calliope found a stone with a deep dip in it, as if, while it was being formed, someone had pressed their thumb into it. The dip was not that big; it would probably hold about two thimblefuls of liquid. But it would be good for Ariana to drink water from. Calliope put it in her pocket along with the *horta*.

At about two or three in the morning they were too tired to go any further. They found a place close to a spring to lie down and, after drinking some water, tried to eat the greens. But uncooked they were bitter and astringent, hard to swallow. Ariana put a leaf in her mouth but couldn't chew it and began to choke and retch. Horror-struck, Calliope managed to get the leaf out and to help Ariana wash the taste away with some water from the stone cup.

Starving hungry, and with no other options, there was nothing they could do but try to get some sleep. Heinrich gathered some branches from a hardy juniper tree to cover themselves with. It was all they had to protect them from the biting cold. They slept fitfully, with Ariana between them, sheltering her from the wind with their bodies.

At the first light of dawn, they set off again. Calliope had seen a monastery marked on the map. Any abbot or monk would help a traveller and, as all were known to be supporters of the resistance, they had nothing to fear. The thought of a meal, and perhaps a bed for the night, kept Calliope going through the next long hours. Ariana grizzled for a bit but then fell asleep again. Calliope would have expected the little one to start to seem heavier the longer she carried her, but instead when she'd picked her up that morning she seemed lighter than ever, like a grain of chaff that could blow away on the wind. The prospect that the child could die of starvation loomed up in Calliope's mind and bile rose in her throat. No, no, no, that couldn't happen.

As the sun rose in the sky, they neared the monastery. Calliope almost cried when its solid bulk came into view in the distance, the bell tower topped by a stone cross. She and Heinrich quickened their steps, eager to reach the sanctuary the building promised.

'I hope they have bread,' said Calliope, her mouth watering, 'and perhaps some chicken or lamb. Eggs would be perfect for Ariana. They might give us some hard-boiled to take with us.'

'They probably won't have much,' warned Heinrich. 'You know how the Germans have pillaged people's supplies across the island.'

'I know,' answered Calliope, noticing how he distanced himself from his compatriots by calling them 'the Germans'. 'But I'm enjoying my fantasy meal, so please don't spoil it!'

Heinrich smiled, his sombre mood of moments earlier suddenly transformed. 'So why stop at eggs, bread and meat?' he joked. 'What about honey cake or baklava? Myself, I'd love some salami or sausage – we'd eat it every day at home. Or perhaps *Kartoffelsalat*... umm, delicious.'

'All right, now stop it!' groaned Calliope, holding onto her belly beneath the sling. 'This is torture!'

Laughing, Heinrich took her hand. 'Come on,' he encouraged her. 'The sooner we get there the better.'

At least we're together, thought Calliope, loving the feel of his large, strong hand holding hers. At least I'm not doing this on my own with Ariana.

They were only a hundred metres away from the monastery now. It seemed very quiet. Too quiet. Calliope had expected to see some of the monks moving around the compound, perhaps working in the vegetable garden. But there was no one.

As they got closer, the light-heartedness she and Heinrich had just enjoyed deserted her and a feeling of foreboding descended. There was something wrong here, she was sure. She cast an anxious glance towards Heinrich. His face was expressionless, but his pace momentarily faltered.

Abruptly, he stopped. 'Wait here,' he said, indicating towards a huge cypress tree. 'I'll go ahead and see what's going on.'

Calliope shrank into the shade of the tree, leaning against

the trunk to support her legs, which were shaking and quivering with hunger.

As soon as she saw Heinrich on his return, she knew that something was dreadfully wrong.

'There's no one there,' he said, tersely. 'It's completely abandoned and it looks like there was a struggle. There's blood on the walls and everything's been destroyed – beds, chairs, tables, all chopped into sticks. They've tried to burn it down, but I suppose the stone was too thick to catch.'

Calliope listened to his words open-mouthed with horror. So there would be no sanctuary here, no place of calm contemplation to rest their weary souls and bodies.

'Wh-what happened to them all?' she asked, pointlessly, because Heinrich would only be able to make the same guess as she could.

Heinrich shook his head. 'There might be some things we could use,' he said. 'I should go back and take another look.'

'We'll come with you,' said Calliope firmly. She was not going to be separated from him, even for a few minutes. What if he didn't come back? The thought was unbearable. If there was danger in the monastery, they would face it together.

Inside, it was worse than Calliope had imagined. Rage rose up in her as she saw how the maximum damage had been done to the monks' humble possessions. At first she thought that looking for anything to salvage was pointless. She wondered if it was sacrilege to even consider taking something from this sacred building. But then Ariana gave a pitiful whimper and Calliope steeled herself. She was doing this for the little one, for her precious niece, and she was sure that God would excuse her actions.

Picking through the wreckage, she came across a cup that was only a little chipped, which she pocketed. Then she found a pan, dented but still whole. She stared at it for a few moments. Was it too big, too heavy, too bulky, to carry?

Heinrich appeared by her side. 'I found this,' he said, proudly. He showed her a canvas bag, the type the monks used to carry around their Bibles and prayer books when travelling to distant villages to take services.

Calliope almost cried with happiness. They had left the village with nothing but the clothes they stood up in and now they not only had a couple of invaluable possessions but something to carry them in. She handed Heinrich the cup and the pan and he put them in the bag.

'Any food?' she asked, hopefully.

'I haven't found the larder yet,' he replied. 'Come and look with me.'

It was hard to make their way across the kitchen to the pantry as the floor was littered with broken furniture and smashed crockery. Part of the ceiling had collapsed due to the fire. Calliope wondered momentarily whether the rest of it was about to descend upon their heads, but she pushed the thought firmly out of her mind.

It was clear that the storeroom had been ransacked. Wine bottles lay in a shattered, red-stained heap on the ground. Jars of honey made from the monastery's hives had oozed a sticky amber gel that lay in still pools on the shelves and floor, about which flies swarmed. A sack of potatoes had been emptied and stamped into a greyish mash.

It was a hideous mess and completely wanton. And then Calliope saw them. Two or three potatoes that had rolled into a corner and lay, a little battered and bruised but still whole. Edible. She grabbed them quickly, as if there were someone else there who might get them first. Bitterly, Heinrich put them in the bag. Calliope could sense how he was hating this, how much responsibility he bore for the destruction caused by his compatriots.

As if reading her mind, he kicked out angrily at some shards of pottery. 'Bloody war,' he swore. 'Bloody soldiers.'

'It's not your fault.' Calliope had said this to him before, but she knew he always carried the guilt of what Germany and Germans had done. She moved towards him to comfort him. He allowed her to give him a brief embrace and then pushed her gently away.

'Let's see what else there is to salvage,' he said, through gritted teeth. 'We need anything we can find.'

But there was nothing else usable in the kitchens apart from a knife with a broken blade and a teaspoon, which they took with them before making their way back outside. As they left, Calliope spotted a monk's cassock, thrown to the stone-flagged floor. She shuddered to think of what might have happened to its owner, but they needed the fabric. She picked it up and it joined the stash in the bag.

As well as growing vegetables, most monasteries would keep chickens so that they had a regular supply of eggs.

'I guess the Germans will have taken all the hens,' she said to Heinrich. 'Or slaughtered them. But there might be an egg or two in the coops. It's worth a look.'

The chicken houses were as empty and abandoned as the rest of the buildings. Calliope searched and searched among the straw in the nesting boxes but found nothing.

'We should get going.' Heinrich looked anxiously around him. 'It's not safe to stay here long.'

They walked for hours, sometimes climbing steeply, sometimes scrambling over limestone rocks and scree. Ariana was silent. She drank water greedily whenever Calliope offered it, but other than that she was almost motionless. Calliope wished she would cry and scream. Crying and screaming was what healthy babies did when their needs were not met. And Calliope was not meeting Ariana's needs. Not in the slightest. But the little girl just looked around her impassively with her chocolate eyes.

When they stopped for the day, Calliope insisted that they

light a fire to cook the potatoes. She used a piece of glass she'd taken from the ruins to get the grass and twigs she'd gathered to burst into flame. When the potatoes were done, she wrapped two in some leaves to keep until the next day and then chopped the third one in half. She smashed one of the halves into a mush for Ariana. At first the little girl turned her head away, but eventually Calliope managed to get her to eat a little. Was it enough? Calliope hardly thought so. When it was clear she wouldn't take any more, Calliope and Heinrich divided the remainder between them. Calliope tried to savour each tiny mouthful but she couldn't. Her starving body compelled her to eat her miserable portion in a split second.

When she lay down to sleep, she felt every bone of her body on the hard ground.

She was woken by Ariana whining and moaning. Immediately alert, Calliope scooped the child up and cradled her. She was burning up with fever, her forehead hot, her beautiful eyes glassy, her skin sweaty.

'Heinrich!' Calliope shouted. 'Ariana's sick. Oh my God, she's really sick.'

Heinrich jerked awake and leant over to the little one. He rested the back of his hand against a bright-red cheek. Calliope stared at him, willing him to say that she was overreacting, that it was nothing, that Ariana was fine. But his expression was grim, his mouth pinched into a tight line.

'I'll get water,' he said. Previously, he'd torn the cassock into strips to use as nappies and whatever else they might need. He took a handful of fabric to the stream to wet it and then came back and handed it to Calliope. Carefully, she wiped the child's forehead and cheeks, praying that the cool, refreshing spring water would bring her temperature down.

For a short while, it did. But before they had walked much more than a mile, Calliope could feel Ariana's skin against hers, so hot it was almost scalding.

No, no, no, she repeated to herself, over and over again. She had lost her twin sister, her parents and grandparents... Ariana was the only family left to her. She could not lose her, too.

Heinrich took a turn carrying Ariana to give Calliope's shoulders a break. It almost made Calliope cry to see how gently and tenderly he cradled her small body and kissed her curly head.

'Sometimes I think this island is nothing but hills and rocks,' he groaned as he helped Calliope over a narrow ledge with a precipitous drop into a wide river gorge below.

'It is,' she agreed, once she'd reached safety on the other side. She remembered the SBS men saying the same thing. 'But until the war, I always thought it was the best rock in the world.' She glanced down at Ariana, whose tiny hands were tightly clenched against her chest. 'Now I'm not so sure.'

Eventually, they began to descend towards the south coast and could even see, far in the distance, the vast expanse of the Libyan Sea glimmering under the sun. They found a grove of cherry trees and feasted on the fruit until Calliope said they must stop or they'd get terrible tummy ache. Heinrich used his service revolver to shoot a wild rabbit and, even though they were closer to civilisation than they had been when they'd cooked the potatoes, they abandoned all caution and lit a fire. Ariana's fever still raged, she had no appetite for the little food they had, and Calliope could hardly bear to look at the tiny child's flushed and shiny face.

'I think it's pneumonia,' she whispered, as if scared to give full voice to her fears.

Heinrich grimaced. He opened his mouth to speak but shut it again without saying anything. There were no words. Ariana was desperately ill and there was nothing they could do about it.

On the fourth day, they were not far from the coast when the storm came. Calliope saw the dark clouds gathering and buffeting above them. She clenched her fists and hoped that the north-easterly wind would blow the storm past them. But her hopes were in vain. The clouds opened and the rain came down in sheets. The little group of three were caught in the open, nowhere near any kind of shelter. By the time they reached an olive grove where the tree canopy provided some protection, they were soaked through.

Ariana mewled and moaned, too weak to make a baby's usual lusty cries. Calliope undressed her and wrapped her as best she could in the strips of fabric from the monk's cassock, but the child shivered and trembled even while the fever rose. As night fell, she got worse and worse. Every laboured breath rasped and her face was no longer red but deathly pale. Calliope sobbed quietly as she cradled Ariana in her arms. Pneumonia was a surefire child killer.

Looking up at the overcast sky, Calliope saw a lone vulture soaring on a thermal high above, searching for the scent of carrion. A terrible dread settled in her stomach and a tight band of fear tightened round her chest. The bird was waiting. Waiting for little Ariana to die.

Heinrich went to look for food and scout out the beach. Any British trying to evacuate usually had to hole up in caves while awaiting a boat, and he hoped he might find news of an imminent arrival. While he was gone, Calliope gave in to the tears that had been pricking behind her eyes for hours now. A motionless, burning Ariana clutched to her chest, she wept and sobbed until she felt she had cried all the tears in the world.

She could hardly believe it when Heinrich returned with good news.

'It's tonight. A caique will come, take you to a ship. All being well, you'll be in Egypt by daybreak.'

It took a moment for Heinrich's words to sink in.

'That's... wonderful. But wait – what do you mean *you*? Us, surely?'

Heinrich made a dismissive gesture with his head. 'If there's room.'

Normally Calliope would have protested, insisted that she wouldn't go anywhere without Heinrich. But she had to put Ariana first. Ariana needed to get off the island and to somewhere she could receive medical care as soon as possible. Calliope refused to contemplate that the infant might not last that long.

That night, under the feeble light of a crescent moon, they waited on the beach. They could already hear the splashing of the oars signifying the arrival of the boat that would take them out to the larger ship when the shooting started.

Gunfire, coming from behind them. A hail of bullets ringing around their ears. The realisation of imminent death, just when they had thought they were safe.

CHAPTER 43

CRETE, JULY 1943

Heinrich flung himself onto the pebbles, pulled out his revolver, took aim and fired. He was quite composed. Calliope, shaking with terror, wondered how he could face his death so calmly.

'Get to the boat,' Heinrich hissed at her. 'Stay low.' And then, as she hesitated, 'Now, Calliope!'

Calliope ran, slipping and sliding over the stones. She felt as if she were in a dream where, however hard she tried, she could not speed up and was not getting anywhere. The hunger that had gnawed at her stomach for the entire journey had been dispelled in an instant but, though the pain had gone, the weakness of the near-starvation meant she could barely summon the energy to move. She had to though, for Ariana.

She reached the water's edge and sloshed through the shallows until it was up to her knees. The boat was just ahead and the oarsman leant forward to grab her as soon as she was near enough. A bullet whistled past her ear, close enough for her to smell its acrid, burning odour. A flashback took her to the village, its charred remains, the burnt bodies littering the streets. She choked, gasped for air, tried feebly to climb aboard.

The oarsman helped her and, as soon as she was over the

side, began to row as if his life depended on it. Which it did, thought Calliope, as she crouched down, arms tightly wrapped round Ariana's limp and floppy little body.

'What's a baby doing here?' asked the rower. He was Cretan, a resistance member doing his bit.

'I can't explain,' answered Calliope. Where was Heinrich? 'But you need to wait for my... er, my colleague. Another fighter for the cause.'

The oarsman shook his head. 'No can do, lady,' he replied. 'We've got to get out of here.'

Calliope's head sank until her forehead rested on Ariana's damp curls. The child was cold, her skin clammy and deathly pale. Was that a good thing? Had the fever passed? Or was she about to die?

'Is there a doctor on the ship?' she asked. Crazy question. Of course there wouldn't be.

The oarsman laughed. 'No idea,' he said. 'I'm just here to get people out there. Though I must say, it's usually British men, not Greek mothers and babies.'

They reached the ship where it lay out in the bay, gently swaying on the current. Awkwardly, and with great difficulty, Calliope hauled herself and Ariana up the ladder. Once she was aboard, she looked back to the shore. It was too dark to see clearly, but the gunfire had stopped some minutes previously. That could mean that Heinrich had seen off the enemy. Or it could mean that he had been killed.

The captain approached over the deck. 'Welcome aboard,' he said, in the clipped English tones Calliope had become accustomed to over the months spent with Laurie and his comrades. 'We'll be in Egypt in no time.' He smiled, and then seemed to register Ariana. 'Oh! You have a, er, a baby. Right. I see.' Having initially given the appearance of someone whom nothing could fluster, he now looked distinctly nonplussed.

'She's sick,' blurted out Calliope. 'She has a fever and she's dehydrated. She's barely eaten in days. She needs milk. And a doctor. Is there a doctor on the ship? Will there be a doctor, in Egypt?'

'Yes, of course,' answered the captain, registering the panic in Calliope's voice. 'I mean, no, no doctor on board, but when we land...' He coughed to clear his throat. 'Um, I'll radio through when we get a bit closer.'

'But we can't leave yet,' Calliope wailed desperately, knowing there was no time to lose to get Ariana the medical care she needed, but also unable to contemplate leaving Heinrich. 'Hein— my colleague – he's still back there, on the beach.' She avoided saying his obviously German name. Would the captain believe he was truly a deserter? Would he think it was a ruse, that they were playing some espionage game here? Desperate confusion and despair swept over Calliope. She didn't know what to do, what to say. She should be happy she'd reached the boat, but it wasn't that simple.

'I can't wait.' The captain stared into the distance as if he didn't want to see Calliope's pain. 'It's too dangerous. We've got to get into safer waters as soon as possible.'

'Please,' begged Calliope, 'please, we must wait for him. He's...' She couldn't finish the sentence, did not have the words in English, or in any language, to explain what Heinrich had come to mean to her.

'Sorry.' The captain turned and left Calliope on the foredeck as he returned to the bridge.

Calliope looked back at her island as it became nothing but a dark outline and then disappeared. She'd probably never see it again. Ariana was dying and everyone else was gone, including Heinrich.

There was nothing to ever go back for.

CHAPTER 44

CRETE, 2005

An audible silence greeted the end of Callie's story. Each member of the assembled group was stunned, breathless, as if unable to digest the epic tale of hardship, survival, suffering and escape that they had heard. There was a long pause before anyone spoke.

'So,' ventured Ella, her voice trembling. 'Heinrich – did he make the boat?'

Her words opened up a huge chasm.

'Yes,' said Callie. 'By some miracle, he swam out and made the boat. In Egypt, he joined the SOE, and undertook several missions with them before the war ended. I was shipped to England as soon as the Mediterranean was safe enough, and eventually he joined me there. He changed his name from Heinrich Schmidt to Harry Smith, became a naturalised British citizen and that was that. He never mentioned being German to anyone.'

Calista gasped. 'I never could have imagined,' she breathed. 'Even when you told me yesterday that he deserted, I didn't imagine that you two stayed together, got married...'

Ella was sitting motionless in her chair, a stunned expression on her face. 'So Grandpa Harry – his name was actually Heinrich? And he was *German*? That's crazy. I never knew. How did I never know?'

Callie held her hands up in a gesture of apology and regret. 'I'm sorry,' she whispered. 'We thought it was for the best. Germans weren't popular in England after the war. Heinrich is Henry in English, and the diminutive of Henry is Harry. That's the name Heinrich chose to go by.'

There was silence for a moment as everyone digested the news.

'And Ariana – she must have... she—' Ella stopped, shook her head, began anew. 'Did she die after all? Despite you getting to Egypt? She must have done, because...'

Calista began to silently weep. A dread weight pressed down in Callie's stomach. She didn't know how to answer the question. Didn't want to answer the question. Dealing with Harry/Heinrich had been the easy bit compared to what was coming.

Sophia, who was sitting next to her mother, gently took her hands and held them, whispering soothingly in her ear. Eventually she looked round to Callie, Ella and George, who still sat, motionless, as if frozen in place, despite the blistering heat.

'I think we should call it a day,' she said, softly. 'Mum's tired. She... well, anything takes it out of her these days. I'm sure you understand.'

As George translated, Ella jumped up so quickly she almost flew out of her chair. 'Of course,' she replied, hastily. 'It's been a lot to take in. We'll be off. Won't we, Gran?' She addressed her final comment directly to Callie, who nodded wearily in response.

Once their farewells were said, Callie and Ella made their way to the car. It was stiflingly hot inside.

'The air con will kick in as soon as we get going,' said Ella, confidently and with a cheerfulness that was clearly forced. 'Let's head straight down to the beach, find some loungers. We should be there by' – she flicked her eyes towards the dashboard clock – 'four thirty-ish. The perfect time for a swim, if you ask me.' She pressed a button to turn the radio on and fiddled with the tuning button until Greek music drifted out to fill the small, confined space inside the car.

The drive to the coast seemed to go quickly, but perhaps that was because Callie wanted it to last for ever. Those assembled in the garden thought they had heard it all, but they hadn't.

Once they'd parked up, Ella and Callie trudged to the beach, the sky above a thick blanket that pressed down on them with unrelenting heat. Ella found two empty loungers in the first row to the sea, made sure they were positioned perfectly to benefit from the shade of the parasol. Inviting Callie to sit down on one, she plumped down on the other. She lay back and put her hands behind her head. After a moment, she sat back up, swung her legs over the side of the sunbed and leant forward towards her grandmother.

'That was really intense,' she said. 'How are you feeling? It – I can't believe that story has been inside you all this time, and you've never spoken of it to anyone. Such a life-changing experience... And as for my grandad. Honestly, Gran, why did you never tell me?'

Ignoring what Ella had asked, Callie fiddled with the strap of her sandal. She should take them off, feel the sand between her toes. It might ground her, bring her back down to earth, make everything seem real again and get rid of the hazy, dizzy feeling that wouldn't leave her. But she didn't. She just sat, looking down with unseeing eyes.

'Ella,' she burst out suddenly. 'There's more.' She met Ella's eyes with an agonised gaze. 'There's a question that none of you asked so I didn't answer it. But I have to address it now. You need to know.'

Ella stared at her grandmother, her face pale beneath the tan she had acquired over their time in Crete.

'The thing is that...' Callie's words petered out. She couldn't do it. Couldn't say it.

'What?' Ella interjected impatiently.

Callie looked out to sea, at the expanse of turquoise water stretching to an endless horizon. She'd thought about it before and perhaps she should simply do it. Wade out, through the shallows and into the deep, and then swim and swim and never come back. That would be easier than what she had to do now. She thought back to her young self, the numerous perilous journeys she had made criss-crossing the mountains, the armed patrols, bullets and bombs she had faced without flinching. And now a few words threatened to overpower her.

'Gran, Ariana dying, you know it wasn't your fault, don't you?' Ella spoke softly, reaching out her hand to lay it upon Callie's. Her grandmother let it lie there, though she wanted to snatch it away. They had all assumed that Ariana hadn't made it. When Callie told the truth, the full truth, Ella wouldn't want to know her, let alone touch her.

'Ariana didn't die.' The words blurted out, no longer in Callie's control. 'She survived. Somehow, I don't know how, she got through the journey and, as soon as we landed in Egypt, she was rushed to hospital. It was touch and go for a while but, with milk and good food and the doctor's ministrations, she pulled through. It was a miracle. I thought that I must have pleased God in some way for Him to be so generous in saving her. I became much more religious after that. Which, after all, is what led us to where we are today. If George hadn't seen me at church, none of this would have happened.' Callie fiddled with her wedding ring, turning it round and round. The heat had swollen her fingers and it didn't move as easily as usual. Perhaps it was an omen.

'So – she died at another time?' suggested Ella, trying to fill in the gaps. 'Not during your flight or on the voyage, but later on in Egypt, or...'

Callie's heart skipped several beats. Her breathing was fast and shallow. *You can't stop now*, her inner voice hissed at her.

'Ariana did die at a different time,' she agreed. 'But not until much, much later.' Callie rubbed her hands on her knees. 'The thing is, Ella, that Louise was your mother, obviously. But Louise was not my child. Louise was the English name that Laurie gave to Ariana for her second name. When we left Crete, we used that name for her. Just as Heinrich wanted to be Harry to fit in, we felt Louise would help the child to fit in. Ariana is your mother.'

Ella's hand shot involuntarily up to her mouth as she stifled a gasp of alarm, her eyes wide, her face blanched even paler. 'I don't understand. I don't get it. What do you mean? All this time... all my life... I've thought that you were my grandparents. But you weren't. Aren't. I...' Her voice tailed off, lost in her disbelief and stupefaction. She stood up, sat back down again, stood up again, shaking her head, her eyes moist, sweat beading on her forehead.

'I don't understand,' she repeated, over and over again. 'Why did you never tell my mum the truth? Or me, for that matter?'

Callie hung her head in shame, avoiding meeting Ella's gaze. 'I... we, Heinrich, sorry, Harry and I, we thought it was for the best. That she was so young she'd forget about Calista and accept us as her parents, that she'd be happier not knowing about the tragedy that took her mother and father away from her, not knowing that she was an orphan.'

Ella stared at her grandmother who she'd just discovered was in fact her great-aunt as if she'd never seen her before in her life. Callie had expected to be crying by now but found herself surprisingly dry-eyed. It was as if all the tears had been spent and in their place was a void, a nothingness. A chasm of wrong decisions and choices as deep as Crete's river gorges that she couldn't put right. She had no further explanation to offer Ella. There were no words that could take away the deception Callie had practised.

'I'm going for a swim,' Ella said, brusquely.

As Callie watched her stride down to the water's edge she felt more exhausted and ashamed than ever in her life before. It was too much for a person to discover, out of the blue. Ella had come on this trip to help her grandmother, not to find out that everything she thought she knew about herself wasn't true. The guilt that washed over Callie like a tsunami threatened to drown her.

Would Ella ever get over the shock? Would she ever forgive Callie? Callie simply did not know.

CHAPTER 45

CRETE, 2005

They drove back to the B&B in silence, Ella's lips narrowed to a thin line, her eyes focused solely on the road. She escorted Callie to her room and then turned away. 'I need to get some fresh air,' she said, addressing the wall. 'Don't come after me. I'll be back later.'

It was past midnight when Ella returned. Callie had been lying on her bed in her room in the dark, feeling the heat of the day subside as night fell. She should telephone Sophia and tell her that she and Ella wouldn't be coming to the village next day, couldn't come. If they did, Callie would have to explain her terrible secret to Calista and, in her frail state, this knowledge might hasten her end. Eventually it was too late to call anyway.

A soft knock at the door alerted her to Ella's return. She came to Callie's bedside and sat down in the armchair.

'I'm trying to understand why you did it, and how you did it,' she said. 'You explained about not wanting Mum to be an orphan – or not to know she was an orphan. I get that. But did no one ever ask for her birth certificate or challenge you about whose child she was?'

Callie snorted derisively. 'It was a world war, Ella. We

escaped Crete as refugees, with nothing but the clothes we stood up in. And in fact, in Heinrich's case, not even that. He dumped all of his possessions, clothes, gun, everything, when he swam to the boat. Lots of people didn't have papers or passports.'

Ella shook her head. 'I'm trying to imagine Grandpa Harry hauling himself on board wearing his birthday suit.' She gave a wavering half-smile at the thought. Callie's heart leapt. Was she beginning to forgive? To accept? It was too quick, she knew, but the idea of Ella hating her for the rest of her life would kill her more quickly than any disease of old age that could possibly befall her.

'If Ariana – Louise – hadn't been so sick I would have laughed at the sight,' agreed Callie. 'But I think her remarkable survival was a catalyst for our decision not to tell anyone the truth about you or him. We had been through so much and we both felt that the only way that we would be able to move forward with our lives, to build new lives – because that is what we had to do – was to start completely afresh, to forget the past entirely, to reinvent ourselves.'

Ella exhaled loudly. She ran her hands through her hair, still matted with salt, leaving it sticking out at odd angles. 'I'm wondering what Mum would have thought if she'd known who she really was,' she murmured. She looked confused and bewildered, like a little girl unable to comprehend the world, and Callie's heart turned over for her.

'We honestly thought it was for the best,' Callie reiterated, whether to persuade herself or Ella she wasn't sure. 'We truly did.' She stared into the distance, as if she could see through the wall and back to that impenetrable past and understand better for herself why she and Heinrich had made the decision. 'Of course, if we had known that my sister was alive – well, then, everything would have been different.'

A long pause greeted her words.

'When are you going to tell my— Calista?' asked Ella, falteringly. 'And how?'

'I don't know,' answered Callie, truthfully. It had felt huge enough to tell Ella and, though she had known that was only the first step, at that moment taking the second seemed impossible. Knowing she had inadvertently stolen the years Calista could have had with her child was enough to cleave her heart in two.

'You should probably do it sooner rather than later,' said Ella. She opened her mouth to say something else, but shut it again. Callie knew what was on the tip of her tongue. That Calista didn't have that long. That Callie must do it before Calista died.

'Tomorrow?' suggested Ella. 'There's no time like the present.' She twiddled with an earring, a silver key, turning it round, righting its position, then looked at her watch. 'Well, today actually, as it's gone midnight.'

Callie inhaled deeply, let the breath go in a long sigh. 'All right,' she said. So they would be going to the village that day after all.

She thought she would not sleep that night, with so much on her mind, and with her routine so disrupted by going to bed so late. But in the end she slept soundly and didn't wake until ten. Ella had saved her some breakfast, but she could hardly eat or drink. Her stomach roiled and contracted in fear of what was to come.

On the drive to the village, three large birds soared overhead.

'Look!' Ella pointed through the car window. 'What are they? Eagles or something?'

Callie shook her head. 'No,' she replied. 'They're vultures. There must be a dead animal, a sheep or a goat. Perhaps a cow. They'll make quick work of it...'

'Eeeuch,' squealed Ella. 'Nasty.'

'Well, it might seem so.' Callie closed her eyes momentarily to block out the vision of the vulture that had wheeled above their open-air camp as little Ariana had been fighting for life. That bird had been robbed of its prey. That was the main thing, wasn't it, that she'd saved Ariana from certain death? Not that she'd never told her or her daughter the truth about her real parents. 'But actually vultures play a vital role, cleaning up carcasses and stopping the spread of disease.' When she was a child she had once found a goat's skeleton, and marvelled at how the vultures had stripped the bones bare, leaving the wind and rain and time to do the rest.

'They just look so sinister,' replied Ella. 'And these ones are big.'

Callie nodded in agreement but didn't say anything further. They would be in the village soon. In fact, here they were, at the parking place. Ella pulled over, stopped the car. Callie's legs felt as if they weighed a hundred tons as she clambered out. They began the steep uphill climb.

'I think I should talk to Calista alone,' said Callie. 'While I'm doing that, you can tell Sophia and George.'

'OK.' Ella readjusted her huge sunglasses. 'I mean, I'm not exactly sure how I'm going to bring the subject up...'

'They'll want to know why I need time with Calista,' responded Callie, unequivocally. 'All you need to do is explain the reason.' She deliberately made it sound simple, because she wanted to believe that it was.

Entering the house as George opened the door, they heard music playing softly from the kitchen. Sophia was kneading dough to make bread while Calista dozed in a chair in the corner. After they'd drunk a cool glass of lemonade, Callie asked if she and Calista could go somewhere private. Sophia helped her mother to a room Callie had not been in before and which had not existed in the house she grew up in. Like the rest of the property, it was elegantly done up in a way that seamlessly blended the old and the new, complementing the traditional style of the architecture. It reminded Callie of the B&B; all muted colours and natural materials, spacious and restful.

A good room in which to blow someone's life apart? As good as any, she supposed.

Sitting next to each other on a small sofa, Callie took her sister's hands in hers. The only way to do this was to speak from the heart and hope Calista would understand. After discussing a few trivialities – the weather, a forthcoming festival in a neighbouring village, a litter of puppies born to a friend's dog – Callie knew she needed to get started.

'I have to tell you something,' she told her sister. 'It's – I'm not – it might be hard for you to hear,' she continued, falteringly.

Calista nodded. Her skin was paper thin and soft, her palms cool. Callie gripped them tighter.

'It's about Ariana,' Callie continued, 'and Ella.'

Calista raised her filmy eyes to Callie. 'I think I know already,' she said. She spoke so quietly that Callie had to strain to hear. 'I think I guessed. Something about the girl... she reminds me more of me than of you.'

Callie's blood chilled in her veins. How could Calista know? It was impossible. They were identical twins; why would any grandchild look more like one than the other? But then she met Calista's gaze and she understood that Calista was correct, had guessed correctly.

'Ella is my granddaughter, isn't she?' Calista paused, biting her lip in that gesture she'd had since childhood. 'You rescued Ariana, she survived, and you raised her as your own.'

Callie tasted salt in her mouth and realised that she was crying, tears pouring down her cheeks. Unable to speak, she merely nodded.

'I knew it from the moment I laid eyes on her,' Calista went on. 'She has something of Laurie about her, don't you think?' She took a deep breath before continuing. 'I want you to know that I understand. That I would have done the same. That it's what I would have wanted. You saved my Ariana's life, and then you gave her a good life in England. You thought I was dead and so you were right to claim to be her mother, and Heinrich her father – much better that than the poor mite believe herself to be an orphan.'

Gulping back sobs, Callie tried to respond. 'But – I mean – you aren't angry with me? You don't – you don't hate me?' she stuttered, finding it hard to formulate the words.

Calista, clearly exhausted from the intensity of the discussion and the emotion, shook her head. 'Of course not. You're my sister, my identical twin. I've felt as if a part of my soul has been missing for decades. And now here you are. I could never hate you.' With these words, Calista also began to cry. The two sisters held each other and cried and wept and sobbed for many minutes.

It was some time before Callie was able to speak. 'Thank you,' she gasped eventually, breathless from weeping. 'Thank you for forgiving me.'

Calista laid her tired head back on the sofa cushions. 'Nothing to forgive,' she murmured. 'Nothing at all.'

CHAPTER 46

LONDON, 2005

'Grandma, what *is* all of this?' Ella had her head in one of the huge wardrobes in Callie's bedroom. A couple of weeks after the revelations, during which Callie and Calista had spent every moment possible together, she and Ella had returned to London for a brief visit. The intention was for Callie to tie up some of her affairs and for them both to collect winter clothes and coats. Ella had decided to postpone her world tour indefinitely and they were going to go back to Crete together and stay until— Well, no one wanted to put into words until what, but they all knew that Calista's cancer was advanced and incurable.

Ella hauled a plastic storage box out of the wardrobe, and then another. Behind these was a pile of shoeboxes of various shapes and sizes.

'Oh, yes.' Callie entered the room and stood by the door, looking sheepish and shamefaced. 'They're just—'

Frowning, Ella pulled an envelope from one of the boxes. The address was written in Greek and, although she'd started to learn the language, she had a long way to go, and reading was especially difficult. 'Who's it to?' she asked. 'Who are they all to?' She gestured towards the stack she'd built on the bedroom carpet. 'There's no stamp or postmark on any of them – so they've never been sent?'

She stared at the envelope in her hand and then at Callie.

Callie walked across the room and sank down on the bed. She had always been so hale and hearty, but these last few months had taken it out of her; all the emotion, the pressure of trying to make up for the lost years, the regrets... It hadn't been easy.

'In my head and my heart, I never really came to terms with Calista's death,' she explained. She spread her veiny hands out on her knees, fingers splayed, and stared at them. 'So I wrote to her, every week for over sixty years. I told her all about Louise and then all about both of you and then, once Louise was gone, just about you. I told her all the things I thought a mother would want to know about her child and grandchild, and probably a lot more besides, that she would have had no interest in.'

Ella's eyes watered as she regarded the person she had always known as her grandmother. 'Oh gosh,' she breathed, faintly. She pulled another box out of the wardrobe. 'So it's all here. Our entire history.'

Callie nodded. 'I'm sure most of what I wrote is deathly dull. And there are so many of them! In the other wardrobe, under the bed... I should get rid of them all, now we're clearing up.'

'No!' Ella's cry was loud in the small room. 'No, this is amazing. We can take them to Crete and read them to Calista... you or George can. I want to know all this stuff too, but I think it'll be a long while before I get anywhere near being good enough at Greek to read it myself.'

Despite everything, Callie smiled. 'Good luck with getting all of these onto the plane! You'll have to charter a cargo flight,' she replied, dryly.

Ella laughed. 'There must be over three thousand letters here,' she said, doing a quick bit of mental arithmetic. 'So yes, perhaps you're right about taking them with us. But I could parcel them up in shipping boxes and send them by sea. People do that all the time with their things when they're moving countries or continents.'

Callie felt newly exhausted at the thought. 'As you please, my dear,' she answered. 'As you please.'

A month later, in the full heat of summer, Callie stood in the doorway of the little house she'd rented for her and Ella back in the village that had been her childhood home. The entire family had agreed that Callie had done what anybody in her position would have: rescued the baby and taken her to safety. Tonight, Sophia was hosting a celebratory feast for their homecoming. Stelios, now in his seventies, would be there, and Eliana, too. They, Calista and Callie were the only ones still left who remembered the war years, who had lived through that time of brutality and fear and death. Because of Calista's condition, it had been decided not to tell anyone outside the family the truth about Ariana/Louise or Ella.

Callie was weary. Her bones ached, her back was hunched, her knees sore. She was constantly short of breath. She could hardly believe that she was the same person who had trekked back and forth across the mountains on dangerous and daring expeditions to aid the resistance. Ella had been teaching her to be proud of her past and not to dwell on the things that had gone wrong, the choices she wished she had made differently. Even now, her great-niece was sitting with her twin sister and listening as George read from the archive of letters that Callie would have binned if it had been up to her.

There were some things Callie would never share, though. Her infatuation with Laurie, her heartbreak when he had chosen Calista over her. She could smile wryly to herself about this now, as she recalled the pain she had felt at being overlooked. But she had been young, and young people feel things so much more deeply than the old.

Her regret that she and Heinrich had never had children of their own. Callie had been pregnant several times, but each time she had lost the baby. She had read recently about pregnancy lupus and recognised many of the symptoms. The Stuart Queen Anne was believed to have had the condition, resulting in her seventeen pregnancies leading to only five live births, and those babies dying in early childhood. Medical progress had come too late for Queen Anne – and Callie.

But it wasn't just her crush on Laurie and her thwarted wish to have a child of her own that still dogged her, even now, after so many years, and after this incredible reunion with her twin sister.

There was something else. Something that she had spent the last six decades trying to obliterate from her memory, but which must have been ever-present because why else would she have written all those letters?

Callie retreated back into the simple house, with its pretty blue shutters and doors and garden gate, and sank down onto the cushioned bench in the tiny living room. Elbows on the table, she put her head in her hands and closed her eyes, trying to banish the self-recriminations that still plagued her. When Ella asked her why she looked so sad or what was making her heart so heavy, it was easy to lie and say that it was because she had only just been reunited with her long-lost sister but would soon lose her. And of course that was a cause of enormous, ineffable sorrow. But it wasn't the only cause.

Callie's mind went back, as it had so often before, to that terrible day in 1943 when she had arrived in this very village to find it ablaze, a slaughterhouse of death and destruction. She had checked her sister's pulse and found nothing. And then, a little later, like a miracle Ariana had crawled out from beneath her mother's body and, dumbfounded and utterly traumatised, stared pitifully around her. Callie's one instinct had been to save the child, to get her away from the carnage. Of all the inhabitants of the village, Ariana alone had the chance to live, with Callie's help.

Callie had wanted to take Calista's body with her, away from the Nazis and the fires, to hug her and kiss her one last time and give her a decent burial. But there was no way she could carry both Calista and Ariana. So she had snatched Ariana into her arms and left. She and Heinrich and the child had journeyed on and on until they reached the coast and the possibility of freedom. Had somehow, by God's grace, managed to save the child not only from the horror of the village's destruction but also from all the horrors that confronted them during their flight.

She had told her sister and Ella everything. Almost everything.

Everything except one last thing, the thing that she had spent over six decades pushing to the back of her mind, trying to ignore because she did not want it to be true. The secret she would take to her grave.

In the split second in which she had made the decision that she had to leave her sister and take Ariana, on the periphery of her vision she had seen something, something she had had to ignore because there was nothing she could do about it. It had not even really been a dilemma, because a dilemma indicates that there is a choice and in this instance there had not been one, or not a realistic one anyway.

As all this ran through her mind in the way that it had many, many times before, Callie recognised what she was doing. Trying yet again to justify something to herself that had no justification. She breathed deeply, in and out, attempting to slow her heart rate. She could hardly allow the thought to properly articulate in her mind.

At that moment, Ella rushed in.

'Gran!' She had opted not to change what she had always called Callie, saying that it felt too complicated. 'You need to come quickly. Right away. It's Calista. She's—' Her voice broke, but she didn't need to say more.

Callie hauled herself to her feet as quickly as she could, and allowed Ella to help her over the threshold of the tiny cottage and down the steep steps to the street. Hastening over the cobbles, the pair were silent, focusing on their own thoughts.

In the family house, Calista lay in her bed. The room was cool and dark, and a gentle breeze from a fan ruffled the fine net curtains. Sophia, George, and other hastily summoned relatives were gathered around, silent, their heads bowed.

At Callie and Ella's arrival, more chairs were brought and space made for them. A short time afterwards, Calista took her last breath.

EPILOGUE

After her sister's funeral, Callie sat in the church for hours, alone. She could have prayed for her own forgiveness, but she didn't feel she deserved it. Her thoughts returned to where they had been when Ella had come rushing in to call her to Calista's bedside. Would God understand that she had done what she thought was right at the time? Was that enough? She wished she could leave her pain here in the church, which had seen so many births, deaths, christenings, weddings, funerals, commemorations and celebrations and surely understood the frailties and inadequacies of the human soul. She heaved herself up from the high-backed chair and slowly made her way to the wake, which was being held at the house.

Next morning, she got up very early, just as dawn was breaking in the east. She put on her sturdiest shoes, and took an umbrella she'd found in the house to use as a walking stick. She had a small rucksack that Ella had bought her a few years ago, saying that it would be better for her back than carrying a handbag. Stowing away a couple of bottles of water and some bananas, Callie regretted the absence of Bourbon creams. Stupidly, she'd forgotten to pack any on this return visit, and there'd been none available at the airport. Just giant Toblerones, expensive sandwiches, and more brands and makes of perfume than Callie could even imagine existing. She'd seen the prices, and the extensive and unnecessary amount of choice, and commented to Ella that she'd never seen the like, but Ella had merely laughed and told Callie she needed to keep up with the times. But Callie felt too old to keep up with anything these days.

She let herself out of the house. Already, her legs felt heavy and unwieldy, her hips stiff and awkward. Her head throbbed. Resolutely, ignoring her many aches and pains, Callie placed her sunhat upon her head and set off.

She'd worried whether she would remember the way, but it was as if her feet had never forgotten. They led her, step by step, along a route she had once known so well and trod so often. Past the bakery and over the stone bridge. Past the vegetable garden and the old sheepfold, now the plot of a spacious detached villa. Past the spot on the riverbank that once resounded to the thwacks of laundry against the stones. Today, it was deserted in the early morning, but in any case the women had washing machines nowadays and did not need to spend hours a week on such back-breaking work.

It was September but still warm. On the olive trees, the fruit ripened under the autumn sun, and the bramble bushes hung heavy with luscious blackberries. Callie plucked a few, savouring the earthy sweetness. When they were children, she and Calista would have been out with their tin pails, picking as much of this free bounty as they could, returning home with mouths, tongues and chins stained purple. Callie had a sudden, sharp yearning for that child she had once been, and was no more. She wished she could step back in time and start her life again, and do it differently, and better.

Plodding on, she tried to regain the rhythm she had as a young woman, the swinging gait that helped her to cover huge distances using minimal energy. But she was old now and everything hurt; her feet, her legs, her back and shoulders. Her heart.

She sat down to rest under a spreading oak tree where the upturned soil indicated the recent presence of wild boar. After eating one of the bananas, in the shade and stillness, she began to feel drowsy, her eyes closing. She was so tired. How she longed to lie down and sleep. But not yet. She needed to reach her destination.

Hauling herself to her feet, Callie got back on the path, the tap-tapping of the walking stick umbrella and the thrumming of the cicadas the only audible sounds. She had been walking for two hours and she still had a long way to go. As the sun rose higher, so the route became more exposed. Looking up into the arcing blue of the sky, Callie recalled when it had been thick with enemy aircraft, bombers and fighters, and then with the planes and gliders that had brought the *Fallschirmjäger* in their thousands, those terrifying Sky People whose arrival had been the harbinger of doom for the island, death dropping down all around them. She could almost hear, in the still air, the sound of George's gurgling laugh turned to silent terror before he was shot.

Goosebumps rose on her arms and Callie suppressed a shudder before determinedly pressing on. It crossed her mind that Ella would be wondering where she was, but there was nothing she could do about it. Perhaps she should have left a note. But what would she have said?

It wasn't an epic journey, rather one she would have found normal and commonplace back in the day. A long walk but not particularly arduous or hazardous. But that was when she was in her twenties, not her eighties. The mule tracks had faded to goat paths and now were not even that; no trodden grass or trampled undergrowth to guide the way, just the sun and her instinct, dormant for so long but now awakened.

Hours later, she arrived. As the ancient stone walls of the

mitato hove into view, Callie paused to take a breath. Surrounded by weeds and undergrowth, the tiny hut itself still stood strong. In the sheepfold, rabbit droppings replaced those of sheep and goats, and to the side of the hut the spring bubbled with as much calm vigour as it ever had.

Callie perched on the low sheepfold wall, where once she and Heinrich had sat, falling in love and contemplating a future that was not guaranteed for either of them. Her worries about how, if she and Heinrich survived, they would be able to be together after the war had been unfounded. Once he'd fought for the British and arrived in England if not a war hero, at least with a very respectable backstory of bravery and valour for king and country, no one had really questioned where he actually came from. Why would they? They believed his cover story. Callie and Harry had settled down to a quiet life devoted to each other and Louise and all had been well.

Soon, Callie became too tired to sit. She slithered to the ground and, sheltered from the wind in the lee of the wall, she lay down and closed her eyes. If she had hoped for some respite from the thoughts that had tormented her since her confession about Louise's true parentage, she was disappointed. Fresh doubts and recriminations immediately assailed her. In her mind's eye, she was back in that terrible day, overwhelmed by fumes and panic, not knowing what to do, which way to turn.

Little Ariana had crawled out from under her mother's body and gazed around her. Callie had grasped her in her arms and cradled her against her chest. That much was true. But then, as she had turned to run, on the periphery of her vision she had seen it. She had seen her sister's eyes flickering with the faintest sign of life. She had seen it and yet she had not stayed. Instead, she had run and run and run until she was far away from the village and Calista. The only thing on Callie's mind had been to save the one who could be saved – Ariana, that tiny, innocent baby. Calista, even if not dead yet, was certainly dying. Callie could not carry both her and the child. She had taken the only decision she could. To rescue Ariana and do whatever she could to get her to safety.

And ever since that dreadful day, she had chosen to ignore the possibility that her sister hadn't died. Because what if Calista had made it after all? What if she was alive? If that were true, it would have changed everything.

Gradually, the sky darkened above Callie's prone form. It was a cloudless night and, one by one, the stars came out and twinkled up above her, the very same galaxies and constellations that had once looked down on Callie and Orion as they guarded the sheep and goats and waited for Heinrich to come.

Callie felt a slight shudder of the ground beneath her. Something large and warm appeared, softly panting. Orion. The faithful dog lay down beside her, nestling into her side, greying nose resting on his paws. She reached out, stroking his soft fur, patting his loyal head.

She wasn't sure how much time passed before a shiver of wind brought the scent of someone that made Orion prick up his ears, then rise to his feet, wagging his tail. A few seconds later a shadow momentarily blocked the moon. Immediately, Callie knew who it was. She'd recognise that form anywhere.

'It's me,' said Heinrich softly. 'I'm here now. I couldn't stay away any longer. I need you, Callie, I love you. Come with me and everything will be all right.'

Before Callie could answer, Orion gave a soft bark of approval, or agreement. Smiling, Heinrich lay down beside her, and together they gazed up at the heavens above until all three fell fast asleep.

A LETTER FROM ROSE

Dear reader,

I want to say a huge thank you for choosing to read *The Letter from the Island*. If you enjoyed it, and want to keep up to date with all my latest releases, just sign up at the following link. Your email address will never be shared and you can unsubscribe at any time.

www.bookouture.com/rose-alexander

If you liked *The Letter from the Island*, and I hope you did, I would be so grateful if you could spare the time to write a review. I'd love to hear what you think and it really helps new readers to find my books for the first time.

I love hearing from my readers – you can get in touch through social media or my website.

Thanks,

Rose Alexander

www.rosealexander.co.uk

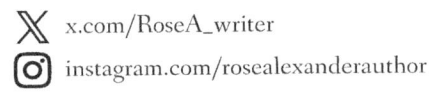

X x.com/RoseA_writer
instagram.com/rosealexanderauthor

AFTERWORD

The Battle of Crete took place in May 1941 and claims many firsts. It was the first occasion when paratroopers were used in such numbers, the first primarily airborne invasion in military history, the first time the Allies made widespread use of decrypted German messages from Enigma.

This book is concerned with the final 'first'. It was in Crete that the German war machine met with widespread resistance from a civilian population for the first time. The Cretan resistance is far less well known than the French. And yet scholars and historians cite it as one of the most successful mass insurgency movements ever.

It's estimated that over 20,000 ordinary Cretan people lost their lives during the German occupation of the island. But under the resistance motto of 'liberty or death', they bravely fought on for four long years, driving the enemy into retreat until, finally, the German forces on Crete formally surrendered to the British on 23 May 1945.

ACKNOWLEDGEMENTS

Thank you, as ever, to my brilliant agent Megan Carroll at Watson, Little, for all her support and encouragement. And thanks also to the amazing team at Bookouture – there are so many wonderful people there who make each book happen, most importantly for me, my fabulous editor Kelsie Marsden who has helped me to write the best books possible. I couldn't do it without you all! Final thanks to my long-suffering family who put up with me shutting myself away to write for hours and days at a time.

PUBLISHING TEAM

Turning a manuscript into a book requires the efforts of many people. The publishing team at Bookouture would like to acknowledge everyone who contributed to this publication.

Commercial
Lauren Morrissette
Hannah Richmond
Imogen Allport

Contracts
Peta Nightingale

Cover design
Emma Graves

Data and analysis
Mark Alder
Mohamed Bussuri

Editorial
Kelsie Marsden
Nadia Michael

Copyeditor
Jacqui Lewis

Proofreader
Anne O'Brien

Marketing
Alex Crow
Melanie Price
Occy Carr
Cíara Rosney
Martyna Młynarska

Operations and distribution
Marina Valles
Stephanie Straub
Joe Morris

Production
Hannah Snetsinger
Mandy Kullar
Charlotte Hegley

Publicity
Kim Nash
Noelle Holten
Jess Readett
Sarah Hardy

RAISING READERS
Books Build Bright Futures

Dear Reader,

We'd love your attention for one more page to tell you about the crisis in children's reading, and what we can all do.

Studies have shown that reading for fun is the **single biggest predictor of a child's future life chances** – more than family circumstance, parents' educational background or income. It improves academic results, mental health, wealth, communication skills, ambition and happiness.

The number of children reading for fun is in rapid decline. Young people have a lot of competition for their time, and a worryingly high number do not have a single book at home.

Hachette works extensively with schools, libraries and literacy charities, but here are some ways we can all raise more readers:

- Reading to children for just 10 minutes a day makes a difference
- Don't give up if children aren't regular readers – there will be books for them!

- Visit bookshops and libraries to get recommendations
- Encourage them to listen to audiobooks
- Support school libraries
- Give books as gifts

There's a lot more information about how to encourage children to read on our websites: **www.RaisingReaders.co.uk** and **www.JoinRaisingReaders.com**.

Thank you for reading.

Made in the USA
Coppell, TX
03 November 2025